THE MINORITY RULE

THE MINORITY RULE

Alexia Muelle-Rushbrook

BOOKS IN ORDER OF TRILOGY:

THE MINORITY RULE

THE MINORITY RULE:
BEYOND THE FENCE

THE MINORITY RULE:
INTO THE FOG

First paperback edition

November 2022

ISBNs:
Paperback: 978-1-80227-835-4
ebook: 978-1-80227-836-1

www.alexiamuellerushbrook.co.uk

For Mother Nature,
May we learn before we go too far

ONE

"I do not want to be a mother."

There, I've said it. Out loud, with more than a mirror or cat to listen. No one has moved. I'm not entirely sure anyone has breathed for a few minutes. I wait, unsure if I am going to be screamed at, banished, abused, or all of the above. The wall clock is the only thing I can hear – I've never noticed it before, now it is as if it is keeping my heartbeat...or counting down to my demise.

"What?" Mum finally answers in a whisper, through clenched teeth.

"I don't want children." I take a deep breath and decide to explain myself. "I've thought a lot about it and it's just not what I want, I want to—"

Mum cuts me off with a slap and I try not to flinch. "I'm not hearing this, you selfish, ungrateful girl! How can you be like this? You want to bring shame on us all? Oh! This cannot be! It's Kate, isn't it? She's put ideas in your head! Ah, well she would, she is barren – all of them are! No, no this is not to be, you'll do your duty and that's that. Not be a mother?! What greater honour is there? The human race is dying out, but you are too selfish to care!"

Selfish?! I've had enough. I've been harvested three times this year. Technically, I probably already am a mother, a biological one anyway. They would never tell me, just in case I tried to steal the baby, like women did at the beginning of the Project. The Powers That Be didn't consider that desperate women will do what they can – whatever they need to – to get their babies back. Being told they were helping to save humanity wasn't enough, they wanted their babies, not to so-called 'donate' their eggs to other women. I don't want babies, but even I am not sure about mini-mes out there; raised in a petri dish, then in a SurrogacyPod, if no viable uterus is available. What kind of start is that? Of course, not all will have survived, but surely some have by now. Sometimes I wonder if one will ever find me. Maybe they'll look like me or love science too. Who knows? It doesn't pay to dwell on these things. Humans are in decline and I'm supposed to want to save them.

I'm just not sure it's the right thing to do. Not like this.

My time of independence is running out. I've held out as long as I can, applied for every extension possible, lied about the reason constantly and told of my joy at one day being matched and given the chance to breed. Good grief, I sound like my uncle talking about one of his heifers coming of age. I'd like to visit him again, the countryside is clean and fresh, with fewer reminders of The Fall, The Fertility Project, and although they're everywhere, the Powers That Be are less obvious.

Less obvious...unseen, unheard, invisible. Yep, that sounds good right now.

The lecture is continuing. I've stopped trying to reason or explain. Mum is screaming at me. Grandma, too. I'm ungrateful, unworthy of the privilege I've been given and generally worthless unless I breed.

It's depressing, out of a population of desperate, infertile would-be parents, *I* am the one who is highly fertile. I've been tested multiple times – that leaves you with no dignity. It does however determine the rest of your life from the age of 18. What education you will receive – to what degree you will be useful to society – and how. I got lucky, I had proven myself and excelled in science – biology especially. The natural world fascinates me, and this bought me time. Time to be, time to learn, time to grow. To look for another way out. At a cost though. They would not allow all those eggs to go to waste, so while I learn, I must still contribute. I hate it, it leaves me weak, exhausted, and hormonal every time.

Leave her, she's just having a donation hot flush.

How I'd love to make people eat their words as they say that to me! 'Donation' suggests willingness, suggests volunteering. I am not. I do not. I agreed as the only other option was worse. Become the cow. Learn no more. Rear the babies.

No thank you.

I remember the day of our test results. Posted on the wall for all to see – like a seating plan at a wedding. Everyone huddled around the notice board, anxious to see what their grade was: 0, meaning totally barren, no hope of children – freedom, I thought; 1 or 2 indicating varying degrees of infertility. Mixed hope, matches would be iffy, tests continued, but you could have some input in the direction your life took; 3, meaning fertile. The now rare Golden Goose. What everyone hoped they'd be; everyone, but me.

I stood there in the huddle, looking at my name – Maia Woods – and shook my head gently. It is ironic. Mum liked naming in the hope of fertility, the hope of what's to come and what I'm supposed to want – 'Maia,' meaning 'mother.' Well, she was right, I am a 3, just like my siblings, just like her and the majority of my extended family. The only exception being

I would give anything to be a 0. Guilt and fear washed over me; fear for myself, guilt for everyone around me seeing 0 or 1. Tears flowed down their cheeks. We're raised in the knowledge that life excels with children. No children, you'd better hope for a scholarship, to win the lottery or that your family is rich and well connected to the PTB (Powers That Be). No links – no prospects. You'd better enjoy the life you're assigned – because that's where you're staying.

Even then, we're supposed to rejoice, taking 'our place in the essential role of a happy, prosperous society.' We're well indoctrinated in that from a young age. No rebellion is welcome here.

To consider what could be with a lower score possibly isn't helpful to my state of mind. The 'what ifs' haunt me. Kate – the friend my Mum likes to blame for every thought I have that doesn't match hers – she's a 1, or used to be. She was downgraded to 0 last year after retesting. She, however, is happy – she was matched with her high school boyfriend (also a 1), married him and they both got the jobs they wanted. They come from wealthy families, well, adoptive ones, which Mum uses against them constantly. 'A wasted opportunity to continue the family name' – because somehow infertility is their fault.

If they're extremely fortunate, they may receive a donor baby one day; but realistically with low grades, they are statistically unlikely to ever be parents. That hasn't stopped them finding peace and happiness though – and that is what Mum can't abide me seeing, just in case I get 'selfish ideas.'

Kate had stood beside me when I saw my results. I saw the tears in her eyes, she saw mine. Despite knowing they were for different reasons, we empathised with each other's pain as well as our own. True friendship that would survive any trial.

I wish the same could be said for Theo, but he proved less loyal when the going got tough. So much for 'forever.' I had looked over to the boys' results sheet, seen his score of 0, turned round to see him reading my score, then walk away, shaking his head.

We'd discussed all this for a year or more. I wasn't expecting it to be easy, but we'd promised to fight the system together – regardless of how tough the opposition was. We'd met at high school and quietly turned from lab partners to friends to soulmates without ever really saying anything. We just understood each other – until we didn't, apparently.

I thought he just needed time to think and process everything, but the coming days proved me wrong. He grew more distant, colder, cruel even, as the days passed.

"A 0 and a 3 are never going to be matched – stop dreaming, applying for consideration is a waste of time and resources." It was like listening to my mother – but worse as I'd come to rely on his words as a place of sanctuary and now they were only causing pain. "It's time we grow up and accept our paths – our *separate* paths." How those words cut me!

I still dream about him now. Six years later, his words still haunt me, his betrayal – the ease of his betrayal, that at a moment's difficulty, he dropped and ran – and seemingly didn't look back. He applied for and was granted a university spot in another Hub – where, I never did find out. I heard conflicting rumours, but all resulted in him leaving and never coming back. His parents told Tim (Kate's now husband), that he was offered a job alongside his studies and hoped his marriage would soon follow. I stopped listening after that and thankfully Tim never mentioned him to me again (probably after being told off by Kate as we had made a pact not speak of Theo), but whatever the reason, I wasn't subjected to verbal reminders again and just left with my own thoughts to torture me.

Though we don't speak about it much, Gee-Gee is the only one who seems to notice the duration of my pain; I feel she always seems to just know. Gee-Gee is my great grandmother – something of a mouthful, so the family all call her Gee-Gee. At 89 years old, she still works in the laboratory every day. Professor Georgia Beaufort to the rest of the world, she holds one of the highest ranks within the PTB as The Director of Fertility. Each Hub has a Governor for every division (for example, security, agriculture, fertility, or finance). They answer to the Director who oversees their sector for the entire United New Earth (UNE) and sit on councils with the Generals from each Hub and President Generals from each State. There are 12 States across the planet, all of which are governed by the Powers That Be.

As such, Gee-Gee is a true believer in the UNE and as one of the founders of The Fertility Project, she may be wise and understanding, but me looking to her for refuge from the PTB is entirely pointless. Plus, I think she has secretly spent the last six years hoping I will snap out of 'my independent streak' as Mum calls it. 'No good ever comes from focusing on I' – that has been my mother's daily reminder for me since I was old enough to listen. Maybe she has a point, but even Gee-Gee sighs quietly when she hears Mum repeating this yet again, not unlike a crazed parrot.

She and Great Gramps dedicated their lives to The Fertility Project and their high standing provided the wealth in which I've been raised. Guilt again washes over me. On paper I have everything, I have no reason to complain, every luxury is mine

– except the one I want: *freedom*. Freedom to choose my own path. One size does not fit all.

Mum's verbal assault is continuing, but my lack of response is now encouraging her that I've seen reason. Grandma also seems worn from the argument, but equally hopeful that my rebellion has been squashed.

I sigh. It wasn't voluntary, it just slipped out. Mum takes this as resignation, not despair. I can think of nothing helpful to say. I've had this conversation with myself a thousand times, always with compelling, winning arguments that could not be denied, but apparently, I have none now. This is my last attempt – Matching Day is coming, and I have nowhere left to hide.

Now aged 24, I've reached my limit before being matched and married. Heaven forbid my fertility should run out before I breed!

Most marry aged 18-20, either instead of or alongside studies. All studies finish by 24. You can further yourself within your field, but not swap, change, or remain single. Family values are everything. Apparently, the old world lost its way; family ties were broken, divorce rates sky high, racism was rife, money drove all, to hell with the environment, and generally every man was just out for himself. I'm not entirely sure it's not the same now, just masked differently; though creed and colour is not important, family status is. Those lucky enough to have natural children look down on those with adopted and pity those with none, but not enough to socialise with them much – who knows, maybe they could sterilise with their eyes?! Ignorance and pride are dangerous things. Those with adopted children love them dearly regardless, but desperately hope they are fertile as this is the key to elevation of social status and continuation (or commencement of) a fancier life – with a better house, better food and all the social niceties most people seem to want.

To stop all out rebellion from the lower, infertile ranks, there's the lottery. Once for purely financial gain, now it's also for a baby. It sounds ridiculous – it is – but it works. Dangle the carrot of hope, people buy into the cause, toe the line and even better, cheer you for it. Kate's parents won the lottery. My mum always scorned them for it, labelling them as 'social climbers' who didn't really fit in (apparently). When she realised Kate was barren, Mum asked Dad if they'd be moved out of the neighbourhood 'to somewhere more fitting.' I'd gone red with anger when I heard and was relieved to hear Dad utter words in the negative adding 'that would be ridiculous,' though I was slightly more annoyed when he continued: 'that would just cause unrest amongst other lottery players.' Ever the politician. Never mind if it's right – will it cause a revolt?

Dad takes little interest in his own home; I think Mum drives him to the office more than necessary, but he also seems to genuinely prefer it there and loves his work. He has certainly never really taken any interest in the running of home life that I can recall. As long as all is calm and respectful, he is happy. Grandchildren are a little loud, but he seems to like to see them, though I have often noticed his attentions tie in with a photo opportunity with the press. The image of 'a true family man.'

Hmm.

Mum obviously picks up any slack he leaves and crows to everyone around about her amazing children and how wonderfully fertile they are. Not me of course – Abby and Abraham, my older siblings. Both married young, both proven breeders: Abby with twins and pregnant again, Abe's wife has four children. This is Mum's crowning glory, her source of joy and what makes her the object of envy amongst all her friends – well, actually not just friends, she misses no opportunity to boast of her family to anyone with half an inclination to listen.

You'd think that would be sufficient family credentials; six grandchildren and counting is more than most ever dream of. I try that argument, suggesting I could make a difference to humanity with my research, not through having children myself…

"Don't talk rubbish, girl! Oh! For the shame! Why would you not want to honour the family? Anyone can fiddle with test tubes! You've been blessed with fertility, can continue your family's great name – but no, you seem intent on blackening everything!"

Shame.

That's what I am. A potential cause of lasting embarrassment and disappointment.

She had three children and to achieve true, now unheard-of excellence, all must breed. If one happens to be miserable, well that is just a small price to pay for the prestige she bases all value on.

Gee-Gee has quietly sat in the corner the whole time, stern faced throughout, but totally silent. She now walks out of the room, without uttering a word. "See!? You've disgusted Gee-Gee!" exclaims Mum. "Have you stopped to consider the sacrifices she has made? The work she has done?! All for you – for humanity itself – and you have the gall to sit there and throw it in her face?!"

I'd thought the lecture over. I was wrong. A history lesson is coming my way. Absolutely nothing I don't already know, but here it comes all the same…

"Do you never think of what Gee-Gee has seen? The devastation of disease, the ugliness of greed and wars – witnessing her own parents, neighbours, and friends being killed, homes and cities destroyed in explosions, waiting for the dust to settle only for it to reveal a barren, nuclear infected waste land. How hard she and others worked for the establishment of the UNE, the design of a worldwide order that truly works for all – for a way that ensures humanity survives!" I am not convinced that the UNE order 'working for all' concerns my mother, it serves *her* and that is enough. "You should think beyond *you* for once, apologise to Gee-Gee and take your place in society…and grow up! Ah! To think I almost died for you to be born! *This* is the thanks I get!"

I cannot take any more. I walk away, walk out of the house, Mum screaming after me, but I do not stop. She does once I reach the street, purely because she would never let the neighbours know all was not well in paradise. I know that only too well – keeping up appearances was drummed into me early on. So much so, I do not cry until I get to the river. Then the tears flow with the bubbling water. The therapy of that sound normally soothes me faster, but my soul aches and even when the tears stop, I still feel like a torrent is flowing through me.

I am not unaccustomed to Mum throwing blame at my feet. I said her three fertile children were her pride – this is true – but the third child has been a disappointment on so many levels. She had planned to have a whole litter of babies, not three. My birth had been traumatic and dangerous for us both and Mum had to have a hysterectomy as a result. So, everything, and I mean *everything*, I have done to slightly remind her of this fact has caused us both to wince. Including birthdays; if I could forget them, I would. Instead of a celebration of life, it is just a yearly reminder of near-missed death and lost opportunity for Mum. You would think a mother couldn't be so cruel, but like fertility, it comes naturally to her. I hoped that overtime I would become less sensitive, but apparently, that was easier hoped for than achieved.

I don't know how long I have sat here, but I suddenly feel a presence next to me. I turn to see Smoggy, the aforementioned keeper of my secrets, the confidant I can confess to with no judgement. I sigh, I probably should have limited my confession to the cat. Smoggy is my aunt's and is a large, fluffy grey cat of noble appearance. She has spent many an hour sitting beside me by this river, especially in recent years. I envy her. She gets to spend her days pottering as she will, with no worry of kittens as she was neutered when young.

Infertility in humans caused by disease and wars had spread to some other species, but not in the same lasting, degenerative way and felines seemed largely unaffected. My research at work is linked to this very fact and I spend a lot of time pondering why the still undiscovered disease or virus that caused our decline in fertility isn't also wiping out wildlife – despite some of them wandering into nuclear exclusion areas. The radiation from nuclear war itself caused infertility and early menopause for hundreds of thousands, but even before, and certainly after the wars, other factors were causing a rapid decline in fertility. I want to find out why.

Study material is limited. The PTB are frugal to say the least. Domestic animals are around, but largely in the country surrounding the Hub on livestock farms. Pet numbers are strictly limited, and my aunt has Smoggy under special license. My parents could have pets, they just find no joy in the natural world. I sometimes wonder if I am adopted; I have such vastly conflicting characteristics, it is hard to see how we are related. All having brown hair and brown eyes is hardly compelling evidence, until that is, I look at Aunt Dora or Gee-Gee and then I can see the link.

Again, I sigh.

"Maia?" a soft voice comes from behind me. I turn around to see Aunt Dora approaching. "Are you okay?"

"Fine." I'm hardly convincing, but it seems the right thing to say. "How are you?"

"Well dear, thank you, but you aren't fooling me or the cat."

"No, probably not." I turn back to the water, hoping the answer to life will float past.

Aunt Dora calls me indoors as she walks away; it is more of a command than an invite, yet somehow, I don't mind and follow without complaint.

She lives on the edge of SubHub District One (SH1). She is well-connected and rich enough to be in SH1, but poor and infertile enough to not be nearer the centre. This suits her, she has little in common with her mum or sister (my mum) so prefers to be out of family discussions whenever possible. She loves the quiet and the river, which runs a short distance from her home. I often retreat here when life weighs me down. Sitting at the bank is always peaceful and I enjoy looking at fruit orchards and vineyards which are across the water.

Aunt Dora's husband left her for his personal assistant – such a sad, but true cliché. More pathetic still is that he was granted a divorce on the grounds of being proven fertile with his lover (literally being outed by her pregnancy!), so my aunt was annulled and granted permission to stay in this little spot as compensation. Society celebrated the new union like it was the original and the fact the baby arrived in three months was neither here nor there.

How convenient. Family values – when it suits.

Aunt Dora is, or at least seems, at peace now. She wasn't for a long time. She was rematched (another bandage on society's cracks) and married for three years, but she spent half of that time caring for him as he slowly died from radiation poisoning. Apparently, he unwittingly walked into a radioactive area whilst surveying with the army. The truth of that was debated, but only quietly for fear of causing a backlash. After his death my aunt was left to her solitude and conspiracies were largely forgotten.

Her bungalow isn't large, but is homely and she has a sizeable studio where she paints. The subjects vary, but most are commissions for the wealthy. Over the mantelpiece is a painting of me as a child under the oak tree by the river – just where I had been sitting moments before.

Long has that spot been my refuge.

Again, guilt weighs on me. I know so many have much more to deal with, yet they accept their lot with grace and humility. Why can't I? Why, when I am comparatively well-off, can I not just take the path offered me?

Smoggy brushes around my legs and miaows. Is she trying to tell me something? I've often wondered if that cat doesn't possess powers. I pick her up as I sit on the sofa which seems to please her as she purrs before making herself at home on my lap. This in itself is a therapy – I am at least useful to someone.

"Ha, traitor!" says Aunt Dora, seeing Smoggy as she comes in with tea – the drink that solves all woes in UNE

Britain apparently. Each location in the world is basically now identified by a code. Each Hub is named according to its location within its State. The State is named after the country it replaced – or as in many cases, the largest country it replaced. As an unmistakable reminder of UNE rule, each State has 'United' at the beginning. United Britain, Southern Hub is where I live and although the world is meant to be one united operation, with no ethnic or cultural differences, old cultures remain within the 12 States; even if muted – the English loving (and being mocked for loving) tea is one of them.

"You're the only one she betrays me for, but I suppose we're all staff to cats!"

I smile and chuckle, but don't reply.

"So, you don't want to marry?"

"Who told you?!" I look up in surprise.

"You just did! But I knew that long ago, and Matching Day is this week."

"Oh." I can think of nothing more intelligent to say and turn back to Smoggy for help. I've argued too much today and had my confidence thoroughly trampled by Mum. I believe I'm in the wrong, so expect the same lecture from all. "No, I'm afraid I don't..." I trail off, any thought of finding a sympathetic ear has left me.

"No, well nor did I, it was pushed on me – twice! But I did it, for better or worse."

I'm amazed, I think this is the first time anyone has voiced even half an opinion other than everything being a great honour and privilege, so effective and regimental is our school indoctrination.

"You're not as alone as you think; but it can work and it's up to you to find your silver lining whilst doing your duty.

Obeying the system doesn't mean you can't work it and find happiness."

It is a mixed message, but I'll take comfort and hope where I can. I am not so alone. Not everyone is unquestioning, even if they follow the path set out for them.

TWO

I leave Aunt Dora's with something resembling hope, though I am not entirely sure what I am hoping for. She told me that accepting the system took courage, but so did looking for a balance of acceptance and change; finding meaning in myself – that is what I want. What *is* the point of me?

To have babies. My mum's voice rings out in my head. How she manages to haunt even my most self-assured thoughts! – forever keeping me humble – she'd be so pleased if she knew. I sigh again. I wonder how often I sigh? Too much, is the answer.

I should be heading home, but I am not ready for that so, rather than turning right out of Aunt Dora's gate, back towards the rest of SubHub 1, I turn left towards SubHub 2.

Cities are no more, the largest were all bombed to oblivion decades ago, then as the population dwindled and the Powers That Be took control, forming the UNE, smaller areas were deserted and Hubs formed. Each State (formerly known as countries) has a few Hubs strategically placed and connected by high-speed rail for trade purposes.

Commuting of people is rare; everyone has their place, their role, that is it. Tourism is a big, Earth-polluting no-no and is not allowed, no matter who you are. Each Hub has areas of commerce, arts, design, natural history and preservation, recreation, and entertainment. Why would anyone want more?

Humanity's destruction of the Earth is taught early on in school. Pictures of ruin and rubble are imprinted on each child's mind. No pity is spared as they are shown images of the dead and dying, the mutilated and nuclear radiated, as well as cities of dust and deserts of ash. Why? To make darn sure we understand the damage we have done and how lucky we are to live in a clean, organised, and peaceful society within our Hub.

So, even if you live in SubHub 2 or 3, you are still taught you are lucky. You have a home, a safe one (as long as you are not rebellious of course) and have friends and family (to some degree) – a place to belong. Each SubHub stems from the Central Hub. The nearer you are to the Centre, the better. The Centre has all the niceties that people drive towards and children are all raised in SH1 and schooled in the Centre.

Beyond SubHubs 1-3 is not for humans anymore. Pollution from nuclear and chemical wars is dotted all over. Every year the UNE Army works to reclaim certain areas with varied success. Sometimes small patches of land are secured and can be farmed – or tested on – but Hub expansion is slow, if existent. This doesn't really matter though for as the population continues to age and dwindle, more space isn't the issue, fertility is.

There are trams running between SubHubs all the time, all eco-friendly, solar powered and a necessary form of travel. Cars and lorries are infrequently used and really are only for large deliveries and the Army. Fruit and vegetable farms are dotted in between Hub Districts, some open air, some in specialist greenhouses. Arable and livestock farms are all on the outskirts of the entire Hub and are run and guarded by Army outposts.

Any factories for manufacturing are also on the outskirts or in outposts, but they, along with arable farms, are largely robot operated.

By getting on the tram, my barcode will be flagging big time, but I don't care – let the drones follow me, they do most of the time anyway. Occasionally they stop me on the street and ask where I am going. So far, they haven't called an officer to come and detain me, but it is only a matter of time if I keep riding trams without clearance or apparent purpose. I said tourism wasn't allowed: well moving beyond your district rank is considered tourism by many.

At birth you are assigned a barcode; this number spells out your pedigree, and a chip is permanently implanted into your neck. Once some doctor decides you are big enough to have it tattooed, your left arm and back of the neck declare your pedigree for all to see. You cannot hide or hold your sleeve down if a drone greets you – not unless you want to be arrested of course.

At 18, you have an extra digit of 0,1,2 or 3 added (poor Kate had the indignity of having hers altered when her fertility status changed) and then the final addition comes on the 'joyful' occasion of your marriage, meaning, every step of the way, a stranger can read you.

There are a few people sitting behind me on the tram now. I can hear them whispering my code and wondering where I could be going. This was probably a mistake; I should have just sat by the river and watched the farmers collecting apples in the orchards. Grapes will be soon. I like watching the harvests, a little natural order in our organised chaos. Others are keen on watching as it reminds them of the coming cider and wine, but this isn't as exciting to me as it should be. I used to go to the bar with Theo, Kate, and Tim, but after Theo left, being a third wheel was hardly appealing. Nowadays I just go for the odd birthday or Christmas party… I could go now, but what's the point?

Listening to others whispering, 'what is she doing here?' is hardly relaxing. I suddenly think it is about time I saw Kate. She has left me messages that I haven't answered, not because I don't want to talk to her or because I think she doesn't understand my plight, I just feel guilty…again.

I ignore the whispers and get off the tram in SH2 and walk to Kate's house. Her parents are in SH1, but as a tested infertile, she and her husband were allocated a marital home here. Mum thought it should be SH3, with 'all the other barreners' as she charmingly put it, but thankfully not everyone is quite as cold as she is. The neighbourhood is clean and tidy, but with less ornamentation and smaller homes. Kate lives in a ground floor flat, five streets from the station. I don't mean to pry, but I find myself glancing through windows as I go, wondering behind which doors is the better life and are they all happy?

It is Saturday night, and one couple has their TV on in easy view of the window so I can see that the lottery is on. The excitement in their faces is palpable as they look between their digital ticket and the TV screen. The lottery should just photograph this couple for their advert – it sums up everything in one, soundless image.

My stomach churns: guilt, gnawing at me. Not only can I have children, I can (and probably do) donate towards the lottery. People can *win* my babies. My stomach churns again, this time from nausea, not just guilt. How can this be right? Surely a better solution is to find the key to improved, natural fertility, not winning other people's babies? This is how I can help humanity, find a better, lasting way forward. I have so many theories, things I would like to investigate, if only someone higher up would give me a chance! I have done everything asked of me, followed the steps of the ladder, proven a true and faithful lab assistant, achieved all the grades, submitted reports, boring or otherwise, had great responses, but always found a door closed in my face as I tried to go beyond.

No one expects me to continue work post marriage and stale opinions plague me, such as 'why waste time on a 'breeder'?' – 'maybe her husband will continue her theories' – 'or she can continue after she has hit the menopause' – by which time someone else better will surely have come along and I will have to retire as a grandmother. Gee-Gee was the exception, but she was a founder and had her children while the Project was establishing – and before birth rates dropped through the floor and every 'female breeder' must be preserved and protected for the glory of her family and not exposed to 'the strains of work.'

I had thought, or at least hoped, that Gee-Gee might have helped here and asked for an exception, allowing me to work more – or even better, to work *with* her. She will discuss some ideas with me, encourage me even, but never really help me succeed beyond. I did ask why once; she just said she 'didn't want to show bias or unbalance the UNE's model.' I don't understand. She has no problem standing for issues she believes in and has never shied from an argument so I fear she must believe, despite her own path, I am better use as a mother than a scientist.

Sometimes, I wonder why they educate and train me at all if I can't go any further and am actually just waiting for maternity leave to start. I know the answer really – they're hedging their bets, just in case my fertility fails, then I have some potential 'other' use for society. Also, education occupies my brain because 'the devil makes work for the idle' – a cheerful motto that children are literally taught to chant in primary school.

Oh, if only someone would at least have a discussion with me! No, that can't be. Discussion leads to hope, hope breeds rebellion. No, order must be maintained, I must be squashed. It is depressing, I am answering my own arguments without voicing them.

Aunt Dora's words come back to me – 'find your own silver lining' – somehow, I must.

I am standing outside Kate's home. It is clean, small, and identical to the others. I should walk straight up to the door and knock, but find myself stood on the path, looking through her window. Kate and Tim are sitting close together on the sofa, watching the TV, just the same as the neighbours – watching the lottery, waiting for the numbers to be called out of the antiquated machine. As they do, Kate is eagerly checking her ticket on her watch. She must have a couple of numbers matching as both their faces are lighting up.

For a moment, I share their joy, wishing the numbers to fall their way; they'd make wonderful parents and although Kate says little to me about it now, I know she has always dreamed of a baby. Hope turns to despair; their numbers don't all match. Tim puts his arm around Kate, and I see both have a glint in their eye. I shake my head and walk away. I can't, I just can't.

The conflict that whirls in my head makes me feel dizzy. Maybe I should just take the match offered to me; if I am lucky, I might get a good partner who I can at least like. I don't dare hope for love, I'm not sure I even want it, that just opens me up to betrayal and disappointment. I do envy Kate and Tim though as through it all, they have a loving, trusting partnership. My own parents don't have that, they tolerate each other – at best. Maybe that is something else I fear: being coupled with someone I can barely tolerate and becoming my parents. Matched by pedigree and genetic compatibility, not personality, interest, or desires.

Without thinking, I sit myself back on a tram, back to SH1. The light is fading fast now and although it is still fairly warm from a pleasant summer's day, I wish I had thought to pick up a jacket – preferably one with a collar to stop the renewed whispering about my barcode.

There are fewer people now, probably on their way to the Central Hub for a night shift, but as a 3, they know that work is unlikely to be my reason for travelling alone now. I wish I could visit Uncle Joseph and Aunt Aggie; it is so long since I have seen them. As 0s, they were posted to a farm, and rarely leave it.

When he first became the Governor of Defence, Dad used to take me with him to see his brother. He went for work mainly, I was never sure what for exactly – something to do with checking on security around the fences, but I didn't care as he would leave me with my aunt and uncle while he was busy. I loved it. My imagination ran free, I could play and watch the animals and almost forget the PTB existed. Almost – the hum of drones was never far off, especially if you went near the perimeter fence. Nowhere is 'eyeless,' not even out there, but I still preferred it there and couldn't see why children weren't raised out there, rather than in CH or SH1. I asked Aunt Aggie once while she cooked dinner, but all she did was sigh and say: 'Children must be raised together for the future.' I wasn't sure quite what that meant then, just that the question had caused her pretty face to turn pale and her lip to start quivering. I didn't ask again.

Dad stopped taking me with him when I turned 13. I hit puberty and like everything else for me, life turned towards gearing me for my future as a wife and a 3, an educated 3, but a 3 nonetheless. Then I understood Aunt Aggie. Children have to be raised together, under the same strict regime, otherwise cracks occur; cracks that I would dearly love to fall between.

As I walk into our cul-de-sac, it is nearly dark, but I can still see the houses, all smartly set back from the street, with flowers and bushes nicely arranged in the front gardens as well as on shelves up the exterior walls. Every home is more than twice the size of those in SH2, all with individual gardens – nowhere else has this: communal gardens yes, but not private. Then, standing at the back of the street, larger than all the others, is our house. It is ridiculously large even though Gee-Gee and Grandma live with us. Family stays together, particularly female lines. While young and married, you might live separately from family, but retirement or death often sees the older members living with the younger again. Abigail and her family live two doors down; Abe and his family are in the next street, in a similarly oversized home. One happy, close unit.

I wonder where my home will be? Not close I hope… Ah! Has my own conscience betrayed me? Have I decided to give in and accept the system? The idea still saddens my inner soul, but seriously, what *is* my alternative? There is no 'opt-out' option. I don't want to be imprisoned as an egg donation cow, and although I thought about declaring myself not into men and asking for an alternative match and being made a surrogate, that hardly solves my dilemma. I'd still have children – and a match; plus, it seems insulting to everyone for me to live a lie of another kind. No, better to live a true lie than a fabricated one.

The lights are on in the living room, nowhere else, meaning they are either asleep or all together. Wasting electricity in empty rooms is not permitted, which in this case, is helpful as it means I have half a chance of sneaking upstairs without sparking another war of words with Mum by stumbling into the wrong room. I go around the back, triggering the security light, but that shouldn't alert those indoors; the backdoor opens quietly as I scan in and creep into the kitchen. Reacting to the proximity of sustenance, my stomach rumbles. I open the fridge, select a yoghurt, which is hardly filling, but I can eat it quietly, grab an apple off the counter, fill a glass of water and set off for a hasty retreat…this is ridiculous; my heart is racing.

I make it up the stairs and am just about to close the door when a foot blocks the last couple of inches. I nearly cry out and drop my glass as the light pings on and my mum's face looms.

"Well? Where on earth have you been? No!" she waves her hand in my face. "Don't bother, we know, your dad got a call saying you were on the tram."

Damn drones obviously sent out an alert. Ridiculous things.

"There is no need to go visiting other SubHubs, none whatsoever. If you can't meet Kate in the Centre, you don't need to meet her at all. Your father doesn't need to be explaining to the press why his youngest daughter flouts the rules." She turns, but whips around again saying: "And I trust you want to apologise to me and have decided to finally take the place you are destined for?"

In a few short sentences I feel beaten. If there is a silver lining, I'd dearly love to see it. I just nod.

"Excellent," says Mum, walking out the door.

I don't eat, I don't even get changed, I go to the bathroom and stare at myself in the mirror, hoping to see sense somewhere. I see none and eventually crash into bed, hoping I don't wake up here.

THREE

I wake up to the sound of Mum singing. She does this well and normally it gives me joy to listen to her; however, all her songs this morning seemed to be themed on matrimony and forthcoming wedded bliss, so I fail to feel comforted by the melodies. Apparently yesterday has been wiped away from her memory – all but the final moment of my simple, dejected nod. That may well have been the act of depression and weariness; however, to Mum, it was the affirmation of joy and fulfilment of her lifelong dream. I wish that joy would rub off on me, truly. If I could but take on her simple acceptance of how life is, take genuine pleasure in the order in front of me, I would probably be the better for it.

Mum has assembled every family member possible for Sunday morning breakfast and seemingly been to the bakery, for there is food everywhere. This seems like gluttony to me. SH2 and 3 have never and will never see this kind of wealth. Food is rationed and earnt by all, one way or another. Society has no room for the dysfunctional or dependent, yet Mum thinks it her right to feed us all like superior beings when she sees fit and stores extra allowances for such occasions that she deems worthy. To be fair, all districts have ample fruit and veg (hence the farms and orchards dotted throughout the Hub), but this breakfast still seems like unnecessary selfishness.

'A balanced diet is essential for a healthy workforce' was Great Gramps' philosophy. He had been a massive advocate of this and as Director of Agriculture, he long ago established that everyone, of breeding 'value' or not, was properly fed; and although he died last year, (aged 92), this rule remains fixed into society's code. Meat and fish are scarce for everyone; the lower classes see little of it and what they do see is small in proportion. However, it is nutritionally enough for those who want it.

Farms are small and production low, but animal welfare is paramount. At least that balance has been achieved. Gee-Gee, on a rare occasion of feeling nostalgic, will recount what her parents told her about farms of old, describing individual farmsteads so vast they would expand beyond an entire Hub, about toxic chemicals that would be constantly used to control plants and animals alike, and trees that were cut at an unimaginable rate for more land until they were at risk of becoming a rare species – along with all the fauna and flora that lived amongst them.

Then, disease hit Earth like a plague no one had previously conceived in their worst nightmares, disease that could not be controlled for a generation as it mutated every time they thought they had an efficient vaccine. While millions died from this worldwide, natural disasters also increased; earthquakes and tsunamis struck some areas, but wars sparked everywhere. No one could decide how to act, and everyone wanted more than the next country, more land, more money, more produce, more trade – more of more and more again. Gun wars turned to nuclear, cities were flattened, and entire states left toxic.

It was this worldwide chaos that left the world in such a state that the Powers That Be became necessary. People say the

PTB had been watching and waiting: key members of almost every organisation imaginable, actually sleepers, waiting to rise. Others say they were just the ones that rose behind other leaders at the right time; and where others failed to communicate, they succeeded, forming the strict and effective network of the UNE. Whatever their origin, they have become a well-oiled, highly efficient, global organisation. An organisation that my family takes great pride in belonging to and working for, in their various forms. You'd think I am about to say, 'except me.' I'm not. Despite my sorrows, I do believe in the work of the PTB. Listening to my lectures as I grew up, seeing how the world was, I see the need for *most* of it now. The Earth is not the vibrant, welcoming place it was. Wars, pollution and disease saw to that. Huge chunks of land are totally unhabitable and the sea is still dealing with the pollution of decades of overindulgence and disasters. We do need to live in our Hubs, for our safety if nothing else. The trade transport links to other Hubs and commercial outposts work. But – ah! There it is! *But,* I feel I have more to contribute. I could help work on the beyond, if only I could study how wildlife has coped – if it is coping? Then hopefully some lessons could be learnt for us. There must still be room for improvement in the UNE – does life need to be *so* restricted? Does anyone want to talk about it? Structure is important, yes, though surely not to the point that discussion is vetoed so categorically.

"Maia!" Mum's squawk brings me from my musings with a jolt. "Quit daydreaming and pass your father the butter!" I comply, muttering an apology. I should try to make more effort. I don't want another argument and my head is still aching from yesterday. "Eat, girl! Don't wait to be served, you need to start thinking about serving your husband and caring for your family!" Nope, even meekness isn't going to stop the lecture, though this was said with a smile.

Not even Dad is going to sit this one out. When he speaks his tone is different to Mum's and always sounds ready for a press conference – slow, to the point, not really inviting questions, though he might at the end – if there's time: "Maia, your mother and I are very happy you have decided to take your match without further delay. You have proved yourself at work, Richard told me your work is excellent and until you have children, you are welcome to stay on, but it is time you are a role model; I must have all my family leading by example. I do not want to be receiving calls from the Security Services saying their drone has flagged you on trams to outer sectors, it is totally unnecessary and just sparks questions – answers to which I doubt are useful or logical. There are plenty of lovely areas is SH1, or even the Centre, visit those if you must wander." He pauses a moment. "Good grief, Peter wanted to send an officer in case you were going to the fence!"

Hmm, would looking at the fence be *so* dramatic? Would someone else considering the beyond be so bad? Of course, I voice none of this. I had no intention (then, at least) of going to the fence. I've heard enough stories of people trying to wander beyond and either being detained or 'lost' as a result. Horror stories or true, I don't know, but like the Bogey Man, it is a fear to be encouraged in the young and unlike Santa, something not to be corrected in the old.

Peter Lloyd is Head of Security Services in the Southern Hub. Dad, as Governor of Defence, is his boss. Peter is an odd man of medium height who thinks he is a giant. He walks around with his head slightly tilted skyward whenever possible, the rest of the time surveying the room like he is considering stealing something. Whenever he visits Dad I do my best to be elsewhere as he makes me uncomfortable. If it wasn't for family connections, I would ask how he got his position, but as bloodline means everything nowadays, it takes little explaining as he is second cousin to President General Fairfax. His Deputy, Mark Jones, is the actual brains of the Force and Dad, along with anyone else who has sense, calls him if it is at all possible. I doubt Mark would have called Dad about me, but I suppose it doesn't matter who did.

"You really should be careful, the trams aren't always safe at the moment, there's issues with…well, just be careful."

Issues? Now, of course I want to ask more. I'd not seen anything, but had heard of rumours at work that there was some unrest in SH3 to do with housing. It hadn't entered my head yesterday.

"I'm sorry Peter was distressed. I was just riding the tram—"

"Yes, yes." Dad stops me short, glancing at Mum who is cooing over Abigail's pregnant belly, not paying any attention to us. "I told your mother I'd say something, let's leave it there."

"So! Big week, hey sis!?" grins Abe, sitting down next to me; he's been on the phone outside until now. "Finally getting matched! That'll be you soon!" He nods towards our sister, Abigail, chuckling, making his cheeks dimple. He has always been handsome, and age has improved his looks. Only two years older than me, we should have been close, but we have always been like chalk and cheese. He and Abby are close, and are very similar: brown, tidy hair, brown eyes, slightly toned, beautiful skin, share a sense of humour (at my expense normally) and both embrace the roles set out for them. Abe went straight into a logistics business apprenticeship, quickly climbing the ladder, married Isobel, and had babies soon after.

Abby, who had no intention of working, married Luke as soon as matched and gave birth to the twins 18 months later. True poster children for Mum and Dad's cause.

"Wednesday, huh? Big week all round!"

"Oh? Why's that?" I must have missed something as he clearly doesn't just mean me.

"Hmm, yes," mutters Dad.

"What is happening?"

Dad fidgets in his chair as he says, "Oh, there is an exchange happening between Southern and Midland Hubs."

"*Really?!*" That happens so infrequently, it can't fail to spark interest.

Isobel, Abe's wife, jumps in before he or Dad can answer: "Pappa says it is because Colin Evans is a moron and they want to cover his mistakes up, labelling it 'a restructuring and opportunity to diversify bloodlines.'"

Oh crap. Why do I think that includes me? I fear Matching Day being this week too is unlikely to be a coincidence.

"Colin *is* a moron, getting the President General Fairfax's grandson killed was just the cherry on top of what can only be called a short, but pathetic career. It is enough to blacken the title that Great Gramps dedicated his life to. Good riddance, they should have been harsher than demoting him to Governor of Agriculture in the Midlands Hub. I only hope the next guy is actually up to the task of Director!" Abe is insensitive enough to ramble on with Gee-Gee next to him and actually looks surprised when she corrects him.

"I hope *she* will do her duty as Director of Agriculture, honouring my husband and the PTB admirably. I can't say she was my *first* choice, but I hope she will prove worthy. Colin proved a liability beyond anyone's imagining. Taking

31

his granddaughter, Anthea, and Angus Fairfax on a trip to the outpost was stupid beyond words. Letting them walk out on a minefield…well, it was a blow beyond reckoning. Two young lives absolutely wasted. And both had promising careers ahead of them. President General Fairfax has every reason to hate Evans – he took out his heir!"

Hearing anything close to a decision within the PTB that Gee-Gee dislikes or that at least wasn't her first choice is a rare moment indeed. She gently shakes her head, as if trying to dispel other thoughts, ones she doesn't want to voice.

"How many are coming from the Midlands?" I ask gently.

"Enough!" chips in Dad. "It has sent the Defence team into a spin as they and the Housing Secretary prepare for new posts, houses, etc. All done in a hurry too, nothing like a bit of forward planning."

"Well, I hope they prove useful as Gee-Gee hopes, otherwise it is just extra work for no good reason," adds Abe.

At the mention of her name, Gee-Gee sits up straight. She is apparently not willing to continue doubting the newcomers as she replies, "All will be well, trust in the system, Abe."

A little surprised, Abe can't help raising his eyebrows. I think Gee-Gee looks tired, and ask if she is okay, prompting her favourite saying when she thinks things need concluding: "Yes dear, I just need R&R." Rest and Relaxation. Sounds good; she certainly seems to hold a lot of faith in that phrase. From a little girl, I remember that being her 'go-to' answer to any stresses she heard of, whether talking to family or to colleagues about work. I have never actually seen her take her own advice though. If she isn't in her study, preparing to consult on some project, reviewing test results, or in her lab, she is watching others trialling yet another 'something interesting' as she calls it. The nearest she comes to rest or relaxation is times like now, but somehow, looking at her face, I doubt this qualifies.

Great Gramps' death last year has really taken its toll on her. She has been grey haired as long as I can remember her, but elegantly so; her skin could easily have been 10-20 years younger, and her mobility is nothing short of remarkable.

Until recently, I might have joked and said she had been sipping from the elixir of life. If she had been, Great Gramps' death has stopped her. She is just as dedicated to her work and not disinterested in family life, but the sparkle in her eye has gone and clearly the recent disappointment of Great Gramps' successor's epic failures of office (even setting aside unwittingly leading a young couple to their untimely deaths) has been more than she wanted to deal with. For her own sake, she should probably leave agricultural affairs to those actually in charge of it.

Technically, the Director of Fertility has little to do with such things; however, I suppose after a marriage of 68 years, working as a true partnership, founding part of the PTB and The Fertility Project, asking her to step back would be like asking a bird not to fly.

To have a love like that, one that can alter your innermost being, can hold you up every day of your life, through good and bad, you stand together and build everything else around – that is something truly to be envied. If only I had that. I sigh, yet again, but thankfully no one notices. They are too busy discussing the new arrivals, who is leaving and whether they think it worth the aggravation.

"Of course, this could mean something really exciting for you Maia!" Mum has joined in the conversation. "I think there is an excellent chance of a substantial match for you, maybe you holding out all this time has actually been providential!

Oh, I wonder who it could be? Stephen – have you seen the list? Anyone you think likely? Surely, Match Day being this week isn't a coincidence, have you looked? Yes, you must have…I hope you have consulted to get your youngest daughter a worthy match?"

Mum is cooing with delight at the very idea that I fear. A 'high profile match' is absolutely not what I want. If I think I have no freedom now, and drones alerting me getting on a tram are annoying, then a whole new level of restriction could potentially be coming my way.

"Beatrix, you know I cannot be seen trying to sway matches, that is not my job."

"Yes, yes, but '*not be seen*' is not the same as '*do not do*'… come, *have* you seen the list?"

"Yes, I have, you have two days to stew. I will not discuss it and give you ideas."

This vexes Mum, but it certainly doesn't deter her. Grandma, Abby, and Isobel gladly join in with her predictions – I smile as I internally liken them to cackling hens, but say nothing. Whilst their prattling is depressing, it at least leaves me to quiet contemplation. Dad takes this matter as concluded and goes onto business chatter with Abe and Isobel's husband, Luke.

"You'll find your place, Maia, trust the system." Gee-Gee's words come at a whisper, but are clear as a bell. "Nothing good ever comes without a little work, trust me." She rises to leave, gently squeezing my hand as she goes. A tear comes to my eye; that was the first bit of physical comfort I have felt for the longest time and the words were undoubtedly meant to reassure me. I wish I had her faith right now. I will try to take solace from her belief and hope it sparks some of my own.

The Minority Rule

* * *

No one else noticed Gee-Gee's words or that I had none for some time after she left. I was hoping to slip off and quietly do something on my own, but when I try to leave, Mum makes it clear she has other ideas. I am to be presented as a picturesque doll on Wednesday, just in case my future husband or in-laws think about rejecting me on grounds of being scruffy – heaven forbid they actually see me as I am! I say this to Mum in a dry, sarcastic voice, but she either misunderstands me or choses to as her response of: "exactly my dear, that's the spirit!" isn't exactly what I was going for.

So, off to the shopping centres of the Hub we go. It would seem this is a premeditated manoeuvre as the shop assistant is waiting for us with a selection of dresses – none of which I would have chosen for myself. However, Mum looks at me with pride, pride which if I'm honest, I don't think that I've seen before, and for a moment I pretend this situation isn't forced.

Being paraded is wearisome, though in my teens I enjoyed this to a degree. Under PTB decree, all purchases must be 'needed' and are rationed accordingly. When with Kate and some other friends from school, I wanted to look good, and although I had no false illusions of being the prettiest, I knew which styles suited me and the whole scenario was fun at least.

'Fun' isn't a word I would ever use to describe the few family shopping trips I went on growing up. Mum groaned at everything I glanced at, let alone picked up, and Abby quickly established herself as the 'pretty sister,' often reminding me that next to her I am average at best. She decided that the rations were best used on her, not me, so instead passed her clothes to me when she tired of them. This was not entirely Abby's idea, it is actually another PTB mandate to minimise waste, but if you heard her speeches as I received her hand-me-downs, you'd be forgiven for thinking it was.

I have always struggled to tame my hair and found makeup unnecessarily time consuming. Kate has tried helping me with these things, but to little avail. She is beautiful anyway and effortlessly so. Her blonde hair is perfectly tidy whether worn up or down, her blue eyes shine without makeup, and I don't think I've ever seen a spot on her skin. I'd be jealous, but Kate doesn't flaunt it and she has such warmth of spirit that begrudging her any of the above just seems silly. Unlike my mum, who openly despairs of me, Kate's mum enjoys teaching her how to be 'girly.' She is the only girl – only child – but that's not it. The difference is, well…Kate's mum, I believe, loves her exactly as she is.

Satisfied with the dress code, my hair is now Mum's 'target.' The PTB states: 'Hair must either be short or collected in a bun, so a drone or officer can scan at any time without delay. For social or genuine practical reasons, the neck may be covered; however, should a drone request a reading, the left arm must be exposed and presented immediately. Failure to comply will result in detention and potential prosecution for obstruction of order.'

I choose long, but collected in a bun. Mum now wants fancy arrangements. I tell her this is impractical. I don't win. Returning home, I catch my reflection in the tram window. I have to look twice as it doesn't look like me – someone almost pretty, I grant you – but not me.

FOUR

Monday morning alarm – great, two days left.

I get up and rather than delay by having breakfast or having to listen to more of Mum's chatter, I grab the apple that I left in my room on Saturday and make my way to the tram. It quietly passes by streets and businesses until it delivers me just outside the lab, which adjoins the Southern Hub General Hospital. The Science Laboratory in the Central Southern Hub is enormous and apparently the biggest of all the Hubs in the UNE. I'll probably never see any others in person, but I have seen videos of labs from other States and some of them look just as impressive as ours, even if not quite as large. We receive research, video calls, and reports from all the Hubs, but never or hardly ever physically meet. North America is largely unhabitable now – it was bombed so badly during the wars when Gee-Gee was young, along with a lot of Russia and Asia, that the majority of it was declared 'gone' and the PTB haven't dared try to probe there since. Once, a couple of years ago, President General Karl Roberts from the Northern Hub of United North America visited for a PTB summit (which is even rarer still, as most of those are held virtually). Everyone wanted to meet him and the staff he brought with him. If visits from Hubs on the same continent are rare, visitors from so far away are almost unheard of. Literally years can pass in between non-trade visits, so their presence was truly fascinating, almost like aliens from outer space!

I was thrilled to spend a little time with Professor Millar while he was here. He visited Great Gramps and Gee-Gee a lot at home and they spent hours chatting locked away in their study. I wished they would include me more, but as so often is the case, I was left wondering. My boss, Dr Richard Brown, told me there wasn't enough time for all the assistants to chat to the Professor and it would be wrong to give me preference because of my family – like that had proved so useful to date! I at least got to sit in on one lecture on fertility in United North America's population. His research and theories on viral changes over time and studies on how they mapped mutations from combined viruses and radiation damage were compelling and made the foundation for many of my day-to-day investigations.

The lab is bustling today, not unlike when Professor Millar visited. I ask Susie at reception what is going on. She says visitors from the Midlands have arrived and 'everyone' is in the lecture hall. By 'everyone' she means everyone important – so not me; I'll have to wait.

Susie enjoys the superior knowledge that comes from reception and even more, enjoys taunting others who want to know. Luckily, she has a limited power of holding her tongue, so it is only a matter of time before she tells someone, and the chain of whispers can begin.

By dinner time I am proven right and the new visitors – well, residents! – begin to appear out of the lecture hall. My apple didn't last long, and I am hungry, so I wander to the canteen. The room is absolutely packed to the point of being claustrophobic. I wonder if this is how the viruses started – the original ones that caused a multitude of pandemics and halved the population in a matter of ten years. We're now vaccinated for these, so they're largely controlled, if still existent; however, it is easy to imagine how they took hold if people were constantly living in such close proximity.

Houses, even in poorer areas, are spaced, streets are organised in blocks, and sectors designed for isolation if necessary. Also, all the newcomers would have been isolated at home for two weeks prior to travelling here. Normally only a quarter of these people would be here at once and I suddenly feel overpopulated.

No one else seems to care – they are laughing, joking, and discussing whatever theory or event is interesting to them. More food than normal is being consumed, rubbish dropped all around; who cares, hey? – this room is full of the elite. I shake my head; we study history so much, but learn so little.

Security personnel are also double the normal number and all armed. This isn't entirely new, security is in every building, it just isn't always quite this obvious. Every sector of the Hub has officer stations. Every doorway I've ever walked through is logged; the barcode on my left arm ensures that. Put simply, a door will not open without scanning you and if you don't want an up-close conversation with one of the multiple armed people nearby, leaving your arm exposed for scanning is the way forward.

It is clever really; make the convenience of having the door open for you seem like a blessing, so no one thinks to question what the PTB does with all your data. I don't believe for a second it isn't tracked and analysed. However, I, like everyone else, embrace it to the point of making fashion items to hold the sleeve up. While considering this, I fidget with my sleeve, telling myself I *can* unroll it at any time…I can, but won't – obviously.

My arm is suddenly grabbed and I turn to see the welcoming smile of Kate.

"Hey! How are you? This is crazy, right? When have you ever seen so many here at once? Everyone has crawled out of their labs to see the newbies – you'd think they were a new species!" Kate is always beautiful (even in a lab coat) and has an infectious smile that can lighten every mood, which instantly works its magic on me. "Where were you at the weekend? I thought you might pop over – or call me back at least?"

"Sorry, I really wanted to…I should have…" I trail off, not wanting to lie, but also not wanting to confess how close I was to her house. I am still confused and embarrassed by my Saturday travels.

"Never mind! How are you feeling? *Nervous* – sure you are, that's normal." She is answering her own questions by reading my face, but it is nice to be understood. I let her babble for a few minutes, just giving the odd 'mmm-hmmm' in the right places.

"So, what brings you out of the greenhouses?" I ask when she has finished.

"Ha-ha, well, I heard people talking on the way in about new arrivals overnight and I wanted to see if I saw anyone interesting – not that I'd know anyone, but you know, it's something different, right!? Why they have to come in at night, I don't know. Surely, day travel is okay by now?"

"I don't think so. No one does it – or not willingly anyway. Grandma despises the idea, I remember Abby asked her once about it and she burst into tears; crying that it was what Grandad did and died horribly as a result. I'm not sure that is entirely true, I think he actually went into a radiated area on foot, but her reaction was so severe, Abby never asked again. I did ask Dad, he said the radiation flares in the worst areas are less at night, so train travel is just safer then. Plus, he thinks the view of the destruction upsets people so much, it is better to travel in the dark and leave people none the wiser."

"Maybe, but I rather like the fairy tale image of people arriving and that's hard in the dark!" I just laugh at this, although I share her interest in seeing new arrivals, I'm not sure there is anything fairy tale-like about their coming. "Come on, your handsome prince could easily be in this room right now... now, which one *is* he?" Kate starts glancing around the room. I beg her to stop, I'm not laughing this time and thankfully she instantly gets the hint.

"Okay, I'll stop, but don't forget to look anyway!" she says, winking, as we sit down at the nearest empty table.

"Yeah, yeah. Anyway, how are all the seedlings today – any breakthrough crops?" Thankfully Kate's love of plant life is her weakness, so anytime a conversation needs diverting, I know to resort to asking about it.

"All well, thank you. We have some exciting new yields from some of our veg and newest fruit trees. We have really improved genetic modification too and increased disease resistance, meaning fewer chemical controls or only natural fertiliser is needed. It's really exciting to see the difference a few generations have made; if it carries on like this, next spring we hope to have enough seeds to start production on some of the Hub farms. Tim has some on the community allotment back home already, he wanted to test a few out of the lab and the results are better than we'd hoped for!"

I'm happy that they work together and have an equally content, fulfilled life together, but I'm suddenly struck with jealousy that she has this: the simple pleasures in life, as well as the complex, tackled as one. I don't mind being single, in fact I would prefer to be valued as just *me* first and foremost, but society hardly allows this train of thought, and I suppose ultimately, I do want what Kate has – though I still bear the scars of hopes dashed.

"It's so wonderful you have each other to share your work."

"Don't give up, you might find that soon – just because it hasn't happened the same as with me, doesn't mean it can't happen…"

I know she is right. I also know she wants to say 'just because Theo left you.' It is the unmentioned sentence, but we both know it is there.

"Look, your dad is here!" I follow her gaze and Kate is right. He sees me, nods with half a smile and turns back to his guests. He clearly has no intention of introducing me right now.

"I better get back to work, I'll catch you later." I smile at Kate as I get up, happy to get out of the room and back to the relative peace of my lab.

I am curious, but decide not to wander about any more after work and instead go straight home. Dinner is promptly served at 7.30. Neither Gee-Gee nor Dad are anywhere to be seen. Mum mutters that she wouldn't have cooked so much if she had known they weren't coming home. I can't help wondering why she thought Dad especially would be home early today when he hasn't been for years.

Mum and Grandma talk of nothing but the new arrivals. By all accounts they and their respective friends have spent the day 'newbie spotting.' Of course, they have absolutely nothing useful to impart and no actual knowledge gleaned; however, they somehow find enough to discuss to satisfy them both well into the evening.

If Dad or Gee-Gee returned, I didn't hear them, nor see them the next day. This didn't sit well with the gossip train but meant I could once again escape and largely repeat yesterday's activities of quiet work until evening. It was wise that I enjoyed peace while I could, as when I got home preparations and instruction from Mum for tomorrow's Match Day were extensive.

Most of the instructions were verbal, some practical – I would argue, all unnecessary.

FIVE

I had hoped to quietly go to the Matching Ceremony alone. I will be the first to admit this was a naïve hope, but it was something to cling onto. I also had daydreamed of methods of escaping – mostly to the country. Maybe a few minutes of freedom would be worth dying for? Possibly, though I doubt they would just shoot *me*. That was what happened to rebels of old, particularly if they were feared to be bringing disease back into the Hub – just shoot them down with a drone like a rogue wild animal and leave them to rot. Now, if they detected a breach from the Hub, they would send a drone, scan me, and send Enforcement Officers to catch me. Then what? I don't know; details of detainees are vague, prisons exist, but in outposts and mostly sentences are lifelong, regardless of severity. Precious few people talk about the past if they do come back, which in itself is enough to cause fear and compliance in the masses. I just know, with fertility falling at the rate it is, they won't 'waste' a 3.

If Mum knew I was weighing ways to get myself shot or detained outside the perimeter fence while she dresses me up, she really would have a fit. I've decided surrender is my best form of defence for today. If I truly have no escape, if causing a scene won't gain, I may as well observe, at least playing the role of obedience. If I am to find a silver lining, maybe it is best spotted by observation. Worth a go, right?

I like natural colours, ones that allow me to wander largely unobserved. Pink does not allow for this. Pink is the colour I am in. Not bright, praise be, but pink nonetheless. On Abby, fine, any of my nieces, great, just not me. The dress is also tighter than I would like, but does at least flow somewhat.

"Yes, quite lovely, see, I knew you had a figure under those jeans and jumpers!" declares Mum. That is the closest to a compliment I am going to get from Mum so I'll take it. "Oh, you should have seen me at my Matching Day – I was younger than you of course, but *so* pretty. Yes, I think your dad could have done much worse! I was nervous, everyone is, but it is so exciting. Oh, the joy! *Three* children married!"

I want to pipe up and point out that today isn't my wedding day, but Dad arrives, ready to leave and so saves me the effort.

I feel sick. Actually sick. Sitting in the Grand Hall of the University, I wonder if I could make it to an exit unseen. I can't keep my legs still; I am shaking that much. Mum is getting fed up with my nerves, scolding me through gritted teeth for fidgeting.

"If I could, I assure you, I would stop." I grind my teeth back at her. I'll pay for that later, but it is all I can do to cope right now. Others are filing in, some I know, some not. They all look as pale as I must be – or would be, if I wasn't plastered in makeup courtesy of my mother. Most of the soon-to-be matched are younger than me. There are a few 20-24 year olds, but the majority are 18 and freshly primed for matches and fertility tested to boot.

I glance over the older boys, trying not to look like I am in the viewing gallery of some sort of weird market. I need not worry really; everyone is doing the same thing – unless they are already coupled and fairly sure their application to stay together has been approved, in which case they are sitting quietly, hand in hand, just waiting for the confirmation. I can't help thinking this was meant to be me six years ago, hand in hand with Theo, just waiting for confirmation of what we already knew.

Maybe I'm wrong, maybe 18 is just too young to *know* we're right for each other. Maybe the PTB, with their scientific and genetic matching is the better, more lasting way for the majority. Build a relationship, a solid one, on mutual respect and a level playing field, be the cog in the wheel they design for you, together.

"Don't look so nervous Maia, he is nice."

Shocked, Mum and I simultaneously gaze at Dad, though Mum vocalises before I do.

"What! You *do* know him? And didn't tell me? Why on earth not?" No reply from Dad. I think he is regretting his momentary attempt at fatherly comfort. Either that or he is enjoying winding Mum up – maybe both. "Well!? Tell us *now* for heaven's sake!"

"Of course I know, do you not think I have been talking to all the new residents the last two days? – well, weeks actually! – not reading every file and sitting in the necessary meetings before they arrived?!"

I'm pretty sure I am witnessing the start of a fight that will continue for some time, especially if Mum doesn't agree with the 'quality' of my match. Despite her pressing for details on the *who*, Dad has held onto the affront that she doesn't know what he does and presumably, therefore underestimates his 'powers' in the PTB. This has clearly annoyed him, and I believe if he could, he'd walk off and leave us here. All my life, that has been the answer to their arguments: one gets too much, the other walks off. In public, they're all smiles – even now, smiles are masking their agitation. In private, sullen glances, grumpy phrases and ignoring each other for days is the norm. They're hardly the model couple they claim to be.

I do not want to be them.

Maybe this is why I have rejected the idea of being matched for so long? Maybe this is why I fear whoever I am about to get called up with now. The idea of becoming my parents frightens me. I do not believe in the system enough – yet they do, for all their differences and squabbles, they *do* follow and promote the status quo. I can't help wondering if they still would, had they been lower down the pecking order and one of the families desperate for a child. However, looking around me, many of these people are 0, 1s and 2s and they are still sitting in the rows, waiting to be called, waiting for their place in society, to be given their order and are quietly accepting the structure in which we live.

Suddenly, the seats on the stage are filled by eight self-important looking officials. The Matchmakers. Four men, four women of varying ages, all from the much larger group who make up the Genetics Committee. They are directly responsible for who is matched with who, what grade of fertility you receive and how many tests and 'donations' you participate in each year.

As they are seated, the room falls silent. One last man comes in, surrounded by extra security personnel: President General Fairfax. Though aged now, he still commands the room, still stands tall and muscular, ready for a battle, physical or verbal. He sits briefly, then rises and addresses the room:

"Welcome everybody! I have the great pleasure of seeing so many bright and promising young people come together today. This is a glorious day, a day of fulfilment for every person here.

I know this is a scary moment for many of you: life from now on takes a new direction, requires adjustment with your new spouse, but together, you can forge a lasting partnership and take up your role as essential members of the UNE, ensuring everyone's future. Never forget that unity is the very essence of what we strive for – Every. Single. Day. The success and future of our planet hangs on the decisions we make today. Not only for the continuation of humanity, but the safe development of and respect for Earth, never again repeating the mistakes of our forefathers."

Respect the Earth. Yes, that is what I would like to dedicate myself to; helping to restore what is damaged. Help with humanity's infertility, but in harmony with nature. That *is* what I want too, just *without* having to personally sacrifice my eggs or uterus – or marry someone chosen for me. *Well, you're out of luck, aren't you?* Great, I'm talking to myself again. Mum suddenly puts her hand on my leg – not to comfort or reassure, but as a (surprisingly strong) weight, to stop my leg from vibrating from fear.

"Now! Without further delay, let us begin. We will call you up to the various tables, the ushers will direct you to which as you come up and you'll be given your match and wedding date."

True to word, the eight officials break into twos. Ushers appear and start calling out names and taking individuals to the designated tables. Couples meet at these tables, some for the first time; some seem pleased, some not.

One couple is thrilled, they are already together and have been matched. Only happy tears for them. Not so much for another couple I had been watching, I'm just close enough to hear: "I'm sorry dear, you're fertile and he is not, this gentleman is your partner now, you cannot think so selfishly, I'm afraid…"

The girl starts screaming; all eyes are on her as her decibels ring throughout the hall. This clearly happens more than the PTB likes to admit as security swarms in effortlessly and grabs her. Her screams increase, but only for a moment, as her red hair is swept back, and a canister is pushed into her neck. She is immediately silent, her limp body is swiftly swooped up by the guard and in a flash, removed out the back.

Her boyfriend had been trying to get to her, but guards were by him, almost before she started screaming. They whisper something to him, what, I don't know, but it is enough to stop him in his tracks. Silent tears roll down his cheeks. He pauses, then darts towards the back door with impressive speed, but he doesn't make it. Instead he is tasered before he reaches the door and is dragged out casually by another guard.

It is like someone is playing a scene from my mind. I've envisaged this scenario a thousand times whilst trying to reconcile myself to Theo's betrayal. For the first time, I actually *see* the genuine fruitlessness of fighting the powers of the UNE. The order laid out by the PTB does not allow for discussion, extension, or expectation – unless it serves them or their way. This couple being together does not serve them. Theo and I would not have served them.

Fighting the system would have ended in separation. Knowing this, I still can't forgive him. Accept maybe; forgive, no. He gave up too easily, he could have at least told me he loved me or made me feel like I was worth fighting for. Star crossed – or fertility crossed lovers – crappy, but romantic. Maybe acceptance is healing to some degree though.

You would think this display was enough to stop proceedings, but apparently not as the ushers continue as if nothing happened. Business as usual. I wonder if these acts of violent drama are deliberately allowed to play out every now and again, just so the PTB can swiftly remind the masses what happens to those that rebel. After all, there's nothing like a good (free) visual aid to hammer a point home. I personally have seen little of this over the years, with just the odd 'removal' on the streets or from a building, but listening to conversations from those who live in SH2 or 3, I realise this happens a lot.

No rebellions are welcome, and they're certainly not tolerated.

The room is half full now, but I still feel claustrophobic, not unlike how I imagine a goldfish feels in a bowl, unable to escape the beady eyes that are watching its every move. I suppose I had mentally considered the boys of my age who I knew were unmatched but, as no one appealed to me and, until three days ago, I had still planned on somehow avoiding this, I hadn't allowed those thoughts to multiply. Then, the newcomers had arrived, and I was pretty certain I would get a newbie; so guessing was *really* pointless. I wasn't wrong.

Almost everyone I know is gone, certainly all the 2s and 3s. Lucy from my street is probably the only 3 of my age left (or the only one I know anyway), and she has just been called up with one of the new guys. I wish I could say we were friends, but she, like so many in my neighbourhood, is full of her own self-importance and according to her, I don't take enough pride in my position.

Lucy got really angry at me once for asking her to pick up her own litter. I was polite about it (well the first time!) and I actually thought it had been a mistake originally, but she informed me it 'was the lower people's duty to clean up' and as I didn't concur, we have barely spoken since. Petty, but true. Being a 3 is a lonely position if you don't share the superiority complex that apparently *should* go with it. I wasn't the most popular girl at school, far from it, but Kate and I had a nice group of friends that we would hang out with.

Until, that is, grading day.

Then slowly, the cracks began to show. The social hierarchy changed, and people resented me for something I have no control over. Everyone's attention was turned from education and speculation of the future to focusing on the direction that *was* now theirs, not what they *hoped* it would be. Schoolground chatter and gossip of girly dreams became unreachable for too many and envy is a powerful enemy.

I was doubly isolated as the dreams of the other 3s weren't mine; the one person I hoped would stick with me, didn't; and my best friend, though loyal, was torn between her group and mine. Fast forward six years, and here I am, listening to an odd looking, pale, thin, little man call out my name, pointing me towards a table with a computer screen and a little box of cards neatly placed on it. Sitting there are two members of the Committee, both smiling at me, but with no warmth. They are clearly tired and want this done, I can see it in their eyes.

The man on the right, slightly plump and balding, asks me to confirm my name and present my left arm for scanning. The woman checks her screen and fishes out a crisp, white card from the box. Almost everything is digital and communes with your watch, which despite the simple name, it is a small device of numerous functions and many impressive implements can extend from it as it acts as a phone, organiser, internet access, library, map, camera, and fitness assistant (to name just a few of its basic abilities).

No number or machine is private, every drop of data flows through the Hub's immense network. Only very special things are printed, intended as a keepsake for generations to come. Here is mine:

Congratulations on the joining of:
Mr. Maxwell Rivers & Ms. Maia Woods
3:3
To Marry 18th December 2123
13:00

Whilst digesting these few words, I am asked to present my watch. Without thinking, I unlock it with the barcode on my left arm and then hold out my right arm across the desk so my watch can be scanned. Immediately a notification flashes up:

Maia Woods:
Donation:
October 20th 9:00 a.m.

My heart sinks: one consolation of marriage had been no more donations. It would seem I am wrong; they are going to maximise my production before my marriage. I hold my stomach instinctively.

"Oh, don't worry dear, you'll be ready to get pregnant in December."

The lady meant this kindly, so I just about pull a smile, but my stomach is twisting so badly that I am struggling not to vomit. So much so, that I have actually forgotten to locate the person who my card is congratulating me with. I look up, a man is standing next to me, looking equally as embarrassed and, dare I say, as ill, as I feel. He is a few inches taller than me, slim, but slightly muscled, has olive brown skin, black hair, and dark brown eyes that I am relieved to see have a glimmer of kindness, not arrogance, to them.

Maybe there's hope.

"Hi," I whisper, holding out my right hand, "I'm Maia."

"Max." He takes my hand and briefly shakes it. "Hi… Wow…Okay…" He fidgets. Great, he is as awkward as me. That's good – I think?!

The lady at the table addresses us: "If you both go into meeting room 8, you can sit down with your parents, chat and get to know each other. More details on marriage, housing, etc will be passed down in due course. Congratulations, may you be blessed in your union and serve the UNE faithfully."

I can't find any appropriate words, so I just bow my head and force a smile. As I step to walk away Max's speech stops me in my tracks: "Thank you, Ma'am, I am sure we will strive to make the UNE proud."

I take it back.

He is a believer.

There is no hope for me.

SIX

Max and I silently make our way to meeting room 8. We glance at each other a couple of times with nervous smiles, but there is no communication. Our parents are already waiting for us and we are greeted enthusiastically, if not entirely warmly, by all. Dad has clearly spoken to the Rivers at length before as their manner to him is familiar, almost comfortable. I can see Mum is annoyed by this, but as she hasn't got to marry their son, I don't feel too much sympathy. I view the three strangers, desperately looking for hope that this is a good thing. Max has already demonstrated he believes in the system, so really, I'm probably searching for a needle in a haystack, but if I'm to find my silver lining, I may as well start here.

Max's dad looks like him – or rather, Max looks like a younger version of his dad. If Max ages like this, he will still be handsome when he is older. Dr Henry Rivers is his name. I'm yet to hear what he is a doctor *in* as my mother is making up for lost time and chattering at such a speed that asking my own questions would be fruitless. For now, I'll just have to take in the information provided from Mum's verbal assault.

Currently, she seems to favour Max's mum, who I am *really* unsure about. Her features are completely different to Max's or Henry's. Her skin is soft and pale without a blemish – she's definitely not a gardener! I could shake Kate's hands blindfolded and know it was her!

Mrs Rivers looks stern and I imagine it would take a lot to truly make her laugh. I say 'truly' as she chuckles, but it seems insincere or forced. Her dark blond hair is immaculate. I don't think a single strand is allowed to be out of place before she leaves the house each day. Right now, my hair is tidy (thanks to a thousand pins) but she'll probably have a heart attack when she sees me on a normal day! Dad is also keen to talk to her, and now I hear why – she is the new Director of Agriculture, so not just Mrs Rivers, she's *Director* Rivers.

Just when I thought my heart couldn't sink any further!

Mum is absolutely beaming – of course she is – this is another claim to power, another family connection to the top level of the PTB, and a family continuation of Great Gramps' title. Mum – well most of the family actually – had been annoyed when Colin Evans had inherited Great Gramps' job. He had fallen into it by default really as he was a relatively junior Governor of Agriculture at the time, but directly in line and for various, potentially unfortunate reasons, was most in position to take up the role quickly after Great Gramps' health had declined rapidly.

Not only does this mean Max will have been well and truly indoctrinated from a babe, but it will also mean the chances of me slipping somewhere into mid-SubHub and quietly living in peace are extremely thin. Max is the only son. We, therefore, must be the poster couple, joining Midland and Southern together, a united front for the future of the UNE, perfect examples of what the PTB strives for, blah blah blah… I can hear the speeches already and want to cry.

I feel my eyes welling up and my lip starts to quiver. If Mum sees me cry, I'll be in trouble – what's new? I stare at the floor and breathe slowly, desperately trying to stop the room from spinning when my arm is gently touched. I look up in a hurry, surprised to have been noticed as it has been several minutes since anyone has even mentioned me.

"So, Maia, I hear you are a research scientist? Who do you work under?" Dr Rivers definitely has a kind expression; his smile is refreshingly warm and his tone inviting, not examining like his wife's. I don't doubt he sees my moist eyes, but he makes no mention, just gives my arm a gentle, reassuring squeeze and waits for me to answer.

"Yes, yes, I am, I work under Dr Richard Brown, studying fertility influences – do you know him, sir?" Mum should be proud, I've swallowed my tears and delivered a polite, well-presented sentence, just as she has practiced on me for a lifetime.

"Richard, hey? Yes, indeed, well this is good news, we will be working next to each other for I am taking over the lab next to his for my genetics studies. I must say, I was sorry to leave my lab in the Midlands, I had everything just 'so,' but when I saw my *new* home – well, the extra space and resources can't fail to excite me!"

"*Henry!* Must you talk about laboratories constantly? Come, we have much more important things to discuss and thankfully, to save us, here I believe comes the Housing Association to show us where our son is to live!" Director Rivers is clearly not a science fan; though I suspect it is more a case of not liking the conversation to be centred on anything but *her*, for as soon as she has regained direction of conversation – even that which touches on the scientific – everything seems wholly interesting to her.

After a few minutes, the representative from the Housing Association walks up to us holding her screen out as she calls out mine and Max's details. "Okay, lovely, I'm Claire, I am your Match Coordinator, I'll just scan you both and ping you your housing details. Tomorrow at 9 a.m. we will meet there and go over the catalogue for furniture etc. It has already been painted and cleaned, so really there'll be no delay…ah, though no rush, I see they have delayed your wedding for extra donation…lovely, lovely."

I fail to see that as 'lovely.' Claire is holding her screen with her left arm so I glance at her barcode – a 0, so the 'loveliness' of donations is unknown to her; she might use a different word otherwise. I roll my eyes, but keep my thoughts to myself – good job they haven't worked out how to display them on a screen like everything else I do, otherwise I would be seriously screwed.

"Well, I'll see you there tomorrow at 9 anyway, best to get everything sorted early, I'm sure it is very exciting for you both! Your dress will need submitting by Friday – I *assume* you have a family wedding dress?" She now turns to my mum for affirmation, which of course, Mum gives with pride, adding it has already been used by my sister. "Oh, excellent! Well, the seamstress will adapt it to your size, pop it into her at 11 a.m. on Friday please – I've booked you in." A few taps of her screen seem to satisfy her; she has done all she needs to. "Lovely, lovely, well, I'll let you get acquainted, I see you have dinner tonight in the Central Hub, lucky you, don't let me keep you, see you in the morning!" And with that, she trots off to the next group.

I glance at my watch; her 'ping' was actually a seemingly endless number of emails, directions, and guidance notes. The title of some makes me cringe. I glance up, Max is also checking his; I watch his face as he scrolls through – he grimaces at about the point I did and looks up at me, blushing a little.

I chuckle; he at least has the same reaction to the cringeworthy as me. 'The First Union' and 'The Fertile Couple' aren't exactly what I want to be reading right now. Sex Education in school was interesting. The basic 'birds and bees – how to...' was bad enough, but then the nitty-gritty mixed with the 'doing of one's duty' and 'abstinence is a punishable crime' was enough to freak out any teenager.

Rest assured, if you are able to have children, you *will*, and the PTB *will* check that you're trying to conceive regularly.

I already knew there would be monthly health checks. Skimming over the messages, I can see the dates for these are already booked – the first a month after the wedding. The email threats of counselling if 'compliance is questioned' – I doubt that means sitting on a sofa and talking about my childhood.

I remember one of the educational videos I was made to watch at school on a yearly basis. In it you see a lady with 'issues' with her husband. They were non-specific to what defines 'issues' exactly, but the point was a failure to attempt natural conception would result in highly unpleasant techniques (I added that bit, they used the phrase 'supported procedures' whilst detailing things that make you want to run away and hide). If that fails, privileges are revoked, and you enter the 'Artificial Insemination Programme.'

When I was about 15, I innocently asked my mum (only once!) why we couldn't just be artificially inseminated if babies were so important. Mum's reaction was colourful, to say the least and I was in no uncertain terms informed that was a shameful way to conceive and a poor example to the family values that everyone works so hard for.

Now, I saw this as somewhat of a paradox; the family is artificially put together, what does it matter if the baby is conceived artificially too? But no.

"A.I. is for the last attempts and for the lab, not the happy, active family where natural is available and right. Proper union is the building block of the UNE, Maia."

My conclusion is, regardless of how Mum paints it, it is purely done to ensure compliance to UNE rule; as if they control bedroom activity as well as everywhere else, there can be no room for rebellion. Whatever the reason, the man standing about two metres from me is going to be closer to me than I'd like in less than three months' time. I shudder involuntarily; I think Max notices, but by the look of his face, he has similar freaked out thoughts of his own.

I suppose it doesn't matter if you're a believer or not, the realities of actual compliance with the rules *is* frightening. Well, I hope it is, my only comfort is that he is frightened too. We're told that's normal – it is, right?

Mum is already counting the grandchildren. Totally ignoring me, she is gleefully recounting the family successes in fertility to my future in-laws, declaring I am sure to be as fertile as my siblings. "Ooh, to think she might have twins like her sister – maybe as soon as this time next year!"

"Yes indeed, that would be wonderful, however one would be quite sufficient!" Great, both mothers are as bad as each other. "I have held out for just such a prospect for our only son – matches in the Midlands just didn't meet my requirements. I was beginning to lose hope until *this* wonderful opportunity presented itself!"

"I'm not sure that the President General thinks his grandson dying is a 'wonderful opportunity' my dear; however, it has allowed for previously unimagined change and development."

"Yes, quite Henry, I should have worded that better. The President General is still here somewhere, and I want to maintain a good relationship with him!"

My dad nods at this. Politician's approval. They'll get on just fine.

"What do you do, Max?" I decide it is time I actually learnt something about him, rather than listening to parental boasts or swamp myself in fearful thoughts.

"I'm an architect." Phew, not another politician in the making! I ask what kind of architecture interests him; this seems to give him pleasure as his face lightens as he replies: "I have been given a post evaluating development and structure within the Hub, working alongside the Botanical Department to maximise gardens that climb our structures. I am hoping to prove myself and in time be allowed to look at further expansion and restoration."

"Yes, yes, dear, but keep that to yourself! Why go into danger zones needlessly? Haven't I told you a thousand times: the fertile don't need to risk themselves where the less fortunate can more safely tread?" I have to repress a chuckle here; Director Rivers might as well have said: 'You're far too important for that, let one of the expendable, infertile do that.' My mum immediately backs her up. A cold shudder again goes through me – two unwavering, unfeeling mothers is more than I want to contemplate.

"Yes, Mother, but there is much to learn out there and even within the Hub, I would like to help improve life for all parts of the Hub, especially the poorer – maybe that would help with wellbeing and fertility…who knows, I was thinking—"

The Minority Rule

"Maxwell, enough!" The glare from mother to son is enough to make father and son stop and stare.

Apparently, that tone is well rehearsed as neither men seem to want to move in case they anger her further. Max gives a little bow and says no more. She clearly wants to control, but lighten the air as Director Rivers shakes her shoulders slightly, smiling as she turns to my dad.

"It is wonderful to hear our youth wanting to help; however, I keep telling Max, he must earn his position, learn from his elders, and fully understand how the UNE works... *walk before you run, my boy!*" Her sideways stare at Max then bears straight through me as she says, "Maia, I hope you will help Max settle into the roles you are both destined for."

"Indeed, Madam." I can manage no more. I feel like a mouse facing the farm cat. I'd like to squeak and run.

"Oh, no need for 'madam,' I'm to be your mother-in-law. No, no, in private you must call me Mary – in public, Director Rivers, of course, but at home, Mary."

She may say this smilingly, but I feel no warmth. I do somehow feel a degree of understanding towards Max though. We have known each other for little more than an hour, yet I am pretty sure we have had a similarly 'interesting' upbringing. I'm not sure whether to take this as a glimmer of hope that he isn't a complete drone – or just confirmation that he has been moulded well enough that any independent thought is easily squashed.

Conversation continued to be dictated by our mothers way into the evening. We had gradually wandered to the restaurant for a government paid meal that all newly matched couples and their families receive as an ice breaker.

Food, even at restaurants, is normally well restricted and, despite my mother occasionally using up more rations than she is meant to, even we don't normally eat as well as this. Along with the importance of UNE rule and quietly 'taking our place in society for the prosperity of all,' we are also well versed on the sin of waste and gluttony. This applies to possessions such as furniture or clothing, but extends to anything physical – including food, so on many levels, this lavish meal seems too much for me.

I would love to make an exception and enjoy it, the variety is second to none, but my stomach is still in knots and it is cruelly affecting my ability to relish the taste. I eat as best I can, 'encouraged' by Mum glaring regularly at me. We may both regret this later, but I will do my best not to waste it by vomiting.

Max and I have barely spoken; I think we have both silently decided there is little point while the others are here as if one parent doesn't mute us, the other does, and it just makes the effort of trying tiresome. We have, however, shared a few mutual grimaces and even chuckles at whatever they are saying over us. I am not saying I am *hopeful,* just that there is *hope.* My soul yearns for hope, so although I am no nearer to *wanting* this match, I *need* there to be something to hope for. I cannot entirely write him off for his indoctrinated replies because, like a fly on the wall listening to the conversation, I realise I am doing the same thing. Somehow, I must hope this is a shared survival response, not an inbuilt belief. If it is a belief, I am absolutely doomed. 'I' will become 'we,' and 'we' will be set by *him,* and *I* will cease to matter…as long as I have babies. I shake my head involuntarily and am spotted by my dad; he looks quizzically at me, but chooses to ignore me. I need to stop talking to myself in public (even if internally) before someone decides to lock me up as a crazy person.

I am thrilled when everyone finally says goodnight. A slightly awkward peck on the cheek from Max and his parents sees me free to hop onto a tram. Mum and Dad chatter on the way home and I slip off to my bedroom without much more than a "night, night." I am sure Mum would love to discuss Max further, but as I've no doubt tomorrow will be long enough, I am not going to indulge her now.

SEVEN

My alarm wakes me abruptly at 7 a.m. I set it before nodding off last night having decided that gives more than enough time before I have to meet Max at the house. Mum clearly disagrees as I walk into the kitchen to:

"You're late! You're not even dressed!"

"Good morning, Mum, good to see you, too. I have nearly two hours, the house is twenty minutes by tram, I can get dressed and drink tea in that time."

"Hmm, but what about your hair? You'll never tame *that* in time!"

"I'm not going to try; Max will have to take me as I am."

"What?! That is not the attitude. No, no, come, you have no time for tea…" she says, opening the hall door.

I ignore her, pouring tea into my mug, probably not my wisest move, but I have woken up determined to amuse myself while I comply with society's rules. Let's make sarcasm my silver lining today.

"We will *not* be late, you hear me?!"

"Pardon? You don't need to come with me."

"What? Of course I am coming! I must see where you are to live, make sure the house is just right and choose your furniture. You will only get one chance to choose for several years, so you must choose wisely! Jane told me her daughter had a very small catalogue to choose from last year; I'd like to think *my* daughter will have a better selection, but I keep hearing alarming reports of cutbacks in supplies – again! And of course, your father refuses to put in a request! Maybe Mary or Henry have already put in a request? Mary doesn't seem the sort to take 'no' for an answer or to be happy with second-hand, low class…no, no, we can't have the Midlands Hub outdoing the Southern – no, no!"

"Mum! I hate to burst your bubble, but everyone has cutbacks in supplies and what does it matter what furniture *I* choose? *I* have to live there – well, Max and I, so surely, *we* can claim the right to choose our own furniture. It is about the only thing I've had options in my whole life."

"Psh! Ungrateful girl, I have chosen well enough for you until now." Mum is clearly missing my point, but I suppose that is nothing new. While I'm thinking of an argument that has the slightest hope of success, she comes out with yet another trump card. "Plus, Mary said she would be there, and you can't let her choose for you." Yep, that's me done for. My house, along with my husband, will be chosen for me, down to the selection of my kitchen cutlery.

Mum continues her babbling all the way to the house; she has an opinion on everything from the number of people on the tram, the weather, the neighbourhood, who she thinks is influential here, whether it is *really* the best area; and then last, but no means least, my choice of dress and hair (I see nothing wrong with trousers, shirt, and casual jacket – apparently, I look like I'm going to an interview. Oddly enough, that's exactly how I feel).

A pregnant lady gets on the tram with a toddler. This is all the encouragement Mum needs to continue her lecture on the joy and wonder of being a 3. She coos at the child. Now, don't get me wrong, he is cute, and I am genuinely happy for the mother. She looks the absolute picture of happiness – to be honest, she is actually a much more compelling advert for motherhood than my sister or sister-in-law have ever been. They gloat in an ugly, arrogant manner; this lady beams with natural, sweet pride while Mum oohs and ahhs and asks when the baby is due. If I had a sister like this lady, maybe I wouldn't feel so pressurised and frankly, bitter. However, I am what I am, and although I would dearly love to find my peace, I cannot see it being achieved by copying this lady's path to happiness.

Thankfully the lady is going for a hospital check-up, not getting off at our stop because, were I to find her my new neighbour, Mum would constantly compare me to her. I step off the tram into an area almost identical to the one I got on at.

When the Hub was designed, uniformity was certainly in the architect's mind. Directions on my watch dictate my steps and after walking a short distance, the little red dot flashes, telling me I have reached my destination. It's 8:45 a.m. I want to boast of my time keeping, but as I am about to, the front door of the house slides open releasing Claire, who excitedly greets us as she bounds down the path.

"Ah, lovely, lovely! What do you think, Maia?! Is it not a lovely house?" Taking my cue, I look up. It is smaller than our current family home, but is made in exactly the same style. Although nothing in the Hub is unnecessarily adorned and everything is minimalist using prefabricated and recycled material, botanical arrangements feature heavily on and up every building. Flowers, herbs, shrubs, and trees are on every conceivable surface – partially for beauty, but also to provide sustenance and clean air. The whole street is made up of about a dozen moderately sized homes, each one like the next except each has different displays of flowers – mine has a pretty purple arrangement. I hope I don't have to tend the garden; flowers have never been my strong point, but chances are there is a street gardener from SubHub 2 or 3, just like there is back home.

"I like the area, yes, a little further from us than I would have chosen, but altogether, it looks well kept." Mum, as always, answers for me. Claire seems a little surprised that there was any doubt the area would be good.

"Oh, yes, of course! All our 3 couples are moved into the best homes. We want the best environment for our growing families! There is a park – perhaps you saw it on the way in? – it is quite lovely, and the preschool is just by it. Yes, everything is *just* right!"

I wonder if this is what zoo animals felt like in the old days. Exotic wildlife is relegated to digital books and video now, but apparently, before the UNE was established (after The Fall of What Was), society had zoos and breeding programmes for endangered species. Many of those are now gone entirely or if still alive, in fallen areas where we can no longer go, but I wouldn't blame anyone for likening zoos of then to Hubs of now. Okay, Hubs are larger and more elaborate, but certainly SubHub 1 is designed for optimum care of breeding stock and although there are no bars, the PTB surveillance and barcoding certainly feels like prison to me.

"Ah! Max and Director Rivers! Excellent timing, welcome to your new home!" Claire waves her arm through the air, showcasing the building behind her as they approach.

"Thank you, I like the flowers." Ha-ha, I don't think Claire was expecting that response as she turns to see why the flora should be what captures Max, not the actual house.

We share a smile at her confusion and I can't resist subtly mimicking her tone and adding: "Yes, I thought them *lovely,* too."

Mum understands, but disapproves (there's a surprise), so glares at us both. Happily oblivious, Claire giggles sweetly, leads us up the path and through the front door. Inside is as I expected – clean and clinical, like every other home in the Hub. The reception hall is light, but not warm and leads into an open kitchen, dining and living room which spans the majority of the downstairs, the only exception being a study and bathroom. We have three bedrooms and a bathroom upstairs.

"Only three bedrooms?" Mum looks concerned.

"Oh, don't worry, we can easily upgrade to a larger house if more than two babies come along – plenty of time for that! With fertility dropping, sadly most people don't need upgrading, but of course, the PTB will be thrilled to upgrade if necessary!"

"To be sure, Maia comes from very fertile blood, I have no doubt she will need more room before long. Her sister has twins you know and another on the way! She took a while to conceive a second time, but I have no doubt she will carry on now she has got going again and her brother has four children! To be fair his wife has a lot to do with that, but fertility is clearly strong in *my* blood!"

Bragging like this is so unpleasant to listen to, but Claire and Mary seem thrilled. I just want the ground to swallow me up, especially when I spot that Max is also smiling as he listens to my mother.

Claire pulls her cataloguing system out of her bag, lays it on the kitchen island and logs herself in with her wrist. The room is filled with holographic items as she opens up the system. I now see the great advantage of the houses being architecturally the same as holograms are cast in the appropriate places around the room.

"Now, shall we get started? Here's the first option, we can mix and match as we go, or you can just choose a whole set. I'll slowly flick through, tell me if you want to lock or tag an item to consider."

I wish I had my mother's enthusiasm for this; she looks positively overjoyed at the number of items shining around the room. I just feel overwhelmed, and it is already obvious that my opinion is of little interest to her as she pokes images. Mary is not much better, in fact within minutes it seems to have turned into a competition to see which mother can select an item first. I have images of them taking credit for the selection in years to come.

Max quietly walks to me and whispers: "What do *you* like? I'm a simple, no-frills kind of guy, but if we don't choose for ourselves now, we're going to be living in replicas of parents' homes." A sigh of relief, mixed with a smile comes out of me. Max is absolutely encouraged by this as he finishes with: "I know this is awkward as hell, but I want *my* life, *our* home, not *theirs.*"

"I'm on board with that."

To my surprise, I *am* on board with him. I have known him for less than a day, fought meeting him for six years and still resent the idea of having life dictated, *but* maybe, just maybe, he could be an accomplice to change or freedom – that's probably asking too much, but I must search for something resembling my silver lining – whatever form that might come in.

With my newfound hope, I start looking at items properly and untag some of our mums' choices. Max follows my lead. Some of his selections are interesting, but I figure some things have to be compromised on and frankly, his choices are better than my mum's will ever be. On the whole we seem to share preferences and he actually has a nice eye, so after a few minutes of conjoined attack, both our mothers sit back, adding their opinion for added effect and self-consolation, rather than expecting compliance. It feels good to choose something, however unimportant.

Upstairs, Claire does the same thing, setting out the catalogue in each appropriate room, ready for items to be flicked through.

"Now, baby rooms – they can be redone or ordered as you know a time scale, but we'll default a few selections for you until that time. Bathroom – you can either repeat from downstairs or select again, and then there's the master bedroom…"

I'm guessing 'separate beds and no baby items' is not the answer Claire is after here. Max and I seem to have run out of mojo, and if it wasn't for the fact my mum has started to take over again, I would happily have slipped back downstairs. "Let's just go with basic, default for upstairs; the bedroom included."

"Okay, lovely, lovely, nice and straight forward – an excellent example, Maia." Well, that wasn't my intention, but I am glad that Claire approves as it has the added bonus of stopping Mum objecting to not running through whatever options she would have preferred.

Selections finally done, I feel exhausted. I am worried about any suggestions of continued 'together time' – in fact

I worry if I will eternally be subject to someone else's diary. I am relieved to hear that Max and Mary have to attend a 'newbies' meeting in the Central Hub at 2 p.m. and Mum wants to stop at a friend's house on the way home. I am a little less pleased to learn she has arranged for us all to have dinner at 7 p.m.; however, at least that gives me six hours to myself and the day is bright and warm. I refuse my Mum's invite onto the tram, repeat the awkward pecks on the cheek to all, and start walking in the direction of the river.

EIGHT

It did not take me long to find the river and although this part of it is less familiar to me, I easily wander down its bank into more known territory. There are so few spaces in the Hub that I can forget the PTB or feel remotely unwatched; and although I know there are cameras and drones here too, they have the grace to busy themselves at a distance, allowing thought to feel less checked.

I pass a few people, but do not stop to say more than a polite hello or remark on the weather. On the other side of the river, people are again at work on the orchards or in the greenhouses which seem to run for miles. Kate loves visiting over there, she has the greenhouses next to the lab, but these are truly enormous. Apparently on the outskirts there are more, but as that is Army and robot domain only, I don't suppose I'll ever get to see it. Had I been a 0, or 1 even, they might have considered me military material – *'the making of the strongest family'* as the adverts say. But no 3 is allowed to apply for the Army, and in truth, I'm not sure it's for me any more than motherhood. I would have perhaps liked the option. Seeing other places and alternative roles in life would have been something to consider at least.

As I reach my favourite spot, the sun is really hot, and I am glad to take refuge under my tree. On cue, Smoggy appears to sit next to me. I am not sure where she was before I arrived, but my regal friend wastes no time in greeting me. To my surprise, and apparently Smoggy's displeasure, another cat also appears. Smoggy hisses at the ginger tabby, but he is seemingly undisturbed by her feline expletives and walks up to me as though she wasn't there. I stroke them both, one on either side of me, and once Smoggy is convinced my attention can be divided amiably, silence resumes.

Calls of "Squash! Squash!" in a high-pitched voice suddenly disturbs our peace. I am guessing my ginger companion is 'Squash' as he tenses as he hears the calls edging closer. Then a second voice, which undoubtedly belongs to Aunt Dora, joins the calling, this time for Smoggy and Squash in a comical "Smoggyywogwogwogggyyyy…Squaassshhh!"

Smiling to myself, I sit out the calls as I can hear them approaching and neither cat moves an inch in their direction. Aunt Dora appears first, mildly scolding me for not moving, but I laugh and remark that as I wasn't being called, I thought I'd wait. Thankfully she laughs, too, muttering that I'm as insolent as the cat, turning in time for the owner of the other voice to appear.

Standing before me is a lady I know by sight more than personal experience. Over the years she has been present at larger, extended family gatherings as she is great grandmother to Aunt Dora's late husband. I've also seen her at Hub meetings on the odd occasion, but she is always quiet, always on the outskirts, and whenever possible it would seem, always quickly back at home. Her house isn't that far from here, but I am surprised to see her cat so far from home. I am about to voice my surprise when Aunt Dora solves the riddle.

"Maia, you remember Mrs Addams? Well, she and Squash have just moved in with me."

"*Really*?!" I need to work on my default responses. I am so surprised I can't think of anything else to say. I was only here a few days ago and nothing was mentioned. Aunt Dora's house had no sign of imminent change – and frankly, I thought she was so relieved to live quietly alone. I can't think what brought this on so suddenly, but I collect myself enough to add: "Yes, of course; good afternoon, Mrs Addams."

"Hmmphh, no need for the *Mrs Addams*, dear, *Eve* will do just fine. All this title business just makes me feel old." She winks saying this, for she *is* old. In truth, she is probably the oldest person in the Hub. I remember her 100th birthday party – I must have been 10 or 12 at the time, so I think 'old' is a fair, though possibly not flattering, description. That said, she looks remarkably well for one of her age, and although she walks with a stick, she has just one and moves as fast as many twenty or even thirty years younger. Her grey hair is neatly arranged, and I'd imagine her blue eyes are as bright now as they were when she was in her twenties.

"Yep, your aunt has had me dumped on her, those rotten hmmphh PTB want me house and want to put me in a nursing home to die under their control, no thank you, I've kept to me self all this time, I ain't goin' when they want now, hmmphh."

I am shocked and amused by her speech. It is clear by her tone 'hmmphh' is code for swearing, without her *actually* swearing. She isn't really pronouncing anything, just producing a mixture of a grunt and mumble, with an altered tone for (presumably) whatever word she'd actually like to insert into the sentence. It is also clear this woman is no push over, despite having lived so quietly.

Aunt Dora looks nervously around her, including at the sky – I can only conclude she doesn't want drones picking up our conversation. She walks nearer to the river where I am now standing and speaks so quietly I can barely hear: "Eve found herself in a difficult spot, I think it my duty to care for her, she is family to me after all and as we're both outsiders to the general norm, I think it only right we stand together – come what may."

A cold shudder hits me, despite the heat of the day. "Are you okay, Aunt Dora?" I whisper.

"Yes, yes, my dear, I am fine. Eve isn't always so well...in her mind I mean, and I cannot let the PTB discard her into a home."

"Wouldn't she receive specialist care there?"

Aunt Dora shakes her head. "No, my dear, I think, perhaps happily, you misunderstand the purpose of a nursing home for people such as Eve...*care* is not the objective. No, she must never go there, the PTB must *not* hear her talk, you must promise if you are to visit me, *never* to repeat what she says, especially if she says something odd or unusual."

I stare at Aunt Dora, trying to process what I am hearing.

She stares at me without blinking. "Do you promise? I must have an answer *now*, or we'll have to part."

I feel my eyes boggle with surprise, but instinct replies for me: "Yes, of course, I'd never betray you!"

I do not understand, but I do recognise fear in Aunt Dora's face. I am unbelievably curious, but I can see I am not going to get answers, not today anyway.

Aunt Dora smiles, sighing with what I can only imagine is relief. "Dear girl, I know we can count on you." She steps back and increases her volume saying: "Ha! Smoggy is not sure of our new housemate. Squash doesn't seem to respect her reign quite as he should!"

Taking her lead, I look at the ginger tom, wondering what he did to earn such a name. His features aren't squashed, everything seems fine…he is actually a handsome boy, so I ask:

"Why is he called Squash? Did something happen to him?"

"No!" Eve laughs at me. "He is as fit and healthy as can be! When he was a tiny kitten, he reminded me of a little butternut squash, so that's what I called him. My brother's grandson bred him and let me have him once he was weaned. That was the last useful thing any of my family did for me, hmmphh ungrateful lot."

Aunt Dora suddenly looks panicked. "Let's go have some refreshments! Maia, will you join us inside? It is so hot out today! You must tell us about your match. I have been waiting for an update. How did it go? Is he handsome? Your mother is pleased, I know, I had *her* update pinged to me – full of her delight!"

I answer her questions as we walk towards her bungalow. Both cats follow like well trained dogs – which is odd considering how recently Squash moved in. Aunt Dora is clearly happy to distract Eve and Eve seems interested enough in my match to forget her mention of past grievances. I cannot pretend to not want to ask a thousand questions, but am also glad of a sympathetic ear to relive the last day or so's events.

"Well, at least there is promise there. Not every match starts as well…or ends as well for that matter. I hope he proves worthy my dear, hmmphh, poor Dora here got lumbered with my great grandson – and look how that turned out!"

"I loved him in the end, Eve, and we found our path, however short. Believe in the matching system, Maia, it will see you right."

I struggle to decide if Aunt Dora completely believes this or if this is said for the benefit of more than myself. She seems anxious as we walk past the neighbours' gates and only relaxes once she has the kettle on the go. It is actually too hot for tea and I really need to be getting home if I want to avoid Mum's wrath, so although I would dearly love to continue this conversation, I will have to wait. I make my excuses, hug both affectionately goodbye and make my way back into the heat, pointing in the direction of home.

NINE

As the kitchen door slides open, Mum immediately starts humming 'here comes the bride.' I can just about see how this was nice in the days of old when marriages were spontaneous, chosen or in any way a joyful union of an in-love couple. However, as I am neither in love nor joyous, this tune does nothing for me – other than irritate. It doesn't help that Abby is also sat in the kitchen providing a backup chorus.

"I'm looking forward to meeting Max, Mum says he is lovely," beams Abby. "Gee-Gee is coming home early with Dad, she wants to meet him too, though I think she knows his mum already – she muttered something to that effect on the phone when I called to invite her."

"Of course Gee-Gee knows her, she has Great Gramps' role now, they would have had video meetings when she was in the Midlands Hub – or *he* would have if not her...Director Rivers was only *Midlands Governor* previously, ah, but what does it matter? She *is* Director of Agriculture now and you will be her daughter-in-law – such an excellent match! A pity Max hasn't taken a more political role, but that might change now he has moved, but if not, your children will be in excellent line for positions of power!"

I am sure a mother's speech is supposed to comfort, reassure, build up, and generally support a child. In fact, looking at Abby, our mother's speech does just that for *her*. For me, it constantly produces a cold, frightening chill. How can one who gave birth to me understand me and my hopes *so* little?! If I must have children, I hope I do a better job at raising them to be happy for who they are, not what someone else wants them to be, even if their opinions differ to mine. I am not going to argue with Mum, it is a waste of breath. Out of obligation, I offer assistance, but this is declined in favour of me 'preparing myself for guests.' Ignoring the insinuation, I gladly take myself upstairs until I hear Dad and Gee-Gee's voices. At least with more people around, Mum's attention will be better divided.

The Rivers are prompt in arriving and dressed nicely without being over the top. Mum is verging on over the top, but plays the role of hostess well. I feel sorry for the Rivers, their three to our nine (plus children) must be overwhelming. Mum is determined to display the Woods' fertility in whatever way possible. I don't know why she bothers; the match has been made, the Presidential General has approved it, and death is the only thing that will stop this marriage now. Whether the two families like each other really isn't a concern of the Matchmakers, and as Dad clearly had a leading hand in this, I think Mum's display is extra unnecessary. Even so, I suppose I should want harmony. Conversations flow relatively easily, mostly allowing me to observe rather than participate. Grandma and Mum are both keen to quiz everyone, Abby and Isobel are mainly fixed on controlling the children, and neither father seems overly attentive, but do assist when prodded by their spouses. Abe is interested in Max's posting and Gee-Gee is in discussion with Mary. They clearly do know each other; however, I am not convinced they know each other for the right reasons as their tones are a little strained. What they are saying is correct and amiable, but I am sure there is a hidden code of past disagreement.

"It is lovely to finally meet in person, Professor Beaufort, I have seen you on video calls so many times with George, but I must confess, I never expected to physically meet. Coming to the Southern Hub seemed so unlikely!"

"Indeed, life takes unexpected directions."

"I hope to continue the good work of George – Director Beaufort – of course bringing new ideas of my own, while ironing out some mistakes."

"Such as?" Gee-Gee's tone is not amused, "I presume you mean Colin Evans' mistakes, not my late husband's."

"To be sure." It is a little bit like watching two animals circling each other, sizing the other up, saying nothing particularly of interest to the observer, but saying plenty to each other. "I have nothing but respect for George's work."

Dad joins in with: "You have a lot of work to plough through – past and present. I know I have more than usual at the moment."

"Yes, I am sure an influx of new arrivals didn't help with that!"

"True, but thankfully things have gone smoothly there. Hopefully you will soon find the swing of things."

"No doubt, no doubt. I plan to hit the ground running, Stephen. That's the only way I do things; there's no point in jogging along."

"Sometimes a little R&R at the appropriate time solves many a fall, Mary," says Gee-Gee.

The Minority Rule

I definitely feel like I am missing something as Mary stares at Gee-Gee. A wordless power struggle is flashing before me that no one else seems to see. What on earth is Mary planning on doing as Director that threatens Great Gramps' memory so badly? Mary suddenly shakes off Gee-Gee's stare, smiles, and says:

"You're probably right, Professor, but I don't mean to be a wallflower and relaxation never did come easily to me."

"When you get to my age dear, the importance of reflection at the appropriate time is well established."

Mary nods recognition, but doesn't reply.

Henry interrupts my observations by turning to me. "Well, Maia, things are moving along nicely with the wedding plans. Mary was concerned about your age, but I've seen your results – most impressive. It is a shame more people aren't as fertile as you – the figures for this year's eighteen-year-olds are truly worrying. If this rate continues, those in primary school now will be 95% infertile."

"Yes, well I've already said she's worthy of our boy." Mary doesn't seem keen on Henry leading this topic.

I'm not keen on people discussing my fertility at the dinner table, particularly when they have seen results I will never see. I wonder how Mary got to her position – being in the right family no doubt, but fertile women so rarely get anywhere academically, let alone become governor or director. Positions like this are reserved for men or infertile women; and for the majority, even if you want to work after your children reach adulthood, the jobs available do not lead to high(er) office.

Mary must have pushed incredibly hard when Max was in his teens; possibly this shouldn't surprise me – our short acquaintance has shown she is one determined woman.

I should admire her, I suppose; if I am to accept my role as wife, I should aspire to her achievements, but if I have to be so cold and driven, I am not sure her method is worth the personal sacrifice.

"How are your parents, Director Rivers?" (I am still not comfortable calling her Mary, despite being told to). "Have they moved with you or do they live with family in the Midlands Hub?"

"Well, thank you, Maia. My brother and his wife live with them and care for them as necessary."

I am increasingly curious now. Had she said, '*my sister,*' I wouldn't have been shocked, but for parents to live with a son when a daughter lives, well, this is curious indeed. Abby *will,* in time, live with our parents. There has never been any question of this. Abe will live with Isobel's parents as she is the only daughter. That is just how things are.

"Oh, that's a shame they couldn't come with you." I say this innocently as a gentle probe in case this was a new arrangement thanks to her relocation.

"Oh, no, this is how things were anyway. It all works well. Pour me a little wine, will you please, Max?" As Max complies, Mary holds out her glass in her left hand.

I have a habit (for better or worse), of reading barcodes. I like reading pedigrees, which I admit, is a little two faced as I hate anyone reading mine, but right now I am not sorry as I am fascinated by what I read. At the end of her code is a 1… Mary is a 1?! How is that possible? How did she have a baby as a 1? That has never happened to my knowledge.

I start hypothesising answers to my riddle: Is Max a lottery baby? Surely not. He looks like his dad…Was Mary downgraded? There's no sign of that on her code…Is Max a donation baby from a donor mum? That's not common practice – to put it mildly! Why would they agree to that…? What is Henry? I now look for Henry's code.

Annoyingly, he is sitting so his arm is out of sight. I really don't want to make my newfound mission obvious; that would be embarrassing. I consider asking for things to be passed to me…a drink, condiments, but sitting as I am, I don't think I will be able to see anyway. I will have to wait.

Gee-Gee has started talking to Henry now. They clearly know each other too. Why this wasn't a more obvious acquaintance before, I am not sure. He is a geneticist, of course he knows the Director of Fertility! Henry's respect for my great grandmother is clearly apparent as his tone has changed whilst talking to her. She seems interested in his conversation but not overly encouraging – or rather not at the dinner table as she remarks:

"Yes, indeed, I think we should discuss this at the lab. Your new research sounds intriguing, and I would like to look into it further." At least it is not just me she won't discuss work with for long at the table!

Conversation flows on and I have to wait until it is time to clear up the plates to continue my attempt to read Henry's barcode. I know Mum is expecting me to help clear up and for once, I am happy to comply. As I politely reach past for one plate, Henry passes me his, giving me just enough time to see his code ends in 3. Walking past from behind a short while later, I glance at his neck, just in case I was mistaken.

Nope, clear as anything: 3.

Perhaps not as subtly as I should, I go around the other side of the table, looking at Max's neck. Pedigrees match and both are 3s. What doesn't match is the maternal familial code.

Mary is *not* Max's biological mother. Okay, this isn't the biggest revelation in the world, plenty of people have children they are not genetically related to, but it does open up so many questions: *how* was a 3 and a 1 matched? That doesn't happen. Ever. *How* did she rise up to be Director? *Who* is she?

While these thoughts race through my head, one thought of consolation comes to mind – if she isn't Max's *actual* mother, he is less likely to be like her. Okay, Nurture v Nature is an issue, but at least genetically, he isn't her.

TEN

I have been escorted by my mother to the dressmakers and thoroughly poked, prodded, and pinned by the seamstress as she prepared to alter my wedding dress. Mum is delighted with her involvement; I am just happy to have gotten through it without too much drama or added misery. The rest of the day is my own. No meetings, no dinners, both sides of the adjoining families have work-related meetings and I am free to do as I please.

I messaged Kate when I realised and thankfully she was able to get time off this afternoon, so I have the comfort of her companionship. Of course, Max figures heavily in her immediate questioning. She has a way of making the grilling almost fun and for a while, I forget that the whole scenario is fake. I am grateful for this; this attitude is the one I need to adopt if I am not going to become a very bitter old woman – one that makes made-up grunting sounds instead of swearing, like Mrs Addams. I've not forgotten her or Aunt Dora's earnest entreaty to keep any conversation with her to myself. As soon as I can, I want to visit again as not unlike the mystery around Mary Rivers' past, my mind has so many projections to the possible truths that I feel the need to at least try to find out more. I consider confiding in Kate, but my promise to Aunt Dora rings in my ears. I have never seen her look so solemn or so afraid – or so conscious of drones and neighbours, which makes me conclude that confiding in even Kate is not right or wise.

A promise is a promise.

No, the enigma of Mrs Addams will have to stay undeciphered – or rather *unshared*. I very much doubt my curiosity will allow me to not privately consider why that seemingly unremarkable old lady should hold any knowledge or opinion that the PTB doesn't want voiced. Trying to think about what little I *do* know about her hasn't produced much enlightenment. She is one of the oldest residents in all the UNE, I remember reading that, or Mum talking to Aunt Dora about it a year or so ago…Okay, that is an achievement, but hardly one to cause fear. She has lived quietly in her home in the corner of SubHub1 for as long as I can remember.

I'm pretty sure boys from my year used to make up stories about her home being haunted or some such rubbish – the typical go-to answer to why someone lives quietly and tries not to interact with noisy neighbours – which of course probably just confirms her reason (whatever that may be), to keep to herself. 'Live and let live' or Shakespeare's 'To thine own self be true' aren't exactly popular theories these days. I am actually surprised Shakespeare is allowed to be read – I suspect we aren't shown all of his works.

So much literature from before The Fall is forbidden and destroyed now. Anything that doesn't help maintain the ideals of today had to go; however, the occasional, seemingly random piece of art from long ago exists.

Of course, it isn't random if it proves a point that the PTB like – and Hamlet isn't exactly a happy tale of past days, so I suppose the PTB thinks it helps highlight the need for today's strict order – though I expect any text can be twisted to one's teachings if you pronounce them authoritatively enough on the young and impressionable.

Okay, so Mrs Addams is off the conversation list, but as Kate chatters on about Max, I am considering asking her opinion about his mother. I'm not sure why I am holding back. Kate won't repeat anything I ask her not to; Tim might unwittingly, but he isn't here, and Kate definitely wouldn't. Something tells me to wait on that one, too, though, at least for another location. Central Hub is not the place for real confidence – there are cameras, drones and lord knows what other devices covering every conceivable inch and angle of this place. Officially declared as being for our security, I can't help questioning the need, but know better than to *actually* question it.

Last year a man set up a stall outside the University questioning the necessity of so many cameras. He had a small, curious crowd listening to him, but not for long as a drone called security, who then dragged him off in record speed. Some of his audience were also detained and only released once they were able to chant the PTB speech pitch perfectly for the awaiting press. They all said the same thing so there was no way it was anything but scripted: "I am glad the security services were quick to respond to such unwarranted, misinformed conduct as was witnessed by myself. Any doubt the PTB surveillance is for anything other than ensuring optimum function and peace in society is disturbing and not something I wish to contemplate."

The protagonist himself disappeared and neither press nor notable personnel seemed to question where he went. There was the odd rumour – all presuming prison. I did hear Dad talking about a relocation soon afterwards, so I wondered if that was for him or his family as they also seemed to vanish. Call it what you will, the PTB's power to silence is impressive.

"Are you listening to me?"

Crap, the honest answer is 'no' but I chuckle and say, "Of course, you were asking about Max, my house, where it is, if my mother was pleased…"

"And then?" Kate is grinning, but I can see I've annoyed her a little.

"I'm sorry, I got distracted, what were you saying?"

"Hmm, what distracted you? I'll tell you if it was more important than me asking about food." She smiles properly; I'm forgiven. If only everyone was as kind-hearted and open as Kate – if only *I* was, I'd live a less frustrated life.

"Nothing is more important than food! – certainly not my musings of husbands, in-laws, and things I don't understand – where shall we eat?"

Kate doesn't answer straight away, but looks at me quizzically, her blue eyes fixed on me, reading me in a way only a true companion and kindred spirit can. After a moment, she squints, as though she has read enough, grabs my hand, and says: "Okay! Well, that can wait, let's eat! Tim is going to eat with his uncle tonight and I'm not going to eat alone – come, I have a dessert voucher saved up and a chocolate mousse which I'm dying to meet!"

I am dragged into a familiar little café, one we have visited many times – and one that does indeed have a fabulous dessert menu. I also have an unused voucher which is handy as a chocolate mousse for two is not enough to truly enjoy its delights. The waiter recognises us as we scan in at the doorway, and he swiftly ushers us to a quiet corner and presses the menu button on the centre of the table, causing the hologram menu to flash up before us. "I doubt I need to ask, ladies, but you are welcome to peruse the menu before you decide." We glance at each other, giggle, and confirm that we are creatures of habit and our choices will indeed be 'the usual.'

"So, you said Tim is with his uncle, you mean Bruce, right? Is he Okay? I haven't heard him mention him recently."

"Ah, yes he is all right, Tim chats to him every so often, but I couldn't tell you the last time Tim visited him in SH3 – he gets fed up with extra drone checks, but last week Bruce called up in such a state, Tim decided he would go help." I look at her, eyes wide open, willing her to continue without saying anything. Kate gets the hint, but whispers the next bit. "Have you heard about issues in SH3?" I nod. "Well, Bruce rang up Tim for help as apparently he has been applying to the Council there and had nothing but failed promises."

"Oh?"

"Bruce loves his greenhouses in SH3 and has really got a lovely system there. As you know, he volunteered to go down there long ago – much to Tim's Dad's displeasure; he still hasn't made his peace with him not wanting to stay in the Central Greenhouses, even if it's such an obvious choice for him, what with his wife's family and home being there – not to mention he would never have made Head of Horticulture up here! Anyway, I digress, Tim and Bruce have been cross referencing projects occasionally, testing seed, you know standard 'green-fingered stuff' as you call it."

I laugh as she clearly intends me to.

"Well, one of Bruce's greenhouses failed. I mean epically failed – heating or irrigation or both apparently – and the shortages were causing residents to get angry." I stay silent, but that would certainly explain the reports of unrest in the SH3. "Bruce was trying to get the Council to apply for rations from SH2 or 1 while he rebooted that greenhouse, but they were ignoring him, only saying he had to manage with what they had. We doubt the Council even bothered consulting beyond their own walls. They had their rations, so decided the issue couldn't be so bad and just sent the Security Services after any protestors – which of course, worked its magic as no one in their right mind is going to stand in front of them. So, it was left to Bruce to find a solution. He managed to get the greenhouse fixed, but all produce is behind in growth, so he called Tim to see if he could supply anything edible or soon to be – *anything* to pacify the residents. We had a meeting yesterday with the other horticulturists here and came up with a list of plants to donate without rationing changing up here. Tim is now delivering said goods."

"Hmm, sounds like a lot of unnecessary stress. The Council should have just referred the Horticultural Departments to each other to begin with."

"If *only* it worked as simply! We should have involved the Agricultural Governor to approve the donation, but we figured with all the changes and the new Director, getting an answer would prove untimely and poor Bruce was stressed enough!"

"Ah, my new mama, huh?! Is she striking fear into people already?"

"Ha-ha, yes indeed, I think the Council have heard of her reputation and are already too afraid to consult with her."

"Any idea of her background?" I ask coyly. Kate catches my eye as I ask, again quizzing me silently.

"I had hoped *you'd* be the source of info in that department – all I know is those that *know*, have hinted she is not one to take lightly."

"No, that much I worked out myself, I was just curious to the…" I stop here as I'm unsure how to end my own sentence and don't want to say too much. I pause long enough to be saved by the arrival of food. It smells heavenly and happily distracts Kate long enough for her to start chattering in another direction, meaning for the remainder of the meal we stay on topics mainstream and mundane.

"Well, that mousse was worth waiting for," grins Kate as we get up to go. I scan my barcode on the table centre piece, the bill flashes up and I double scan my barcode to confirm payment directly from my bank account. My watch pings a receipt, the entrance door opens as we scan out and we wave our thank you to the waiter as we leave. The chocolate hit was definitely worth it.

"Katie, Maia?! Ah, how *lovely* to see you both!" We both turn around to identify the vaguely disguised sarcastic voice that is greeting us.

"Lucy! How are you?" Kate is quicker to civility than me (as usual). I suppress a groan and tell myself not to roll my eyes. I doubt that Lucy has anything to say that I want to hear. I know she chats to Kate sometimes (always adding an '*i*' to Kate's name as though she is trying to mother her), but if we have spoken in the last six years, we have never ventured beyond the basic niceties people exchange on the street whilst trying to pass each other as fast as possible.

"Well, very well, thank you – excited for my new adventure!" She looks at me, grinning, clearly expecting me to understand. It takes me a second or two longer than it should, but then I remember that she was at the Matching Ceremony too.

"Ah, yes of course, you have just been matched. Congratulations." I'm proud, I managed to recall my inner fake-but-real, upper-class 3 voice. Lucy beams. Obviously, she likes her match.

"Thank you! Yes, I am *sooo* pleased, I finally have a match worth accepting. Papa turned down everyone for the last five years and I began to think he wanted me to be an infertile old maid." Kate grimaces a little here. Lucy is so insensitive; she clearly notices, but doesn't mind giving offence.

"I didn't realise your dad was the one stopping your matches..." I am about to add in some sarcastic remark about her being repellent enough on her own, but the crafty cow second guesses me and butts in with:

"Oh, yes of course! And now, I am going to be the wife of a future minister. Maybe even Governor one day as Jonny's Papa is Finance Minister in the Midlands Hub, so he *has* to follow in his father's good stead."

Although titles do tend to follow in families, I'm not sure it works quite as simply as that; however, the effort of correcting her seems too much, even if my nasty side would like to wipe the grin off her face.

"I *suppose* I should congratulate you, Maia. I saw you being matched rather well too. I can't see how you deserve such a position – of course your dad weighed in over mine I suppose. Ha! good luck to Max, says I!" I should have corrected her, hateful grublet that she is.

"*Lucy.*" Kate's monosyllabic attempt at reprimand.

"Oh, never mind, *look* at my ring!" She produces her left hand for us to view said ring. It is a waste of breath mocking or educating her; I know that. Lucy has been spoilt, pampered, and generally puffed-up all her life; nothing will change that now. Her sole purpose in life is to be adored and adorned, so gaining a fat engagement ring from her prefabricated fiancé is pretty fitting. Kate produces some polite admiration where I can't be bothered, even though I know she is as bored as I am.

"Anyway, we're *all* luckier than that silly girl, Lilith, at the ceremony the other day – you can't have missed her, Maia. What a stupid scene to make; as if she didn't know that she wouldn't be matched with her infertile boyfriend!" Kate turns to me for translation; news clearly hasn't reached her about that part of the ceremony, but Lucy jumps in before I can speak. "It was such a tragic display. Papa says education needs to be more thorough if youth don't see the fruitlessness of such schooltime romances. He thinks it better if we don't have them at all, and I think him quite right if that kind of thing is going to happen, it is just unseemly. Fertility is bad enough as it is so no one is going to match a 3 with anything but a 3. Even *you*, Maia, saw that sense back in the day – or was it Theo? Probably, but anyway, *that* silly girl will regret her display of insolence and only have herself to blame!"

Now, here is one use of a self-centred, spoilt gossip – they love the sound of their own voice and don't know when to shut up. Leaving aside what she said about me (for which, I would love to commit some act of violence against her), I am pretty certain her father would not have intended for her to voice his opinions on the street in the Central Hub and I daresay they were his musings over an evening meal with family only and a glass of wine or two in hand. I hate the very sight of Lucy's father. Dr Oldman is Head of Genetic Correlation. Dubbed as 'Dr Donation,' he is responsible for embryo collection and just thinking about him and his cold, bony fingers, along with his equally cold utensils, makes my skin crawl.

"Why, what happened to her?" Kate wisely asks as I am still considering whether to retaliate to Lucy's careless comments.

"What do you *think*?! She has joined the Artificial Insemination Programme. Like it or not, she'll make herself useful and serve society as a cadet – best place for her! Papa says she'll settle there well, no point trying rehab like Mama suggested – the results are iffy at best."

"The AIP? I thought she'd be rematched after…?"

"After *what*? You can't be *that* clueless. The PTB aren't going to waste resources – or another fertile match – no, Papa says that is just not effective. Much better to rematch the jilted; after all, *he* did nothing wrong and can continue in civilised society."

I must admit I had not given much thought to the 'after' for that couple at the ceremony. I knew it wasn't anything good and that they would remain separated, but I had assumed the girl (called Lilith, apparently!) would have gone through some attempt at extra training or counselling (the cynic in me says '*reprogramming*') before being enrolled with the Artificial Insemination Programme. Lucy called her an 'AIP cadet.' I can't help thinking that the AIP makes you more cow than cadet – which is saying something as I already feel like a cow. Like everything the PTB wants to threaten with, but not give details about, little is known about the logistics of the AIP. However, routine egg harvesting and pregnancy seemed to figure regularly in what information we were fed at school.

"And him? The boyfriend?"

"Who cares about him?! He is infertile and can get a job like everyone else, I daresay. I doubt anyone will rush to match him again. Why would they? Or maybe he took his match after he came round?!" Lucy finishes her sentence with a cold, but hearty laugh. It makes my stomach churn; how can anyone be so unfeeling? I really want to leave now, but Lucy is still rambling and Kate is too polite to walk away, despite me doing my best to edge backwards.

"Can you imagine being harvested for another ten or more years?! No, thank you! Then you'd be glad for early menopause – one more donation and only *my* babies after that! Oh, I can't wait!"

"You have another donation too, huh?"

"Yes, yes, but that's okay, I have every intention of being pregnant by Christmas if at all possible! Well, must go, things to do!" Lucy spins round, flashing us a look at her ring again and giggles as she goes.

"Isn't she just a joy?" I sneer.

"Quite, but don't pay her any attention, you know she is thoughtless," says Kate.

"I don't envy Jonny, whoever he is. I wonder what her future in-laws think of her?!"

"I doubt they care too much; they are in the Midlands still, so are unlikely to see her beyond video calls."

"Oh, they didn't move too?"

"No, my mum was talking to Lucy's; apparently they have three sons, Jonny is the youngest, and as Finance Minister of the Midlands Hub, they are required to stay there."

"Hang on! He is the third son?" Kate nods. "So, he is in fact, unlikely to follow in his father's lineage? Ha-ha! Oh, *why* didn't you say that in front of her?! I would have crowed that one all day!" Petty, but true. I would have enjoyed throwing that back at her. Kate mocks me, but we both laugh heartily.

Kate and I decide to walk a while and head towards the park. I haven't been for some time and much of the grass is now brown due to a lack of rain, but it is still a beautiful area and I love the old trees. There are younger, smaller ones that have been planted more recently, but it is the big ones that are the most awe inspiring. The tales they could tell would probably shock and amaze in equal measure.

We have been walking silently for a while, but I don't mind; true companionship doesn't always need words and our silences have always been comfortable. I am actually a little surprised when Kate does speak, especially as her tone is quiet and serious: "So, you have another donation?"

"Hmm, sadly. I was hoping the last was the last, but apparently not."

"When is it?"

"October 20th. Why?"

Kate fidgets with her sleeve before answering. "No, no reason, just wondered when you have to start your injections."

"Soon…Why am I *that* grumpy you want warning of my hormones?" I laugh trying to lighten the mood. Kate does laugh, but not fully. I don't understand, I am the one that gets violated, so why does she seem nervous?

"Ha-ha, no…well, maybe a little, but you can't help that. No, I was just asking."

"Are you okay?"

"Of course!" Kate gazes around as though searching for something, but says nothing for a while. Suddenly she asks: "Did you hear about the pregnancies in SH2?"

"No!? Really?! When?!"

"I only heard yesterday. I thought you'd know…but then you've been off for three days with your match, of course. Both ladies live near me. Apparently, they both had stomach pains within a day or two of each other so went to the doctor's, who couldn't find anything so did a blood test, and then a scan to confirm it. Can you believe it? Your boss is interviewing and analysing them to see how this has happened."

"Wow, this is unprecedented; do you know what grade they are?"

"1 and 2 – one of each."

"What?! Okay, this is *really* exciting!"

"It is. I know as a 0 my chances aren't great, but if these two women can get pregnant, surely there is hope, right?"

Kate is looking straight at me, her beautiful eyes holding mine with such a plea for hope, I really don't know how to answer her. Not honestly anyway. I have seen enough fertility studies to know that 0s do not have any hope – not even a glimmer. To be graded 0 every part of her reproductive system will be effectively dead. I struggle to comprehend how a 1 has regained enough to support a foetus – a 2 is exciting enough; a 0 just seems too much of a stretch to dream of. I desperately don't want to shatter her dreams, but surely giving false hope is just as cruel?

"I'd really need to see some data to even begin to comprehend how this has happened and absolutely, it is encouraging, but I don't want to lie or give you false ideas, Kate – oh, *please* don't cry! I'd love to say something more optimistic, but—" The words tangle in my mouth. I feel like I am crushing my best friend's dreams and don't know how not to.

Kate finishes for me: "But I'm a 0 and pigs can't fly."

She bursts into tears and so do I. Neither knowing what to say to the other, neither can stop the tears. We hug instead.

ELEVEN

I have agreed to meet Max today. I am more nervous about this than I was for the family dinner because now we have to talk without interruption. I am not sure if I am nervous to find out we have thoughts in common, and I actually could like him, or am afraid to find out he lives up to my fears. Either way I am being silly as I have to find out sometime.

Before we parted last night, Kate tried to comfort and reassure me all would work out well with Max. I am grateful for this, but her obvious sorrow of being childless weighs on me. I don't know how to help her – if I could donate my fertility to her, I would in a heartbeat, but even if it existed, black market uterus exchange probably isn't the answer to either of our problems – and liable to get us killed if it did!

I try to put my worry for Kate aside as I step on the tram, having managed to escape the house with very little interaction with any of my family. Mum just caught me last minute with "Surely you're going to dress up?" which of course, I dismissed with: "Must go!" I heard her grumbling to Grandma as I stepped outside, but thankfully the exact words didn't reach my ears this time.

Max is going to meet me in the Central Hub. I'm not quite sure what we are going to do all day, but it is at least warm and sunny. I can only hope that's a good omen. I smile as I spot him; Mum would be so annoyed as we are both simply dressed in jeans and shirt. What attire she thinks *is* appropriate, I am not sure, but I am fairly certain jeans aren't included. We greet with another awkward peck on the cheek, but this at least makes us both laugh.

"I think we need to work on that one."

I chuckle. "Yes, otherwise eternal bruised noses could be on the cards... *So!* What do you want to do today?"

"Well," Max says shyly, "I was hoping you'd have some ideas, given as you were born here, and I've been here less than a week."

Fair point. I suggest food – who doesn't need to eat? Plus, it is near midday and by the time we have pottered through a few streets, I am definitely hungry. I was too anxious for breakfast, but hunger has overtaken fear for the time being. Max has similar tastes in food, so mutually choosing somewhere is straightforward and I am pleasantly surprised to learn he is a talker. Not an in-your-face, opinionated, loud talker (Lucy comes to mind), but an easy going, interesting, dare I say, funny, talker. Really quite different from our previous meetings where most things were said in a low, unassuming voice. After eating, we just stroll for a while through the streets towards the park, chatting about interests, work, houses, family, etc as we go. It is odd, it actually feels like a date – like a real one, not manufactured. I find myself split; part of me hates the idea that the PTB matching does know best, and I could have been woefully wrong to resist, but the other part is sanguine, even if only mildly, that the future might be pathing out better than imagined. I want to hold onto this feeling and not revert to my default mistrusting, reserved stance, nor hold onto my general depression for my prospects.

Without really paying attention to our direction, we have wandered towards 'The Aviary.' Here lives a variety of poultry of different shapes and sizes. People come here to see the birds and purchase their ultra-fresh free-range eggs. The birds live in giant open areas of the wooded section of the park, but there are also enormous, walk-through aviaries where a selection of parrots live.

Apparently, the President General has a soft spot for parrots, so made this exhibit for all to see and has a farm dedicated to the production of their feed. I am told that the idea caught on, so every Hub has a similar attraction. Anyone who is afraid of birds would absolutely never visit as you go through a series of netted doors before walking into the aviaries where you are then up close and personal with whatever birds that want to greet you.

Mum always refused to take me, citing: "I was defecated on once and that was enough for a lifetime, plus, those unclean parrots are also foul-mouthed!"

I tried explaining that whilst unpleasant, poop will happen from all species (I was reprimanded for that) and that if any birds were 'foul-mouthed' that was a direct result of foul-mouth humans talking to them as they only mimic what they hear.

"Well, that may be so, but I am sure that is just evidence the place attracts the wrong class of people as far as I'm concerned – no, there are much better places to visit, Maia."

By class she meant *grade*; as obviously only infertile people swear, but I gave up reasoning and had to wait until my mid-teens when I was old enough to go with friends alone. Thankfully, Max has no such hang ups and doesn't duck away as birds fly past us while we walk along the sandy pathways. He also laughs as much as I do when one parrot tells us to leave in no uncertain terms.

We wander back towards the Central Hub early evening and Max suggests we find somewhere playing live music as well as serving food. I ask what kind he likes and am overjoyed at his answer of "Anything but jazz." I suspect it is largely thanks to Dr Donation playing it every time I go to his clinic and it being the last thing I hear before I 'donate' my eggs, but I just don't like or *get* jazz. Of course, Mum loves it – which, I suppose, is just one more thing to add to the long list of how incompatible we are. Anyway, the relief of not having jazz played at home (when it becomes *home*), is certainly welcome.

"Huh, you have that monument too? Probably every Hub has one."

I turn to see which monument has caught Max's attention. There are several around the Hub, all for someone or some statement that the PTB want to remind the people of. This is one of Earth. Half depicts a beautiful, green and vibrant planet with an abundance of fauna and flora. The other half mirrors the first, but displays a post war, post Fall, world. I hate looking at it. I have seen the images a thousand times at school, all are graphic and burnt into my brain. This monument just forces me to relive those images. Which of course is the point. The PTB want, no, *need*, humanity to constantly remember the damage we did through selfish greed, hate, and destruction and not forget the objective of the UNE.

'Lest We Forget' – that's the title engraved on the base on both sides of the globe, but there is a sash surrounding the globe with a poem written in red:

Lest we forget
The damage we caused
The greed and the hate

Alexia Muelle-Rushbrook

The needless disgrace
The sorrow and loss
And the hollow cries
Tears that flowed
From weeping eyes

The death and destruction
The rubble and ash
The misery that lasts
And the blood-stained sash
Every woman and man
Made to stop and count
The cost on the Earth
As the piles did mount

Greed and destruction
Is no longer our way
Guardianship of Earth
A calling for all everyday
Together brings harmony
Hatred must cease
A united future
Turn sorrow to peace

I feel a lump in my throat reading this. I always do. I agree with the poem, but it again reminds me I haven't found my path to peace or unity and I feel the reproach of non-compliance. I wish I felt the comfort of following that 'united future.' I feel like I have spent my entire life following the path set out for me, but continuously find myself stumbling into the ditch next to it, not treading the path itself as intended by society. And every time I do step onto the path, all I can do is look back at the ditch, wondering if my answer lies in the cold, muddy water. I sigh. Too long have I followed my conclusion that it is easier to be sad than attempt the peace that I am told is waiting for me.

"Are you okay?"

"Hmm…? Yes, sorry I was just wandering off into my own thoughts – sorry, it's a bad habit. When you meet her, Kate will tell you I am very rude and often drift off – I promise it's not deliberate! I do *try* not to!" I surprise myself by realising mid-sentence, I genuinely want Max to think well of me and not think I am disinterested in what he has to say.

"It's okay, I wasn't saying anything profound, so you didn't miss much. Are you sure you're okay though, you seemed deep in thought?"

Max is watching me. I've been told in the past when I am silently thinking, my eyebrows twitch. I can only presume they do this in time with my thoughts, but I would rather they didn't as it seems unfair to give away how animated my internal conversation might be – not to mention how *frequently* I talk to myself.

"I was just thinking about that monument. It disturbs me."

Max pauses for a moment and looks back at the modelled Earth. After a few moments silence, he turns to me with a speech that the cynic within says is the PTB's indoctrinated answer, yet his words strike a chord; and even though there is nothing new in what he is saying, somehow it sounds different:

"I think that is the point, it *wants* to make us uncomfortable. Here in our cosy Hub it is easy to forget our history as well as what is beyond the Hub now. The damage is not assigned to the past, it is very much present, we just don't see it. We can't erase the past, but we can remember, learn and do better. That is what the PTB strive for – being better Guardians of Earth, not destroyers, whilst securing humankind's future and giving everyone peace and meaningful structure."

"Yes, and that is what I want to help with – making a difference, be useful, not just—" I stop, realising that I am not talking to Kate (*how* has he made me this relaxed, so quickly?!). Confessing all my thoughts to my husband-to-be after four days acquaintance is probably not conducive to future happiness – I should at least wait a week to say I don't want children. It took 24 years to tell Mum, surely a week is enough for Max?!

"*'Not just'…?*"

Crap. My mouth really is too big sometimes. *This* is why I should only talk to myself. It would stop embarrassing, potentially detainable, certainly anti-establishment, confessions. I can feel myself going red, but can't stop that any more than I can think of a feasible ending to my sentence.

"Not just…sit at home and raise babies?"

Ground swallow me up… swallow me up…

I can't read Max's thoughts; his expression isn't giving anything away. He is just looking intently at me, holding my gaze with those soulful eyes. This could be a test – a way to catch me out, test my loyalties – not that it took long to worm something stupid from me.

I have tried to reply a couple of times, making what I'd imagine are fish mouth impressions, but I have failed to actually say anything. I have however managed to bite the inside of my lip – which should remind me for a few days at least to keep my mouth closed.

Max suddenly shrugs his shoulders, smiles, and says: "It's okay, I always thought that was a bit mean on 3 women…well, *some* 3 women. I can see some would choose nothing else, even given the choice. Mum made it clear *she* doesn't entirely fit the rule." He winks at me.

My heart is racing, but I have to laugh, even if quietly. I wonder how the PTB would react if they realised they have potentially matched two radical thinkers? Though I do *not* want to be classed with his mother any more than I do my own.

"Be careful where you voice that thought; mentioning anything close to not following the rule has caused more than one argument for me." I'm almost whispering, mainly because I'm too relieved to be able to find volume.

"Ah, yes, from your mother, no doubt. I understand not living up to one's mother's ideals." He pauses, glancing around to check we are indeed alone before softly adding: *"Have faith Maia, I think, together, we can make a difference."*

TWELVE

Well, I had thought I was nervous yesterday morning and whilst that had turned out to be the nicest day I have had in a very long time, I am less convinced my luck will be in again today. Yesterday, Max and I had stayed together until late in the evening, wandering around the Hub, eating, chatting, and although doing nothing significant, it felt liberating.

I am hopeful of at least having the makings of a true friend; in all honesty, this is one hundred times more than I had dared hoped for. I tell myself not to get entirely carried away, but I have little happy butterflies mixed in with the nervous ones in my stomach. The nervous ones are all attributed to the fact I agreed to Sunday dinner with Max and his parents (though I think it was more of a summoning than invitation by Director Rivers). I do not require Mum's instruction; I have dressed up (albeit slightly) and am as ready as I'll ever be for my first solo meeting with the future in-laws. I have yet to dare ask Max about his parentage – I doubt if today is the right day, but I also doubt I'll resist checking barcodes again, just to reaffirm I wasn't dreaming before.

"Ah, I'm glad to see you have dressed more appropriately today, Maia – not a total improvement, but an improvement nonetheless."

"Morning, Mum, you look lovely too, thank you so much for your encouragement."

"Tish, if I don't try to educate you, who will? And if Mary thinks I don't, well, that looks bad on me." I roll my eyes. For someone with a catchphrase of 'no good ever comes from focusing on I' she sure does like focusing on herself. Of course, I am not going to voice this opinion as realistically, it is pointless.

"Maia? Are you going to the Rivers' today?"

"Yes, Gee-Gee, for lunch."

"And hopefully she will remember all her manners and answer all their questions politely as she has been taught," adds Mum derisively.

I would like to say this doesn't annoy me, but it does. I am 24, not 10, and even at 10 I knew how to behave at other people's houses. A few swift clips around the ears had seen to that at an early age and I quickly learnt not to move or speak out of place in Mum's presence, lest I irritate her. It has only been in the last few years I have managed some kind of 'back-chat' and in all honesty, that is minimal too.

Silence is golden.

Gee-Gee only really nodded when I replied, both of us ignoring the babble of from Grandma and Mum that has followed. I look up to see Gee-Gee staring at me. Once she has my attention, she pushes a mug of tea slightly in my direction, picks up one for herself, tilts her head in a subtle nod and walks towards her study. I am surprised to say the least, but pick up the mug and follow her, assuming that is what I am supposed to do. I pause behind her as she scans her barcode for her door to open. Only her study and Dad's require their individual code to open the door. Every other door opens for any household member or doesn't need one (the bathroom for example). I have seen the inside of Dad's study more regularly than Gee-Gee's and I rarely go in there more than once a year.

Gee-Gee has always been exceptionally private about her space and I can't say I blame her. Mum sees it as her right to rattle around every other room at will, so having somewhere out of her way frankly sounds magical to me. Gee-Gee's study is actually a mini apartment with a lounge, bedroom with en suite, and her study. The annexe was added to allow for more space due to so many generations living under one roof. This room is large and was originally designed to allow for Gee-Gee and Great Gramps to share office space – his desk remains in one corner, although nothing is on top of it. I am surprised by how light the room is. From the garden you can't see in here as the windows are darkened and flowers climb the exterior walls, making the room truly private; however, from within, you would never guess.

Gee-Gee sits at her desk without saying a word and gestures for to me to sit down – which I do without questioning. My mind is racing through every possible cause for me being called in here, it has literally been years – the last time was when Theo had left, and Mum had given me a speech on how pleased she was that 'my fruitless endeavour was over.' I had borne it as best I could, but Gee-Gee had come home towards the end and pulled me in here to give me a hug – the one and only hug I received from a family member in this household at the time, and it was so desperately needed that I really didn't take in my surroundings.

Now I look around. Everything is clean and orderly as expected. There are paintings on every wall, and almost all I believe are Aunt Dora's, as besides the signature I recognise the familiar, warm glow that she captures in her work. I am particularly struck by the painting that is hung in the centre of the far wall. It is a version of the monument Max and I discussed yesterday. How bizarre I should see it on two consecutive days, when normally I pass it by without stopping. This version is however not identical to what is on the plaza; it has the Earth divided the same – one side destroyed, one not – but there is no sash and no poem. Just an inscription on a plaque attached to the frame:

'Being Guardians of the Earth gives us no greater right to be here than any other species'

A simple sentence perhaps, but one that hits home. I can't begin to imagine how many species of bird or animal are on the Earth now. We all know the figures of how many were damaged and killed by humankind's actions because the PTB make sure that we can recite them. I have often pondered on what right we had (or indeed have) to dictate the lives of other species. Why did it take such an extreme point in time for humanity to stand back and truly recognise the rights of other species that walk, fly, or swim this Earth? Will we always wait until the eleventh hour before we act? Or will it be too late next time?

"I've never seen this version before."

"No, probably not, though all the Directors have one – a reminder that we have a huge responsibility on our shoulders to do what is right for all. I look at that every morning before I leave so I never forget the importance of what I do and for whom I do it."

Gee-Gee stares at the painting for a moment; her eyes are sad and weary as she does. She sighs. I recognise that expression as one I myself must pull when deep in thought. If I manage to get to her age, having worked as hard and achieved so much, I will consider myself blessed. Of course, I haven't seen all she has or endured half that she has. Maybe I am wrong to liken myself to her. It's my turn to sigh; I'm feeling guilty – *again.* Oh! For a day when I feel I have done well! She obviously hears my sigh as she suddenly turns to me, narrowing her brows, saying:

"Maia, it pains me to see you so unhappy. It always has, you don't know how much." She pauses, shaking her head. "You're a good girl, you don't belong in this house now and I truly, fervently, hope this match will prove the answer for you. Although I know very little of Max, I am told he has an honest, intelligent character, and he certainly seems gentlemanly. I wasn't sure he could be, but I am hopeful that of him I was wrong to judge…*but never* lose your guard with his mother. Please promise me that. I can't say more, I should have said less, but couldn't stand by and watch you wander into that family blindly."

If I wasn't confused and nauseous before, I definitely am now. I have a million questions, but don't know where to start and I can feel my lips forming fish impressions again – apparently it is the weekend for me to be speechless! – but I must say something, for Gee-Gee has stood up as though our meeting is adjourned.

"Gee-Gee, you can't leave me with that! Surely—"

"I'm sorry Maia, I must."

"But you tell me not to go into that family blindly, whilst giving me nothing to see with?!"

"My dear, you have your wits and know how to use them – *that,* I'm sad to say, is far more than the majority of *our* family is blessed with. Take Max, marry him, and follow your path together. Be happy. Build a true friendship – love will surely come in time. Build your own family. I know you say you don't want that, but there you must think beyond the now, beyond the just you. Don't twist your face like that, my dear, it may sound like an insurmountable task now, but you *can* do it. I did it and love my family very much – *despite* some of their failings – failings that have weighed on you and given you a dark view, but now is your chance to free yourself of their ties and form a stronger, healthier future. For yourself first, but for all as well. I want you to live a quieter life than I have known. That woman is a threat, but as long as you don't forget your guard, your peace is still within your grasp. Trust the system; all will be well if you do. You *will* flourish. No, I can't say more. Promise me *now*…you *will* keep this to yourself and remember my advice always?"

I stare for a moment, but say nothing; no argument or question comes. I can see there is none to be had. Her tone and expression are equally earnest, true, and unrelenting.

"Of course. I promise."

"Good girl. Now, I must go."

Gee-Gee kisses my forehead, gently takes my arm, and leads me out the door. Once in the hallway she affectionately squeezes my arm and releases it, scans her door with her left arm to lock it, and silently leaves the house.

THIRTEEN

I think I stood motionless on the spot for a good ten minutes, only finally disturbed by the sound of Mum approaching. I ran upstairs, mind racing, replaying everything Gee-Gee had just said. Going over it wasn't helping though; I had more questions than answers. Why tell me anything if she can actually tell me nothing? If Gee-Gee is uneasy about Director Rivers, why have I been matched with her son? Who isn't actually her son...which is another mystery. Why will no one tell me a full story? I am entrusted with intrigues, but no details. I am repeatedly told to trust and follow the system, but not to understand it. I have my wits, but am to retire them the moment I get pregnant. Maybe I would be less against having children if I didn't have to sacrifice everything else to raise them! I want to scream. The frustration of it all is overwhelming. And now I have to compose and present myself at Max's house to be fully scrutinised by his parents. As if that wasn't frightening enough – as if *Mary* wasn't frightening enough – without Gee-Gee confessing that she also fears her to some degree.

I am not sure how, but I have arrived at Max's looking composed. I have dug incredibly deep to find my inner chi and I'm very much hoping it lasts for at least the duration of this meal. I was told to arrive at 1 p.m. It is 12:45 p.m., so in my books, this is an acceptable arrival time. Wine bottle in hand (donated by Dad, though he doesn't know it yet), I scan my barcode at the door, and I hear the security system ring and announce my name.

Thankfully, Max doesn't leave me waiting for long and his welcoming smile undoubtedly helps to reassure. The peck on the cheek doesn't involve clashed noses this time (that's two in a row as we also parted without crashing into each other last night), so we're making progress there at least. Inside, the house is as cold and clinical as I expected. I had a glimpse at Mary's decor choices when she and Mum were trying to out select each other at our new house; so, with that, plus her cold manner, I would have been shocked to find she was a hoarder of more than the most basic ornaments.

"Ah, Maia, it is lovely to see you, is that for me? Wonderful, very kind, do come in, Mary is in the kitchen – ah no, you don't need to help her – best leave her to it. If I am the chef, do come help, but Mary prefers to master her own course." A warm and amusingly candid greeting from Henry helps my nerves a little as he ushers me into the dining room.

"You cook, sir?"

"I do! And enjoy it too – but please don't call me 'sir,' I feel old enough as it is, and I hope you will see me as family by-and-by." Henry's smile is as reassuring as his son's. I am very glad of this, as living in absolute fear of both in-laws would be too much to ask.

Conversation flows for a few minutes, nothing exciting, just general chatter, but it does help to distract and relax me – until the kitchen door opens.

"Maia! Welcome, welcome…Henry, why have you not sat Maia down and offered her a drink yet?"

Wow, there is no mistaking the cold chill that comes in with Mary. It may only be the 5th of September and still warm outside, but no one would guess with this woman in the room. The sudden difference in the attitude of both men is palpable. Henry immediately pulls out a chair for me to sit on and offers drinks as directed. Dinner is brought out and it smells divine – which is helpful to restore digestive order as my stomach is still in knots thanks to the morning's events.

I naturally take the meek demeanour that Max and Henry have adopted which seems to please Mary as she chatters away, only really requiring very basic responses as she tells me how pleased she is with the neighbourhood, how easy access to the Central Hub is from here and how quickly she was able to get all her belongings just as she wants them. I can't help looking around the room again at this remark, as the 'all' I can see would have taken two minutes to set out, not the days she implies.

"To be sure, I still have much to establish at work, but I am certainly making headway there too," Mary continues. "Unfortunately, though, it does mean my time with you today will be shorter than I had anticipated. I must go into work, there is just so much to arrange, but there will be plenty of time for us to chat more once I am settled into a routine and you're both married."

"Yes of course, I can well imagine you have a lot to become acquainted with in a short period of time. It must be difficult moving to a new Hub, leaving family, and starting a new job!"

This was meant as a kind, empathic comment, but Mary stares hard at me. I have no idea what she thinks I mean – or could possibly mean – but she narrows her eyes, holding my gaze, which frankly, can only look confused. Then as quickly as her stare had started, she drops it, smiles, and says: "Quite dear, very true; however, I am very much equal to the task and I believe the rewards in every direction will be worth any initial hardship."

"Of course." That is all I can manage. Internally I am praying Max and I don't feel the need to visit here too often. Our new house isn't too far away from here, but just enough out of her commute route to (hopefully) make her visits sporadic at best.

Mary carries on talking and all three of us let her dominate and direct each topic, adding where invited to, but not more than we think she will find tedious or bordering on the opinionated. I am not sure what time she has to return to work, but it can't come too soon as far as I am concerned.

"So, Maia, I called your Coordinator, Claire, to ask a few questions and arrange a few details—"

"Why?" Max surprises me, as he suddenly looks annoyed – as am I, but I am trying to restrain my displeasure at her interference.

"Why, indeed!? To arrange details, I just said that, and I don't like your tone, young man."

Max sucks in his bottom lip. I think he has conceded, but apparently, I am yet to learn his mannerisms, as he shakes his head, releases his lip, and says in a firm, but quiet tone: "Mother, I would rather you do not do such things, the details can be arranged by myself or Maia." Mary reddens with each word and I am sure she is about to spit a few choice words of her own when she is surprisingly mellowed by Max who calmly adds: "You have so much to do already."

"That's sweet of you," Mary says, smiling, "but it was no trouble and I wanted to ensure there was no chance of bringing the wedding forward. It seems so far away; I was sure you'd be married in a month, six weeks at most, upon arrival here."

"Were you able to bring it forward?" I am not certain if I am supposed to speak now, but the question almost asks itself. I am also not sure what I hope her answer will be.

"Alas, no. Claire was quite adamant your date is unchangeable due to your donation in October. They want you to have eight weeks for your hormones to realign."

Yes, because me not conceiving in the first month would be terrible. I sigh involuntarily. One day I might actually learn to control these sighs. One can only hope!

"I share your frustration, Maia. It speaks well of you that you are eager to move on with Max – you are a lucky girl, but I feel you are also well matched for my boy." Mary is smiling at me, but I wish I felt comforted by her approval. "However! One more donation is not *so* bad; and Max, you can at least settle yourself into work in the meantime."

"You start tomorrow?" Henry finally says something – it has been a good ten minutes since he has done anything but eat. By the look on Max's face, Henry already knows the answer to his question, but he answers all the same. I daresay this diversion tactic is well established in this household. If my dad cared to be around more often, he would probably use a similar technique to distract my mum when he thinks she is becoming too forthright or abrasive.

"Yes, I met with Mr Stanley and his team last week, but start officially in the morning."

"And you will do very well there. I have no doubt you will climb the ladder and quickly rise to better roles – I will certainly be doing my best to promote you." Nope, Mary isn't done meddling.

"Mum, you know I am *in* the role I want."

"*For now*, but I trust in time, you will rise and keep on rising. I lead by example."

"Yes, and I thank you and I am proud of you for your example, Mother; but you know I do not wish to follow your political role and want to do more with architecture – maybe with surveying too—"

Mary cuts him off with no more than a wave of the hand and a tut. Max falls silent. Last night, he was full of chatter and ideas for improving housing – in structure and horticultural usage (I told him Kate and Tim would love to share ideas on that one). He told me more about wanting to help research and develop beyond the scope that is currently laid out for us, and frankly, his words had warmed my soul. I didn't tell him then, maybe I will one day if I muster up the courage; but he gave me hope that I am not so alone in wanting more. In these few moments, I realise his ambitions are as stifled as mine, the only difference is he is a man and there is a chance of him shaking the chains of his mother. I look up and see him smiling at me. He is annoyed with his mum, I can see that, yet he still smiles at me. It could just be coincidence that our genetics match, but maybe, somehow, the Matchmakers know we come from similarly oppressive mothers and need each other as a means of respite. Maybe we can be each other's salvation – or at least a support while we rescue ourselves. Or better yet, a little of both.

FOURTEEN

I don't think we were actually holding our breath, but the moment Mary leaves the house, everyone seems to breathe easier. Henry immediately relaxes and takes over conversation. His tone is quietly authoritative whilst being kind and interesting – and what's more, *interested in* what Max and I have to say. He apologises for his wife's manner, laughing as he states 'you get used to her way' – which he might have, but I daresay not *easily*! They have clearly learnt to act one way with her present and another when separate. Exhausting as that may be, I understand the logic – and the need.

"So, Maia, what is it you are really interested in at work? Is there a line of study that truly inspires you?" I can't tell you how happy I am that he has asked me this. I am shy to answer; normally, no one else cares enough to ask me, even out of politeness, but if this is my only opportunity to impress or spark interest – or just relate my thoughts properly – I am not going to not answer now!

"Well, I have several ideas and thoughts that intrigue me surrounding genetic influences regarding fertility. It is my belief that it is not just pure congenital or hereditary conditions that are determining our fertility successes and failures; I think epigenetics is playing a huge role in the human race's evolution."

"Nature verses Nurture?"

"Exactly."

"Yes, the nuclear radiation has been proven to change the mapping of our genes – more than just causing early menopause for the majority…"

"Yes, but I mean beyond *just* radiation – that has certainly been well studied – obviously with more study required as things change and continue to mutate as they are; however, I think—"

"Of course, vaccines have long been blamed for influencing how inherited genes are expressed – some vaccines were altered, but largely this is just people looking for an excuse…"

"No, I don't mean vaccines; I have reviewed the studies (at length thanks to Dr Brown) and the ones we use today really have no evidence of influencing, activating, or deactivating genetic code. Certainly not to the degree of infertility we are seeing now. I believe there are other influences at play, possibly a combination of them, that are modifying our gene expression, causing us to seem healthy, but are effectively causing widespread sterilisation; potentially whilst in utero *and* in developing adults."

"Well, that is a theory and a half – how is your research going?"

"Slowly. I am yet to find anyone that wants to fully back my research, so what I have done has largely been an offshoot of something else I have been *asked* to do – hence having more data on vaccines and radiation – though I must say, I have far from discounted the radiation. Radiation influences are undeniable and absolutely lasting, I just suspect that its effects are coupled with another element as yet unknown to us."

"Do you have a leading suspect?"

"Ah! Well, a virus or bacteria would be the easiest to go undiscovered – a virus that doesn't affect our notable health –

or one that rides off another, hence why we haven't discovered it. I have considered nutrigenomics; but we are so particular in how, when, and where our food is produced, I think that unlikely. Especially as our food is now entirely locally produced; if the cause, for example was from radiation or poisoning of one soil or water source, infertility would be localised, not worldwide as it is. As I said, vaccines are continuously and so rigorously checked now, I think the modern ones are highly improbable suspects – obviously never say never, but there are so few chinks in that armour, I think radiation plus virus would be my initial leading area of investigation." Henry doesn't interrupt this time, but listens to me intently. I decide to continue while I finally have someone's undivided interest: "I think the virus is likely to be airborne, it is not impossible it is transmitted from person to person; however, because contact between Hubs is few and far between and disease precautions so thorough, my instinct tells me to look at airborne first."

"Hmm, you definitely make some interesting points, Maia. As you know, my heart and research lie with genetics. I have dedicated everything to mapping DNA and its reactions to our world to find out why we are increasingly infertile. I am amazed you have not been redirected to me sooner – even before my son was in need of a wife. My lab in the Midlands was in regular contact with the teams here and around the world – we are always looking for different angles, new faces (well, brains!) to expand our scope and research alongside. You would fit in very well with our current and future work. How is it you have been hidden so?"

I pause, not wanting to trap myself in an improper remark, but also not wanting to miss an opportunity. "I do not know…

possibly because I am a 3 – and a girl, so my priorities are *elsewhere.*"

"Indeed…yes, but no…" Henry scratches his head for a moment. "Maia, would you like to work with me? I instantly feel we would be good together. I must spend the next few days organising so will be no good until at least Thursday; but please, come find me on Thursday in my lab. I will talk to Richard tomorrow in our meeting and see if I can't steal or at least share you with him – if that is okay by you?"

Not wanting to break out in the hallelujah chorus and embarrass myself, I take a deep breath, but I can feel my mouth curling big and wide with such a beaming, genuine smile; the like of which I can't remember my face displaying. Someone is listening to me! Wants to work with *me!* "Absolutely, I would be honoured!"

"Excellent, I shall organise that – oh, I am so pleased! A daughter-in-law *and* a colleague!" Henry gets up to leave, smiling as he does. A smile to match my own. Maybe here is my silver lining. "Okay! Right, I am going to prepare myself for the week ahead and leave you two to do something other than listen to me. See you soon, my dear – Max, I told you all would be well here." He gently places a hand on his son's shoulder, squeezes, and leaves the room chuckling to himself and humming a tune I do not know, but instantly like. My heart could sing too; I feel *real* hope. I turn to Max, hoping we haven't bored him or that I haven't agreed to something that he is going to disapprove of, but I am relieved to see he also shares my smile. He takes my hand, initially as though he is passing on the squeeze from his dad, but he doesn't let go. We both gaze at each other, neither of us say anything, but my heart beats in a way that I didn't think it could anymore.

Eventually, Max stands up, suggesting we go out as the day is still bright and inviting. A walk sounds perfect, so we set off – with no absolute direction, but it doesn't matter one bit.

We have been walking hand in hand for some time without speaking, just taking in the scenery. The silence is amazing, it feels like I am walking with an old friend, not a new acquaintance or a person who has been thrust upon me by society. If only I had known this was possible! The hours of dread and fear that I could have saved myself!

Gee-Gee's warning is still ringing in the back of my head. I am concerned that she could disapprove of my working for Henry. She has been far from encouraging towards any of my thoughts regarding further studies of late and although her warning was against Mary, I can't now help wondering if I was meant to include Henry in that warning? How am I to know if everyone is so vague? Besides, Henry and Max have made it quite clear they have learnt to manage life with Mary rather than exclude her or fight her. I see no reason why I should try another tactic when this one seems to work for them. I'm not sure if Max has learnt to read my mind, but he suddenly speaks.

"I know Mum is challenging."

I say nothing, I was taught to be silent if I can't say anything nice. If given a minute to think, I am sure I can come up with some pleasing phrase, but Max thankfully saves me the effort.

"She is, don't worry, I am not blind to that and her dictations for my future normally weigh on me greatly, but—" He pauses, turns to me, and takes my other hand, collecting them both in his. I hope his heart is racing, as mine is. He looks straight into my eyes, then to the floor, then up again.

"But I have a new hope, a hope that we don't have to live in the shadows of our parents. I want to do better and...and I *want* to do it with you by my side."

He is staring at me, which would normally rattle me, as from anyone else, this is usually the precursor to some negative verbal assault; but he is smiling, patiently waiting for an answer without a hint of the judgement that would come from almost every one of my family members. In this moment, I realise I need to escape my family ties if I am ever to expect more from myself or others. Blind faith or ignorance? – time will tell, but in this moment, I decide to make him my confidant and place my bets on him.

I sigh, but for once it is a happy one, a hopeful one, one that accompanies a smile to match his as I return his gaze; trying to find the words to reply to him. Again, he saves me the effort, this time by leaning forward and kissing me. Yep, that'll do. No words needed.

FIFTEEN

This week I wake up grinning. Proper, big, wide, cheesy grinning. I have slept solidly – no weird or tortured dreaming like I normally do, just sound, undisturbed, joyous sleep. I keep telling myself not to get carried away, not to run before I walk, but I feel good, and I don't want to waste the feeling.

Maybe genetics do know best. As a scientist, I should possibly be less surprised by this, but I have witnessed so many matches that miss the mark. I resent the choice being made for me, but must confess my reluctance may have been misplaced – or maybe just well timed? I can hypothesise all I want: the fact is, today I have hope and I am going to enjoy it.

Even Mum's verbal assaults seem less heavy. I avoid lengthy conversation by telling her I am running late, leaving her wanting more information, but just about satisfying her that all is well with the Rivers.

On Monday I was eager to get to work and could see everyone was busy when I arrived. Dr Brown was darting around, preparing for a board meeting, but called me into his office to update on proceedings. He was really thrilled with the discovery of two pregnancies in SH2 and had already interviewed and started profiling them. The cause of their fertility changes is not obvious at all and he has theories flying all over – some more plausible than others. I was hoping my role was going to be more; however, as usual, he got towards the end of his presentation and revealed I am in a minor support role, following through tests decreed by others, not pursuing my own ideas. This is nothing new, but it is just as frustrating as ever. So be it. I am at least part of the team and it is exciting... plus, maybe things will change soon?

Thursday seemed to be taking its time arriving, but I was happily distracted in the meantime. Max and I met for lunch every day and again in the evenings after work. We just walked, talked, and then found somewhere to eat, but it was (*and is*) such a welcome change from the lonely monotony of my own thoughts. I haven't seen Kate, but she messaged to ask if Max and I would go out to dinner with her and Tim on Friday. I am looking forward to that, but at the same time am nervous to see her, especially as I know she will want any news on 'how' the SH2 ladies became pregnant. It is too early to know, if we will absolutely know, but nothing suggests a 0 is going to regenerate her fertility and I know that is the news she is longing to hear.

I haven't seen or heard from Henry since Sunday and I was beginning to let a little pessimism creep in, fearing that something would change between now and then, but I need not have worried – I didn't even need to search for him!

"Ah, wonderful, you're early! Good morning! Shall we go up?" I have to chuckle at the slightly backwards greeting as I walk into the lobby, but warmly return his salutation and follow him to his lab, listening to his small talk as we go.

Henry watches the lab door slide itself shut, turns to me, claps and rubs his hands together and declares: "Okay! Well, good and somewhat iffy news." I grimace at his words, trying to hold onto the 'good' and praying the 'iffy' is manageable. "No, no don't look beaten! It isn't *so* bad, we just need to pace ourselves. I've had numerous meetings this week – who knew scientists love to chatter so much, hey?! When I was little, I always had this image of them squirrelled away in a darkened lab, with only their mice and hamsters to talk to!" Henry proceeds to heartily chuckle at his own joke, his smile and laughter is warming (just like Max's – no, don't start daydreaming). I wait for him to stop chuckling, but when he does, he obviously needs a reminder of topic.

"So, what came of your meetings?"

"Ah! Indeed, well many things, but regards yourself, I met with a little more opposition than I'd hoped – turns out you're right; the general consensus is young, female 3s should not be high ranking in business or science as it is likely (and desirable) that you'll soon require maternity leave, and you must set a good example for others as you marry and raise a family."

"But surely I have some use until then – even *after* then, but certainly until? And I could pass on my works and findings?" I'm pleading, I know, but I care not for my pride.

"Yes, yes, my dear, that was my argument precisely – so, I had to think on my feet a little and I can but hope you are amenable to the angle I took, but I used our future father/ daughter in-law relationship to our advantage, saying that you could pass on any research to me when you have to retire from active work yourself to focus on children, but in the meantime, can act as a useful part of my team. Now, I am sure you would rather you didn't have to work *through* me, I can see in your face that pains you somewhat, but truly, that is the best I can offer for now…that, and my promise to include you and if we can, nay, *when* we can, we'll review things."

I don't know how to reply. My eyes are filling up, my vision blurring, I am telling myself to breath slow and steady. Henry is staring at me, obviously waiting for a response, but he can see me welling up and takes my hand. "I'm sorry Maia, this really is the best deal I could broker..."

"Sorry, no, you misunderstand me," I splutter. Breathe, Maia, breathe. "I am so grateful, so *happy* – yes, you're right, obviously I'd like to carry on working, but your offer is more than I've dared hope for – *'thank you'* isn't really sufficient, but—"

Henry sits back, smiling: "Maia, I instantly feel you are a breath of fresh air. I should like to (mostly) keep our conversations *here* professional; but for today, I must tell you how happy I am to see you matched to Max. He has a joy in his step that I haven't seen and feared I wouldn't see; we manage, he and I; but Mary...well, you can see Mary is a strong force and I think you already understand him and he you – a blessing! – such a blessing! and I wouldn't wish a difficult marriage on... well, never mind that! But, safe to say, if I can help you here, I will, and I think we will do great things together."

I can hear the hallelujah chorus again in my head. Don't get me wrong, of course, my best-case scenario would have been that Henry had persuaded the PTB that I can work and, well, not have *any* children or, second best: continue work *and* have children; however, both those are dreams to shelve. I think my best dream now is to work, use my brain and collaborate with Henry – and if children do come along, strive to be a good mum, a better one than I have known. Let that be my example to the next generation. Being realistic, this *is* my best choice. It is already a thousand times better than anything my family has offered me and in these few, short days, I have finally started to form a new dream and mindset. A self-fulfilling purpose. I don't want this new, optimistic me to fall back to sleep.

I thank Henry as heartily as I can without shedding happy tears. I am so touched by his welcoming spirit and can unquestionably see where Max inherited his good nature from. How Henry was matched with Mary is such a mystery to me, neither character nor genetics seem to be compatible. Henry and I discuss plans (I have agreed that in the lab, I will call him Dr Rivers; however, unlike Mary, who I wish to eternally call Director Rivers, I am happy for the relaxation out of hours). He outlines study suggestions; we brainstorm and form a way forward. I am to continue for two days a week with Dr Brown until I am married, giving me chance to round off my experiments there. Next week, while Henry finishes organising the labs and his staff, I will mainly be in my normal place; however, come Monday week, I have a new direction here. It feels amazing.

SIXTEEN

In the mist of all the newfound joy and promise for the future, I am also lamenting not having been back to see Aunt Dora yet. Curiosity and concern have been mounting up, so when Max says he has to work late today, despite being tired from so much change and planning, I decide to make a visit to Aunt Dora after work.

As I walk down the path to her front door, Aunt Dora surprises me by opening it abruptly. "Ah, Maia, at last! I am so glad you have come!"

I am about to apologise for not coming sooner, but Aunt Dora grabs me and pulls me into a hug. I'm surprised, but happy for the embrace and hug her as affectionately as she does me. As we stand back to part she holds on my right arm, slipping onto it a simple, yet pretty silver bracelet. "Sshh, that'll do, come in, come in, I'll make tea!"

Surprise and propulsion cause me to be silently led inside. Possibly two weeks ago I would have protested, if only a little, asking what was going on, but as everything is different and Aunt Dora far from her normal self, I find my default reaction has changed to mute. I am directed towards the sofa, next to which, is Eve, who is fast asleep in a lounge chair.

I am too confused to ask what is wrong, so just sit silently, staring at Aunt Dora, waiting for an explanation. She fidgets with a cushion, playing with a loose thread as though it is the only thing in the world. Amazed by her lack of attempt to speak, I clear my voice loudly and wave my right arm at her whilst pointing to the bracelet with my left hand.

"Right, okay, *that* is a signal blocker."

"And you have one of those *because...*?" I stare in bewilderment and as speak, I clock her arm: "You have one, too – *why* exactly?"

"You promised to keep any goings on here secret...this just ensures neither you or nor I unwittingly break that."

"Okay, but I'm going to need a little more info please. Where did you even get these?"

"Me. I made them." Apparently, Eve is not asleep.

"Eve and I are concerned about the listening capabilities on our watches. Mostly they are just used for adverts and algorithms, but they can do much more. If Eve is to live peacefully with me we cannot take any risks."

"How do you know our watches are or can be tapped into like that?"

"Coz I made 'em."

I am not sure I have blinked since the start of this conversation; it seems so farfetched.

"Hmmphh, don't look at me like that, you ain't the only girl with a brain. I know what them hmmphh things can do, coz I designed them. The almighty PTB haven't worked out how to better them yet. Hmmphh, so-called whizz kids." Eve falls silent; if her eyes weren't open, I'd think she was asleep. She is physically awake, but in all honesty, I cannot tell if she is still lucid. I jump out of my skin when she suddenly returns my gaze with wide, piercing eyes and declares: "Ha! I'll stop 'em listenin'! Hmmphh! Hahahahaha! I ain't gone yet!"

With that, Eve sits back in the chair and starts gently snoring. I can't take my eyes off her just in case she starts up again as quickly as she went off. Eventually, I turn to Aunt Dora, silently pleading for some sort of sense. She watches me for a moment, sighs, and says:

"Maia, there is much I don't fully understand or know. Eve has always been good to me and since Ray died, I have been the only family she has known. Some died in an accident, some she doesn't see – I don't know why, she won't talk about it...What I *do* know is she is now not well and needs me. She says some things that don't make sense at all, and some things that do, but sound treasonous. It could all be fabricated, but had she continued as she was, it would only be a matter of time before she was caught saying the wrong thing and..." Aunt Dora tails off, unable to finish her sentence. She doesn't need to; treason – proven treason (verbal or physical) – has only one penalty. The PTB aren't known for giving many second chances and anything that undermines their rule is unlikely to make them lenient, even if it's a little old lady in the twilight of her life with fading health.

"Did she really make these bracelets?"

"I *said* I did." Well, if I don't have a heart attack by the end of this visit, it'll be a miracle. How does Eve sleep and wake so quickly? She snores and breathes slowly, so I don't see how the sleep is being faked!

"If you have these bracelets and they really block PTB surveillance, why worry about surveillance?"

"Because these can only be worn in here," explains Aunt Dora, "you must always remove it before you leave the house and put it back on when you arrive. I'll leave one in the drawer of the console table for you."

"What happens to them outside?"

"Nothin', they work just fine," grunts Eve, "except every door you walk through or drone that detects you will mark your watch as unreadable and you'll have hmmphh drones and officers around you faster than you can say your own name."

"So, barcodes are still active, just the watch isn't?"

"Precisely – the watch is working; it is just muffled so they can't hear you."

"Clever. How is it the PTB haven't found that you have these bracelets?"

"Hmmphh, coz they don't know I made them. They may have their own by now, probably do, but these still work fine, so they haven't updated much of significance after all these years. Hmmphh, youth don't always come up with the gadgets – wisdom ain't for the young."

"Wow." I am lost for words. "So, you were a…robotics designer? How is it there are no gadgets here?" I ask, glancing around the room. "Actually, I think you have *less* than before, Aunt Dora?"

"Yes, Eve and I discussed this before she agreed to live with me – no robots."

"But if you were a—"

"I *know* what I *know* and *know* I don't want them. Hmmphh, I thought you were making tea, Dora? Or shall I sleep? – You, *you* could sing to me…that's bound to make me sleep. Do you sing like a cat? Squash?! Squash! Come sing with the girl!"

Eve settles and falls asleep again. I'm not sure whether laughing is appropriate or not, but I can't help smiling – I think it more a coping mechanism than genuine mirth. I feel lost trying to keep up with her outbursts and can see why Aunt

Dora has trouble deciphering the truth from the ramble. I turn to Aunt Dora for guidance, she nods to me to follow her to the kitchen. As we leave, Squash arrives, possibly answering his mistress's call. He jumps up next to her and sits as though on guard.

Whilst in the kitchen, Aunt Dora asks about Max, so although I give an abbreviated version, I happily recount the last few days'events as we return into the living room with tea. Eve is awake, stroking Squash, humming to herself, paying no obvious attention to us. I am fairly sure she is listening though.

"I am pleased my dear, you deserve a good match," says Aunt Dora. "I look forward to meeting him, I think he sounds like he is worth casting my eye over!"

"Do you want me to bring him here? I did consider it, but thought I should ask first?"

"Hmm, good point. Well, I don't plan on being a total recluse – in fact I can't be – maybe give it a little more time until we decide to bring him into our circle of (partial or complete) trust, but let us hope he is worthy!" Aunt Dora suddenly looks tense again. "Ah, that does remind me to ask of you a favour."

"Of course, how can I help?"

"I need to visit some clients and run a few errands – I've tried holding things off, but I really can't much longer and I don't like to leave Eve alone for long, so I was hoping—"

"I can stay with her, when do you need me?"

"Saturday?"

"Name your time and I will be here; I have nothing arranged that can't be postponed."

"Are you sure?" Aunt Dora's whole body relaxes.

"Absolutely, Max and I were only going to the Botanical Gardens. Sunday is as good as Saturday for that and I'm sure your errands are best done on Saturday – here, I'll message him now to tell of the change of day and that'll be that." Without delay I tap my watch, causing the menu to pop up, select messages and email Max. As I am about to press send I pause and ask: "Can I send this now? Or shall I send it when I leave and have taken the bracelet off?"

"Now should be fine, but maybe it's best to do when you leave, just in case the system logs a lag in sending."

"Okay, I'll send it in a bit, I should go anyway, the sun will be setting soon, and I've been going to bed a bit late all week." Not that I mind one bit; walking in the dusk, hand in hand with Max has been worth it. "There have been some lovely sunsets though."

"I'm more of sunrise kinda girl," smiles Aunt Dora, "I love the light on the canvas and don't mind early starts for it. I love the sunset; I just don't tend to have the patience to paint well at the end of the day."

"Hmmphh." For the seemingly hundredth time, Eve has made me jump. I'll get used to her abrupt starts eventually. "Red sky at night…Shepherd's delight…Red sky in the mornin' …Shepherds warnin'."

Eve speaks slowly, dragging out each word, then grumbles "Hmmphh" for no apparent reason. The whole time she looks down at Squash who has curled up on her lap, totally ignoring her speech and movement. He at least is obviously used to her. She suddenly jolts up her head, eyes bearing through me and declares: "Are you the Shepherd? Or the *sheep*? – Hmmm." Eve scoffs. "…Or the *wolf*? There's *always* a wolf…*Look out for the wolf.*" Her eyes lower briefly, but then are back up, narrowed, and fixed on me. "Are *you* the wolf?!"

I laugh and without thinking reply: "I've been called the black sheep by Mum before, but never the wolf."

"*Ha-ha*! I like this one!" Eve laughs to Aunt Dora, nodding at me, "...*the black sheep*! We're all black sheep, just some work harder to pretend they're white."

"Does it matter?" I'm honestly not sure if I am having a meaningful discussion or encouraging folly.

"Hmmphh, of course it matters! No point pretendin', you'll only get caught out eventually. The wolf *will* find yer."

SEVENTEEN

Kate, Tim, Max, and I are all supposed to meet for dinner tonight straight afterwork – no dressing up or pretentions; just friends spending time together. Max, I know, is a little nervous, but when his mother isn't around, he seems to talk to anyone easily enough and I don't doubt that Kate and Tim will like him. He messaged to say he was running late at work again, so I text him the address and head to the restaurant alone. As I scan in, I spot that Kate has arrived first as she is sat at the bar, sipping whatever white wine she has ordered. As I approach, she turns, hops up and greets me with the same affectionate hug that I am always welcomed by.

"No Max?" Kate is looking around me as though I have hidden him somewhere. I laugh and tell her he is late. "Ah, well, snap, Tim too – though certainly not by choice, he had to run back to SH2 after we heard reports there was an accident near our house."

"What? Oh no, is anyone hurt? – Is your house okay?!"

"No and yes, thankfully. It is bizarre, apparently mid-afternoon one of the carrier drones – you know, the big chunky ones that carry furniture and big orders? – well, one of those crashed into the side of a house down our street and blew up!"

"How?!" I half squeal. "What the hell was it carrying?!"

"No idea, I suppose that is what they are investigating now. Good job it happened mid-afternoon when no one was home – well, one of the houses is empty now anyway." Kate pauses, gazing at me, apparently deciding whether to add the next piece of information. I ask why it was empty (thinking someone old had died perhaps) and Kate coyly plays with her wine glass as she replies: "It belonged to one of the pregnant couples – you know the 1 couple I told you about?"

Yes, of course, how can I forget? Brushing over the fact this topic made us both cry last time we met, I carry on, hoping for a less distressing outcome now. "Have they moved already?"

"Yes, on Monday; both couples were moved at super-fast speed."

"Was the house destroyed?"

"No, the drone smashed into the upstairs wall, ricocheted into the house behind and then landed in the allotment garden and blew up."

"That is so weird. I'm no detective, but you would think if the PTB wanted to cover some tracks there, they would crash the drone into the house properly – and blow that up?"

"You think it wasn't a coincidence?"

"You think it *was*?"

We're both staring at each other. I don't know about Kate, but I have shivers running up my spine just thinking about this scenario.

"But why destroy or *try* to destroy the house *after* they leave? That makes no sense."

"Unless they are sending a message?"

"To whom? Surely, they did nothing wrong? Besides, no one knows how Rose got pregnant – not even Rose!"

"I'm guessing her husband had something to do with it?"

"Ha-ha, aren't you funny?" mocks Kate. "Yes, I don't think parentage is an issue…though I'm sure you're going to tell me they will DNA profile the baby to be sure."

"Certainly."

"Maybe the PTB know how already?"

"Well, if they do, they are wasting a lot of resources having Dr Brown investigate. I have spent most of the week with his team researching little else – and before you ask, we have no answer yet I'm afraid."

We both pause, silently considering how bizarre the scenario is. Drones so rarely malfunction it makes the news every time they do. Thousands of various-shaped drones take to the skies in the Hub every day – so much so, they are largely ignored. I only detest them when they notably follow me. The ones that are going about their business delivering goods make no difference to my day, so it is quite shocking to hear someone now has a building repair job because of one.

Feeling the need to use the bathroom, I leave Kate to order me a drink and excuse myself for a few moments. When I return, only a middle-aged couple are sat at the bar. As I look around the room I just see strangers' faces, but suddenly hear Kate's voice coming from a seating area around corner. She is talking to Tim who has obviously just arrived so I don't hesitate walking to them. I am about to say hello when I overhear the end of his sentence:

"…Well, if you don't hurry up and ask her this time, how will we ever know?"

I stop dead in my tracks and feel myself going beetroot red. At speed, my mind tortures me with possible explanations to this sentence: maybe it's nothing to do with me, maybe it is – but is something nice…Tim's tone doesn't sound light-hearted though; so, I doubt it. What has Kate been trying to ask me? I've frozen behind Kate, but she turns around when she sees Tim staring up at me. None of us know how to respond. I (involuntarily) shake my head and shoulders and sit down next to Tim.

"What will you never know?"

They both fidget in their seats, glancing at each other, then at the table. Neither speaks; Kate opens her mouth a couple of times, but nothing comes out, and Tim hasn't moved his mouth at all.

"Come on! What is it?! I thought you could tell me anything?" I am actually hurt that Kate has had something weighing on her shoulders that I don't know about – especially if it involves me.

"I can…I do…oh, please don't be angry!" She grasps my hands and cups them in hers across the table. Her eyes are so earnest that only a very cold person would not be moved.

"I can't be angry with you Kate, but I can't help either if you don't speak!"

Kate gulps. She says 'Okay,' but then says nothing. I'm trying my hardest not to be obviously frustrated, but this *is* frustrating. "Did you hear that Lola had her baby?"

"Who?"

"Lola, she lived in SH2 until last month when she moved to SH1—"

"Another surprise pregnancy?" I would have heard of this surely?!

"No, no, the baby was developed and born in a SurrogacyPod."

I am really struggling to see the link…struggling more not to snap… patience is a virtue… patience *is* a virtue… "Is she from accounts at work? I half remember something about a surrogacy new arrival?"

"No, that's Tess in accounts; she and her wife had IVF, her wife carried the baby. No, Lola is (or was) in the canteen, you know her; black hair, my height, cute, but bordering-on odd little laugh? – Oh, anyway, that doesn't matter! Her baby arrived safe and…and *that* was made possible because of her cousin. She is a 3 and applied to donate one of her eggs specially to Lola and her husband." Whoop, there it is. The penny has dropped. If I was beetroot before, I am not now. I am white, absolute white and feeling ill. My hands have started to shake, even though Kate is holding them. I pull them back and rub my face while Kate obviously decides she has started, so may as well finish: "Apparently, there are a few cases of donation grants being accepted if the donor applies for a couple to receive their egg. The donor has to be of sound mind and character – and proven a productive producer – which you *must* be after all these harvests! I know it is a lot to ask, I know…" Kate tails off her sentence, running out of steam, so Tim speaks for her:

"We have wanted to ask you for a long time, Maia. We had made our peace it wasn't going to happen and hope for a lottery win; but who knows if that'll ever happen – and when we heard you have one last collection—"

"You thought you just had to ask."

"Right."

It is my turn to be silent. I have no idea how to answer this. My silence has given them both courage to speak as they are now laying out the details; how I apply, when I apply, I don't have to include a specific sperm donor – though I can. I think if I ask, they have their laptop ready to produce here and now with the form primed and ready to ping up in front of me – sign with my finger on the pixelated line.

Where to begin? How to describe the confusion in my head – and indeed my heart. Only days ago, I was thinking how I would swap my uterus gladly with Kate so she could have the children she so desperately wants. Were they just empty thoughts? Here is a potential opportunity to give Kate what she so desires – but my initial, gut-wrenching reaction is to say absolutely: no. Am I only a fair-weather friend? When put to the test do I turn tail and run? No, I will love Kate until the day I die and never see a truer friend. So, will I give her my egg and watch her rear my child? *My* child. Doing this could feasibly see Kate and I raising children at the same or similar time – siblings, in different households. Surely that is just too much? A step too far?

But I have already donated eggs – three times a year (it will be four this year), for six years. I can only assume I am highly fertile from the fact they keep harvesting me, but also from what Henry alluded to when he spoke of 'my impressive results.' Highly fertile is defined by 10-15 eggs per harvest. If I average 12 a time…

This line of thought is not conducive to happiness. I know these figures; I just don't normally choose to remember them. How many of those eggs survived and are already across the globe? Not in this Hub, but shipped to others where people have won them. Why would Kate having one be so bad? She would be a wonderful mum. But I would see it and know it was mine. You can't ignore a truth in front of you…

"I can't decide this now."

"Of course, of course, it is a huge thing. I'm sorry, I just—"

"*We* just *had* to ask," cuts in Tim, "I hope you can forgive us."

I close my eyes, briefly shutting out their earnest, hopeful, yet anxious expressions. I open my eyes and feel a solitary tear roll down my right cheek.

"There is nothing to forgive."

EIGHTEEN

I am half praying that Max calls to say work has detained him and he will have to postpone so I can go home; but the other half is praying he arrives quickly so we can change topic and distract me. A distraction would be fantastic about now. Thankfully he hears my prayer, as while the waiter is asking if we are ready to order, Max's handsome face appears behind his shoulder. Concealing current emotions (temporarily at least), I jump up and briefly, but affectionately kiss him on the lips and swiftly turn to introduce him to Kate and Tim.

They also seem relieved to have someone new to redirect and lighten the mood as they openly greet him. I am thankful. This meeting means so much to me; I need the two people who have carried me through everything to include Max and form as strong a friendship with him, as they have me. I can't ignore the fact that the decision they have just handed to me threatens the bonds of our friendship, but resolution to that is for another day. Now, we chat, laugh, and eat. Just as friends should.

The rogue drone figures heavily in conversation. Tim, having come straight from the scene, has little more actual information, just more description of the crash spot. We again go over the oddity of it all, meanwhile trying to also make light of the damage, as luckily it wasn't as destructive as it could have been.

"Did my flowers survive?" Kate asks Tim.

"Which?"

"The gladioli."

"No, sorry – none of the allotment did."

"What? Damn it! They were just blooming so beautifully!" Turning to Max and me: "I had some particularly beautiful blooms this year, I'd been tweaking some new variations at home as well as work."

"I thought you grew veg?"

"Yes, mainly, but I have some flowers too – Ha! Dave was getting quite jealous of my new ones – he and I had a little competition going. I suppose he'll claim he won now! Hey, do you think he sabotaged the drone to take me out of the competition? If my gladioli at work are killed too, I'll know it was him!"

"Who is Dave?" asks Max innocently.

"Oh, don't ask her – she and Dave are constantly competing to out-bloom one another." Tim rolls his eyes as he laughs at Kate. "I'm sorry honey, but I think Dave has a good chance of winning this one – *without* foul play!"

"Dave is Head of Botany in the Botanical Gardens," I explain, "he is a really lovely old man. His wife makes the sweetest jam and brings homemade scones into the greenhouses. I always try to time my visits to Kate at just the right time to share in the bounty!"

Max smiles. "Ah, we're still going there this weekend, right?"

"The Gardens? – yes, on Sunday. Hopefully the weather will hold; I think it is meant to."

"Good, I'm keen to go. I've had a quick tour around some of the greenhouses, but I'm mainly sticking with the planning team to begin with until I know where I am. I've already got ideas for structural changes to allow for more botanical gardens on buildings – but maximising space for not just ornamental plants, but improved bee activity and veg for homes – so we're not just relying on greenhouses."

This is like music to Kate and Tim's ears. Max's ethos is one that has long been established – in fact the PTB have actively pushed and encouraged it from their beginning from what I understand. However, like so many elements in life, those in power think they have concocted the perfect solution, so any embellishment or suggestion of change sounds like heresy. The three of them are now so happily engaged in discussion, throwing about ideas and ideals, it truly warms my heart. If I can but hold onto this feeling and these friendships, all else should seem like less of a task.

What a mixed evening! Kate and Tim left on one tram, Max and I another. Both pairs affectionately parting, promising to see each other again soon. In terms of my best friends' and fiancé's first meeting, I couldn't have asked for more. Oh! But their request! Where to start unpicking that one?!

"Come on, we're getting off," says Max suddenly.

"What? No, we have another couple of stops yet."

"No, let's get off and walk the rest," he says standing up, taking me by the hand.

I'm tired and really should get home as I need to be at Aunt Dora's for 8 a.m., but can't resist him, so follow without further protest. We point ourselves in the direction of home (well mine, he now has very long walk or needs to catch another tram). We walk along, arm in arm. Without really thinking about this specifically, I've missed this sensation so much, yet it feels entirely new.

"So, what is it?"

"Hmm? What is what?"

"Whatever it is that made you ignore what I was saying on the tram."

Crap. I must have zoned out again. On the tram I was leant on his shoulder, daydreaming. If asked I would have said we hadn't spoken; however, by the look on his face, I'm guessing I didn't hear him talk to me.

"Did I? I'm so sorry, I didn't hear you, I must have been daydreaming."

"Yes, I got that part, I was hoping to have better luck now."

"Sorry – what did you say?"

"Nothing noteworthy – just how I enjoyed the evening and can see why you like them so much – but that isn't what I want to discuss now."

"What is?"

"What has concerned you so – did your meeting with my dad not go as well as you hoped yesterday? I know we haven't had chance to talk about that properly yet—"

"No, I am very grateful to your dad, he has provided me with great hope."

"What then?"

"I must have just been daydreaming about—"

"Don't give me that; your eyebrows were in full gallop, so I know you were considering something important."

Dammit! I knew I should have plucked them out! Or at least should wear a big hat – even in the summer! A fringe might work, but I don't think one would suit me. I instantly cover my eyebrows with my hands, cringing with embarrassment. "I'm going to have to pluck them out."

Max chuckles, "Please don't, that would look odd, and I love them just as they are."

Well, that just melted me. I stop and stare at him, hands still on my forehead, but he gently pulls them down to my side, continuing to hold the left hand, but releasing the right, taking his free hand back up to my face; pulling me in and kissing me, whispering, "Don't change a thing," as he steps back.

I expel a sigh. A happy, blown away, catching my breath, kind of sigh. He knows exactly how to take down my defences.

"Now, what *is* wrong?"

I tell him, openly and honestly what Kate and Tim are asking of me. He doesn't interrupt or question until I finish telling him my confused thoughts, the reasons for and against, and the complications of either option. In fact, he doesn't say anything, we just continue walking silently, hand in hand until I ask what he thinks. Now it is his turn to sigh. He blows out his cheeks, slowly releasing the air before replying:

"Honestly? I don't know. I see exactly what you are saying from both angles." He shakes his head. "I can't lie, it would be pretty weird to see your friend walking around with your daughter – maybe *our* daughter – or son, for that matter. Your nature versus nurture argument would literally be tested in front of us…"

"I know."

"But I am not unsympathetic to their desires, especially as we are hardwired to want children…Don't stare at me like *that*! You received the same education as I did!"

"You're right – about all of it – but what *is* the answer?"

"I don't know. Think on it a while longer…" Max stops, turns to me, and gently says: "Promise me something?"

"What's that?"

"You'll always discuss things with me. I don't want to live in secrets, even if the truth is difficult."

I look up at him. How is it, after years of loneliness, he has come, so wonderfully, at just the right time? I hope this luck doesn't run out. I step up to him, so there's no space between us, he holding me, me him, both of us smiling.

"Always."

NINETEEN

"Ah, Maia! Prompt as always, thank you my dear!"

"My word, you have enough bags – have you ordered a Solarbug? Surely you need one to deliver that painting? It is too big to lug onto a tram!" I say looking Aunt Dora up and down as she clutches an enormous oil painting and various bags filled with smaller pieces of artwork.

"No, but I am regretting that decision. I just hate being driven alone by a drone. At least on a tram you normally have an operator – or can forget to some degree if there isn't. Do you think I have time to order one?"

"Of course, I'll do it now for you before I see Eve." I quickly order a Solarbug on my watch to arrive as soon as possible and then remember to put on my bracelet. I wave my wrist at Aunt Dora to prove that I haven't forgotten.

"Excellent! It is still taking me time to get into the habit. Thankfully, Eve doesn't forget that one yet. She has had breakfast; I've left instructions in the kitchen for lunch, and I'll be back hopefully long before dinner – you'll eat with us?" I smile and nod. "Lovely. Now, I can't really prepare you more for today, you'll just have to see how the day goes; she has had difficult spells the last few days – one minute, she is her normal old self; then as though someone flicks a switch, she can be confused, angry, sad, occasionally comical, sometimes—"

"It is okay, we'll do very well and be good companions for one another, I'm sure."

"I can't thank you enough for this. Eve is family to me and I shall not let her down, but I do worry—"

"We'll worry together; your family is my family – blood or not. Look, your Solarbug is here – off you go!"

I help her load the Solarbug. I share her dislike of them – not that I am going to tell her that, I don't want to risk her refusing to use one when she really does need it. Talking to robots and drones is just the norm, but talking to a faceless one while it drives me around just doesn't feel right. I go back inside and straight into the living room, entering quietly in case Eve is asleep, but she is stood by the window, watching the Solarbug disappear with Aunt Dora in it.

"Mornin' little lady. So, your aunt has gone on a drone, hey? Practical I suppose. And now you're to watch me – or hopefully entertain?"

"I'll certainly do my best. How would you like to be entertained?"

"Sing to me."

"Sorry, I rather not, I'm not—"

"Hmmphh, some entertainer – don't want to sing. I used to sing, you know? Just for fun, but I do love music."

"Then why don't you sing to me? I'd love to hear you!"

"Hmmphh, I don't sing anymore. Your mum sings."

"Indeed, and very well. I love to hear her."

"Hmmphh." This could be a long day if everything I say displeases her. "She's an awkward woman."

"Who?"

"Your mum, *obviously*. Nothing like your aunt, shame you ain't hers really." I have to chuckle. That is a thought I have had several times over the years. "I bet she is happy now. Three children, all 3s. Odds of that these days are slim."

And don't I know it? "Yes, Mum puts high value on our fertility."

My dry comment makes Eve turn to look straight at me, but all she says is, "Hmmm."

I start prattling on about anything and everything I can think of. The weather is an old faithful, but work, my family, hobbies, painting, reading, the cats (probably her favourite, so I revisit that topic more than once – which the cats love as the more we talk about them, the more Eve pets them). Eventually I can see Eve is tiring, so I let her sleep and go into the kitchen to prepare whatever Aunt Dora has left for me. We eat together, but Eve soon falls asleep again, so while she snoozes, I sketch in a pad of paper that Aunt Dora has left on the side table. Hopefully she will not mind, it is so rare I have the opportunity to sketch at all, let alone on paper! I see the practicality of everything being digital and how the touch screen system understands and, if required, re-fonts our handwriting is impressive; but occasionally it would be nice to receive an actual letter or write a report for real. Access to trees (farmed or otherwise), is so limited though, I know that cannot be.

"So, you like this Max?"

I jump a little. Yet again, Eve has managed to catch me out. How does she do it? I am beginning to think she enjoys it as I see a little smirk as I recover myself.

"Yes, I do."

"Do you love him?"

"It's too soon for that – I hope to – the fact I like him is more than I'd ever imagined possible…and that has happened faster than I dared to dream of."

"Hmm, time is relative. You know when you know. Sometimes it creeps up on you, sometimes it hits you with a brick when you least expect it – but probably when you most need it. By the grin on your face, I'd say you know."

"I'm not sure, I'm trying to be 'all-in' and really, I suppose there is no harm in speed, it's not like I have options! It's just past experience has taught me caution – I'm not sure I can be *this* lucky…"

"Hmmphh, luck doesn't change, it just ebbs. It's up to you to catch it when it comes in and decide what to do with it."

"You're probably right. I have just spent so long fighting against this moment, it seems too good to—"

"Look, if you got dealt a good one, keep it, don't let fear of success cause you to fail."

"I am going to have to write your sage words down." Eve laughs at me, but doesn't reply. I watch her face as it slowly turns from a smile to frown. Whatever memory she has just recollected, has not been a happy one.

"Which was it for you with Mr Addams?" I'm worried I'm bordering on dangerous territory here, but it is the first question I think of and need to attempt to cheer her up again.

"Ha! The brick!" The biggest smile spreads over her face. Thankfully, recollecting Mr Addams seems to bring her joy. "We just knew. We were a quirky pair, made for each other, even in the most difficult times. Hmmphh, be glad you weren't there *then*—" Eve's face has fallen sorrowful again. How much she must have seen over the years!

"I can't image how difficult it was to live through all the changes as you have – to see the Fall, if only part of it."

"Hmmphh, the Fall took a long time, Maia, much had happened before my time, but possibly the worst was when

I was young. Mine was the generation of the biggest change I suppose: the swap over, the better path, striving to do better – that's what aging *should* be for." Eve stops for a moment. "Pfft… Be glad you have the structure of now – and the innocence." Eve falls silent and is almost motionless, with just a very gentle wobble of the head. She clearly has a plethora of memories and emotions running through her mind. I am itching to ask her so many questions, yet her peace of mind is so delicate, I am reluctant to test her. "Yea, my Tom and I rode some storms." She gazes at her bracelet, twists it around her wrist and whispers: "Why didn't you finish these first?"

Now, I am dying to ask, but she has drifted into another one of her hazes and I am not sure what to do. Aunt Dora says she frequently switches from one frame of mind to another, and I get the impression there is no dictating which. So, I wait, and possibly for the first time I see what you could describe as 'the switch' – just like someone suddenly clicked their fingers in front of her eyes, Eve blinks into awareness; this time continuing to twiddle with her bracelet, but saying nothing.

"Did you design that with your husband?"

"Hmm, yes. Though he never finished it. He was too impatient and thought he had the answer without it. Fool."

"So, you were both IT engineers?"

"Yes, though officially, it was him. I was raising children for twenty years, but Tom always designed with me and I him. Until the last—" She closes her eyes, grimacing, and her lips start to shake. I am sure she is willing herself not to cry as she tightens her face further.

"Once the boys married, I did more still, but still I stayed under Tom's shadow; we thought it best. He was a suspicious man – what good it ultimately did him! So, we kept newer tech to ourselves for a bit." Eve grins. "Ha! Some of the things the kids used to play with would make the PTB weep!"

"How many children did you have?"

"Two," whispers Eve as her face drops. I think I have said the wrong thing. "Two boys… both are gone now."

"I'm so sorry."

"Hmmphh, not your fault, tis mine," she says, shaking her head softly from side to side.

"That's not true, I'm sure."

"Pfft, you don't know. *Good.*"

I don't know whether to leave the conversation or pursue it. I'm curious – *so* curious, yet it doesn't seem right to ask more if she doesn't want to say.

"They should have died of old age. *They all should have!*" The distress on Eve's face is heart breaking. Pain and suffering reflect in her eyes and though fair skinned anyway, the colour has drained from her face in an instant. However curious I might be, I can't bring myself to make her talk about it.

"*Oh, Mason.*" She mutters quietly, but then bursts into tears saying: "*The bastards got them!*" Her tears have turned to wails and I don't know what to do. The sight is horrible. I try to sooth her, but she pushes me away. I try to think of what to do; in the end, I just sit in the chair next to her, which is only just big enough for us both, though neither of us is large. The uncontrolled body quakes that came with the wailing stop after what seems an age. I am desperately trying to find the words to say, but they all seem insufficient to calm her grief. I go to hold her hand, asking if there is anything I can do to help. She doesn't reply at first, so I gently ask again. This time she looks up and gruffly exclaims: "Leave me! Do not ask the price I pay!" but rather than push me away, she leans on my shoulder. I pull her in for hug, both of us gently rocking and tears silently falling down our cheeks. "*I must live with my disgrace,*" she whispers. I have never heard such sadness in a sentence.

No words of comfort come to me; I'm not sure any will do anyway. A tune does though, I don't know where from, but the melody plays through my head, so I sing it as well as I can. Mum would do better, but Eve squeezes my hand, so I hope I will do.

TWENTY

Aunt Dora comes home early evening and enters the house so quietly that neither Eve nor I wake up. We eventually fell asleep when the tears had run out. Neither spoke again, just one resting on the other, joined by Smoggy and Squash at some point as they curled up next to us, making use of our motionless slumber. I vaguely hear a click in the distance and open one eye just enough to see Aunt Dora crouched in front of us, taking a photograph. She smiles when she sees I have spotted her. Her smile is warm and affectionate – it has always been such a comfort to me. Regardless of trials she may be going through, for me at least, she has smiled, hugged, and comforted me whenever I visit. I am sure my entire childhood would have been a lot more painful if it wasn't for her care.

She helps me gently lean Eve onto the opposite side of the chair, miraculously not waking her up and we go into the kitchen, leaving her and the cats to snooze.

"I hope you don't mind me photographing you, but that was too wonderful to miss – the light was reflecting on you so beautifully! – but that aside; it fills my heart to see you both bonding."

"No, I don't mind," I reply smiling.

"I'm sorry I was gone so long – how was today?"

"Well, we had an *interesting* day!"

"Good, interesting?" Aunt Dora pulls a nervous expression as she asks. "Or are we talking, 'no, you won't stay with Eve again,' kind of interesting?"

"Ha, no more 'I couldn't explain it, even if I wanted to, *interesting*' – but of course, I'll stay again when you need." Relief washes over Aunt Dora's face as she relaxes her whole body. She starts telling me about her day which thankfully went well delivering commissions and booking a few more.

"I don't want to take up all your Saturdays, but if we could repeat this every so often, I'd be so grateful. Eve was self-sufficient until recently and is mostly pretty mobile, but her mind plays such tricks on her; living alone is just not safe – even without the added *complications*. To be honest, if she hadn't chosen to live away from most people, she would have landed in difficulties earlier."

"I can see that. We had some straightforward conversation, but some was so riddled... though I have to say, also very wise! She is a remarkable lady."

"Ha! That she is! But she has tortured and locked herself away for so long."

"Yes, I witnessed her grief this afternoon. Her sorrow is enough to break even the coldest heart, I think."

"Did she tell you anything?" Aunt Dora scans my face in a way I haven't seen before. I can't help thinking she would like to examine me just in case I know too much. I hardly think that fair when she has brought me into this scenario, not the other way around.

"What are you worried she has told me? Surely I have done nothing to earn your mistrust?" I can't hide the hurt her tone has caused.

"Maia, I trust you more than anyone, you wouldn't be here if I didn't. If anything, I am worried *for you*, not because of you. I know you question the rule – *though you follow it* – don't get me wrong, but you want discussion, room for change and improvement, *they* want silence while they rule."

"You yourself told me to follow the rule whilst looking for my silver lining! I am just following your advice! And I am hoping to have found it – or the start of it at least."

"And I couldn't be happier, my dear. But all the more reason for my caution. I always knew Eve held a darkened past, but it is not until lately I have begun to see the depth of the darkness that haunts her."

"Do you know who Mason is? She cried out his name?"

"Her eldest son. He died along with Frank, his brother, both wives, Tom (Eve's husband), and Mason's daughter and son in law."

"How?"

"Some accident; they were visiting Mason's workshop which was on a farm on the outer rim and a drone malfunctioned – I think Mason had been experimenting with drone capabilities and miscalculated. He wanted to celebrate his wedding anniversary by showing off his latest design, but it ended up killing everyone – or almost everyone, in the immediate family. Eve was on her way to join them, but had been delayed and arrived to see a burning pillar of fire. My Ray wasn't there as he had his exams and was to follow on the next day. I didn't know him then; he was only 17. He and Eve then lived together until we married."

"I don't know what to say, that's horrific." I have cold chills running down my arms and back. A scene and loss like that just seems beyond comprehension. "So, Ray was the last of the family?"

"No, Frank, Eve's other son, had a daughter, she had a daughter too and there's now a great-great granddaughter, she'd be in her late teens now I suppose, but Eve hasn't seen any of them in years. There was a lot of anguish after the accident, and they left Eve aside."

"So much for the bond and importance of family. How could they leave her alone like that?"

"Hmm, you can't pick your family and blood means more to some than others."

"Eve blames herself, but if she wasn't there, how could she be to blame? And if it was her fault, why did she say, *'the bastards got them'* to me earlier?"

"Hmm. I don't know. I do know she and Tom used to work on tech together. Maybe Tom – or Mason? – was playing with a drone she hadn't finished or had miscalculated on and that caused the fire? Maybe she just meant the drone got them?"

"Maybe." I'm not sure if Aunt Dora believes her own suggestion or if it is what she hopes I will accept. It doesn't add up though and does not account for Eve potentially holding a secret the PTB want to silence her for – which they must if Aunt Dora is concerned enough to move Eve in, wear devices that block others, and is hardly willing to leave the house. A miscalculated drone sounds more like an excuse the PTB would use, not threaten murder because of.

Aunt Dora has started preparing dinner, but I keep catching her glance at me. I am sure she is trying to weigh up whether I am satisfied with her hypothesis. I can't decide if I am going to let her think I am or if I should push for more now. I decide the softly, softly approach may yield more fruit. It may also drive me to distraction, but I don't think a tantrum or ultimatum will get me anywhere. It wouldn't work with me and I unfortunately think we are more alike than I care to admit at the moment. Suspicion, reserve, and measured responses have been indoctrinated into us. So, I take a deep breath and ask if I can help.

"Hmmphh, here you both are." Eve's stick comes through the door before she does. The door slides back as designed without hesitation, but Eve knocks the retreating edge with the stick as though it were stuck. Aunt Dora scowls, but doesn't rebuke. "You back then? Sell your paintings?" Aunt Dora nods with a half-smile. "Hmmphh, little Missy here is more like you than you know – though sings like her mum."

Ha! I'm not sure who looks more surprised, but I speak first. "High praise, Eve, thank you."

"Aye, you'll do well."

"You got her to sing? Well, I never thought I'd hear that!" exclaims Aunt Dora. I laugh, it was a surprise to me too and not one I plan on repeating, but I am happy to see recounting it made Eve smile.

Eve doesn't respond now though. In those few seconds between entering the room and sitting down, whoever holds the cruel switch in her mind, changed the channel. This time, not to a different train of thought or even emotion, but to blank. If she were a screen, her eyes would be filled with white noise. There is no reaction and seeing it brings a lump to my throat that I cannot swallow.

I look over to Aunt Dora. She has seen too, and I believe her face mirrors my own. The cruelty of disease and aging is distressing to watch. So many ailments have been cured or lessened over recent decades, but so many still elude the scientists who work so hard to map and seize them. The brain is such a complex organ – fertility has proven complicated enough and we can't even find what is deactivating or depressing our capacity to breed, but this is nothing compared to full comprehension of the brain. So fascinating, yet so heart-breaking.

TWENTY-ONE

"Are you okay?"

"Hmm? Yes, why do you ask?" I'm pretty sure I haven't been daydreaming this time…

"You just seem quiet."

"Am I normally loud?!"

"No, I suppose not."

Now I feel bad, I was a touch sarcastic, and Max looks a little dejected. I was only jesting, but I think he took it as me being evasive. Maybe I *am* being evasive. Eve and Aunt Dora have been weighing heavily on my mind this morning. I know I promised not to live with secrets from Max, but this isn't really my secret to share – not yet anyway.

I need to lighten the mood and take my mind off worries. I've promised to take Max to the Botanical Gardens and let him tell me about the various fauna and flora. Some I know from visits with Kate and Tim, but I am happy to hear another perspective. The gardens are huge and beautifully coloured all year round – in winter more in the hot houses, but still, the whole place is seriously stunning, and it is easy to spend a whole day wandering through the different sections and feel like you have moved through multiple countries; the topography and plants are that varied.

"I love how peaceful it is here," I say gazing into the trees. "Do you come here a lot?"

"No, not really, not unless I'm with Kate or if work is stressful – though I tend to go to the river for my therapy."

"Hmm." Max is smiling but says no more.

"What?"

Still nothing.

"What made you 'hmm'?"

"It just amazes me how similar we are."

"Really? The river in the Midlands was your solace?"

"No, the river in the Midlands Hub isn't near where I lived. But I do love water and find it relaxing, so my therapy is – or *was* I should say – *was* going to the Botanical Gardens there, where I'd wander around and sit by the waterfalls."

I suddenly feel goosebumps up my arms and neck. "Hmm, indeed." I'm smiling... no, I can feel myself beaming. Max stops and takes my hand – which just increases the goosebumps, which I didn't think was possible! I squeeze his hand and gently tug his arm to carry on walking. I'm not sure what to say so leading him to the waterfalls here seems the best thing to do.

Once there, Max's reaction is as anticipated. He loves the architecture and gives me descriptions on the design and structure. It is wonderful to see it anew through him. Kate always focuses on the plants alone; Max understands and enjoys the construction, layout, and choice of plants – all way beyond my simplistic 'it's beautiful.' There are some benches near us and deciding to have a break, we head towards the nearest. Even they are designed in harmony with the surroundings, all using recycled material, perfectly complimenting the concept the architect had in mind. A message is inscribed on the back of the seat which makes me pause before I sit down. Max follows my gaze and reads the inscription aloud:

All those who find themselves swept along by life's madness, pause a moment and find peace with me.

THE ARCHITECT

"Well, that could have been written by me!" says Max, still holding my hand as he sits down with the biggest grin on his face. "Maia, will you join me in finding peace?"

I don't reply, but sit down immediately beside him, returning his grin. He puts his arm around me, and I lean into him. We silently watch the water flow in front of us and I instantly feel the peace. This place is perfect. Perfect not just in aura, but in company and it works at soothing some of my worries, if only for a while.

"I wish we could just stay here," I whisper. That was all Max needed to turn to me to kiss me; one hand on my jawline, the other around my back. Now I definitely don't want to leave! Is this too good to be true? I need to stop doubting myself. How have I gone from so sad, pessimistic, and lonely, to worried, but hopeful in such a short period of time? … Ah, the power of a little change and hope! I think the biggest change is not the prospect of love, however wonderful that may be, but the realisation someone is listening and believes in me – helping me believe in myself, and genuinely envisage a future both in and beyond the narrow frame that I am told I should want.

"If I knew this was possible from being matched, I wouldn't have hidden from it for so long!"

"So, you *did* hide?!" Max looks amused more than anything. "There we differ. I wanted out as fast as I could, Mum just didn't like the Matchmakers choices."

"But how did she manage that? To postpone I mean?"

"She got me to apply for extensions – same as you, but I'm guessing you filled yours in without asking!?"

"Certainly. And I had more than one argument about that!" I feel myself rolling my eyes at the memory. "Waiting for love or even the right man wasn't high on my mum's list of concerns – any more than my education."

"Nor mine, she just wanted a match with powerful links – she wants me to 'follow her lead up the ladder' as she calls it."

"Yes, I got that impression – hence both our mums crowing at our match. Before we met, I was afraid you'd share their dream, and I would eternally be a trophy housewife."

"I can assure you, I neither share their dreams nor wish to make you into anything you are not. I've nothing against the roles our families have taken, but our paths don't need to be so linear. I am certainly not convinced about mum's idea of a powerful family dynasty."

"Would you like to be Agricultural Governor or Director one day? You have excellent knowledge and understanding of botany which I'm sure extends to agriculture."

Max's face falls. "You sound like my mum – she'd like nothing more."

"I didn't mean to sound like your mum – I want to know what *you* want, not her. I have no desire to push you to roles you don't want, just encourage those you do." Max nods, but is clearly still thinking of his mum's desires. After pausing briefly, he continues with:

"In fact, I think if we had a bunch of kids and one girl was infertile, she'd do everything possible to make *her* Agricultural Director – continuing female empowerment in the family as well as us proving successful in fertility. For her, that would be the dream complete."

I cringe at the thought of an extended family dynasty, and resist the urge to tell him off for even slightly comparing me to his mother because a more pressing point has come to mind and now is my chance to seize the opportunity to ask:

"Max, how did your mother do it?"

"What do you mean?"

"You just said it yourself; only infertile females are truly empowered now – with top positions I mean – so *how* did she marry your dad, have you, *and* become Director?"

"You know she's infertile?"

"I saw her barcode."

Max doesn't reply. He sits back a little, chewing on his lip, looking anywhere but at me. He is still holding my left hand and begins playing with it slowly, more out of distraction than affection, I think. I'm considering whether I should ask again or change the subject – maybe now wasn't the right time? – when his grip suddenly tightens, and he hurriedly says:

"I don't know much."

"But you do know *something*?" I ask softly.

"Hmm."

"Such as?"

To call him reluctant is an understatement. I still don't know whether to push or leave him. Maybe in time he'll open up. We said we'd have no secrets, I plan to keep to that, but also don't plan on blurting out everything I've ever thought, done, or considered in one day to him, so, it is fair enough he should do the same. Vexatious or not, I will probably have to be patient. I lean back against his arm, watching the water flow. He again wraps his arm around me, but neither of us speaks.

I have no idea how long we have sat this way, but my arm is going numb, so I rearrange myself, causing pins and needles to shoot up and down my arm as the blood resumes its normal flow. I've given up on waiting for a reply and have been so absorbed in my own thoughts I am surprised to hear him suddenly speak, especially as he is still on our previous topic.

"She didn't *have* me." I don't dare reply – not that I'm sure what to say anyway. I had guessed as much from the barcode differences, but I am not going to tell Max that. I want him to tell me in his time (and hopefully end my perpetual guesstimates). "She, Mum – Mary, I mean – isn't my mother; she married Dad when I was a newborn and brought me up as her own. I've never heard anyone mention to her that I am not actually hers, whether out of ignorance, respect, or fear… well, I leave that for you to decide. Dad only told me after he'd had an argument with Mum once. She was furious and didn't speak to him for weeks afterwards. Then one morning, she flipped."

"She was violent?"

"No, no…though I would be lying if I said she was *never*, as plates did smash a lot in Dad's direction. No, *this* was a good*ish* flip – creepy as hell – but she suddenly started chatting, smiling, and laughing like nothing had ever happened. Although the weirdest time didn't last too long, she never alluded to the past again. I even wonder if she trained herself to forget. I genuinely believe she thinks I am her *real* son."

"But adoptive parents do love their children like that – certainly Kate's do."

"Of course, but they don't pretend to have *given birth* to them. At our induction here, I heard Mum talking to our guide about the maternity ward as we passed the hospital. She said she remembered the day I was born and how beautiful I was and how she knew her son was magical straightaway. She wouldn't have seen me then, so *how* is that possible?"

My goosebumps are back, but these are definitely not good ones. How do you train yourself to forget things? Surely deeply repressing something isn't healthy?

"Do you know who your real mum is?"

"She had an accident and died before I was born – no one will ever speak of that time. I asked Dad a thousand times when I was younger, but he always froze as though he was expecting Mum's wrath to strike him from afar. I even tried my grandparents, but I got a similar reaction, mixed in with tears. Eventually I found it easier not to ask."

"Which grandparents? Do you know of family from your real mum?"

"No. I once found some of my newborn baby photos with a couple that looked the right age. I asked Dad, but he never had a chance to answer as Mum rushed in, took the pictures, and ripped them up, declaring 'those people are nothing to you' – I think they must be my grandparents, otherwise why would they have been printed? No one prints photos unless they're special, right? But they never tried to contact me if they are. Dad's parents have always been around. They were really unhappy when we moved here, but they live with my aunt and cousin, so coming with us wasn't an option. Mum's parents have had little to do with me – which, given the family values everyone rates so highly, I always thought odd."

I am trying to digest what Max is saying. All this information has actually done is add questions to my pile, not answer anything.

"Do you know what kind of accident your mum had?"

"She fell downstairs and was pretty much gone when Dad found her. They kept her in a coma for a bit; I was born at seven months by caesarean, and she died soon after."

I squeeze his hand tighter, but can't think of anything to say, comforting or otherwise. He is right: the lack of family ties is odd. Even my dysfunctional mob stick together, even when I wish they didn't.

"What do your granddads do? – for work I mean?"

"Dad's is an accountant. Mum's is in the Army, Captain of the General's Guard. Why?"

"So, in a position to grant favours or exceptions maybe?"

"Like, a 1 marrying a widowed 3, you mean?"

"Precisely. Though I'd still wager there's more to it than that as your dad would have been young and fit to marry another 3. So, there had to be good reason for not. It's just, what *was* the reason? Hmm, so many directions of inquiry…" I can feel my imagination running away with scandals and theories – mostly implausible as even with connections such a grant of marriage, to my knowledge, is unheard of.

"Can you not look so amused?" retorts Max. "This is my life you're considering. And maybe, just maybe, the secret is best left." I look straight at Max and instantly feel rebuked. He has probably tortured himself with theories over the years and only felt pain and frustration when doing so. Watching me light up with enthusiasm at cracking his code is hardly going to be helpful.

"Sorry. Of course, I should have thought."

"I am curious," says Max more gently, "I just don't want to be the subject of an investigation. I've got this far by going forward, not looking back."

"I get that, I really do, but to a certain degree, you need to know the past – or deal with it at least – to be able to move forward, to heal, to not repeat mistakes made by yourself or others. Not repeating mistakes sounds pretty good to me."

"We won't repeat our parents' mistakes. For starters, I think we've started by liking each other and if we are blessed with children, we won't put pressure on them to be any one thing. Mum was always so harsh, even when she went back into part time work. I thought she might relax once she was working, but she didn't. I think she actually pushed for me to excel harder, as though it was a way of proving to the PTB she could do both roles well simultaneously."

"What age were you when she started work?"

"Seven."

"What?! So early?" Hell, if I'd been told I had only seven years to wait, I may have complained less! 16 is more the standard answer – if mums go back to work at all.

"I know, I received a lot of stick at school for having a working mum. She dropped me off at school and went into her secretarial role at the Agricultural Affairs department for a few hours. Of course, I never told her I was bullied about it, but none of the other kids understood why my mum worked. She was itching to, and I heard her begging her dad not to 'retire her' as she put it. By the time I was 16 she was in full-time work and rising ranks fast. I think I was 18 when she made Governor of Agriculture back in the Midlands."

"It's curious then, that she doesn't advocate a change in the rules, allowing other women to follow her lead? I heard her tell you she leads by example."

"Yes, but she also enjoys the distinction of being given special licence and powers. If everyone has that, that is hardly a distinguished position, is it?"

Good point.

I nod my head on one side, acknowledging the truth in what he says. I will try not to pester him by continuously questioning, but I can tell I am going to spend a lot of time mulling over the conundrum of Mary Rivers.

TWENTY-TWO

Kate emailed me on Sunday night. When I saw her message flash up on my watch, I wasn't sure I even wanted to read it. I had just left Max and was full of giddy, girly-joy and feared opening the message would burst that bubble. However, after twenty minutes of not opening it, the effort of ignoring it was weighing on me, so really, I should have just opened it immediately.

The message is relatively short and sweet, apologising for dropping their request on me that way, telling me she wished she'd asked me earlier and in a less clumsy fashion. Honestly, I'm not sure it would have made a great deal of difference. She finishes with:

'I will respect your decision either way, but if you do want to consider or apply for this wonderful gift, then here is the form you need to fill in, we have completed our section already. Much love, as always, Kate xx'

The form requests I write an essay answering: 'Why I believe the nominated couple deserve my egg.' I have spent all week trying to write the darn essay because Max suggested I write it, even if I ultimately decide not to submit the application. I've written a hundred drafts and have finally finished. I haven't spoken to Kate all week and she hasn't messaged again. I forwarded my final draft to Max this morning before breakfast to see what he thinks and am now waiting for him to have lunch with me in the café nearest the lab. I am not nervous about seeing him, but I am so fidgety that I am driving myself crazy. I will be glad when the decision is made and declared.

It feels like he is late, but in truth, I think I left for my break slightly earlier than I should and Max has a longer walk than I do. My watch pings. I click on my message thinking it is likely to be Max saying he can't make it or is late, but as it opens I realise he has returned Kate's application form. Scrolling through, I am surprised to see he has filled in the optional section of 'sperm donor.' I am trying to digest what this means when Max grabs my shoulder and kisses my cheek before sitting down coolly in front of me.

"Ah, good, you've seen it."

"Yes, just now – you've filled in the sperm donor section?"

"I have. I can't pretend I think it easy to potentially see someone else with our child, but I am also not sure I want to see that same couple with just *your* child – so better together in everything."

"And you're all in? What made you decide? I can't."

"You."

"Excuse me?"

"Your application – I read it and if you believe what you wrote, they deserve a child. If my children are out in the world in unknown corners, I think I would rather know the couple truly deserves the child and will give it the childhood and love we'd want them to."

"So, I should sign and submit this then?"

"That is your choice entirely, I'm just letting you know I'm with you, either way."

Max's face is serious, yet not hard. I feel my expression is hard – well, hard-set at least. Maybe I should read my essay again, if it is good enough to convince Max perhaps if I read it again to myself… Oh, who am I kidding? I already know I believe what I wrote, I am just not sure I am prepared to drive that wedge in between myself and the one friend with whom there has been no wedges. A child-shaped mini-me is definitely a wedge. Is it one I can get over?

"What are you thinking?"

"Hmm?"

"You're chewing on your lip and have sighed at least five times in thirty seconds – *talk* to me!"

"I am just weighing it up."

"Do you believe what you wrote in the essay?"

"Yes"

"Then you have your answer, surely?"

"Yes, I do."

"And yet you sigh again! You are worried about the consequences still. You can't know how we will feel until it happens. I hope that seeing the joy it brings them will throw away any doubts we have now."

"Yes, but with that I could throw away, or at least severely tear, the one friendship that hasn't failed me – sure, my aunt has always been a friend, but it's different—"

"I understand, I do. I've had to leave my friends behind and we can say we'll video call each other or watch virtual matches together, but it isn't the same – and this is an entirely new kind of separation – but if you don't do it—"

"I'll blame myself for their childless sorrow all my life."

Max nods. Ugh. I haven't much time left to decide, so my procrastinating can't go on much longer. Max has ordered something, but I'm not sure I can eat. I lean my head on my hand, pulling at my hair. I frustrate myself with my own indecision.

"Have a muffin – it's chocolate," says Max trying to sound upbeat.

Okay, I can eat. I'll call it comfort eating, but I'll have to get fruit too, my FitWatch app has been flashing at me recently for not eating what it considers a balanced diet. It also doesn't like my lack of jogging. I love my walks down the river, but rather than visiting the gym (which I have never seen the point of), I have satisfied the app by jogging a few times a week instead of walking; however, I haven't done this in weeks. I've just been too distracted and was hoping the amount of walking I have been doing would be enough, but I'm guessing the number of stored up food vouchers I've been using hasn't balanced out.

"I think you're going to have to introduce me to your gym," says Max suddenly.

"Are you a mind reader?!"

"No, your watch is flashing red and so is mine – I saw you stare at yours…"

"Ah, okay. No, I don't go to the gym – don't look at me like that! I'm more an alfresco kinda girl. Do you like the gym? – *Of course, you do!*" I roll my eyes. I am sure everyone except me loves the gym at some point.

"Ha, yes, though I'm up for a run if you prefer. I've been meaning to look into virtual teams, I was in a local football team at college – nothing major, just for fun."

I never have really enjoyed watching virtual sports, it gives me a headache. Guys (or girls) running up and down a pitch with a virtual ball with a team doing the same thing in another Hub has always fascinated me for the technology of it, rather than the game itself. There are worse games to watch though, so if Max takes that up, so be it.

"Well, if I am to stop this darn watch flashing at me, telling me I'm getting fat and my eggs are in danger of rotting, I had better run at some point soon."

"I don't think your eggs will rot."

"But you *do think* I am fat?!"

"No!" Max has immediately gone beetroot red and is stammering, searching for a complement or a more politically correct phrase. I shouldn't tease him, but I am mildly ashamed to say I like watching him squirm.

"Ha-ha, that was too easy, calm down, I'm joking. But if the app doesn't report me to the Genetics Committee for reckless behaviour, my mother will if she spots the warning light on my watch."

"Well, I'd love to see the river that you love so much, so why don't we go for a run tomorrow?"

"Ah, slight issue – Aunt Dora has asked me to go again."

"Oh, is that going to be weekly?"

"I'm not sure, but I do need to help her if I can, I'm sorry."

"It's okay – well, I would mind less if I could come…"

"Well, I think Aunt Dora must have pre-empted that one. She says she won't be as long as last week and was wondering if you'd join us all for a picnic in the afternoon? If you prefer not to, I understand, it's just…"

"I'd love to. I am keen to meet Dora – and indeed Mrs Addams."

Hmm, well I am keen for him to meet my aunt. *That* is a meeting I've been longing for since the moment I liked him. Meeting Eve – well, that one I am less anxious *for* and more anxious *about*. Well, that is tomorrow's issue. Now I have work to go back to and have an email to send…or delete.

TWENTY-THREE

"Ah, Maia, you're back – may I borrow you?" Henry enthusiastically greets me as I walk through the door. "I know you're not supposed to start until Monday, but I wanted to show you a few things. I've been mapping out some of the theories already and have some of the team pulling up old data to re-run through. It will take a while, but if we can cross reference fertility rate with blood types – and exposure to various elements and whether any known disease or virus was present at any point – we may begin to see a different pattern if we look anew."

"It will take years for some though, as we'll have to test the same patient at regular intervals, record where they were, what they ate, when they had which vaccines, family history..."

"Oh, we have that already, so we have the foundations. We are just aiming to trial different subjects to see if they all have the same response we expect – and if they don't: what are the variables? I am hoping to see this virus of yours rear its head. I rather fancy discovering it."

"You and every other geneticist!"

"Indeed, of course."

"You said you already have the data to start examining past responses – I have asked for this a million times and was told it isn't collated in that manner or I wasn't allowed to see it—"

"My dear, you just have to knock on the right door." He means this kindly, but I can't begin to verbalise how exasperating this is. Obviously, I suspected this was the case. I have been blood tested more times than I can count and although I earlier half mocked the alerts of my FitWatch app, I am fully aware that data is collected and reviewed somewhere. Glancing over the top files that Henry is showing me, I can plainly see that many of the things I've been itching to review and investigate have long been charted.

"Why would the PTB not want to share data? How are we supposed to solve a riddle with no clues?"

"They do share, just with the select few. Minority rule cannot be managed if everyone has the same information."

I'm not sure how to take this statement. Of course, Henry is right. Society has to have levels of knowledge and clearance in order to control the masses. I get that – *mostly*. However, I am not sure Henry totally likes it either as his face is sombre –- in fact, his expression at the moment is not unlike when Mary is in the room: matter of fact, saying what needs to be said, but avoiding too much probing.

"But that is *so* limiting. So many discoveries must go unfound." *And so many minds left stunted.* I'll leave that bit out. I am very grateful to Henry for whatever breadcrumbs he'll drop me and am fearful that if I get too greedy, too soon, he'll retreat, leaving me more frustrated than ever.

"Baby steps Maia, we can't run before we walk." Well, there's a metaphor I can do without. I'm being oversensitive, I know that, but today I am tired of thinking about babies. Though, here I must laugh at myself. Am I not studying graph upon graph of data relating to people's abilities to have babies? Maybe I have chosen the wrong scientific field if I am going to be pushed over the edge by a metaphor! "I am sure you find this frustrating, but believe me, gently is the approach to take. We don't want to rock more boats than necessary as we go." Looking at Henry, I suddenly realise he isn't just talking about research, he is talking about *me* doing research.

"Do you mean *me*? – that *I* rock the boat? *How*?" I am searching his face for an answer as he isn't saying anything, he is just rocking in his chair slightly, twiddling his thumbs. "Why am I more likely to rock the boat?! Please answer me!" My eyes are filling up as I am hit by a wave of frustration, confusion, and anger – my three faithful friends who seem to follow me everywhere. "It can't *just* be because I am a female 3. Other female 3s have worked in the lab until they had children…"

"Yes, indeed they have. Sit down, Maia, please; you are very pale. I really don't know what to say…just that the PTB employ who they employ and release more detail to some than others. I told you I met with opposition to you joining my team – Dr Brown for one was keen to keep you, so it is not that you are not good my dear, just that life isn't linear; and it's best to do things slowly, so ripples are not noticed."

Henry is managing me. I'm not stupid, I can see that, but I can also see that throwing a tantrum will not help me and he is likely to be right. I am grateful he wants to help at all. I am sensible to the fact that he doesn't have to. I will try to be patient and bring no undue attention to myself…Oh crap. Kate. My brain has quickly jumped to an issue. If submitted, that application will likely cause a ripple. Well, there is nothing for it, I'll have to ask Henry his opinion about the whole egg donation idea…

"I see. Hmm." Not quite the 'yes do it' or 'no don't' I was hoping for. "Do you want to do it? You've told me the pros and cons, I understand that, but where does your heart lie?"

"If I knew that, we would be having a conversation about me having already submitted the form or not at all, as I would have deleted it."

"Yes, okay, but—"

"I'm not sure about losing my friend. It is a noble cause to give her happiness, however—"

"It would be up to you to choose *not* to lose a friend. That takes time and commitment."

"So, if it was you seeing your child raised by another, you would make your peace?" I suddenly realise that as a 3, he almost certainly does have children in other Hubs, just the same as I do. "I don't know why I struggle with the idea of a SurrogacyPod – I know there is a loving pair of arms waiting once born – but nine months in a box of tubes and synthetics reminds me more of…" I stutter, trying not to say, 'creating a monster.' I suppose I have put so much focus on the natural world and the natural abilities of life that even though amazed by the achievements of man, I am also saddened it has come to this. I want to restore natural function, not encourage the manmade.

"Have you seen the SurrogacyPods? I mean *actually* seen them and the team that cares for them? Not just on video?"

"No." I have to admit I am judging without witnessing – though whose fault is that? Again, the PTB hardly invite students round for tours, and staff in those units are so closely screened, the notion of volunteering to work there or just visiting is absolutely ridiculous…until now apparently!

"Right, come on then." Henry puts away all his work, gently, but hurriedly pushes me out the door, locks it with his code and leads me out of the lab into the maternity ward of the hospital. I am too shocked to question, but every door we go through will be reading my barcode, which is surely flagging me as being in totally the wrong area. I will be amazed if this doesn't at least result in another lecture from Dad on 'the importance of staying within one's bounds.' Though I do wonder if that buffoon Head of Security, Peter Lloyd, won't also come and detain me. Earlier in the week, I saw him marching some poor lad through the main plaza of the Hub. He had two officers following him, but neither appeared to be impressed or bothered by his charge, so I think it was more for show than need – and I would argue the show was quite pathetic, but I really don't want to be detained and considering only twenty minutes ago Henry was telling me to not make ripples with the PTB, frankly this whole exercise seems unwise.

"Okay, here we are – look, Maia."

Overwhelmed, I have just been blindly following Henry's lead and not really taking in the surroundings of each corridor. Now he has come to a stop in a corridor, I look around and follow his gaze. There, through a glass window is a large room with SurrogacyPods arranged like little petals of a sunflower. Placed in the middle of each 'flower' is a table, monitor, and chair, which is presumably where the nurse sits to observe. Medical equipment, other monitors and graphs are all around the sides of the room and nurses are gently going back and forth, checking over each pod and the data that's displayed on the SmartTablet the end of each one. In the pods, I can see foetuses of different sizes and ages, each flower containing what I assume are different age groups. All are tucked up in their amniotic fluid, snug and peaceful. If they were in distress, you would see it, either physically or on the SmartTablet. I can faintly hear music playing – they are playing it to the babies. Henry pulls my arm and directs me to another window. There is another room of SurrogacyPods, this time containing twenty pods with foetuses in later development to the previous room. One of the nurses is sat in the middle of the flower reading a book aloud. I can't hear her or see on her system what she is reading, but I can see from her movement she is animated, so she is acting out whatever story is in front of her.

"See, Maia, these babies know love before birth. Okay, it isn't their mum talking to them in the womb, but these nurses do their absolute best to ensure they are the next best thing. I do also know that if a baby has been allocated, the new parents are encouraged to come and read or sing to the baby as it grows. Max himself lived in one of these pods for two months and I am eternally grateful for them and the staff. Science has gone way beyond the intensive care of old and it saved Max – and by proxy, me too. I understand and share your worries about seeing your baby in the arms of another, but by all accounts, do not let fears of the *how* they grow stop you from saying yes – if that is what your heart chooses."

"And the PTB? I thought I was to avoid drawing attention to myself?"

"Softly, softly, we will get there, and we can always spin your application in a manner to suggest not only wanting to fulfil your friend's dreams, but further the PTB mandate – worded to please all parties." I silently open up the draught of my application and show it to Henry. As he finishes, he takes a step back, just slightly lifts the corner of his mouth to one side into a smile, nods his head and whispers: "Perfect."

TWENTY-FOUR

Eve has spent most of the morning asleep, or if awake, not knowing who I am. Aunt Dora left while she was sleeping, but before she did, told me Eve's confusion has been significant over the last couple of days. I am not sure if this means her introduction to Max later will be easier or harder, but I am not particularly looking forward to it. I am not convinced that a picnic by the river is the wisest choice either. Aunt Dora says that neutral ground is best and not wearing the bracelets is necessary so as not to spark a perilous comment from Eve; but as the river is flowing calmly at the moment, relying on water flow to drown out drone surveillance is a tad risky. At the same time, Eve can't be shut indoors 24/7. That itself is a prison sentence and although I know Eve's speech is sometimes concerning, maybe the PTB's interest in her is more imagined than either Eve or Aunt Dora realise. I can but hope.

"Hmmphh, are you ready for your picnic? Where's the food?" Rather than being startled by Eve's sudden communication, this time I am startled because she actually made sense for the first time today.

"Aunt Dora is bringing the food with her. Can I get you anything in the meantime?"

"Hmmphh." I take that as a no and I carry on sketching the fruit bowl. For some time Eve doesn't seem to have anything else to add and even the cats are so uninterested in us they go outside through their cat flap. I am trying to get the shadow effect correct on an apple when Eve asks: "So, your match is comin' to meet me and Dora? Mmmh, suppose that means he's a goodun?" She sighs quietly. "Dora has already tried reasonin' with me. Waste of time. I'm as likely to forget who you are in a minute. Darn fog follows me everywhere."

"Fog?"

"In me head – you ever walked in thick fog, Missy? Especially when it's patchy and you find a clearin' for a minute?" I nod. "Aye, well if you have, that's the nearest I can describe my thoughts." She pauses, running her tongue inside her cheeks, shaking her head as she thinks. "Pfft, and that's probably on a good day. When I am at least *aware* of the fog. Dora tells me I'm getting worse." Eve lets out a long, deep sigh. So deep, she looks deflated afterwards. "Arses will win one way or another."

"Who? – How?"

I am desperately hoping for answers, but it is too late, she has walked into the fog again.

Max arrives shortly after Aunt Dora returns home, and they greet as old friends with genuine warmth and affection. It isn't until this moment that I realise the degree of importance that I have placed on them liking each other. Conversation is set to standard chatter, but with a hint of familiarity, and I cannot help wishing that this is my nucleus family and not a collection of misfit offshoots. I am a misfit, but the wonderful thing is, with them I don't care – and even better, don't need to.

Max admires some of Aunt Dora's work, so she proudly leads him to view the picture above the mantel of me as a little girl sat under the big oak by the river.

"You'll see that tree shortly, for that is where we'll eat. It is Maia's favourite place on Earth, I believe."

"I have heard much of the peace of the river, so am keen to see it. You have captured the serenity perfectly though, Dora."

"Thank you. You might like my most recent painting of Maia – would you like to see it? It is nearly finished."

"Recent? I didn't know there was a recent one of me?!" We are ushered into her studio and there, on the easel is a large painting of me, Eve, and the cats, all asleep, but lit up by glorious sunrays from the window. "You've been busy! You only took that photo last week!"

"And the image stayed with me, so I had to paint it."

"It's beautiful, truly." Max seems genuinely taken by it.

"Hmmphh, you've made me look old again." How an old woman can creep up on you, I'll never know, but I will need some sort of incontinence underwear if Eve keeps it up. I cannot repress my mirth however as I see she has had the same effect on Max. I did warn him, but just as Aunt Dora warned me, experiencing for oneself is vastly different than purely being told.

Introductions made again, all seems okay. I express concern regarding going to the river being too much for her, but Eve insists she is fine, though does consent to a wheelchair being taken for her to sit in – by the river of course, not as a means of transport – that is *obviously* unreasonable!

Enjoying our time together, I begin to muse on the idea of this kind of meeting being a regular occurrence. Eve has been quieter for a little while – not switched off or asleep, just thoughtful – when Aunt Dora asks Max about work and then drifts onto his family. I think this risky; however I suppose in reality that is a pretty standard direction of conversation and no harm should really come from it. I am not sure if harm *has* come, but when Eve hears Max's surname and suddenly joins in, it does produce extra pause for thought:

"What did you say? *Rivers? Which Rivers?*"

"Do you know a family of Rivers? I suppose it isn't an unheard-of surname."

"Pfft, yeah, *maybe.*" Eve squints whilst looking up and down at Max. "You look like one."

"One what?"

"A Rivers."

Max grins. "I am a Rivers, so that is handy."

"Cocky one, are we? Hmmphh. Not all rivers run true."

I'm not sure which of the four of us is wider eyed. Eve falls silent again and Aunt Dora, not wanting to continue the discussion, starts remarking on the work going on across the river. Some of the apples are clearly ripe as men and women are busy harvesting. They are too far away to hear their conversation, but some of them are singing a jolly tune and the sound of their melody floats across the way to us.

"If you pluck an apple from one tree and plant it in the shade of another, which tree does it belong to?" No one answers Eve. If the others are like me, we are trying to decide if Eve has some wisdom to impart or if this is just another one of her random musings. "And if that apple grows into a tree and bears fruit, is it the fruit of the first tree – or the second that cultivates it?"

No. I don't know how to respond to that. I probably should. The nature versus nurture debate, in whatever form, always intrigues me; but before answering, I glance over to Max, smiling.

However, my smile doesn't last as he looks grave – wounded even. My capacity to respond is instantly distracted from the general philosophy of Eve's question to the notion of possibility that Eve could indeed know a story of the Rivers family.

"You can't change genes," says Max solemnly.

"Ah, but you *can*, for better or worse; they can be altered, and then the fruit might be rotten."

"Or that apple rolls away from the tree that stole it and bears fruit on its own land."

Max stares straight into Eve's eyes and she into his. Both a little pale. Both absolutely stern. Neither blinking. Eve finally breaks the stalemate as she bows her head, smirks slightly, and says: "Touché."

Aunt Dora and I tried to rescue the mood, but it took some doing. Max recovered sufficiently once we got Eve back inside – more so when she went to sleep – and she at least is seemingly undisturbed by any remembrance of conversation. We stay a while longer, long enough to make me think we have finished on a good note and as we leave Max suggests taking a walk up the river. I happily agree, but when we get there he doesn't hide his anger for long.

"How *could* you?!"

"How could I *what*?" I ask as chills race up my back and neck.

"You told them about my mum, didn't you?!"

"No! – No, I did not!" It hadn't occurred to me Max is looking stern and pale because he is harbouring anger towards *me*. I was too wrapped up in the mystery of Eve's comments. "I told you Eve says odd things."

"Yes, very odd…so it is just coincidence that I tell you the secret of my family one minute and the next that old lady is coming up with metaphors of stolen fruit and rotten apples?!"

"I admit, the timing is strange, but I swear, I didn't say anything…but even if I had, you didn't actually tell me anything particularly condemning, plenty of people are brought up away from their birth parents, so—"

"I told you that in confidence. Actual secret or not, it is not something we talk about – or want talked about. I don't want to hear Mum's squawks about privacy or being ungrateful to her again." Max is welling up. My heart aches for him; I know those feelings. Feelings of despair and anger at your own family for how they have brought you up and how they have made you feel.

"You're not rotten, Max. You never were, nor will be. And I promise, I said nothing to Eve or Dora – or anyone else."

Max gazes longingly across the water for a few minutes without moving. Finally, he turns, hugs me, and whispers, "I know." He steps back, barely looking at me. "I'm going to go. See you tomorrow."

With that he walks away, leaving me to watch him disappear. I don't reply. I don't know how, and if I did, I doubt it will make a difference. I just stand, staring across the water. Hours later and I am still staring across the water, watching the ripples in the moonlight. Feeling as lost as ever, just when I had begun to feel found.

TWENTY-FIVE

I wandered home in the small hours. The last time I did that was when Theo left. He had dropped his horrid speech about going our separate ways and had walked off much the same as Max did – just minus the hug and 'see you tomorrow.' There was no 'tomorrow' then. He kept away from me and soon left the Hub entirely. I have told myself it isn't the same and not to panic, but the feeling of déjà vu, seeing the similarities of their silhouettes disappear from the river and leaving me alone watching the water is a hard feeling to shake.

I haven't slept much and have spent too long staring at myself in the mirror again. I don't know what answers I think my reflection will give me?

My stomach has rumbled numerous times. It is a welcome distraction from self-pity so I go downstairs in search of sustenance. It is late morning and with any luck Mum will have gone out to see friends.

"Ah! Finally!" Nope, my luck has ebbed out this morning. "I've been waiting for you, Madam, it's time we had a mother-daughter chat." Oh, dear Lord, please no, why start now? "Don't roll your eyes at me. I was hoping not to as well, but your father and I agree it is time I did so you realise the importance of your duty."

"I'm pretty sure I have had that drummed into me already, so it's okay, I get it. You got your way, I'm marrying." I internally add 'I hope,' but really, even if we hated each other, that wouldn't be enough to stop the match now.

"You're missing the point. Of course, you are getting married, that was never in question – just when, *not if* – so you can quit looking smug. I am not talking about *that* duty. I'm talking about your duty to donate."

Okay, not only am I annoyed, but I am also confused. "I haven't refused that either…"

"No, but stopping out half the night with a boy, *even if* he is the one you are to marry, is not acceptable. You are booked for a donation and although I am pleased you like him, *those* activities are *not* to be enjoyed until *after* you are married." Mum is staring through me. She says she is pleased I like Max, but her stare makes that seem improbable. She is pleased I am matched and for the family connection, but I don't believe for a second she gives a monkey's beyond that. And to assume that me being out late means anything? – well, I am not sure I can be bothered to defend myself!

"It's nice to know you have that opinion of me."

"Pfft. I've a good mind to have a word with his parents, they should share our desire for you to seamlessly fulfil your donation duties before you wed."

"Please do, I'd love to be there when you have *that* conversation."

"Why, you *selfish*, headstrong girl! Do you take nothing seriously?! You'd think with your family and work – and future prospects! – you'd be more grateful…and *respectful*! Gee-Gee was right to point out the time you came home. We all share a concern in the shame you could bring!"

"*Gee-Gee*?!" Now, that does hurt. So long has she kept out of such conversations, it wouldn't have occurred to me that she would have any part in this current exchange.

"Yes, we *all* share the same desire to see you stop flittering about! Maybe we should set a curfew?"

"I am TWENTY-FOUR! I am NOT abiding by a curfew."

"Really? We'll see about that when I speak to your father."

"DO."

"And you can stop narrowing your eyes. I hope I have made my point. Pregnancies outside marriage – particularly before donations – are *not* to be. Do you hear?! The only gossip I want to be centre of is of envious housewives, wishing they had our luck and fertility. Not because my daughter is a dirty stop out."

"Are you done?"

"For now, yes. But do you have no apology?"

"What *for*?!"

"What for? *What for*?!"

"Yes, what for? For being born? For being fertile? For repeatably donating when told to? For trying to make a difference beyond my fertility? For not being a fake doll like you, perhaps? For not having sex? – because I haven't – or is it just me *breathing* that upsets you?!"

I don't wait for a response, although there is one; let her spit feathers in her own time. I walk out of the house and keep walking. I'm fuming, frustrated, and feel beaten. Normally I'd go to the river, but I've been there enough for one weekend and am unlikely to find solace. Kate is still waiting to hear about my application, but honestly, I haven't the energy to talk about it now, so am not going to see her. It'll really annoy Mum if she finds out I have applied to donate my egg to Kate. *Good*. Well, if I needed a reason to push me over the edge for a decision, here is it. Not a noble one; I wish it were. In truth, I had already decided, just not had the courage to actually press send. Indecision over, I press send now.

Thanks Mum.

I go to work. Yes, on a Sunday. There should be fewer people in, so even more opportunity to work on my projects – and avoid discussion about anything other than work. This plan works for an hour or so; the lab is empty, and I potter between two adjoining labs happily. I am pouring over data on my computer, blocking out any thought as best I can, when suddenly a door in the adjoining room opens.

The sound of nearby movement is subtle, but it is enough to stop me in my tracks. I can't see who it is as the connecting door is almost closed, so I decide not to speak, hoping whoever it is will soon be on his or her way and leave me in peace. This plan is soon thwarted however as the door slides again, facilitating a second, much louder person.

"Don't you walk away from me, Henry! Are you telling me you knew already?! Are you out of your mind?! First, I hear you are employing her here, then you take her for a tour of the maternity ward, and *now* I receive a call saying she wants to donate an egg – *our grandchild!* – to her infertile friend! *What are you playing at*?!"

"I'm not 'playing' at anything. I'm actually trying to work."

"Don't give me that crap! Answer me! I demand it! Don't forget how you have all this new space and clearance! I'd *hate* for you to be demoted."

"Don't threaten me, Mary. It won't wash anymore. I have proven myself beyond your arms, thank the Lord, and I told you when I agreed to come here things would be different. What I do is for Max and his happiness – and *mine*. Stop meddling where you're not wanted."

She must have hit him, as the speech is followed by a thud, then silence. I am beginning to wonder if they have left, but I can just about hear what I can only describe as frustrated, heated moans – angry ones – no, *seething*.

"You think Max's happiness is going to be achieved by seeing our grandchild with that barren girl?" Mary is gritting her teeth, but trying to change her tone, presumably trying a different line of attack to her previous, literal attack.

"Max *chose* to sign that application. Maia didn't ask. You know children are only classed as grandchildren if raised with paternal or adoptive parents, not donor. Even so, yes, *my* genetic grandchild will be with Maia's friend. I gave Maia my blessing, not that she needed it. She cares deeply for another. Maybe you might want to remember what that was like? *Caring* for more than self-interest."

"Hmm…and look where that got us."

"Indeed. Hindsight is a beautiful thing." Henry's tone is dry, much drier than I've heard from him before, either with or without Mary being present. "And as for you mocking her friend for being barren, do you forget you, yourself, are barren likewise? Surely your pretence of playing mum hasn't *actually* fooled you?"

No answer. The seething release of air that I can only imagine is coming from Mary has intensified though and it continues for some time until she finally speaks again.

"If you want Max's happiness so badly, why are you risking it by letting Maia in all areas? Hmm?! Tell me that!" Mary is again gritting her teeth and apparently refusing to answer or even acknowledge what was previously said to her. "You say he likes her and she him – then why jeopardise or muddle their future with visiting maternity wards needlessly or donating eggs? Helping others is all well and good, but sometimes it pays to think of oneself first."

"Oh, relax. I only took her to see the SurrogacyPods to show how much love goes into them. Are you not curious for discoveries of science? There is so much to learn and discover. Maia has a curious mind; you can't simply stick her in a nursery and say '*breed.*' You of all people should understand the absolute set rule isn't for everyone."

"I preferred it when you were just focused on the science. Surely, you see the importance of those eggs? She wouldn't be delayed in marriage if she wasn't—"

"More fertile than the average sow – yes, I know. She is remarkable, even better than her sister's more recent results, which were way above average. Look, be patient. One egg won't alter the course of things and showing leniency to some of the general population on occasion is good – it isn't going to cause all out rebellion and besides, most people don't even know anyone willing to consider specific donation. Plus, it helps prove Maia is on board with PTB rule of donation and she is trying to help the future betterment of society."

"Pfft. I hope you buy your own tale. Whether you have a point or not, you are treading dangerously. You think you have made your own way up the ladder? Well, I suggest you make sure you are right about this or you may find a few rungs kicked out from beneath you. Then you'll be glad to look to me for help again."

"Mary, if I tumble down, so do you."

Henry abruptly pushes his chair back, scraping it on the floor noisily, before speedily passing the door to the lab where I have been hiding to reach the door he came in through. I don't see Mary, but she sounds like she follows him out, though I suspect they go in different directions down the corridor once they are able to.

My head is spinning, heart heavy and my eyes are filled with tears. I must have been holding my breath on and off, so now, once able to breath undetected, I gasp out loud, as though I have been underwater. Where do I begin with that conversation? How do you unpick so much information?!

'A curious mind'? That is what Henry said I have. Well, right now, I wish I had anything but. I run my hands up my face and fingers through my hair, pulling it as I go, compromising my bun. The band holding it up breaks free and my hair falls into a mass around my shoulders. I pull my hair forward over my face, slump onto the desk, and sob silently.

TWENTY-SIX

Meaningful work has now gone out the window for the day as my mind will not settle on anything. I decide not to stay at the lab for fear of Henry returning. I am worried he saw me as he passed the door to leave, and if he did, I am not ready for that conversation yet. I also don't want to talk to anyone else. Running might help and will have the added bonus of stopping my FitWatch app from flashing at me – but I don't want to go to the river – so, to the gym it is.

I can't really remember the last time I came here, though it looks exactly as I remember it – which is like every other building – minimalist, but clean and tidy. A ridiculously muscled woman in her thirties is on reception. She clearly loves making use of the gym and her enthusiastic greeting is probably energising for normal gym goers, but I just feel tired listening to her overly chipper greeting.

"Welcome! Ah, Maia Woods! Lovely to see you back, it has been so long! Fantastic to see you! How can I assist you today?"

I wonder what it would be like to walk through a door, and it not announce who you are? Just once, I'd like to walk into a room (that isn't the bathroom), that doesn't either verbally announce me or flash up my information on some sort of screen.

"Thank you. I'd like to use a treadmill."

"Wonderful – would you like a group session or private room?"

"Private, please." The thought of running alongside other people while they experience their virtual chi with headsets on does not appeal; nor does sharing someone's chosen scenery. Today I wish to choose something, however minor, all by myself.

"Lovely. And what scenery would you like? – I see rivers are a firm favourite from your historical data."

"Woods please." I'm steering clear of rivers. "Or maybe I should have a bike? Cycling in the woods sounds nice."

"I'll set you up in a room with both, you can choose then."

"Thank you."

"Woods for Ms Woods, how lovely – he-he – come with me please!" As she giggles to herself, she shows me into one of the private rooms which all stem off a long corridor. If there weren't numbers on the door, you'd never know which was which. "Do you have clothes to change into?"

"No, these will do."

"Oh, no! Certainly not, I'll get you replacements." I don't have time to challenge her because she trots off and back again so quickly. "Here, I'll charge them to your account – enjoy!"

I suppose one helpful use of shared data is when others clothe and shoe you, they get the right size. I step onto the treadmill, starting with a slow walk and with my first step, the walls flash up with images of woodland. It is beautiful. I don't know how they do it, but I am sure the air suddenly smells differently too – earthy, but clean and fresh. I suppose if I came here enough I would know these woods as well as I know the actual river because they use drone footage on repeat – and I don't think they update it as often as some people would like.

On repeat or not, I do find jogging and cycling through these virtual woods calming. So much so, I don't really want to leave. I've nowhere to go anyway. I glance at my watch and realise I have notifications – one being from Max, asking where I am. We hadn't arranged anything specific for today and I really wasn't sure if last night's 'I'll see you tomorrow' actually meant tomorrow. Right now, I'm not sure I want to see him, but not wanting to lie, I reply with my location. He doesn't reply, but to my surprise, ten minutes later, a knock on the door produces Max.

"That was quick!?"

"I was already nearby."

"Apparently so."

"I was walking around, hoping you'd message to meet here – in the Centre I mean."

"I wasn't sure if you needed space, so thought I'd leave you." …*and I have had a stressful day that I don't want to talk about.* Hmm, best keep that to myself.

"It's beautiful in here. Really peaceful. Can I join you?"

"You already have, but sure," I say shrugging.

Neither of us talk, he cycles, I jog. It is nice until I get tired, and realise I am running on empty thanks to Mum cornering me in the kitchen this morning.

"I need to eat; I'll go shower and meet you outside if you like?"

"Sure, but hang on…" Max steps off the bike and in a couple of strides is in front of me, smiling, though a little shyer than normal – if you can know what *normal* is after such a short acquaintance? Either way, it is normal to me and it warms my soul to see his smile. He takes my hands, sweaty as they are, and swings them slightly. "I'm sorry for leaving last night and for doubting you – I know you didn't tell them about Mum; family matters rattle me more than I care to admit. I'm sorry."

"I understand. I shouldn't have taken you there, Eve is a lot to take."

"No, no, I want to know your family and not be so sensitive about mine."

"Hmm, if you learn how to not be sensitive, you better let me know." I quickly kiss him and go to retreat to the showers. I really need one and am definitely glad I didn't run in the clothes I arrived in.

Max grabs my hand, stopping me from leaving and then grabs my jawline with the other hand. "Hey, that's not a proper kiss!" I laugh – well, more of a girly giggle in truth, but it is cut short, and I don't mind.

I wish the rest of the day was as light as that moment; I really am trying to push everything else aside, but my mind is a whirlwind. I don't know whether to tell Max about any or all of the day's events. Bizarrely I think the conversation I had with my mother is easier to relay than the one I heard with his parents. So, when Max asks if I'm okay, I decide to start from the top of the day and see how things take me.

"Well, I can't say I am not glad to not have been there for that one!" Max is heartily laughing. "But, if she does speak to my parents, I really would like to be a fly on the wall and see how that goes!"

"I'm glad you're not taking it seriously."

"You are?"

"No, of course not. I'm frustrated though – and disappointed to learn Gee-Gee agreed with them."

"Did she, though? Did she say that or did your mum use her name as weight for her own daft ideas? I'd wager your dad doesn't know either!"

I'd honestly not considered this as a possibility. I don't want to rely on it as truth though; it is better to be prepared for consistent betrayal and undermining than set myself up for a second fall, hoping my family is less cruel or underhanded than originally feared.

Eating helps to a degree, but my head is banging, so I leave for home early. I'm relieved to leave on a good note with Max and it was helpful to at least partially laugh at my mother. Thankfully, she is visiting the neighbours and not lying-in wait for me when I get home. Grandma is, but without Mum to spur her on her rebuke is annoying, but less provoking. As I turn to leave, she tells me Mum is still angry and I just about contain a '*GOOD.*' Instead, I smile and make a hasty exit in the direction of my bedroom before she says anymore – which looking at her face, she planned to. Gee-Gee however catches me as I am about to scale the stairs.

"Ah, good you're home."

"Yes, before dark *and* undefiled."

"Pardon?! What have I done to deserve *that* tone?" If Gee-Gee is acting confused and offended, she is doing a good job. I feel bad, I've never spoken to her like that, yet I am still angry. It's possible I should be angry at Mum alone, but I expect to be let down by her; I had hoped to be able to rely on Gee-Gee – if not to support me against Mum, to at least not goad her.

"According to Mum, the family thinks I am a dirty stop out and likely to get pregnant before I should, which is ironic, as all Mum has ever wanted is for me to *get* pregnant – but apparently only on a given timetable." Gee-Gee doesn't answer straight away, so I carry on. I am finally venting and it feels good. "And, *apparently*, you are included in this theory and told Mum I need to remember my duty! Which is, frankly, confusing. I have never *not* done my duty and *you* yourself told me to find happiness and build a life outside this family. When I follow that advice – or at least *try* to – I am still told off! So, tell me, *what is the point?!*"

"Your mother has twisted what I said, I'm sorry—" Gee-Gee whispers, pointing to her apartment. "Maia, come and sit down—"

"No! I won't. I'm done listening to this family! I am a disappointment. *Fine.* I'll just have to own it and be a disappointment!"

Gee-Gee extends her arm to me and I think I can see a tear in her eye – though it is hard to tell, as I am holding back tears of my own. Mum probably did twist what she said, but she knows Mum as well as I do, so she should know better than to say anything of the sort to her. Frustration and anger are building up and finally bubbling out. I can't talk anymore, and I certainly don't want to listen to anymore lectures, riddles, or half stories. Tell me everything plainly or nothing at all.

I dart upstairs and lock the door.

TWENTY-SEVEN

As my alarm sounds, my name is called softly. It is confusing as I come round from my slumber, so it takes me a moment to identify the voice.

"Gee-Gee?" I sit up, focusing on Gee-Gee as she speaks to me. She is sat at the foot of my bed. "What the hell? I locked the door! How are you in here?"

"I unlocked it, never mind that, I need to speak to you before—"

"What do you mean 'never mind that'? No, I won't, you can unlock my door?! – What am I saying, *of course you can*, I daresay Mum can too?" I roll my eyes; I can see in her expression it is true. I knew Mum came in, but I thought it wasn't possible when I was inside or had personally locked the door. Apparently, I am wrong. Again.

"Maia, you must know I never meant your mother to accuse you—"

"Yet she did. I *had* hoped you would be my advocate, not the instigator of Mum's attacks."

"And so I am. You know that. I chose my words poorly with her, I am sorry. Your mum was excitedly speaking of a forthcoming pregnancy and I merely wanted *her* to remember the importance of waiting—"

"So, you *did* tell Mum you thought I had forgotten my duty of donation!"

"Will you let me finish a sentence?! I understand your frustration and I deeply regret my part in adding to it." Gee-Gee turns to the door as we both hear movement from outside; someone else is waking up. "Please hug me and don't lose faith in me."

It is hard to deny her affection, even if I am still hurt. I give her a hug, though probably briefer than either would really have liked.

"You'll be married soon enough and can find a more independent way."

"That day can't come quick enough." It really can't. Then at least I can get up and have breakfast without fear of an altercation with Mum or any other family member who wishes to direct or mock me. "Why must it be in December? Surely, I could marry after the donation in October? If I take a month or so more to fall into cycle and get pregnant, what does that matter?" Gee-Gee doesn't answer. "I know, it isn't *the way*, Mary said she tried it – *without* Max or I knowing in advance I might add. I wasn't sure I was pleased at the time, but now I wish her meddling had succeeded."

"Mary's meddling is *never* something you want to see succeed. Remember that, Maia." With that Gee-Gee gets up, turns to me when she gets to the door, nods her head with a sorrowful smile, and leaves.

Questions without answers. Riddles with no clues. Sorrow without clear reason. Sorrow *with* reason – but no one wants to hear. The loop of my life continues. But does it? Today I start a new job properly. Surely it is mine to grasp and expand? The conversation I overheard between Henry and Mary troubles me. Maybe I will have to find a way of parking that in the corner of my mind. *My curious mind.* Dammit! I annoy myself almost as much as others frustrate me. I get up, get dressed, and head to work.

I walk into the lab, the same room that Henry and Mary fought in yesterday. The lab I was hiding in has people working in it, but the door is closed. I wish I had closed the door! Ignorance might have been bliss.

"Ah, excellent, Maia, I think we need to chat." Henry seems to have been sitting in wait for me. He gestures for me to sit down opposite him. I don't really have a choice, so I sit as directed and wait. "Okay. Mm-hmm, yes…how to begin?" I'm not helping you, so you can work that out yourself. "I think you might have been here yesterday?" Henry is looking straight at me, sucking in his bottom lip, clearly hoping I am going to speak. I'm not. I just nod, return his gaze, wide-eyed, feeling oddly defiant. "Yes, yes, and heard – well, heard an unfortunate conversation. You must think very little of me, I wish to rectify that, I didn't mean what you heard—"

"Oh, so I'm *not* more fertile than the average pig?"

"Crap." He closes his eyes and breathes in deeply. "Maia, I am so sorry, that was poorly phrased."

"No, I enjoyed it. I'd always thought of myself as a cow or maybe a sheep. A pig is a real upgrade in farmed animals."

"Oh, I'm mortified." Henry half hides his face with his hands for added effect. "You probably don't believe me, but I had to say something to Mary to manage her reaction – she is not a straightforward person and I've had to learn how to play her game so to speak. She is rather unhappy about your request to donate an egg—"

"Will my application be denied because of her?"

"No, not necessarily. She isn't on the Genetics Committee so has no vote, *but* can make her thoughts known." He pauses, twisting his lips as he presumably thinks of what he wants to say. "I had to think on my feet – I always do with Mary. Challenging her is not for the faint hearted. I said to you it had to be '*softly, softly.*' I wasn't joking."

"I thought you meant with the PTB!"

"I do, but she is a part of them and she is just as difficult as any you'll meet – the sweet girl I loved at school is only a fragment of her personality and—"

"You loved her at school? So you were together *before* you married?!" Henry flashes his eyes at me, his cheeks colouring red, like he had just been caught in a forbidden act.

"Yes, but that is not my point now. The past is gone; we must look forward and step carefully. I am genuinely sorry you heard our heated exchange, but in some ways, I am happy you heard another side to her." – And of *you*, don't forget! Or I am supposed to trust you completely regardless? – "I told you before *(and meant it)*, I think you have a place and a right to be in my team. But nothing here is linear for one in our circumstances. I have to *say* and *do* some things that appear less than straight…to *curve* certain events or decisions to land where *we* want them."

"Follow the rule while bending a little."

"Precisely."

I'm being managed *again*. I can feel it. I am not sure he doesn't actually believe what he is saying though. But I also don't know if what Henry is saying is absolutely true. Part of his speech to her could be taken as him being controlled by her – but not all, and that actually confuses me more. To me, it sounded like Mary was trying to repress a change in Henry, not the other way around. Regardless, I am seriously beginning to doubt if I will ever be 'just me' and allowed to have a thought or opinion that isn't subject to someone else's whim or management. He says *'softly-softly.'* What I hear is *'slowly-slowly.'* I don't need fame and glory. I am happy going under the radar, but I do want to someway, somehow feel valued and valuable – beyond my 'skills' in fertility. I am tired, so tired of feeling muted and muzzled. If this is what life in this lab is going to be, along with everywhere else, maybe I should just quit. I'll get a cat like Eve and Aunt Dora and chatter to it – or maybe a dog. We can run by the river or through the park or orchards together. That would be nice. I daydream of easier things. Maybe I should go simple? But if I did that, working so hard would have been for nothing and I still strive for answers. Answers I'll never find running through the park.

I am preparing to ask more questions such as: Why was my sister tested recently? Why did the maternity ward visit upset Mary? And what *exactly* does Mary hold over Henry? I think he is also considering saying more as his mouth is half open, formulating a word, when he is interrupted by the door to the adjoining lab opening. As I look up so see the figure stepping into the room, my heart stops.

TWENTY-EIGHT

"Maia?!"

I'd recognise that voice and those eyes anywhere. They comforted me for years, but have tortured me for the last six. I am beginning to doubt if I am here or actually still at home in bed dreaming up a perfectly good way to have a horrid morning. I have imagined this moment a thousand times and thought of very possible reaction I'd have and what I would say. Whether I'd grab him, hug him, slap him, kiss him. Run to or from. Cry or laugh. It turns out, I go with: stare in disbelief.

Henry, happily oblivious to my inner turmoil, has seen this as a brilliant way of breaking off from a painful and difficult conversation and jumps into host mode in a blink of an eye.

"Ah! Wonderful, Theo, do you know Maia already? She's starting in the lab with me today. Maia, Theo is one of my brilliant apprentices who I managed to steal as part of my relocation deal! He and his wife have proven invaluable, so I just had to bring them – and of course, Theo's parents are in this Hub, so I got extra points for reuniting them – though maybe less with Ella's parents! Well, best not dwell on that! Anyway, how is the research? What news?"

I feel sick. Theo, who has been coldly staring at me, now blanks me, half turning his back to show Henry what he is working on. I can just about see from the angle – he has been going through some data regarding radiation effects, looking for a possible connection between naturally raised and surrogate born children. The two of them chat away. I hear the words, but my heart is racing and I feel like my blood is fighting against circulation. What blood is running, is running cold. Why today? Why, when I am already feeling so low, does he have to show up *now*? And married, no less. I suppose that thought has occurred to me before, but I had hoped to never see it. I had hoped if he came back, it was because he loved me still and had waited, like I had been for him. I thought I had delayed marriage as I don't want to be a mother and so I could work? True, but had an option been: marry him and have babies; would the honest answer still have been me wanting to delay marriage for six years?

Hypothetical and pointless questions. We physically cannot have children together. He left *me*. His love was not lasting *or* eternal. He was not worth waiting for and even now, he can't even crack a smile or give a glance of some past affection. I am a distraction and nuisance to his work. Why am I here? Will I ever be taken seriously? Enough! I am with Max now. He is better than all this and I can't be dragged further into self-pity and grief. This part of my past is dead to me. Theo killed that part, and I cannot resurrect it.

They have finished their briefing and by now I feel anger more than anything. Cold anger though, not the heated passion I might once have felt. Disdain for myself at once having put so much care into his whereabouts and regrets for the bitter person which that care has potentially led me to be.

Henry is obviously taken with ideas of what they have been discussing – which is annoying as I probably would be too if I had followed it all, not just the parts I captured in between my own thoughts. He directs Theo, who then returns into the lab he came from, nodding to me as he leaves. I minimally return the nod, but say nothing. Henry has seemingly forgotten what we were talking about previously as he starts quizzing me on other research, and this is how our morning looks set to continue and I must do my best to focus on the task in hand. If I am to work here, inner turmoil or not, I will not let him ruin it for me. Ugh.

Just as I am thinking to disappear for lunch, a female head pops around the door from the corridor.

"Is Theo here, Dr Rivers?"

"Yes, in the other lab," says Henry cheerfully.

"Great, thanks, I've just come for lunch if that's okay?"

"Of course, we're going soon, too."

The woman steps into the room, smiling. She has beautiful red hair twisted up into a decorative bun – not like my plain and boring one, one that actually requires care and attention. Her skin, though slightly pale, is youthful and as you'd expect, her face is pretty and her smile warming. Theo must have been expecting her as he enters the room, looking stern as before, but smiles to her as she greets him.

"Maia, this is Ella, Theo's wife, who I stole from the Midlands Hub," declares Henry. "If you need IT support while in this lab, she's the one to call." Oh, for goodness sake, let's rub salt in my wounds and complete my day, shall we?!

"Lovely to meet you, Ella. I hope you are settling in okay?" Mum's years of training me in civility when wanting to scream is finally proving handy.

"Yes, I think so, thank you! Are you new too?"

"To this lab, yes, but I've been with Dr Brown for the last six years – just next door."

"Ah, right! So, Dr Rivers has stolen you from inhouse, not another Hub like us!" Her tone is warm and friendly. If circumstances were different, I can see me wanting to make friends with Ella. She has a calm, genuine aura about her. Shame I'll have to hate her anyway.

"Ha-ha, yes, I have an eye for talent and am not afraid to claim it!" Henry laughs at his own joke; everyone else politely chuckles.

"Maia was always a very keen scientist, even at school." Theo speech is still cold and matter of fact – and certainly not inviting conversation from me, just making a statement to his wife, who counters his inanimate expression with an enthusiastic one of her own:

"You know each other?! Lovely, I've not met Theo's old friends yet; we've been settling in and not had chance! Do you want to catch up?"

"We were just lab partners at school." Cold and matter of fact. Theo flushes with what I think is a little pain in his face, but doesn't reply. Good. I've nothing more to add for *you*. Ella looks a little sad, but true to all good optimists, she lightly shrugs her shoulders and says:

"Ah, well, we can be friends now!"

"Mm-hmm." I smile, I'm cold, but not so cold as to rain on her parade. Thankfully, this is enough to satisfy her. I can't do anymore; so rather than stand about waiting for conversation to finish (Ella is asking Theo something about their home), I decide to make a dash for lunch and whisper to Henry that I'll be back in an hour.

"Did Max ask you about dinner?" I had thought we were keeping our home/work relationships separate, but apparently, he has forgotten this on day one – which is particularly unhelpful when I am trying to dart out the blooming door and he spoke loudly enough to catch everyone's attention.

"No?"

"Ah, well, Mary did only say this morning...Sunday evening, family roast?" Theo looks quizzically at us both. Henry notices, I ignore him. "Maia is my daughter-in-law or soon will be! An added bonus to the move...though *not* why she works here, of course! She has many ideas—"

"I don't doubt it, Maia was always brilliant." A coldly delivered compliment, but a compliment nonetheless I suppose.

"Quite, a real asset, to work *and* family!"

Blushing, I wave at Ella, remembering my manners briefly and dart out the door before anyone else speaks to me, making sure I disappear down the hall before anyone else can catch me. I want to think unhindered, but don't have time to process anything as Max is waiting in the foyer. So, repression it is then.

I greet him as normally as I can. I must be doing okay as he starts waffling on about his morning before we have even walked out the building. Someone has irritated him with their stagnant views – *ha! welcome to my world* – but I let him chatter because it is easy listening and I welcome the distraction.

"Maia?! Ah, lovely, lovely! Max *and* Maia!" I turn to see Claire, our match coordinator, trotting up to us in ridiculously high heels that honestly look like they might break at any moment. "Perfect timing! I am so pleased to have found you both together – and so easily!"

"Did you message or call me? Sorry, I haven't received anything—" I start to check my watch in case I have missed something.

"No, no, no indeed! I have literally just stepped out of a meeting with the Genetics Committee! It is as though an angel swooped in and brought you here, saving me a call! Anyway, lovely news, *so* lovely! Max, your Mum will be *so* pleased, as I did tell her – indeed, I thought it quite impossible, so didn't even ask – but just this morning, I received an urgent call in – which was okay, I only had a dress fitting to attend and really that isn't essential I see that and can go now instead, so really it is lovely timing! Anyhoo! Your wedding date has been brought forward to 30th October! Isn't that just *wonderful* news?!"

I am honestly not sure where I thought her speech was going. I began to fear what she could consider *so* lovely and I think I held my breath towards the end of her speech. Max has hold of my hand and I am not sure who squeezed who the most – or in fact, who is still squeezing the most. I turn to him, he is smiling – no, beaming at me. All the morning's stress melts away and I beam back. I can feel my smile literally spreading across my face. The sooner we marry, the better. No more limbo or waiting on a knife edge. A new start and it has to be better than the mix up I have now – *it has to be.*

Claire is waiting for a response, but also seems to be basking in our smiles.

"Oh, I am pleased. You make a wonderful couple. Oh! Imagine the babies! You'll be a bit sore with cramps from donation for a couple days, but you should be okay after ten days to marry. That was the only available date you see, but now it's yours! Right, I will ensure all is planned and let you know when and where I need you! Must be off! Lovely, lovely!" I would say with that she walks away, but Claire is almost skipping, despite the shoes. A woman happy in her work. As I watch her go, still holding Max's hand, still absorbing the news, I see Gee-Gee walk out of lab foyer. In an instant, the penny drops; this timing is no coincidence. I let go of Max, asking him to give me a minute and walk straight up to Gee-Gee, who stops walking when she sees me approach.

"It was you, wasn't it?"

"Yes." No messing around, no pretending to not know what 'it' is. I can feel my face scrunching up, repressing tears, but a single drop escapes and tumbles down my left cheek, which is soon followed by a couple more. I hug her and she hugs me, full bodied and unembarrassed.

"Thank you," I whisper. She doesn't answer, but squeezes me a little harder and I, too overwhelmed, can say no more.

TWENTY-NINE

I am beginning to realise how many pies Henry has fingers in and although I am still not happy about him trying to manage me, in all honesty, who isn't? My thoughts are a whirlwind in my head, but I must find the key to calming my mind – as well as manage and utilise others as much as they do me. Henry is so excited to share his research, both past and present, it is difficult to know where to begin. After introducing me to more of my new co-workers, he brought me the data that Theo has been looking at (thankfully minus Theo, who seems to have disappeared into another lab again – which I can only assume is where he has been the last few weeks and where, if I am to keep my composure, I have to hope he will stay). The research on radiation effects on babies according to location and means of foetal development is interesting to say the least. The detail of samples is far beyond what I thought I'd ever see. I am still baffled as to how the PTB have such extensive information yet insist on being *so* secretive. How do they expect answers with only part of the known equation? I know I need to put that to one side, but the thought keeps rising in my mind, no matter how often I try to repress it.

"I can't stop going over the same point and keep thinking that this is only part of the tale. It can't *just* be radiation – not when the Hubs are located to minimise exposure and we don't travel through the worst zones. The genetic alteration is continuing, when by now, if just radiation, the fertile population – in theory at least – should have a better success rate of maintaining fertility; yet we *still* hit menopause early, miscarry more than go to full-term, and produce infertile offspring an average of three times out of every four babies born."

"Precisely," says Henry. "So, we need to pinpoint the switch that you describe – and flick it away from degeneration! Whether it be a virus as you suspect, something else *is* controlling our ability to breed and maintain fertility. And whatever it is, it is global and unbiased to Hub, bloodline, or ethnic background. Though, having said that, it does seem some bloodlines have some notable resistance, despite the same environmental factors—"

"Really? Where is the data for this? I haven't seen anything to suggest bloodlines are resistant at all." I start scrolling through the screens for something I have missed.

"Oh, it's not here, it is something Dr Oldman and I were looking at."

"Dr Oldman?!" A cold chill shoots down my spine. Mere mention of him upsets me and I don't need reminding of my forthcoming donation.

"Yes, indeed, he and I have spent many an hour on video calls – though sadly not so much since I arrived, we have both been so busy, but I do plan on catching up with him." I would love to listen in on those calls for scientific reasons, but I doubt that man will ever be anyone I admire or look forward to talking to. "He has observed through his embryo analysis some that are much more resistant to challenges."

My initial reaction is of fascination, but disgust soon creeps in as I realise there is a high chance my eggs are used in his research. As a scientist, it might be reasonably assumed that I would support such research; however, I cannot say I do entirely. I have often mused on the fall of humankind and wondered if our eternal decision to interfere hasn't led to our own demise. Our meddlesome tendencies have historically resulted in destruction of something, and we then have to meddle some more to counter our original alteration.

This cycle can be seen in almost every aspect of human existence, from land management and food production, to the materials we make, use and discard; the laws of our society – and in days gone by, to the differing cultures around us – causing land 'ownership' to be questioned, trades to be threatened or seized, wars started, and countless lives lost as people vie for more power. When will we learn where the line of success is opposed to the line of excess?

I am keen for knowledge and understanding, but not to the point we lose our moral compass. Everything in nature has order and when in harmony, the balance, though not always smooth or so-called 'fair,' is right. I wish to understand the balance and the factors causing it to fail – and hopefully restore it. Something tells me Dr Oldman does not care for my definition of 'going too far' in the name of scientific knowledge or control.

"Maia?"

"Mm-hmm?"

"I thought I'd lost you there, you were so deep in thought!" chuckles Henry.

"Sorry, I have a bad habit of that. Can I ask you something and you'll answer honestly?"

"If I can, yes, of course." That is hardly the straight 'yes' I was hoping for.

"What exactly do they do with my eggs once harvested? I had assumed they grow all of them for adoptive babies. Am I wrong?"

Henry doesn't answer straight away, but fidgets, then cups his chin with his hand, pointing his head upwards. I am not sure if there is a benefit to his pose, but I begin to think he is waiting to be beamed up – or at least hoping for it. Finally, he looks back to me: "Ah, okay. I don't exactly know."

"But you do – but can't say."

"No, not...erm...I don't know *exactly*—"

"But you said you have seen my results—"

"When?"

"At my parents' meal, when we first met, when you said Mary had doubted me because of my age, but you were impressed by—"

"Ah! Yes, that is true. I have seen your fertility results—"

"That is what Dr Oldman showed you, isn't it?!"

"Amongst other things, yes...but hang on Maia, that doesn't mean I have seen what has happened to all your eggs. You have been harvested several times—"

"And don't I know it!" Oops, I should probably try to calm down before I reply as I can see I'll say something self-incriminating in a minute.

"I really am not at liberty to say more. In fact I don't *know* much more; we all have our sectors of knowledge and—"

The door slides open, bringing in three scientists, all hoping to check on their experiments and discuss with us. Yet again, Henry is saved by the door. Yet again, I swallow a sigh, that would love to be a scream, and try to focus on the task at hand.

* * *

To complete my rollercoaster of emotions today, I have agreed to meet up with Kate after work. I had meant to message her, but had honestly forgotten earlier, so when her message came through mid-afternoon, I readily agreed. The day can't get much weirder, so why not tell my best friend I have applied for her to have my baby, too?!

Kate normally has a serene expression, but as I approach her, I am struck by how anxious and tired she looks. She smiles as I reach her and attempts to greet me as though nothing is wrong, but she isn't going to win any acting awards based on this performance. Not knowing a delicate way to clear the air and answer the question she is pretending not to want to ask, I unceremoniously announce that I submitted the application form. I don't think my manner matters though as Kate's anxious expression is immediately replaced with wide-eyed glee.

"You did?!"

"I did – Max filled it in too actually. Obviously, this doesn't guarantee anything, but—"

"But it means I have a chance! Oh, Maia! Thank you!" The hug I receive is enough to clear worries away – not forever, but certainly for a moment. A very different tone of embrace to the one I gave Gee-Gee hours earlier, but just as heartfelt. "Any idea when we'll know?"

"None, sorry, I will tell you when I know."

"Of course…oh! I feel sick! But in the absolute best way! – When do you start preparing? Soon, right?"

"Why, do you want to feel sick together?!" A little dark humour – obviously I know she is just excited. Kate understands and laughs.

"Oh, this is the best! – and after a wholly crappy day! Wow, I really don't care now!"

"Why, what happened?"

"Ugh!" exclaims Kate, "I hate to say it, but your mother-in-law is a piece of work!"

"What? Why have you had a run in with her?!"

"Well, I knew she had a reputation; we'd heard that already, but she has come in as Director with bells and whistles – and possibly grenades! Ugh! She definitely wants to make every part of the department quake at her name." I stare, boggled eyed, waiting for more information. "She is declaring that as Director of Agriculture, she needs to know every plant inside and out and has ordered a complete inventory of every seed, plant, and crop we have – flowers and fruit and veg – what goes in them, where they are, soil analysis, who looks after them – breed, crossbreed, future plans – oh, she is a nightmare!"

"Did Colin Evans not ask for that? – or my Great Gramps?"

"Yes, but not in the same degree of detail, nor all at once. We'd normally just report new findings, present quarterly – she wants it all this week, then monthly. She is pestering every farmer too for livestock and arable details. A 'total agricultural review' – that's what she has declared it as. What the hell she is going to suddenly do with all this information is beyond me! No one can analyse all that in one go, even if she has some fancy wizard kid with her from the Midlands Hub!"

"Fancy wizard kid?"

"She has some red headed girl with her, apparently she graduated a few years early and is an IT genius who is going to be in charge of correlating the information we provide."

"Ella?"

"You know her? Genius or not, to get that position so young, I think she must be from Lady Fairfax's family."

"Why? I don't see the connection?"

"Because she is red haired; the Fairfax family are all red heads." Kate laughs suddenly, "Ha! and have red haired pets to boot!"

"Is that true?"

"Yes! Come on! You must have noticed!? Lady Fairfax has those fluffy ginger dogs, her daughter and granddaughter breed chestnut horses and I think it is her nephew that has ginger cats – it's a well-known joke!"

"I must have missed that – plus, not every redhaired person is from the same genetic family; that is just ridiculous. They may enjoy ginger animals to complement their own tones, but to say that Ella is related to Lady Fairfax purely because of hair colour is daft."

"Spoil sport."

"Besides, she is Theo's wife and that is enough of an intrigue for me."

"*WHAT?!* What do you mean she's Theo's wife? How do you know?!"

"Because I met them both today. It turns out my father-in-law took Theo on as an apprentice and likes him so much he insisted on Theo transferring with him…along with his wife it would seem, who I knew was in IT, but I didn't know she is also working for my mother-in-law. That is just a lovely little cherry on top!" I thought I had taken today pretty well, all things considered, or at least repressed pretty well, but as I make my speech, a tear escapes, and Kate immediately sees it.

"*Oh, Maia!*"

"Don't." I shake my head. We are in the middle of the Central Hub and crying my eyes out here is not wise. "Not here. I can't."

"Okay, then let's walk."

The Minority Rule

Kate silently grabs my arm, linking hers with mine and we don't speak or look at each other until well out of the Central Hub, by which time I have a massive knot in my stomach and lump in my throat. When finally clear of the madding crowd, Kate turns to me, pulls me into a hug and I sob my little heart out on her shoulder.

THIRTY

Somehow this week I have managed to focus on work and enjoy it. I have new samples to work with thanks to Henry and I have squirrelled myself away in one corner, setting up camp quietly so no one minds my presence – or necessarily even notices I am here. This is not an unusual tactic, but it is more useful now than ever as it allows me to clear my mind of distraction. I didn't say too much to Kate the other evening; however her sympathetic, knowing embrace was enough to clear the jumbled fog of my emotions – which I am not pretending to now be bright and shiny, but they are less overwhelming for the time being.

Claire has emailed Max and me details of our wedding. I can't really imagine what brides in the past thought, but I would like to think it was exciting planning their 'big day.' Mum still refers to it as that; however, as every aspect is decided for me, I really see it as more of an event that I turn up to, rather than organise or anticipate with any gusto. Claire asked me to clarify a few things, but as Mum and Mary apparently managed to be copied into these emails, the guest list is done, dress code arranged, menu pre-set, and house and home pre-ordered – all with very little input from me. That said, I am counting down the days. The sooner I get out of Mum's house, into my own and off the 'single and ready to donate' list, the better.

Max is sweet, kind, and makes me laugh. I want to marry him. After years of saying the opposite, the irony in that still makes me smart, but I will not let pride make me fall there. I would much rather Theo had never come back; his presence has only stirred past pain – which had just achieved the finest of covering over it. However, as he seems cold and disinterested in me, I am more than happy to treat him with the same frosty reception. I have only passed him twice in the lab since Monday, both times with others present so ignoring him took little effort – externally anyway.

Max and I have made the gym a regular thing after work – if four out of five nights in a week can be classed as 'regular,' but the intention is to keep it up, and jogging down different virtual paths is nice. Today we're on the beach. I've never seen the sea – not actually – but I love the sound of the water crashing onto the shore and this virtual scene is pretty convincing. I can see why this would become a place to sit and reflect, as well as a place for activity and fun. Looking at the water, I would love to jump in for real – it isn't possible of course, it isn't really there, and although we have swimming pools and parks with lakes, you can't fake the sea. I'd say, 'one day maybe,' but of course, that will never happen.

I wonder if any of the Hubs are near enough the sea to contemplate venturing that far – not now, but in the future? Or is the damage done so severe the water is just too polluted or the land in between too volatile to make trips to the beach possible? Probably. The Hubs were specifically located to be inland enough for safety and potential expansion if UNE plans were successful and enough of society thrives; but as population continues to decline, I hardly see the PTB prioritising holidays to the sea. Society function may be working, we have reduced our emissions, wars have ceased, waste is minimal, our home-grown production is the best it has been in more than a century – two probably – but what good is that if ultimately, we all die out?

"Penny for them?" asks Max.

"Hmm?"

"For your thoughts – a penny?"

"Don't you think it odd we use those expressions when we haven't used pennies or cash for a hundred years?"

"Maybe, but it hardly has the same ring saying, 'a digital penny for your thoughts,' does it?"

"I suppose. Hmm, I suppose so much is virtual now – even here."

"Don't sigh like that. Not everything is digital – I'm not!" Saying that, Max gently kisses me. I hadn't even realised I had sighed that time – pity I don't get paid for those, I'd be rich… though someone else would tell me how I want to spend it if I was. I laugh at him as well as my own cynical mind.

"Come on, let's go, we said we'd meet Kate and Tim in half an hour and we both stink!"

"Well, aren't you a charmer?!" grins Max.

"Just saying what I see – and smell! I'll meet you in the entrance after I've showered."

Kate and Tim are waiting for us in the restaurant with their drinks in hand and ours on the table waiting for us before we have even scanned in.

"Well, this is excellent service!" exclaims Max as we sit down.

Kate looks me up and down. I think she is checking for any sign of concern, though whether it is baby or Theo related news she is searching for most, I am not entirely sure. I shrug my shoulders and smile which seems to put her at ease and conversation flows with ordinary chatter. Max asks Tim about some of the ideas they previously mentioned, causing Tim to fidget as he responds.

"Well, yes, sadly I haven't had the time lately to really expand on that yet...we've had some unexpected challenges."

"Oh?"

Tim continues to fidget and looks like he is chewing his words, testing which phrase is most applicable. I am guessing that Kate understands because she almost seems as awkward as he does, but she stays silent, waiting for Tim to make his own conclusion.

"Right," declares Tim, "we're friends, right? You're going to marry Maia, so, at some point, I'm gonna drink too much and say things wrong, so I may as well do it now, while I'm sober and I can remember what I've said...and apologise if you're offended."

Max silently looks to me for help. I shrug, confirming I am just as confused as he is. He turns to Tim and grins: "Okay, sure, go for it."

"Good. *Your Mother*...I'm sorry, but she really is a heinous creature and what she expects in a week is frankly ludicrous. She clearly wants us all to bow at her feet – well, she'll get it I suppose, but she'll have no friends in the process."

Max stares at Tim for a moment. Tim is clearly waiting for a response and is a little anxious, but I spot a twinkle in Max's eye and realise he is suppressing mirth. A few moments later, he starts chuckling, much to Tim's obvious relief.

"Damn, I'm glad you laughed. I wasn't sure what you were going to do."

"Fear not, I am not under any illusion regarding my mother. Speak freely, I won't repeat it to her. I am sorry though; I did hear her telling my dad she wanted a complete agricultural review across all the Hubs. Dad told her she was going to ruffle a lot of feathers, but she told him she has every intention of doing so and seemed confident those that 'mattered' had her back. Mum has always been like that. She makes the right friends for her cause – and to hell with the rest."

"That's a dangerous path surely?" Tim says warily.

"Dangerous or calculated – or both," replies Max shrugging.

I didn't mean to, but my whole body shudders to the extent all three of my companions turn to me. Mary Rivers, deliberately or not, has established herself in my mind as something to fear and I have to agree that whatever she intends, it is calculated, and she relishes in being feared. I am about to at least attempt to laugh off my display of dread, when the restaurant door opens, stopping me in my tracks, producing another cold chill down my spine, though of a different nature. Tim and Kate, who are sat opposite me, are in a better position to see my expression change, so they turn to follow my gaze. Kate remains silent, but Tim jumps up with a warm, welcoming grin across his face and grabs the newcomer by the hand.

"Theo! Well, this is an overdue surprise! Maia said you are back! Why have you not come to see me? It's been so long since we video called each other I know, but you should have said you were back! How are you?!"

Theo ignores me, but returns Tim's friendly tone and certainly seems glad to have bumped into him. "I am sorry, I had meant to before now, but we've been trying to settle into our new home together – and get into work and see my parents of course. We were delayed starting as we only got married just before we left the Midlands, so had a little holiday when we first arrived at the leisure park—" Theo stops as his arm is gently tugged, causing him to turn to his wife, who until now has silently stood behind him. "Ah, sorry, this is Ella, my wife – Ella, this is Tim, his wife Kate, and Maia, who you met already – and, ah! Max!"

Before Theo finished, Max stood up, ready to shake Theo's hand as soon as he was spotted. Everyone else cordially greets one another as long-lost friends should – except Theo and I, who just nod at each other, making no attempt to close the gap between us. It hadn't occurred to me that he and Max might know each other. I can feel the blood rushing out of my face so I pinch my arm to stop myself falling into a depression. Of course, Henry's son is likely to have met his apprentice. Hey, where would be the fun in them being strangers? Why not just rain on my parade a little bit more for added amusement?!

"Good to see you both, I'm sorry, I meant to look you up once you finished your holiday... So, you've met my fiancé already? Small world, right?!" Too small. Way too small. "Maia, did you know Theo and I were friends? We were studying different subjects obviously, but Dad introduced us when Theo arrived as he was to be his apprentice."

"That's so weird you should be partnered with Theo's old lab partner!" chips in Ella cheerfully.

"Lab partner?" Max turns to me for an explanation.

"Hmm, at school, before he left."

"Oh. Wow," says Max in a funny tone whilst raising his eyebrows, then nods, not really in anyone's direction.

"Wonderful, weird though, right?!" Ella looks a little anxious, "I was hoping to meet some of Theo's old friends – I haven't really met anyone outside work properly yet and—"

"Of course, it must be difficult moving Hubs, I don't think I would like to do it!" Sweet Kate to the rescue. She starts chatting away to Ella and her anxious appearance immediately dissipates. She might be an IT wizard kid, but she is also a young girl, looking for love and friendship, just like the rest of us. I can't blame or hate her for that.

"Why don't you join us for dinner? We haven't ordered yet…I'm sure they can make space for two more here – or move us?" Tim is well meaning, and I will grant you, this is the obvious move when friends meet, but I really don't want to sit down to eat with them. I am going to have to though. If Max is friends with them as well as Tim and Kate, I cannot avoid this, not without dredging up a past that I do not want to discuss. So, if this is to be my new normal, best I work on it now and swallow my pain and pride. Kate gives me a sideways glance, looking for me to back up the invite that Tim has extended so jovially. I force a smile and wave to the waiter, asking for a table for six, which he graciously directs us to immediately.

The table is round, which is handy as I have managed to seat myself between Ella and Kate, facing Max, with Tim to my far right, Theo far left – in sight, but not easy to speak to. I will make note of this seating plan for any future occasions as it works well. Kate leads female chatter, asking polite, friendly, welcoming questions that I can easily follow and comment on with very little real exertion. Ella is 22, she graduated two years early, and won every award going for her IT skills. She is very humble about it, but I think in all fairness, she has reason to boast. Mary headhunted her when she heard of her achievements – which of course are worth promoting as she is a 0. I didn't need to wait for her to say that: rightly or wrongly, I made short work of reading her barcode, despite not being sat at the best angle for it. The possibilities of a barren woman! How envious I am. Mum (amongst others), would say, 'how ungrateful.'

"Do you have siblings?" asks Kate.

"Yes, an older sister. She, her husband, and my nephew live with my parents."

"Ah, how lovely. How old is your nephew?"

"Three years. My sister's a 2 but had successful IVF. She has been trying again, but with no luck so far. At least she has one though, and he is amazing." Ella looks down as she finishes her sentence, her smile turning downwards as she falls silent.

"It is only right you miss them."

"Yes, I know and we video call – it's just—"

"It's not the same, we understand." Kate says softly, glancing at for me for backup – which of course I give.

"Maybe I'll win the lottery! I can but hope! I'd like a family of my own." How easily everyone discusses their fertility – or lack thereof. I suppose it makes sense, that is what society is based on – and educated in the direction of. *I* am the black sheep, not them.

Kate and Ella are chatting away about hopes and dreams of babies – lottery hopes and the anomalies of pregnant ladies in SH2 that inspires optimism for a more fertile future. I can't join in; I will not lie, neither will I stamp on their dreams. I still recall all too vividly Kate's tears when I tried to reason kindly, so I will not try again now. If I were a normal 3, I'd be singing of my fertility prowess. Lucy would never consider holding back on such an opportunity to gloat, in fact I would be expected to crow of my plans to have a huge family. If that's normal, I'm glad I'm not, but Ella does keep looking at me as though I *should* be saying something, *anything,* to tell of my delight, good fortune, excitement… Call it what you will, but my silence is noted.

The boys had been discussing work, but sport has taken over. Max has been sharing our enjoyment of the gym and Kate catches the end of his sentence as our conversation pauses.

"What? You managed to get Maia back in a gym? I've been trying to get her to join me there for years, but she'll only run by the river!"

"And what is wrong with the river?" I ask smirking.

"Nothing, I just like the variation of the gym locations."

"Well, I still prefer the organic variations in scenery along the river, but change can be good."

"Ha! I'll remind you of that when you're next refusing something because you hate change!"

"Mmm, besides, I went to the gym first, Max joined *me,* not the other way around." I stick out my tongue at Kate, mocking her – immature, but she laughs.

"We could all go? Would that be okay? I'm not much for running outside, but do like to the virtual gym." Ella looks around the table, encouraging agreement and attendance with her eyes wide, not unlike a puppy begging for food. And, like all cute puppies, she gets her way as we all agree her idea is wonderful. I'll have to think of a good reason to get out of that later – which is annoying as I've been enjoying the green light on my FitWatch app all week and physically feel the better for it… Hmm, maybe I should just make the effort and go with them.

The meal is done, but we all agree to stick around. I decide to order a round of drinks, so go to the bar to ferry the drinks to the table. To my surprise, Theo follows me, leaning on the bar next to me as we wait for service.

"Hi," he says.

"Hi." The first two words we have deliberately said to each other. I'm not sure what else he is expecting me to say.

"Are we okay? Is *this* okay?" He nods in the direction of the table where everyone else is chatting away, ignoring us. I don't know how to answer that, but I feel myself pulling a face – half smiling, half exasperated. "I wasn't planning on…" He stops. I glare at him, my patience suddenly running out. I've blanked him as best I can all week. I think my unspoken plan was to do that long enough until his presence required no blanking; and my frustrations, by then so well repressed, that I'd forget to be bothered by them. But him bumbling now has foiled my weak plan and I snap.

"Wasn't planning on *what*?! Walking off without a word? Coming back? Telling me you are here? Rubbing your successes in my face? Explaining *anything*? Even *trying* not to be an arse? Huh? …am I close at *all?!*"

"You seem to be doing okay…I mean—"

"Excuse me? You have no idea '*how I'm doing.*' And if I *am* doing okay, it's no thanks to you! Besides, you don't exactly look traumatised by your time away."

Theo pauses, looking solemn for a moment before he says: "Maia, the move was the right thing to do. Do I regret anything? Sure, but it had to be. I had hoped you'd understand and not hate me; that the note, though brief, had helped make—"

"What note?"

We stare at each other blankly.

"I left you a note, on our tree?"

My pride wants me to call him a liar, but looking straight at him, with his dark eyes holding mine, I can see he is in earnest… which begs the question: what happened to it? I don't need to ask which tree; I know only too well he is talking about the big oak by the river near Aunt Dora's. That tree was mine before it was ours and as far as I am concerned, it is just mine again now, but pretending I don't comprehend him now would be childish.

"I never saw it," I whisper. "What did it say?" It may change nothing now, but everything in me wants to know what it said. Theo opens his mouth, then closes it, presumably he is thinking twice about disclosing its contents now. "Please, tell me."

"I'm not sure I remember."

"Liar." I can instantly see the difference in his expression. He sighs, acknowledging being caught out.

"Hey! Have you ordered those drinks yet?!" Max exclaims as he joins us, putting one arm across my shoulders.

"No, sorry, we got distracted." I'm not lying.

"By what?! I thought women were better than men at multitasking?"

"True, but don't be sexist. We were just discussing how odd it is to be working in the same lab again after all these years and how much exciting data we have to work with."

Theo immediately takes up my ruse and talks 'shop.' Despite everything, despite the hurt and anger, it actually feels good to discuss work together. If we can keep that up and make a working friendship…? Yes, I would like that. Who would have thought that idea possible?

Theo and Max order our drinks, so I decide to retreat to the bathroom for a moment. The bar is long and wraps around the room (which is large); our table is on one side; the toilets are down a corridor at the far end of the opposite side of the bar. When I return, Theo, who has apparently been chatting to the barman, gets up and goes to the bathroom, timing our passing perfectly with a structural pillar that is embellished with plants, blocking out the view of the rest of the room.

"Here."

He shoves a neatly folded napkin into my jeans pocket. I am so surprised, I let him and don't get time to question as he strides off into the bathroom. Confused, I somehow propel myself towards the others who are happily chatting and sipping on their various beverages. I sit down, silently running my hand over my pocket to convince myself the napkin is actually there. I am dying to look at it, but tell myself to leave it alone until I get home.

"Shall we watch a movie or catch a play? One is bound to be starting nearby." Tim is enthusiastic. "It has been so long since I went to either – what do you think?"

I want to go home. I feel like the napkin is burning my leg, but everyone else is keen and I can see that Max is as excited at the prospect as anyone. I am not selfish enough to say no, so off to the theatre we go. Movies always seem so regimented; I'd like to watch one that isn't quite so linear – or disturbing. So many depict the world that was, how it fell, accompanied by some heroic, but often tragic story. In all honesty, most are just feature length versions of what we were repeatedly shown at school. As I sit down, I suddenly realise the PTB have craftily succeeded in ensuring the population continues their education long after school finishes – and what's more, we pay them for the privilege.

THIRTY-ONE

It was around midnight before I found myself alone in my bedroom. The evening had ended well, and I admit to having enjoyed myself despite initial reservations. Try as I might to dislike Ella, she is nice. Kate clearly likes her, though I occasionally caught her glancing at me, as if to check she wasn't offending me by befriending her. Were I a harder person, I might have called in that card, but I am not. Embittered maybe, but totally heartless I am not. Plus, Max already has an established friendship with both Theo and Ella, so if Kate (and Tim) like them too, it should make life easier, not harder. I genuinely hope so anyway.

Wasting no time, as soon as I was safely locked in my room, I pulled out the napkin from my pocket. A standard issue, white cloth napkin – which actually I had technically stolen from the bar as they are supposed to be placed in the laundry container for cleaning, not taken home. However, if that is the worst crime I ever commit, I think I will just about avoid prison. Opening up the napkin, I saw Theo's handwriting – not neatly done, presumably because he wrote in haste using the barman's pen, but it is undoubtedly his writing.

I don't know how long I stared at that napkin for before I fell asleep, but it was the first thing I saw when I woke up and I have been sat here in bed, studying it for some time. There are just two lines. Two short lines that mean nothing and everything:

> *I do not know what lies ahead or tomorrow where I'll be.*
> *But know a piece of my heart is ever yours, though I must*
> *let you go free.*

I do not know how to react, so I seem to have frozen – physically at least. My mind is not frozen, but I cannot decide what to think now or how I would have thought then, had this note arrived when it was intended. Would it have helped me move on or torture me further? It certainly would have raised more questions, but as I had plenty of those anyway, I can't help thinking that whoever intercepted this did me a great injustice. In truth, my major injury has always been the betrayal of him leaving without notice and leaving me doubting if he ever truly cared. This answers that. I am sure I could (and likely would) have concocted other lines of woe to torment myself with, but I could have had *that* comfort.

Another level of mystery has occurred to me though. Theo obviously asked for a transfer, but he would seem to be clueless to his path – or maybe I am just reading too much into the first line and he just wanted to leave anonymously without me trying to follow or track him. A clean break is what he intended. I would ask why, but I know. Truthfully, I have always known; there is no secret there – fertility dictated that we could not be. I wouldn't set him free, so he took the step that needed to be made. Had he stayed, I would have followed him like a lost pup until the PTB came after us both. I tremble as I remember that poor girl's scream as she tried to reach her boyfriend at the Matching Ceremony and her silence as she was injected and knocked out. Where are they now? Seeing them, I had finally accepted the reality of our fates, but only now do I forgive Theo. I actually feel lighter for it. Strange really, but I do feel like part of a burden has been lifted. However, someone knows this note existed and deliberately left me in pain. How cruel and heartless they must be!

I could have happily remained in my room, musing over the napkin, but I am supposed to be sitting with Eve again later today. Aunt Dora had said it wasn't going to be weekly; however, so far at least, it is. I asked Max if he wanted to come, but he hasn't really recovered from Eve's 'rotten apple' metaphor and so I think he was glad to have the excuse of having arranged to watch a football match this afternoon with Tim and some of their respective work colleagues. I am glad he is making friends and frankly, I will be more relaxed listening to whatever idiosyncrasies that Eve may or may not come out with, alone.

I wash and tidy myself up before venturing downstairs. I have avoided Mum for days, but I can hear her prattling to Grandma in the kitchen, so that record is about to be broken.

"Ah! At last!" Mum is all smiles, but not particularly warming. "Good morning, madam." Nope, that's not good.

"Morning Mum, Grandma, how are you both?"

Grandma smiles, "Well, thank you dear—"

"Don't '*dear*' her, she does not deserve it," scoffs Mum.

Oh, for heaven's sake. What can I possibly have done now? "Am I missing something?"

"Yes! I have just been speaking to Mrs Oldman!"

"Oh? It's early for the gossip train, isn't it?"

"Insolent girl! – Well, so you might be. I cannot believe you are risking your match! I really thought we'd turned a page on that one—"

"If you are going to accuse me of something, can you just spit it out? I'm not aware of risking anything, so best you say whatever it is plainly." I know I shouldn't speak to her so; I should rise above, but I am yet to learn such a level of humility. I used to be able to batter and bruise from her attacks silently, but now, I just can't help it.

"I have just been told you were seen last night with *that* boy! I can't believe you have back tracked so many years! Disgraceful! I thought we were well rid of him; I couldn't believe it when Trudy told me he was one of the transfers – what on earth for?! He is not fertile! He has no need to be flittering back and forth – no use at all! *And you*! Oh, if I see you pining for him again! No! it will not be – *do you hear*?!"

"If you are about to give me a lecture on duty again, please save your breath. I would suggest you and Trudy Oldman get your facts right before flapping your mouths off. I was there with *MAX*, Kate, Tim, Theo and his *WIFE*, Ella. No, don't bother apologising, you won't mean it."

Dad walks in, looking a little shocked. "Maia, well!"

"Do you hear how she talks to me?! Aren't you going to say anything?!" Dad glances at us both, shaking his head, but says nothing. "Stephen!" squawks Mum.

"Beatrix, she is right. You accused her before waiting for me to check. She was out in a group of six, with her fiancé no less – leave the girl alone."

"You had Dad check?!"

"Of course I did! I wanted to see if Trudy was right! You forget your barcode gets scanned!"

"Hmph, that'll be the last time I check up, it's a waste of time and—"

"And it's a violation of trust! Why can *she* not just ask like a normal person?!"

"Calm down, it's my job to know where everyone is and Mark has always kept track of my children for me – pft! the number of times I had to intercept your brother when he was in his teens!"

"Really?!" This is news to me. On another day I might find it funny, but even if Abe had a teen rebellion I don't know about, it doesn't change the fact Mum is repeatably against me. It suddenly dawns on me there is a high chance that *she* took Theo's note. Challenging her now is fruitless, but she was thrilled when he left and never understood either of us, so it would hardly be surprising. I also remember Gee-Gee's confession that Mum goes in my room, so as much as I would like to keep my new napkin as a reminder, it is safer gone and I will always remember those two lines. While Mum is momentarily distracted by moaning at Dad, I dart upstairs, fold the napkin as small as I can and put it in my pocket. I'll dispose of that somewhere else, or wash it at Aunt Dora's – I don't think the ink is permanent.

Returning downstairs, I expect a second round from Mum; however, instead she attempts some sort of civilised wedding chatter while I eat breakfast. How someone can flit between attack and chatter so easily is beyond me, but she is the master of her art. As soon as I am finished, I get up to leave. I am earlier than I need to be for Aunt Dora, but I can happily sit by the river for a while until I am needed.

"You off with Max?"

"No, Dad, I'm helping Aunt Dora today."

"Good girl, send her my regards."

"Hmph! Dora needs all the help she can get – what on earth was she thinking taking in that old woman? She's not family, yet she has insisted on inviting her to family things and caring for her for years – grumpy old thing! Who wants to live with her?! She's never had a good word to say, looking down her nose at us all I bet."

"By 'good word,' you probably mean, she doesn't gossip, Beatrix? If that is the lady's only failing, I think she can pass unchastised."

"Would it be *so* difficult for you to defend your wife once in a while?"

"From what?" Dad doesn't wait for an answer, instead he walks out of the room, into his study, smirking as he goes, giving me a little wink as he turns to slide his door shut.

Rather than wait for Mum to reload her verbal assault gun, I turn to take my leave, scanning the backdoor so it opens for me.

"Remember dinner tomorrow night – don't dress like that!" I normally try to ignore Mum's parting comments, but this one makes me step back inside.

"Pardon?"

"Dinner, at the Rivers of course."

"You're coming?"

"Yes, obviously. I saw Mary yesterday and she invited your father and I to join you. Pity she isn't having us all, but I suppose that is a lot of people."

Well, isn't that something to look forward to? "I'll meet you there, I'll be out before."

"What? Oh no, that isn't right and—"

"See you later."

I am not waiting to hear more, so immediately walk off towards the river. It is a beautiful day, and several people are out for a walk. Children are playing in the park as I walk past and it is nice to see them enjoying the sunshine, not just playing virtual games with visors on their heads. It rained heavily during the week, making the river current stronger than of late, so I hear it before I see it. I love how the water seems to have different moods – moods that others cannot dictate. I envy that ability!

As I approach my favourite tree, I see a figure sat by her giant roots. This seems like something of a violation, almost as though I have found a thief in my bedroom. I can't remember ever finding someone else sat there before. It isn't a particularly out of the way spot, but it isn't a typical hang out area either. The terrain is easier upriver, which suits me, as it means no competition and it avoids situations such as these. I am considering turning away when the figure turns to me and smiles coyly. He gets up when he sees me approaching, but says nothing. If Mum is tracking me now, she will absolutely wet herself.

Having stared at his note so long, I am happy to see Theo again so soon as he has given my heart a peace that I didn't know was possible: I feel a sense of *closure*. I don't know if it is appropriate, but rather than speak immediately, I walk up to him and hug him. He doesn't push me away, but wraps his arms around me like he used to and I let out a sigh; one that is different to any sigh I have let go before. It is as though a chamber in my lungs has been trapping a little pocket of air for six years and now, finally, I can let it go.

"Thank you," I whisper into his ear.

"What for?"

"Letting me go. Letting us go. But for loving me, as I you."

Theo steps back and so do I, both of us smiling with a hint of tears in our eyes.

"I'm still sorry though."

"Hmm." I nod. Neither of us speaks for a moment. I sit down by the riverbank, leaning against the oak, just like I have done all my life. Theo sits down next to me, but a little further away than of old. Just as it should be. We watch the water pass us by, not saying anything, but the silence is comfortable, not awkward, and neither of us are in a hurry to break the spell. Eventually I check the time on my watch. It is nearly time I went, but it is Theo who speaks first:

"I'd better go. I just – well, you know." He shrugs. There aren't words, but I get him.

"Yeah, I do. See you around." He reaches out, squeezes my hand, gets up and turns to leave.

"Theo?"

"Yes?"

"Why didn't you know where you were going?"

He pauses, rubs his face with his right hand and pulls a face.

"That note is what you wrote originally, right?"

"Yes, identical."

"Then why didn't you know where you were going?"

"I wasn't allowed to know." He shrugs again, walking away. "You only know what you need to, to serve."

THIRTY-TWO

"Ah, Missy, I knew it was you."

"Before or after the security system announced me?"

"During."

There's no logical answer to that, is there?

"How are you today, Eve? You look well."

"Hmmphh, your definition of 'well' and mine must differ. Though *well* is I suppose, about okay."

"So, you *are* well?"

"What?"

I suppress a smile. "Do you need anything?"

"Nothing I can't get meself. Where's Dora gone now?"

"Nowhere, Eve. Not yet. I'm here."

"Pfft."

"Do you want me to bring you anything?"

"No, thank you, nothing other than normal groceries, please." Eve turns to me, narrowing her eyes and twisting her lips. When she does this, I have started a game with myself to guess whether the subsequent sentence is going to be rational or not. I'm guessing 'not' this time. "So... The apprentice maestro has come to perform?"

"Apprentice?!"

"Aye, sing my little one, sing. A folk tune today, if you will." I win – though I also lose, as I do not know any folk tunes – certainly not off by heart. I look to Aunt Dora for help. She chuckles as she picks up her bags to leave.

"Do you know any folk tunes?"

"See! *Apprentice*!" I really hope Eve doesn't mind, but I have to laugh and I'm pretty sure Aunt Dora is laughing too as she shuts the front door behind her. Eve has a comical and unique balance of quick-witted sense and what I can only describe as absurd. I can't help wondering what a formidable woman she would have been years ago when in better health.

"If you let me use my watch or the radio, I could play some folk tunes for you?"

"No! No gadgets. Hmmphhing things, keep them off. Have you got your bracelet on? I don't want no spies near me." I wave my wrist at Eve as proof of my compliance. "Hmmphh, good. Keep it on."

"Do you not draw attention to yourself by being untraceable?"

"Pfft, no. Watch will still ping location, just fudge up audio so no 'flag words' are detected. That's all you need. Fudge 'em up. Ha! Listen to me *now*!" Eve is chuckling towards the ceiling, but seemingly distracts herself quickly as she turns back to me. "Where's your riverman then? Can he sing?"

"Assuming you mean Max, he is watching football, and I don't know if he can sing."

"Hmmphh."

"Eve, do you know Max's family?" No answer, but she is squinting at me. "I got the impression last week that you do. Max was a little upset by your apple metaphor – I believe that *was* a metaphor, right?"

"Pfft. If you say so."

"Do you ever get the feeling everyone knows more than you do?" Eve is looking straight at me, but makes no effort to reply. "No, of course not, you're one of the ones that *knows*, aren't you?" I roll my eyes as I speak.

"Have you ever heard the expression 'ignorance is bliss'?" I nod. "Yeah, well."

"That may be true if I were ignorant of *everything*. If I had no knowledge of there being more *to know*. That could be bliss. But knowing I don't know, is anything *but* bliss."

"Curiosity killed the cat." Eve stops, looking down at Squash who is curled up on her lap, totally uninterested in our conversation. "Not you boy, ignore that."

"Dr Rivers said I have a curious mind. I am hoping that at least has potential to be a good thing."

"Pfft. He hides behind the skirt of his Black Widow. What the hell good is he?"

"So, you do know Henry Rivers?"

"Hmmphh, don't need to. You need more than nine lives in that household."

"Well, that's reassuring when I am about to marry their son."

"A good apple, planted elsewhere, can be worth picking."

"Stop speaking in riddles!"

Eve stares straight at me, but doesn't answer.

"Please speak to me properly!"

"You said stop speaking in riddles."

"Well?"

"No."

"Really?! You clearly want to say something, why not just say it?"

"You have a curious mind. Solve the riddle. Or better yet: don't and live peacefully, like you're supposed to. You ain't a cat."

"No, no I am not."

"Missy, some riddles are best left."

"Then why say anything, if you don't think I should enquire?"

"Because I have spent a long time alone and I like to talk to yer... Plus, I think you're the sort to question even when you're not encouraged." She pauses, then tilts her head and says: "That...and you're leaving the woods without a paddle."

A cold chill goes down my spine, which is a strange sensation as I also feel a hot flush in my cheeks. I'd like to laugh at her continued obstinacy – or even rebuke her for it, but Eve spoke with such a serious expression, I cannot.

"How about you throw me an oar?" I plead.

"You don't want my help." She shakes her head, screwing up her face as she does. I am not sure if she is fighting the fog in her mind, a memory, or the desire to say more. Either way, something is disturbing her. "No, won't do."

"What won't do?"

"Huh? Pfft! I thought you were going to sing, Missy?"

"No, you brought that up earlier and want to change the subject now. Nice try, I don't think your mind is as cloudy as you like to make out."

"Pfft. I wish that were true. I know yer now, but it don't mean I will in a minute."

"But while you do, won't you tell me what troubles you so? Don't shake your head or tell me it's nothing, I know something troubles you. Surely, even if I can't do anything about the past, it will help to talk about it?"

Eve doesn't reply. She doesn't look away either though. As I hold her gentle gaze, I see tears welling up, if only briefly, as she wipes them away. Again, she shakes her head, wobbling her tongue in her mouth as she does.

"A problem shared, is trouble multiplied," she eventually says.

"No one need know – the PTB can't hear us while we wear the bracelets and I'll never repeat anything said in confidence, I pr—"

"Hmmphh, ain't the PTB you need to worry about."

"Pardon? Who else would be listening? *Who else is there*?!"

Eve grunts softly, rolling her eyes, I think at herself, not me, but says nothing.

"Eve, who else *is* there?"

Eve has fallen silent, but I can see she is calculating a response, so as desperate as I am for an answer, I wait.

"Do you know the worst part of dementia? No?" I shake my head and Eve continues: "I thought it was the continuous walk between the fog, feeling helpless to stay in the clearing, instead eternally getting dragged into another patch of nothing, knowing that one day, I'll likely get trapped in that fog. But now, I actually think it's the in between; sitting on the edge, hearing what I say, but wishing I'd shut up, having less or no filter. I've never been particularly chatty, though I like to talk to some well enough, but I ain't one to sit gossiping about the neighbour's dress code or new flower bed or such. I've kept to meself very well all these years."

"You do like a riddle though."

Eve grins and snorts quietly. "Hmmphh."

"I can't imagine what it's like. 'Sorry' hardly begins to cover it, I know, but I do want to help."

"You help by chatting and keepin' me company when Dora is gone. I know well enough she was right saying I couldn't stop at home alone no more. Those arses want me gone, but I'll not let them take me right to die in my own bed when my time is up – *my time* – not theirs. You see the difference? They owe me that much. Pfft, even I didn't think I'd be so long lived – but a promise is that and *I* keep me word!"

"Who did you promise?"

"My family." She whispers. I have a hundred questions, but instinct tells me asking them at my speed will get me nowhere. Patience is supposed to be a virtue – I am trying to exercise this attribute, but it is taking a lot of concentration. "Hmmphh, not that they know it."

"If they don't know you made a promise, does it matter if you keep it?"

"If they want to live, it does."

I can feel my eyes boggling. "I wasn't sure if you were referring to surviving family or a promise to the dead, but obvi—"

"Both. And I have kept it. I *will* keep it. They may not be loyal to me, but I am them; they don't know what I do. Pfft. Fools."

We both sit silently for a while. I wish I knew what else to say, but as I sit here, curious as I may be, even I am not sure that I shouldn't let the mystery be. Maybe it is Eve's right to take her riddles to the grave; perhaps that is the way she wins against whatever wrong has been done to her? In truth, I am a little afraid to know the full story. It would seem that to some degree, Eve has chosen this life…but only since her immediate family's death – so was it a choice? And if it is not the PTB she is worrying about, *who is it?!* There isn't anyone else! Is that the dementia talking? Or the biggest revelation of my life?

I can't ask now, as in my moments of reflection, Eve has fallen asleep – or has mentally stepped into another room. Sometimes it is hard to tell.

THIRTY-THREE

I didn't tell Aunt Dora what Eve had said. She was so happy recounting her day that I decided to let her enthusiasm wash over me. When Eve woke up she didn't know who I was – or indeed where she was – and it took a while for us to calm her. The reality and cruelty of Eve's condition soon dampened both our spirits, so while Eve rested again, we both sat in the garden watching the sunset. I think we had been out there for about an hour, silently letting time tick by, when the backdoor opened causing us both to startle. Smoggy and Squash trotted out first with Eve slowly walking behind them. She still only uses one stick to aid her, but in the few weeks that I have known her she has noticeably slowed down.

"Eve, where are you going? Can I get you anything?" asks Aunt Dora.

"Just out here. I'm fed up of indoors."

"Are you sure? Okay, but you'll have to take the bracelet off." Aunt Dora points to the sky as a drone flies across the end of the garden – only a delivery one thankfully, but she definitely has a point. Eve grunts, but complies, removing her bracelet and leaving it on the windowsill just inside the door before sitting on the bench next to me. None of us speak. I think two of us are afraid of the other saying something problematic and the other looks too tired to start a conversation.

My watch pings, causing us all to stare at my right arm. Eve repeats her grunt as though replying to the device. It is an email from the Genetics Committee. The heading is a reminder for my forthcoming donation and preparatory injections, but as I scroll down I realise it is also a reply to my application. Denied. I close my eyes and shake my head. Poor Kate, how am I going to tell her? I don't know if I am relieved or disappointed – hopefully it is okay to be both.

"Maia, are you all right? Have you bad news?" Aunt Dora asks softly.

"I'm okay." Is there any harm in telling her? I hope not. "I had applied for Kate and Tim to have one of my eggs, but the Genetics Committee have denied my application."

"You did?! Wow, that would have been challenging—"

"I know, but Kate deserves it. I'm not looking forward to telling her they've said no."

"Does Max know you applied?"

"He applied with me."

"Well, there's your issue," Eve says abruptly.

"Pardon, Eve?"

"I told you, you need to learn to swim better."

I look to Aunt Dora, but she seems as baffled as I am. I don't see the relevance in Eve's comment, coded or otherwise. I should be more tolerant, there's a good chance Eve herself isn't sure what she means, but it doesn't stop me replying:

"Eve, if you only ever speak in riddles, fearing reprimand for plain speech, no one will understand you and neither clarity nor change will ever be achieved."

"Hmmphh, one is overrated and who said anything about wanting change?"

"Surely, whether you admit it or not, you want some change? I know I do."

Aunt Dora looks panicked and gets up, pointing to the door. She is right, I should remember where I am and not let my impatience for detail get the better of me. I was doing better with self-restraint earlier. I suppose it has been a long day – no, that's a weak excuse; truthfully, I think I just like to know things…and I am impatient. Mouthing the word 'sorry', I follow Aunt Dora's lead and rise to go indoors. I extend a hand to Eve, hoping she will take the hint without requiring persuasion, but she ignores me, instead sternly adding:

"Besides, you need to know your goal before you kick." Boggled-eyed, Aunt Dora takes Eve by the hand, ushering her indoors. "What are you doing girl?! Unhand me!"

It seems like this action has sparked an episode of confusion as the two tussle on the journey back to the living room. I try to assist, but being double manhandled only increases Eve's outbursts – and turns her coded grunts to full on swearing – so I step back, feeling a little useless. It is painfully sad to see Eve so confused. I am sure she is reliving a past trauma as her face screws up and tears flow. She shouts her husband and sons' names, but the rest is barely intelligible and the distinguishable words collectively make no sense whatsoever. Once inside, she eventually calms, but mutters to herself, not attempting to communicate with either of us.

I apologise to Aunt Dora as I feel I unwittingly started this outburst by asking questions, but she just waves her hand at me.

"No, my dear, this has happened a lot this week. She says something 'questionable' and soon after, an episode like that is triggered whether I comment or not. I don't know what to do." She pauses. "What change were you referring to? I thought you like Max?"

"I do."

"Then why do you need another change?"

"I don't mean Max. I think 'change' might be the wrong – or too simplistic a word – I just can't shake the feeling that there is more for my life than motherhood." Aunt Dora's face winces. How I should think before I speak! I think I have a sympathetic ear, so waffle without thinking of the feelings of the listener – my childless listener! "I'm sorry! How thoughtless I am—"

"Maia," she says softly, "I think it's normal. People often want what they cannot have and take for granted what they can. Sometimes it takes a huge amount of soul searching to accept our situations. The eternal, often trivial, pursuit of happiness can be a sad and lonely path and has ruined many a man and woman throughout history. Some will eternally race for something more, while real happiness comes with the contentment and appreciation of what you have."

I am about to reply, but hesitate. There is undeniable wisdom in her words, but I also feel like she is contradicting her previous advice. "You told me to do my duty, but look for my silver lining and find happiness. Surely that requires pushing the bounds of the system?"

"You can strive for better, just don't miss out on what is in front of you." She pauses, reaching her hand out to mine. "Do you understand what I am saying? If I am contradicting myself, it's because I can see you have a chance of happiness – true contentment – and if you challenge the rule too much, I fear the consequences."

"But what if I can really help and make a difference? What if my greatest enemy is apathy? Wasn't that humankind's downfall? – apathy en masse? No one acting because it was easier not to. It is easier to follow what is known and to continue on the path of immediate gratification than it is to look to what we leave for the next generation, pretending the problem is for another day – or worse, that the problem is fictional. Allowing greed, pollution, and disease to spread caused the almighty Fall. Surely, if anyone can see a path away from further destruction, they have the moral duty to act, even if it isn't popular with the establishment? Even if that establishment is working for the betterment and healing of Earth and humanity, I cannot believe that they have every aspect wholly covered and no improvement can be made. Nothing we do is perfect. To do better, we must constantly question our actions and not be afraid to adjust outside the box. I fear change, but I also fear doing nothing."

As I speak, I feel an energy building up inside and I know I believe what I am saying. Only hours earlier I was wondering if difficult mysteries are best left, but they are not. What if by leaving some mysteries unsolved crimes and atrocities are left covered? Surely this then leaves it open for crimes to continue or mistakes be repeated? If you do not know where you came from, you cannot fully learn, move on, and grow (as an individual or society). Also, no development or discovery was ever made in science or technology through inaction.

Aunt Dora sighs quietly and says, "Just remember you are valuable for *you*, not what you achieve."

I am taken aback for a moment, but soberly reply: "Very few would agree with that, Aunt Dora; to them, I have but one purpose."

"Not to those who matter. Look, you can strive for more, I am not going to tell you not to, but don't be consumed by the need to do—"

"I understand you – and thank you, but—"

"Just enjoy being a married couple, get to know each other properly and take things slowly. Time is precious…and I know I had too little of it with Ray thanks to his quest to help."

"You're right, I know." Ray died about eight years ago. I do remember him obviously, but I never really knew him well, certainly not well enough to have an idea on the truth behind his illness and death. I've mostly thought of Aunt Dora as being just 'widowed' or 'unlucky in love.' To revisit her mystery hasn't honestly occurred to me. Until now. "What happened to Ray? I mean *really*?"

"Phew! That's a loaded question!" She bobs her head whilst wobbling her lips.

"So, there is more to it? He didn't die from radiation?"

"No, no, he did…slowly, but he did. Hmm, I haven't spoken of this with anyone…I don't really know there is anything *to* say. I don't *know* anything; only that he went out on a job with the Army as a surveyor, like he had many times before, and wandered into a nuclear zone…which was *so* unlike him, he was so meticulous with his calculations. The Army report said there was mechanical failure with his equipment, causing him to wander in the wrong direction when mapping a new area. Ray didn't contest their findings, but there was just something in his face – I don't know how to describe it – but something wasn't right. They supposedly found him collapsed suffering from a massive radiation overdose. He spent ages in one of their specialist camp hospitals, but when he didn't die, they returned him to me to slowly fade away here."

"So, it could have been an accident?"

"Hmmphh, hardly." I know Eve's sudden input should not affect me, but once again, she has perfectly timed her speech to make us both jump. "Best way to send a message. Watch him die slowly, painfully. Nothing like making people toe the line with a visual reminder."

"But Ray didn't do anything – did he?"

"No, but they *thought* he did…or was going to." Eve whispers, breaking into a quiet sob. This is clearly news to Aunt Dora as the blood has rushed from her face, leaving her white as a sheet. Whatever she might have supposed, hearing Eve now is different – and it is clear she doesn't think this is the dementia talking.

"What did they think he did?" Eve doesn't answer me. Then suddenly a new question comes to mind. "Which *they* are you referring to?" That makes her look up. She narrows her eyes at me, but it is Aunt Dora who replies.

"What do you mean, Maia?"

"Eve knows."

"Do I?"

"Yes, you do. I can see that you remember."

"Hmmphh."

"So, you weren't making that up? There is another *they*?"

"I'm lost," says Aunt Dora glancing between Eve and me.

"Eve told me it wasn't the PTB I need to worry about."

"What?! There isn't anyone else."

"That's what I said – Eve? Care to help us out?"

"If you knew what you were asking me, you'd keep quiet. You think you need to solve mysteries, well, you don't. By all means, push yourself, learn, discover, but leave alone that which ain't yours to poke into. My secrets are mine. I know enough to keep quiet. So do you. I told you me promise requires silence. Blood and tears have been spilt enough from me and mine. Ray died. You can't bring him back. My Tom, my boys, my – *Oh, enough!* As if I'm not tortured enough! They are best left to rest. If I was in me full capacity, you'd not know as much as you do. You know too much for your own good."

"I know next to nothing!"

"You *know* more than nothing and that's too much. Hush girl! Death comes to those who cross them. Hush! I tell you! Dora, surely you see sense?! Speak to her. I cannot see anyone else lost." Her tone is steady, but tears flow.

"Eve, are you saying all the deaths in your family are connected? The explosion at Tom's workshop – it wasn't really an accident either?" Aunt Dora's tone is quiet yet firm.

"Ugghh." Eve flexes and fists her hands several times before rubbing her face.

"Eve, you can tell us to be silent, but I think I have the right to know why my husband died. Please, tell us, we won't cross or challenge anyone, I just—"

"No! I must bear this pain alone. I'm done talkin' – *good night.*" Eve gets up and walks out the room. I'd say 'stormed,' but truthfully, a lady her age is probably nearer to 'shuffling at speed.' It is effective however as she makes it clear we are not going to persuade her to share. I am surprised to witness Aunt Dora doing the pushing, not me, but I think her peace has also been disturbed and her curiosity now eternally pipped. Something tells me we are going to be sisters in confusion though, not knowledge.

THIRTY-FOUR

Max is sat on a bench, waiting for me, but staring in the opposite direction. It's silly, it's only been a day since I saw him, but I actually missed him. I am hoping that is a good sign. I am not particularly looking forward to dinner with our parents this evening, but a simple walk in the park sounds good at the moment. I didn't sleep well last night. I spent so long replaying and where possible, deciphering my conversations from yesterday, that my mind just wouldn't shut off. I would mind less if I had come to some conclusion; however, I have none, just more questions. I want to focus on what I *can* potentially solve, so today (as much as possible), I will try to stall my thoughts and tomorrow, throw myself at my work. This plan has the added attraction of diverting me from hormonal surges that will soon come from preparatory injections for my donation. I have given up complaining about them as when I did, I was told by Dr Oldman I was 'imagining things as there are no side effects.' Last time I checked, men do not have uteruses, nor my hormones, so although I would still want to use a few expletives towards a woman trying to tell me that, I really shouldn't confess to what I would love to reply to a cold, insensitive man who is stupid enough to say that to me.

As I approach, Max turns towards me. He smiles and briefly kisses me, but seems weary.

"Everything okay?"

"Yes, you?"

"Mm-hmm. Are you sure? You seem tired."

"So do you." Touché.

"I had a long day with Eve."

"Right."

"Did you enjoy your day?"

"Yes, it was nice." Okay, there is something wrong. He normally needs little encouragement to embellish, be it recounting some tale, the score of the match, what he ate – *something*. We walk, but nowhere in particular, and although I would not normally mind a general amble, this *feels* aimless and uncomfortable. I really wanted a stress and tension free day, and this is currently neither.

"Okay, spit it out."

"Excuse me?"

"I know we haven't known each other long, but I can tell when you're chewing on something. You look tired, dare I say it, *grumpy*, and you keep chewing on your lip as though you are refraining from something. So. Spit. It. Out."

"Mmm, and you call *me* grumpy." I roll my eyes as he stops walking to stand in front of me. "Fine, I didn't want to say, but I admit it is bothering me – I *know* Theo and you were together."

"Okay."

"Is that all you're going to say? I thought you weren't going to keep secrets from me?"

"Well, it hadn't really come up and as it's in the past I didn't see the immediate need to— Anyway, how do you know? Did he tell you?"

"Yes, though not now." I stare at him, raising one eyebrow, willing an answer. Surely, *someone* is capable of answering with a full sentence without constant prodding?! "When we were in the Midlands Hub, we were friends and would hang out. Though he didn't talk about the past much, one day, after a game, we had drunk a bit – not that much – just enough to loosen tongues of those who need to get something off their chest. I was getting it in the neck from Mum about applying for another deferral on my marriage when I didn't want to, so I confided in Theo. I asked him why he was applying and not just marrying – he could work the same, so I didn't understand why a 0 would defer. He eventually told me he'd left his heart behind and wasn't ready to move on. I asked why he left if that was the case. He never named you, or really gave detail (about anything to be fair) but said she – *you* – were his lab partner at school and you'd fallen in love, but you were a 3, so could never be."

I know I shouldn't, but I smile at this. It probably isn't nice of me to be pleased someone else was in pain too, but frankly, it just furthers my healing. I can see my smile has annoyed Max though, so I quickly wipe it off my face. It is a good job I washed Theo's napkin at Aunt Dora's yesterday as it could have added fuel to his paranoid fire.

"That pleases you?"

I blow out my cheeks, desperately thinking of an answer that isn't going to upset him.

"Tell me the truth, you promised – do we have a problem *now*?"

"No. None." I made sure to fire that answer out quickly and thankfully, I seem to have dispelled the initial irritation as Max's face relaxes.

"When I heard Ella say you were Theo's lab partner, well, I was surprised, but instantly remembered that conversation—"

"You don't need to be worried. You are right, we were together. *WERE*. That is a past that marred me, I will not lie, but it is past. Theo and I spoke briefly and that's enough to satisfy both of us that what happened was right and we have moved on." I hold his hand and squeeze it. "You believe me, *right*?"

"But you were pleased to hear he was in pain?"

"Yes, wouldn't you be relieved to know a relationship was mourned equally? I am just as pleased he has moved on. His friendship got me through my teenage years – his and Kate's. They were my voices of reason and comfort when there was little at home. His leaving was a stab in the heart, but as it turns out, a necessary one – to prepare for now, for—"

I am not allowed to finish, apparently, I don't need to. Max pulls me into an all-encompassing embrace – which is far better than any bumbling sentences I can come up with.

An hour or so later, we're sat on the tram heading to SH2. I have warned Max that we're likely to receive an ear bashing for such a day trip, but having discussed our denied egg donation, we decide this is news best delivered in person. I can hear muffled chatter from people behind us. Once again, they're reading my barcode and discussing what can be my purpose travelling away from the Centre or SH1 on a Sunday, but the difference this time is, I am not alone. It is not just my barcode they are recounting, and it feels good to have Max with me.

We step off the tram and I watch Max scan his new surroundings as we walk. "Does it look the same here as the Midlands Hub?" I ask.

"Yes. The architecture and general layout are almost identical. Locations differ, but it is clear both Hubs have the same creators behind them. Is this Kate's street? I think it must be as there is a semi burnt-out building over there – isn't that where a drone crashed?"

Following his line of vision past Kate's home, I see the half-scorched house. "Yes, I am surprised they haven't rebuilt it yet. Construction is normally faster, right?"

"Definitely, unless they want the message to be seen for longer," shrugs Max.

"You think there is a message? But what? They should be celebrating the new life that was conceived here—"

"*Should*, indeed."

Another mystery to add to the pile. I need to pick one at a time. Unpick one, don't get crushed by them all.

"Maia? Max?" I turn to see Tim walking towards us. "What are you two doing here?"

"We came to see you, but are you off out?"

"Yes, but only to the allotment where we're replanting. I just stopped briefly, but am heading back now. Kate is there. You're welcome to join us if watching us dig isn't too dull?"

Max and I readily agree and the three of us chatter as we walk. Kate is kneeling by a newly dug vegetable patch, carefully placing out new plants. She hears our voices and looks up smiling; however, being her usual sensitive, intuitive self, her smile quickly turns upside down.

"They said no, didn't they?"

"Yes, I am so sorry."

Tim doesn't catch on until he sees Kate's tears, then just whispers: "No egg?" I shake my head, and he walks over to Kate to give her a hug. I feel powerless to help, so Max and I wander up the allotment to give them a moment alone.

"Hey, how are you?" I turn to see a man grinning at me. Looking at his face I'd say he is middle aged, but his hair is completely grey. I feel like I should know who he is, but I can't quite pinpoint why – which is embarrassing as he clearly knows me. "So, are you going to give me a hug?! I know it's been a while, but you'd always give me a hug when you were younger – or are you too mature for me now?" He flings his arms wide for a hug and suddenly the gesture triggers my memory.

"Bruce?! Damn! I didn't recognise you for a minute!" I splutter into his shoulder.

"Ha-ha, it's the hair ain't it? No black mane anymore!" Bruce is Tim's Uncle, and although it isn't that long since I saw him, he has certainly changed a lot – either that or my memory is seriously struggling.

"How are you? Has Tim roped you into helping?"

"Aye! Yes, I'm okay thanks. I owed Tim for helping me a while back, so here I am!"

"Sorry, I did hear about your greenhouse hiccup! Is that all okay now?"

"Hiccup? That's a polite word for it, it was a bloody nightmare, but yes, we're producing again, so it's all right." He rolls his eyes. "Though we have more issues from above than before, good job the new Director is too high and mighty to bother with me much! Pfft, she's a pain in the arse – you know she wouldn't let Tim replant from the Central nurseries? Ridiculous woman, she's probably never planted a seed in her life!"

"My mother can be a pain, I'm sorry," says Max seriously.

Bruce flushes red. "What? Oh, you've got to be kidding me! – I'm sor—"

"Really, there's no need to apologise." Max is laughing heartily – certainly enough to calm Bruce, who looked tangibly nervous for a moment. I am pretty sure this scenario has replayed multiple times as Max seems used to it…actually, I think he enjoys it.

I introduce Max and Bruce calls over a young man – probably a little younger than me, with mousey brown hair and deep green eyes that almost match the chequered pattern on his shirt. He introduces him as Jay, his neighbour's nephew. I am suddenly doubting my memory recall as I recognise Jay too, only he isn't talking as though we know each other, but I *have* seen him before.

"Hi Jay, do you work in the greenhouses too?"

"No, not quite, I am an apprentice farmer in the SH3 Vertical Farms. My plants don't ever see the light of day. It is nice to see real soil and not wear white for a while."

"Ha-ha, yes I bet. I wear white at work too – in the lab I mean."

Jay chuckles politely, but doesn't reply. I let the men chatter; it is bugging me, but I can't place this guy. Sense would say 'just ask,' but he doesn't seem to know me, and I don't want to embarrass myself by coming out with the cliché 'do I know you from somewhere?' line…hmm, I may have to before the day is out though as it is really annoying me.

Kate and Tim join us after a while and Jay steps away to continue working. He seems shy, but also tired. Maybe it is because he spends too long under artificial lighting, but he looks pale – almost sickly. I make myself wait until he is out of ear shot, then whisper to Kate:

"Should I recognise Jay? – I feel I should?"

"No, I don't think so, I hadn't met him before today. Bruce mentioned he has had a rough ride recently and said he told Jay's uncle he'd look out for him and try to keep him busy."

"That's nice of him. Does he live in SH2?"

"No, SH3, he just moved near Bruce."

"Ah, does he have a wife?"

"No, he lives alone. Bruce said he had trouble at the Matching Ceremony, so they gave him a year to focus on work and – well, *comply* I suppose."

"That's IT!" I said that a little loud, so I check myself; but the penny dropped as Kate spoke and I got a little too excited. She is staring at me, half smiling, half surprised, waiting for me to explain myself. "I *have* seen him before, but don't *know* him – phew! I thought I was losing it. He was at my Matching Ceremony and he and his girlfriend, Lilith, caused a scene and were separated – remember, Lucy was talking about it a while back?"

Kate pauses, gazing sadly over to Jay. "That would explain the cause of his depression. Bruce says he is constantly tracked by an armed drone and his watch is monitored 24/7. I'm not sure what they think he is going to do, but in all honesty, I don't see how that level of surveillance is going to help his mental health." A tear rolls down Kate's cheek, but I don't think the tear is just for Jay.

"I'm so sorry Kate, I had hoped to give you happier news—"

"It is okay, I am just thankful you asked. I knew it was unlikely, but I had to hope." I give her a long, speechless, heartfelt hug. It isn't going to solve anything, but loss should be shared and despite my own fears of being a mother, I do feel Kate's loss keenly. As we step back, she smiles, or rather attempts to. "Besides, I can still hope to win the lottery!"

I nod at her, telling her "Absolutely." To base all her hopes on that seems cruel, but I am not so unkind to point that out. Let her have some hope.

Max reminds me that we need to head home soon, otherwise we risk both our mothers' wrath. He has persuaded me I should appease my mother and go home to collect her and Dad, so after saying our farewells, we head for the tram and then to our separate homes.

As I get home, Peter Lloyd is leaving. My skin crawls just looking at him and when he sees me approaching, he gives me such a creepy grin, I don't know what to do with myself.

"Ah! Maia, I hope your ears have been burning?"

"Pardon?"

"There is no use playing the innocent young lady. This is second time in few weeks your father has had to personally block me detaining you."

"What for?"

"What for?! What for?!" he spits. "Where have you just been? – *again!*"

"To SH2…oh, you have got to be joking!? It is not a crime to visit a friend!"

"Not a crime?! I'll tell you what is a crime and not! Good heavens, you think a lot of yourself telling me – *me, the Head of Security!* what a crime is!"

"But it actually isn't."

He looks blankly at me, then furrows his brows and grits his teeth. "Remember your position, little girl. Daddy won't always save you and you'll be on the wrong, unnecessary field trip, on the wrong day and then you'll wish you'd stayed at home." He nods as he finishes.

I really, I mean, *really*, shouldn't answer him back, but I hate his tone and refuse to be dictated to by this greasy slime ball. "The day you find me on an *actually* prohibited journey, fine, give me your lecture. Until such time, please read up on your job and the laws of the UNE; maybe then you might save an unnecessary journey in your Solarbug and we might both have a better day."

To say he has gone red is putting it mildly. He puffs out his cheeks and turns back to my front door. I am not sure he didn't stamp his foot as he turned (not unlike my spoilt nieces and nephews when having a tantrum) and he is audibly blowing out air as he waves his barcode on the door scanner. Dad answers the door, looking a tad confused to hear Peter's name announced again and quizzically glances over Peter's shoulder at me before speaking.

"Peter? Everything all right?"

"Ha! I wish it were. Your daughter is treading on dangerous ground! She had the cheek to tell me I don't know my own job and I should mind my own business!" Dad seems a little shocked, but doesn't reply. "Well? Are you going to say something? Surely, she needs a lesson in humility if nothing else?! I would like to think in your position you'd want—"

"Peter," Dad says sternly raising an eyebrow. "She has a point. Getting on a tram to visit a friend is *not* a crime. Not necessarily encouraged, but when there is good reason, it is certainly not a crime. *I* and *I* alone will reprimand my daughter, so remember who is the boss of who, get off my front porch and do some actual bloody work! Maia, come in." He gesticulates for me to come in, so I skip past Peter; he even smells slimy – horrible wretch of a person. Once in, Dad shuts the door and shakes his head. "For heaven's sake!"

"Sorry Dad, I know I shouldn't have spoken like that to him."

"Hmm, no, but it won't do him any harm. I've caught him tailing all of our family more than required recently – *you* especially. Have you noticed more drones following you?" I shake my head. "Hmm, well they are. I know you don't go off-piste much, but mind out, I don't need that idiot knocking on my door."

Mum trots into the hall. She is on full steam attack, though apparently, she is ignorant of the nature of Peter Lloyd's visit. My time keeping, cleanliness, and dress code are continuously questioned, and it is taking all my energy to not reply to her. In order to hold my tongue, I shoot upstairs and prepare myself in such a manner to at least outwardly look like I am bending to her whim.

I was hoping Mum's attacks would lessen once at the Rivers'; however, she apparently feels at ease enough with my future in-laws to continue her particular style of education, only moderately curbing what I'd describe as her in 'full swing.' Max innocently tells Henry we visited Kate and Tim; the moment Mum hears this she launches into reprimand mode, with the newly added twist of apologising to Henry and Mary for my thoughtless behaviour whilst reassuring them I have been brought up to know better. She may as well have me sign a disclaimer stating my behaviour is not a reflection on her mothering abilities, because of course, *her* mothering skills are what everyone is judging. I look to Dad, hoping for assistance, but he seems happily oblivious, so it would seem he only plans on rescuing me once today.

"Well," says Mary, "I think it right you told them in person. I am sure they are very disappointed, but the Genetics Committee will have had their reasons for denying you." This on the surface sounds empathetic, but I am pretty certain she is one of the reasons I was denied, even if I cannot prove it.

"I'm sorry, am I missing something here?" asks Mum. "What has been denied?"

"Oh, dear, I do apologise, I thought you knew—"

"What?" Mum is noticeably getting agitated and turns to me for clarification.

"I applied for Kate to receive one of my eggs, but the Committee said no—"

"Well, I am jolly glad they did! Good grief! What were you thinking?!"

"Of my friend."

If Mum could spit fire, she would right now. Her glare is unmistakeable, but to her credit, she doesn't answer. This is one argument she doesn't want to share with the in-laws, but I have no doubt she will with me later. Henry, looking a little nervous, attempts to engage in conversation about the wedding plans. It is clear he has no interest, but I have to commend him for trying to change the subject and to my surprise, Dad chips in. Feeling Mum's stare, I join the wedding chatter, hoping it will dilute the tension. I stand by my decisions, I just really have not got the energy to defend them to her – donating an egg to a friend is something she would never consider and watching someone she regards as a second-class citizen have a baby at my hands is clearly not a noble gesture in her eyes. I can hear her verbal assault in her stare and all I can really think about now is how quickly this meal can be over – so much so, I don't notice the twist in conversation at first.

"So, you'll have your interview straight after the ceremony," says Dad, "a few quick photographs for the press – Claire has some bullet points prepared for you both—"

"Pardon?"

"Which part didn't you understand?"

"Sorry, I think I must have daydreamed…" Again.

"Maia, you really need to pay attention," says Dad, softly sighing. "No, don't apologise, just listen. I know you are not keen on the press, but you should be used to it by now. I do it all the time, it isn't difficult; just remember the pointers Claire will give you – you are honoured to be joining our two families together, for the good of the family, but also the UNE as a whole—"

"I have to do a speech at my wedding?"

"Will you listen to your father?!" Great, Mum is ready to break her silence. Her mouth is open, ready to carry on, but I am saved by Dad clasping her hand and giving it a squeeze. I doubt that is out of affection, just the politician within knowing how to stop a potentially embarrassing outcry. He then patiently informs me that yes, Max and I are indeed expected to give a live interview at our wedding to the UNE News, confirming our joy at uniting Midland and Southern Hubs, leading and encouraging others to follow in our compliant footsteps – ideally gushing at the wonder of our perfect, scientific match that all should trust in – and to put the cherry on top, tell the world how excited I am to soon be a mother. Basically, I am to be the promoter that I have spent years scoffing at.

"It will do well for the world to see our families united. Our names are individually known as Governors and Directors – but openly reminding of our joining can only be to our advantage – I know I for one am keen to see the Rivers' dynasty grow, as I am sure you are Woods, Stephen." I will give Mary her dues. She is unashamedly proud. Okay, she is shrouded in secrecy on one side, but the side she shows she shines without fear of rebuke.

Dad meets her gaze and smiles, "Indeed, I have every intention of promoting my family members – and not just my son."

"Excellent, I am thrilled we are on the same page. Director Beaufort's choices had concerned me and I wondered if you had the same lack of ambition—"

"Lack of ambition?! She founded The Fertility Project!"

"MAIA!" squawks Mum.

"No, no, Beatrix, she is defending her Great Grandmother, I respect that. She is right to take pride, Georgia has given her life as an example of excellence – all but in one direction. No, Maia, let me finish, for she has failed in securing an heir to her works – either by blood or apprentice. She has clear favourites in her team, but no one she has prepared to hand the reins to, which at her age, with retirement (or more), knocking on her door, is frankly reckless. I do not plan to make that same error. Happily despite or thanks to Colin Evans' stupidity, I now have your Great Gramps' reins and I plan to keep them safe. Hopefully, you, Maia will soon have children, now obviously we want fertile grandchildren, but whether male or female, we will ensure that Rivers and Woods flourish."

My parents are beaming. Mary's speech has cemented their hopes. Neither remotely glance in my direction to see if any of it appeals to me or whether I am as power hungry as they are. They are pleased, so what else matters? Mum has started babbling, expressing her delight. I look at Max: he is smiling, but I can see it is a painted smile, not a real one. He is my comfort in this. At least he doesn't share their power-hungry desires. Henry is sat still, listening to everyone. I cannot fully read him yet as although his sad expression doesn't last long, he does not seem quite as filled with the same positive energy that has empowered my parents.

How can Mum be so unfeeling towards her own grandmother? She didn't blink when Mary alluded to Gee-Gee's retirement (or possible death for that matter). Sure, at 89, retirement would be the norm, but Gee-Gee has never been mainstream, and has dedicated everything to The Fertility Project. I'll be the first to admit I have dreamt of being the one to receive 'the reins' as Mary puts it. I long to be included in her research, have all resources and no limits other than my ethics or imagination to line of enquiry. But to sit around a dinner table, declaring her life work is flawed seems...well, ungrateful and disloyal if nothing else. Gee-Gee must have her reasons (and probably a plan – hopefully anyway), but I am sure Great Gramps' death further highlighted that issue. If she suspects that Mary is undermining her, if only in word, then it is no wonder she distrusts her. I feel disloyal and ill even thinking this way, let alone listening to the power prattle that is currently unfolding in front of me. If they could order my eggs to develop in an exact order, gender, and intellectual preference, they would.

"Of course, a son would be great to start things off – taking the pressure of fertile or not away a little."

"To be sure, though, I would not doubt fertility – Maia has strong genes from me!" declares Mum proudly to Mary.

"Oh, yes, yes, but it is easier if the first is a boy. I'd love to have—"

"Okay! Let's take it one step at a time, shall we? Don't we have a dessert here somewhere?" Max can thankfully take no more either. I so wish we were being transferred to another Hub. I know that is a fruitless wish, but I cannot help hoping for it anyway.

"Ah, yes," says Mary, "I'll just get it – no don't help me clear the table – Maia will help me to the kitchen, won't you, dear?"

"Of course." Yes, because that wasn't a question. I get up nonetheless, collecting plates as I do.

"Good girl, you're as good as my daughter now anyway, so it is only right you want to help me." The only pleasure (if that is the right word), from this sentence is it actually made my mother smart a little. Her widened eyes show her surprise and displeasure in an instant; in her mind, despite my vexations, I am hers to boast of and control. I am not sure if Mary noticed her wince, but if she did, she doesn't care. She is claiming me as hers to command and it is sending chills down my neck and back. I follow her into the kitchen and look around as the door slides shut. It is immediately clear she does not need my help as everything is laid out with military precision and the chills spread to my fingers and toes. As I put the plates down next to the sink, Mary turns to me sighing:

"Thank you, yes that is right, the washer is below, I will do the rest, I have a certain – *perfect* – way of loading it that I'll have to teach you. It is the most economical and generally efficient method – here, watch…"

Her 'perfect' method is pretty standard, but I won't be the one to tell her. Mary prepares the dessert, and I am about to pick up the plates when she catches my wrist.

"Maia, I think it commendable, if not a little misguided, that you wanted to help your friend become a mother. It shows a very giving spirit. I wish I had that kind of friendship when I was your age; having to fight for everything is tiring – necessary of course, but tiring, nonetheless. You are so very lucky to be matched with Max and Henry seems keen on championing your ideas – what good that'll do, I don't know, but—" She pauses. I am dying to ask what her fight entailed and how she managed so much. Dare I ask? The voice within is screaming *'ASK! – Even if you have to flatter her a little. ASK!'* I swallow the lump in my throat (and my pride), looking for the meekest, most unconfrontational, humble tone I can muster, but before I can speak Mary finds her words and there is nothing meek about them: "But take care not to push boundaries you do not understand or that will jeopardise more than yourself. My sacrifices have laid a strong foundation – for UNE and family. Know your part."

I would hope my sense would prevail hearing this and I would remember the numerous warnings I have received regarding this woman – and more importantly, heed them. However, rather than finding my meekest tone, I feel my insides bubbling. I cannot cope with yet another person telling me to 'know my part,' 'do my duty' or 'remember my place.' I am doing my best to hold my tongue, but Mary is standing in front of me, silently demanding an answer with her stone expression.

"I know my role." That is not a lie. I know it, I just don't fully agree to it.

My tone matched hers, which is risky, yet she nods with acknowledgment, only verbally adding: "Good. Be sure you do."

I should leave it there, but the bubbling within has apparently taken hold so without further thought I blurt out: "How did you do it? Be a mother *and* become Director?"

Mary narrows her eyes and holds my stare. I hold my position, but hardly dare breathe. I must have lost my mind. I am beginning to wonder if I am going to pass out before she answers, so startle when her stone expression turns to a cold grin.

"You've heard the expression about when life gives you lemons?"

"You make lemonade?"

"Indeed, well, I added some cream and made souffle instead. It cost more, but the reward was infinitely sweeter."

With that, she picks up half of the plates, pirouettes and exits the room. I follow her with the remaining plates, only now looking at the contents. I am carrying lemon souffle.

THIRTY-FIVE

I have kept to myself for the bulk of the last couple of weeks, deciding that I have a better chance of productive study alone. I actually think the longest conversation I have had today is with the delivery drone who brought me lunch. Part of the lead up to my donation is eating what the PTB say, when they say. Three times a day, a cute little drone appears, calling my name, waiting for me to scan my barcode and unleash the meal within. I don't think I eat particularly unhealthily; however, when the Genetics Committee teamed up with the Dietician Committee, there ended any choice of sustenance for soon-to-be-donors.

My watch also now chimes at the end of each day, directing me to the gym, which really takes the fun out of it when it feels forced. However, as the blasted watch only gives me peace once completed, the satisfaction of *fun* is replaced by the joy of *silence*. Max has been joining me in the gym, but I think that is more out of loyalty than enjoyment as I am certain I am lousy company. The accompanying injections readying me for harvest have made me grumpier than ever before and even Kate told me I was a tad short the other day – 'a tad' being her polite way of calling me outright hellish. I apologised, and of course, Kate being Kate, she just laughed it off, but since then I have kept away. I can neither think straight nor behave appropriately, so solitary confinement is best for all.

I wish I had made headway during my time of intensive study. Dr Brown's team seems to have no tangible answer to how fertility suddenly improved for the two ladies in SH2. All other residents were retested and no one else had their grade changed. I have looked over more samples than I care to count searching for a sign or pattern in disease, genetic code or geographical location, and Theo's 'Nature V Nurture' theory for method of embryo development has come up lacking substance. Obviously, studies go on, but every time we think there could be a new avenue, we find another dead end. The thrill of the chase isn't as thrilling as I'd like it to be this week. All I can think of today is I have one day until donation, and I cannot wait for it to be over.

Ella suddenly pops her head around the door, the flash of her brilliant red hair catching the corner of my eye before she speaks.

"Ah! Maia, there you are! Theo said you were working on things together, but didn't know where you were!"

"Hi, err, yes, remotely consulting occasionally – the joy of technology, which you clearly understand!"

"Indeed, yes, it just makes me chuckle when you are in neighbouring rooms."

"Sometimes I think clearer alone."

Her smile drops. I didn't mean to offend her, but clearly she thinks I meant that as a hint for her to go away. She is about to leave so I attempt to correct myself. I think I succeed in my apology, but I really am fed up of explaining my hormones: "I don't mean you! I'm sorry, ignore me, I don't seem to say anything right at the moment – Dr Oldman tells me I shouldn't be affected, but..." I shrug.

"Oh, don't worry, my sister was *sooooo* grumpy when she was pregnant. Hormones do weird things."

I'm not sure that is totally comforting, but fine, I'll move on: "So, how are you?"

"Well, thank you."

"All settled in your role – *well, roles?*"

"Yes, though I don't think I'll make any friends in the second though," Ella says wistfully.

"Oh?"

"Director Rivers is still making herself – and me by proxy as her data analyst – highly unpopular. I am glad I don't live in SH3 right now; they hate the sight of me, I'm sure."

"Why?"

"She has me raking through data for every conceivable plant there this week. The looks we got at our meeting yesterday was enough to turn me to stone!"

Ella clearly just wants to be liked. Every time I have seen her she is trying to convince me or someone else to befriend her. I can't say I blame her, but I don't see how she can be surprised by her boss's attitude – or other's attitude to her boss. "Oh dear, but you've known Director Rivers longer than I have, so you know she gets the job done regardless of popularity."

Ella appears to be a little stunned and suddenly I realise it is quite possible that she repeats everything she hears to Mary. She has a sweet, innocent air to her, the kind that makes you less cautious when talking. Careful Maia, careful.

I am struggling to come up with something more definitively supportive, not potentially criticising, when Ella answers: "True, she is a determined woman. I just wish people wouldn't assume – you know – I'm not her drone."

I smile and nod. How can I not understand wanting to be seen for yourself? Before I can answer, my watch starts its daily song, instructing me it is time to march to the gym. If Ella had an actual purpose to her visit, I missed it, as once she realises what the music is for, she wishes me joy and says she will catch me later. I shut down my system, scan out, lock the lab, and robotically make my way to the gym.

Before I know it, I am jogging down a strangely familiar mossy track, listening to the gentle breeze of a wind I'll never really feel, mixed with the song of birds I'll never see. Normally the virtual programmes fill me with awe at the technical wizardry, but today I just feel sad – so sad, tears fall down my cheeks.

"Maia? Are you crying?" I was so lost in thought; I didn't hear Max enter. I wipe away the tears, force a smile and blame hormones. He screws up his face, puffing out a long, audible breath.

"So, woods today?"

"Mmm, I normally like it here."

"But not today?"

"No, I do, but…" I stop, but Max silently gestures for me to continue. "Don't you wish you could *really* see it – if it exists at all? Doesn't that depress you? That maybe this beauty is lost and the drones don't take new videos because it is all dead?"

"I don't think it is *all* dead, but – wow, aren't you a ray of sunshine?!" Max is trying to make me laugh at myself. Maybe this is the way to snap out of my current 'woe-is-me' feeling. I do need to cheer up.

"Do you think the PTB deliberately make me grumpy, so I am actually thankful come donation day?"

"Well, that's one theory – you could try looking forward to our wedding instead though?!"

I am. Though honestly, I am looking forward to the day *after*. The day I no longer wake up fearing an ear bashing from my mother. She has been on top form since the dinner at the Rivers', moaning at me for not confiding in her or seeking guidance; for letting her be told by the Rivers – and of course informing me what a singly stupid idea she thinks it was to consider donating to Kate at all. All this is thrown at me whilst she repeatedly goes through the programme for the wedding day, which sounds more and more like a PR stunt, not a wedding. I tried softening her blows by sharing how I am feeling now pre-donation, thinking she must remember what it was like; however, all I received was another lecture on the honour of fertility and how proud I should be. On Friday, Abby saved me from further admonishment by going into labour midway through Mum's speech – never have I been so glad to order a Solarbug and wave them off! Mum then preceded to spend the weekend crowing about how clever Abby was delivering a baby in an hour with such little fuss and declaring: 'She is such a wonderful mother. She'll be ready to have more soon, I have no doubt!' Even Dad told her to focus on their latest granddaughter before ordering another, but I don't think she even heard him.

"Are you listening? I'll take your blank expression as a 'no,' shall I?" Max rolls his eyes at me as I grimace as way of an apology. "Yeah, yeah, I was asking if you want me to come to the clinic tomorrow?"

"Erm, no, it's okay, they won't let you in anyway…how about chocolate mousse to console afterwards?"

"Done."

THIRTY-SIX

Despite having been counting down the hours until this is over, my legs feel like stone pillars as I drag myself into the clinic. The outside of the building, like every other in the Hub, is beautifully adorned with carbon-absorbing flowers and trees, but the second I enter, the whitewashed walls echo the sound of jazz and every nauseated sensation hits me at once. I would turn around and run, but the security system has announced my name and the receptionist has appeared from out back, armed and ready to detain me with her bubbly banter.

"Maia! Welcome back! You look lovely dear, come, come, do sit down, you know the drill by now! Everyone is getting ready for you, let me just take some readings..." There is no option as she ushers me to a chair, simultaneously grabbing my arm to scan her system over my watch, sucking up whatever data on me they feel appropriate. "Excellent! It seems you have been doing well recently! Ready for your wedding no doubt!" She winks at me with the most ridiculous grin. "Hey! I've seen your man; I'd go to the gym for him too!" She walks away chuckling to herself. "Two minutes!" she calls as she walks out of sight.

I am considering darting out the door again – my heart is racing, and I really might be sick. I am sure that stupid trumpet is playing out my demise. I have never enjoyed being here, but every trip seems to produce a stronger reaction as the physical and emotional violation seems greater every time. My leg is twitching again; it hasn't done that since the Matching Ceremony and although that turned out far better than expected, I think it a little much to hope my dream will come true here and they won't harvest me again after all. Henry has avoided any conversation alluding to what I overheard weeks ago – in fact he has proved very artful at ensuring that we are never alone in a secure enough location to discuss it. I am sure he and Mary implied that Abby had been tested and harvested since she was married, and that realisation has ruined any peace of today being 'the last time' at all. Abby and I are not close, she is as unlikely to confide in me as I am her; however, I am surprised that news of her harvest hasn't reached me – unless she doesn't know? Is that even possible? A voice within asks if her 'fertility issues' in-between pregnancies were in fact just excuses to harvest again. The fear of eternal probing is resulting in a cold sweat. If someone does not come quickly, *I am* going to run.

A figure suddenly appears. "Ms Woods, it is lovely to meet you, I am Dr Ling, I will be in charge of your donation today. Do come with me!"

Without conscious effort, I get up and follow. I have never seen this woman before, she is middle aged, short, with dark hair scraped back into a very tight bun. The surprise of an unfamiliar face has had the happy effect of distracting me from shaking, but I feel no less overwhelmed.

"I'm sorry, who are you? – I mean, has Dr Oldman left?"

Dr Ling turns around, chuckling. "I hope I am an acceptable alternative, my dear. Dr Oldman has moved onto a new project for the PTB. I am the new Head of Genetic

Correlation. Now, change into the gown and lie down if you will. Toni will get you set up." She points to a nurse who is bustling around in the corner who, when referred to, waves to me and rolls a trolley towards my bed.

And so, the prep begins.

I am totally thrown by the change of faces. I don't know if it is a good thing or not. Why would Dr Oldman leave? He has always been so proud to be in charge here. Surely it must be a new move? His music is still playing and his certificates are still on the wall. Toni has been joined by a younger nurse who introduces herself as Amy. She is petite and cutesy, with a calm, but welcoming voice and enormous smile. I think she looks like someone cut her out of an advert for the ideal nurse.

Since Amy's arrival, the three women have been largely ignoring me, making me feel even more like a piece of meat awaiting carving. Like the irrelevant lump I am, I lay here, awaiting my fate.

"Okay, Ms Woods, we're all set, if you could count backwards from ten for me." Toni injects me as she speaks, I comply. I suppose they assume they don't need to explain proceedings to an old pro like myself.

"Ten, nine, eight, seven, six, fiivvee, ff…"

"Lovely, okay, let's see how many eggs we get today!"

"I was so excited when I saw 'Woods' on our schedule sheet, I was so sure Oldman wouldn't let us have this one!"

"Hmm, well he didn't have much choice, if he wanted to keep charge of The Initiative, he had to let go of here – about time too; he can't have it all. I've paid my dues as his back up long enough – my research is just as good, and we deserve to harvest the best, even if we can't keep them all."

"Have you seen her results? No wonder they have left her unmarried so long. The Professor must be so proud to have her genes form such an important part of the future."

"Absolutely, and every egg counts. Ha! She wanted to donate one to a friend, did you hear?"

"Seriously? Well, that was never going to happen, surely?"

"Don't be daft, of course not! You think the Professor would allow that kind of waste? Golden Chicks don't go to barren nobodies."

"No, but her mother-in-law managed it somehow."

"Sshh, walls can have ears, even here, and that's a web you don't want to get caught in!"

"Hey, is she blinking? Maia? – Crap, is she awake?!"

"No, no, look, here, I'll just top her up though…."

THIRTY-SEVEN

As I slide into consciousness, the confusion of location is replaced by the groan of remembrance. I know where I am, I just want to be gone. They tell me they can work better with me fully unconscious and maybe it is less stressful, but the foggy headache afterwards is unpleasant, as is the notable feeling of being interfered with 'down there.' Sure, I have been spared Dr Oldman's cold and bony touch, but it doesn't really improve matters.

"Ah, good afternoon Ms Woods!"

"Afternoon? How long was I out?!"

"Oh, don't worry, it is only just afternoon. You had an excellent harvest – congratulations!"

Amy looks so pleased, but I cannot share her enthusiasm and I am confused as to why I have been out so long. I remember going in at my normal time – then as Amy continues chattering, I remember her voice as I was going to sleep...

"Are you okay?"

"Hmm?"

"Your eyes just widened as though you felt pain?"

"No, no."

"Okay, let me look..." She pokes and prods, checking monitors. Thankfully, the monitor that is my mind is still my place of solace, for I have just remembered the conversation

I heard as I drifted off – when I think I was supposed to be out for the count. Dr Oldman is in charge of 'The Initiative' – what is that? Some new element of embryo research I'd wager. Yet another use of my eggs that I probably disagree with.

I am fed, rechecked again and an hour later Amy tells me I can go home. I am relieved they have ordered a Solarbug for me, I don't really want to walk through the Hub at the moment, so I will get it to drop me off somewhere quiet. Aunt Dora might be grateful of me sitting with Eve again; they were both so tired at the weekend and poor Eve has been more vague than lucid on my recent visits, so any hope of answers there seems as frail as the lady herself.

Despite being officially released, Amy is still chattering. I am not sure if she has a point or if she just likes talking for the sake of it. She has not said anything particularly interesting although several remarks have been aimed towards my research at the lab – which of course, I cannot go into as unlike her talking over semi-conscious patients, I have no desire to potentially incriminate myself.

Dr Ling obviously thinks I should have left as she looks surprised to see me as she enters the room and begins to address Amy. Hearing her voice, my brain triggers again with the phrase 'Golden Chicks don't go to barren nobodies.' I feel sick with anger for my friend as I think of the pain it would cause her to hear such a sentence, but my growing rage also has a wider scale. Why do we still rate people on fertility alone? Surely these women should have more compassion, or do they not include themselves? Have they somehow risen above social categorisation by being the harvesters? And then, why does it matter who gets the eggs or resulting child? How does that affect the outcome?

Challenging these women will not get me anywhere, I know that. They will trust me as little as I trust them and that will only leave me open to further PTB scrutiny which never ends well – especially if they think I am challenging their decisions or rules. I cannot shake the knowledge of Eve's other 'they.' Are *they* also constantly watching? And if so, to what end? The whole point of the UNE is unity – one consolidated nation – so what are they doing that requires a covert existence?

These are thoughts for when I am out of here. Having dressed and tied my hair back, I make my way to the door. I will possibly blame it on the drugs for a moment's lack of control, but as I step out, I turn to the women and say quietly: "Take care of my Golden Chicks."

Both women stare at me, mouths slightly open. I have to stop myself from grinning. I hate the whole scenario, and I certainly am not amused by what I overheard, but there is no getting away from the slightly perverse joy at seeing someone else sweat when caught out. Dr Ling is about to say something, but I calmly wave a hand and walk to the waiting room where a girl is sat cross legged in her chair by the door. I smile to her and she beams with apparent pride. Looking at her, I think this girl will make the PTB proud; she remembers her position and duty with ease. My mum would probably adopt her over me in a heartbeat. Scanning the front door, I turn briefly to see I was followed so I tilt my head slightly, eyes cold towards Dr Ling, and step out into the autumnal sunshine.

A Solarbug is parked outside with my name flashing on the side of it. I scan my barcode on its sensor and sit down. Those few steps were actually enough as my stomach is starting to cramp so sitting down is very welcome; the preprogrammed destination of 'home' however, is not. Hiding in my bedroom has proved ineffective and I really cannot be bothered to listen to family banter. This morning Grandma suggested I should babysit Abby's twins 'as practice' while she settles with her newborn. Mum looked delighted, Dad indifferent, and Gee-Gee, as seems to be the norm of late, was absent. I worry about her, but I am also so confused by her – now more than ever. Certainly today hasn't helped as I now have the added pain of believing she, not Mary, stopped my application for Kate. Maybe I shouldn't be surprised. The Fertility Director is going to direct with the bigger picture in mind, isn't she? – whatever that picture might be. Well, I am going to direct my Solarbug out of here and to the relative wilds of the edge of SH1.

THIRTY-EIGHT

As I step off the Solarbug, rather than the quiet sound of the river in the near distance, I hear radio chatter. Following the sound, I realise there is a heavy security presence and guards are checking in and directing each other almost continuously. Drones are flying in a steady formation across the sky and the air is anything but peaceful. Detecting my arrival, a drone approaches me, demanding my left arm. I comply and its red warning light switches to green before resuming its path. Whatever they want, it isn't me; but as they are all on amber alert: something or someone is in trouble.

I am in two minds whether to go on with my mission of sitting by the river; it hardly seems calming now. Even the farmers across the water seem on edge and as I watch them, I realise it is no wonder as they have armed security personnel amongst them.

"Maia?"

"Yes?" I was so engrossed watching across the water, I did not hear anyone approaching me. I turn as I reply to see Ella and Theo. I cannot hide my surprise. "Hey?! What brings you both here?"

"I've been called in to help locate an anomaly," replies Ella smiling.

"What kind of anomaly?"

"That's what I want to find out!"

"Huh?" I feel my nose wrinkle as confusion flashes across my face. Ella doesn't seem forthcoming with information; I am not sure if she is hoping I will ask more, or if it is indeed wise to ask more. They both look fidgety. "Did you both happen to be here? Or…?"

"Oh, I've been discussing with Mr Lloyd about using my skills to help with security. I have been building a new—"

"Peter Lloyd?"

"Mmm-hmm, you know him?"

"My Dad is his boss."

"Of course, right," Ella says nodding.

"Don't you already have two jobs?"

"Yes, but IT support is just a first step; robotics is my passion, I've been tweaking gadgets since a toddler, I am hoping to get a full-time position with the security team. Not that I'm not grateful to your in-laws, you must know I am. I just think I can be more useful and hopefully expand tech—"

"It's fine, you don't have to justify yourself and besides, it is great you have ambitions." I wish I could openly have them. I speak to Ella, but can't help turning to look quizzically at Theo. Her answer might satisfy some of my curiosity, but why is *he* here? He clearly understands my expression as he quickly offers his own explanation, though it doesn't wholly convince me.

"It is actually chance we are here at all. We decided to have a day's walking holiday, so I brought Ella here to enjoy the scenery – which we did, *until* her bracelet went crazy."

"Bracelet?" I look down, Ella is indeed wearing a bracelet next to her watch. If she normally wears it, I have not noticed it before, but she definitely seems rather proud of it. On another day, before I met Eve, I hope I'd be forgiven for thinking it just standard jewellery, however recent experience, and the look on her face, makes it obvious there is more to it. Ella plays with silver band whilst sucking in her bottom lip, glancing at me, then back to the bracelet.

"I made it to enhance signals. In my previous home, in the Midlands SH3, sometimes the outer farms would struggle to connect up which made data analysis frustrating, so I started trialling boosters."

"That's clever."

"Thanks. When I pitched to the PTB, they loved it. I got a call from Peter Lloyd personally asking if it could be tweaked to pick up breaks in signal as they were finding weak spots. I said I'd look into it and—"

"And it can! Wow, that's *great*!" I need to mind my sarcasm, that sentence was thinly veiled with joy. Oh crap! – I need to get her away from Aunt Dora's house. If that thing picks up on Eve's bracelets…

"Yes, it turns out it was quite simple, I—"

"No, Ella, no, don't go there, that is a long and *not* simple explanation which I don't need to hear twice today." Theo is still laughing at her as he turns to me. "Trust me, that will turn your day off into night-time before you know it – very impressive I grant you, but unless you have developed an interest in robotics I don't know about, then I'll save you now."

"Sorry!" Ella is laughing at herself; she really does have a sweet chuckle. I feel bad for Theo cutting her off on my behalf; I have no real interest in understanding the mechanics of her bracelet, but I can see she enjoys talking about her work and can appreciate the joy of sharing one's interests. In fact, it is no wonder she wants to branch out from Mary's clasps; explanation, discussion, and embellishment does not exactly come high on that woman's priority list.

"Is your bracelet still indicating now?"

"Yes, see, it is linked to my watch, and boosts signals – there is something around here blocking signals. We were happily walking down the river when the alarm sounded. I called it in to Peter and he sent drones – and sure enough, their programmes glitch. I need to work on my tech more; I thought I had this ready to go, but we can't seem to pinpoint the origin – it seems to be moving – whatever *it* is!"

Moving? I was fearing it was Aunt Dora's house, but that doesn't move. I really need to sit down again as the cramps are increasing, but the sinking feeling about this anomaly is telling me to go and check on Eve first. I make my excuses and watch them carry on down the river; Ella tracking on her watch as they stroll.

The walk to Aunt Dora's is short, but it feels like miles. I get to the door, scan and hear my name called out, but no one answers. I scan again, still nothing; so rather than waiting for invitation, I scan requesting admittance, hoping Aunt Dora has left me as a trusted visitor on the system. The door slides open and I waste no time as I quickly step inside. Smoggy and Squash greet me enthusiastically, I bop to greet them both, asking where their mistresses are, calling out simultaneously. No answer. I check the living room, the studio, kitchen, bedrooms. No one is here.

Returning to the door, I open the drawer of the console table. Three bracelets. I close my eyes and swallow the ever-increasing lump in my throat. There should be four.

I open my watch and call Aunt Dora immediately. Obviously, the conversation will need to be carefully worded, the multitude of drones and security personnel outside will undoubtably be on high alert, picking up on every drop of fresh data, but I need to try and find answers.

Aunt Dora answers on the second ring: "Maia? Are you okay? I thought today is donation day?" Her voice sounds strained.

"Yes, that was earlier, I thought I would visit, but *no one* is home. Are you local? I would love to say hello in *person*."

"Oh, that would be wonderful, it has been *a long day*. Our place of solace? In ten minutes?"

"See you soon."

I go out the backdoor and down the little path in the direction of the river. I really don't want to bump into Ella and Theo again, so decide to take a diverted route to be safer. As I approach the last fork in the path before the river, I hear the familiar tones of Eve. I rush around the corner to see her sat on an old tree stump in a middle of a patch of rough meadow grass that is set to the side of a bridge leading across the river. She is chatting to herself; I am not sure what she is saying, but she seems animated.

"Good afternoon, Eve, how are you?"

"Ah, Missy, you have come to join us?"

"If I may?" She points to a spot next to her. I take my cue, sitting down on the grass. As I am seated, my body groans with relief, but my heart soon races in panic when my fears are confirmed – Eve has her bracelet on. It is nothing short of a miracle a drone hasn't found her already. I don't know what to do: do I grab the bracelet and throw it in the water? Or into long grass? Do I usher her home and hope no one catches up with us?

"You're not very chatty, Missy. We were having a better conversation before you arrived!"

"We?"

"Me, myself, and I. Don't look at me like that…I know I'm alone, physically anyway, don't mean I can't talk to 'hem who have gone."

"Quite right." I smile at her. I probably just pulled a less than understanding face, but I am at a loss to how is best to proceed. If I call Aunt Dora I could draw attention to this location. I whisper: "Eve, you have your bracelet on."

"So?"

"Do you remember what you told me about the bracelet?"

"I made it."

"Yes, but you also told me never to wear it outside the house."

"Hmmphh, I went for a walk."

"Yes, but you've got a lot of strays following you. Look up."

"Hmmphh, flying spies aye? Should have kept me gun. Lost all me toys – well *most* of them. Tom's fault, him and the boys wanted to break the revolution – darn stupid idea. You pick your side, and you sink with it."

"Maia, is that you again?! Ha, I told you it was her!"

Dammit! I turn, but I don't need to, to know who is talking to me. "Ha-ha!" I fake laugh, "Any luck with your mission, Ella?" I can feel myself sweating.

"No, but she's had us go over the bridge three times now!" Theo is smiling, but I think has genuinely had enough of following Ella's signal now. He nods towards Eve whilst raising his eyebrows at me.

"Oh, sorry, this is Mrs Addams, do you remember her, Theo? She is lives with my Aunt Dora now – Mrs Addams, this is Theo and Ella Locke; Ella is an IT expert and is helping the security services detect an anomaly."

"A pleasure to meet you. It is a lovely day for a stroll," Ella says cheerfully.

"Hmmphh." Eve raises her head looking Theo and Ella up and down. "Missy, why are you dancing with wolves? Hmmphh, you're not one of the family, your red hair doesn't fool me – you're no Fairfax." Poor Ella puts her hand up to her head, stroking her hair. She attempts to mutter 'of course not' but none of us are really sure how to respond to such an outburst and Eve hasn't finished: "I see the wolf! You don't hide as well as you think. I'm no lamb for slaughter! Wolf! Imposter! Missy, watch out for wolves, they ain't no friend to the lamb!"

I don't know what to say, but I need to get Eve out of here fast. I think the only thing stopping Ella from realising that her bracelet has located its target is the uncanny irony that the old lady who owns the anomaly is so shockingly abrupt and rude that she hasn't thought to check her screen.

"I'm so sorry Ella, Mrs Addams isn't well, I best take her home. Please forgive her – please, I—"

"No, not at all, my great grandma was… similar in, erm – *health.*"

"Mrs Addams, won't you let me take you for some tea?" I gently squeeze Eve's hand. "I am sure we could both do with a cup?"

"Hmmphh, don't rush me, Missy, I don't have your youth – though you seem pale and sticky – what is wrong with you? Do you have cooties?"

"You do look ill Maia," says Ella. "Is something wrong?" Thanks Eve.

"I'm fine, I had my donation today, that is all. So, a nice cup of tea from Aunt Dora's would go down well, *don't you think, Mrs Addams?*"

"Aye, all right Missy, come on, I'll take you home – but leave the wolf. Just you come. There's no family here."

Guiding Eve to her feet and away, I mouth 'sorry' again to Ella and Theo. They smile cautiously and wave me off, but

I notice they don't turn to walk away. Once we are out of sight, I take Eve gently by the arm, but swiftly remove the bracelet.

"Hey!"

"Sshh, Eve, that has got to go, you're going to get us both killed – look ahead." Just visible through the hedge in the street ahead is a group of armed guards. They haven't noticed us yet, but they are scanning a family who are walking by.

"Wait here."

I run backwards and go down the opposite fork of the path to which we just came, taking care not to be seen from the ground or above. I spot a little wilderness area, not unlike the one we had just been sat in, and throw the bracelet into the long grass, running straight back towards Eve the second I see it land. I am going to pay for all this running later. Dr Oldman's 'the cramps will be minor, if at all' speech comes back to me – what the hell does he know?!

To my relief, on my return, Eve is still standing where I left her, propping herself up on her stick.

"What did you do?" Eve demands as I approach.

"I got rid of the bracelet."

"Get it back. Pandora is the only safe place."

"Pardon?"

"If it is anywhere else, they'll find it. Get it back." She starts to walk away, grumbling as she goes. I feel sick, but do as I am told, asking her to wait for me, but this time I think I have less chance of being obeyed. Of course, completing my retrieval task is not as quick as my drop off and the sound of nearby drones is causing my heart to pump so fast I fear it's going to come through my chest.

Rummaging through the grass, my search seems to be taking an eternity – to the point that I am considering aborting my mission, when suddenly a glint of light catches my eye. I snatch it up and run back to the path. No sign of Eve; I can only hope she has returned home. My more immediate issue is how to avoid the drones *and* the guards in the street.

The drones seem to have set on a flight path in the neighbouring street for now, so I creep around the corner, praying the guards are gone, but instead I see there are three men standing with their backs to me, all fixated on a small figure in front of them. With little choice but to hope they don't turn around, I make a steady, but swift move towards Aunt Dora's which is now less than a hundred feet away. If I was hot and sticky before, I now feel like I have jumped into a vat of lard.

It isn't until I get to the door and have to pause for the security system to grant me access, I dare look back and suddenly realise the small, distracting figure in front of the guards is Eve. I dash inside, but leave the door ajar for a moment; just long enough to hear her reprimanding her audience: "Hmmphh, rude boys! You could be my great-great grandsons! Do you know how old I am? You should respect your elders, did no one teach you that? Huh? Huh?! Manners, what happened to them?! In my day I knew how to ask an old lady with respect!"

"I am sorry madam, as we said, we have to scan everyone that comes through here…"

"So you might, I ain't sayin' you can't, just don't mean you get to be rude about it! Do you want to hear a story about the rude boy and my mother? It'll take a while, but I'm in no rush…"

Eve may be old and increasingly frail, but she can still be crafty! I have to respect that about her!

I seriously hope Aunt Dora has painkillers on standby because boy do I need them now. I slump into a chair in the living room and the cushions feel like they are welcoming me home.

I never want to get up.

My momentary peace is broken as the security system chimes 'EVE ADDAMS' and I hear her slow steps and a shuffling stick immediately afterwards.

"Missy?! Have you got the kettle on?!"

Despite creaking and groaning, I cannot help smiling at her spirit. I get up and make us tea. Eve watches from her chair and once ready, I sit down across the table from her, shaking my head in disbelief – that was definitely more action than I anticipated today. Eve, however, is chuckling to herself.

"I'm glad you enjoyed that."

"Hmmphh, I'll show them who the real revolution is!"

"The what?"

Eve puffs her cheeks. "You best get Pandora though."

"Who? Oh crap, I better call Aunt Dora, I was supposed to meet her ages ago!"

THIRTY-NINE

"Oh, my word, I am relieved to see you Eve! Where on earth have you been?!" declares Aunt Dora, shutting the door in a hurry.

"'Ere and there. I needed air and the orchards looked inviting."

"You went over the bridge?!"

Eve makes no attempt to reply.

"Well, you seem to have stirred a hornet's nest out there. I was scanned by guards to get into my own home, and I think they are starting to do home scans."

"Inside?" I ask. "That can't be good?"

"No, I doubt it."

I fill Aunt Dora in. She was pale when she got home; however, with each sentence, she turns whiter. Eve sits silently as I speak, although I do notice her face twist and chuckle at various points of my tale. As I finish, she gazes solemnly at Dora:

"You'll have to give me bracelets to Pandora."

"Who? I thought you meant Aunt Dora when you said that earlier?"

"No, Pandora. *The box.*" Aunt Dora's eyes widen as Eve speaks.

"Do you know it?"

"Mmm, yes, I've been forbidden to open it – until now, apparently. It's in my room, the slightly odd-looking, carved wooden box under the bed – fetch it, will you, Maia?"

Without another word, I get up and go into Aunt Dora's bedroom. As expected by the PTB, it is minimalist and immaculate. If I had more time, I would study the paintings, but the imminent possibility of a security scan makes me hurry to the bed. Dropping to my knees, I look underneath. There is one suitcase for the rarest of occasions that you might stay overnight elsewhere and next to it, a box. I pull the box out, Aunt Dora wasn't kidding, it is odd. It is wooden with beautiful carvings on the sides. On top there is a figure curled up in the centre next to a handle, I lift it and carry it straight into the kitchen.

"Damn, it's heavier than it looks!"

"Yes, I know." Aunt Dora gestures towards the table, "Put it here."

I put it down as directed. Eve silently stands and approaches the box, lifting the previously sleeping figure into a standing position and gently flips a panel, revealing a mechanical keypad. Eve looks up at us both, raising an eyebrow whilst nodding downwards and lifts a finger to her lips. Once sure we understand, she presses and holds down number 5 on the pad. In an instant, the little figure starts to dance as music fills the room. The three of us stand mesmerised by the delicacy in which this box performs. Eve clearly knows the music is about to end, for she raises a hand, finger poised to type in on the keypad once more. 7-2-6-3-7. The music stops and the box opens. I couldn't even see the lid line clearly through the carvings before, but now the divide is obvious – as is the reason for the weight of the box. It may be insignificant in size, but the box is metallic inside and contains compartments; plus, hiding somewhere within lies the mechanisms for the music.

"Put the bracelets in Pandora. They won't be able to detect them in there," states Eve.

Neither of us question 'how'; it is clearly lined with multiple materials specifically to avoid interrogation, so Aunt Dora just complies, but before shutting the lid, she turns to Eve.

"What else is in there?"

"Reminders of my past. Look if you must; but be quick."

Fearing she will revoke permission, I immediately reach into the box, aiming for an envelope that is clipped into the underside of the lid. I gently pull it out and slide out a small bundle of photographs. Real ones – some of which are older than Eve. On the back of each is a date and names of those captured.

"Your mum and dad?" I ask.

"Yeah, when the Earth was a different place – when she was still crumbling under our weight."

"And this one? Your sons? Oh, I'm sorry, I didn't mean to—"

Eve gently takes the photo, running a finger across the image whilst a tear rolls down her tired cheek. She sighs, nodding her head as her whole chest heaves with the effort. "And that one – *there* – is my favourite with my family together – for the last time as it turned out. That memory will stay with me forever."

I look over the photograph. Eve, and a man who I assume is Tom, are stood in the middle, with eleven other people stood around them in front of building I do not recognise. Everyone is smiling, the sky is picturesquely blue, and there are flowers all over the building, just leaving the entrance and adorning sign visible: 'ADDAMS & SONS'

"Is that my Ray?" asks Aunt Dora.

"Ha, yes, he was still a teenager there, bless him. And his parents are here – Harriet my granddaughter with the beautiful red hair." I point to another girl who also has vibrant bright red hair. "No, not that one, that's my great granddaughter, Penny, the only one but me in that picture who's still alive – hmmphhing girl isn't interested in me now! Though her mother didn't help – she set the poison in her mind before she died." Eve groans, muttering to herself.

I look up at Aunt Dora; she shrugs. It is clear she has not seen this picture before either as she is studying it hard. "Eve, your hair isn't quite white here – you kept colour to a good age – or did you dye it?"

"Hmmphh! Cheeky wench! I kept my natural colour with pride as long as it would last. Not that the family would own me now. Forgotten and betrayed. Cause over kin. Hmmphh to them! I keep the faith!"

As Eve speaks, Aunt Dora turns to the final photograph: Eve's wedding. There she is stood outside a church – an actual stone church (something I have only seen photographed in the Architecture Museum) in a beautiful white dress, with bouquet and beaming smile, gazing up at Tom. He is dressed in a dark grey suit and is matching her smile with such love it brings a lump to my throat. This is the wedding day of dreams. Not a synthetic hope, a doing of one's duty or matching of theoretical probability and genetics. I feel guilty. I still count my blessings with Max, I am so lucky on that score, but I cannot help wishing we had met on different, free terms – had fallen in love and married in our time with excitement and unforced joy. Instead, it is a day I am counting down until it is over – and praying the days *after* leads to him looking at me like Tom did Eve all those years ago.

Between hopes for myself, I cannot take my eyes off the photographs as they lay across the tabletop. The scenery in the older pictures is as fascinating as the subjects themselves with places and times so long forgotten – and now totally alien to this generation. As I inspect the pictures, one common theme catches my eye. I am briefly distracted by Squash entering the room, his glorious ginger coat shining as it catches the light coming through the window. I stop to pet him and suddenly recall a conversation I had weeks ago with Kate. I had mocked her for pointing out the family only breeds ginger animals and that all red heads are related to Lady Fairfax – statistically that is a daft conclusion, but standing here, I am starting to see a link.

"Eve, who did you say gave you Squash?"

"My great nephew. Why?"

"Your brother's grandson?"

"What of it?" Eve is squinting at me while my brain is ticking.

"And he likes ginger cats? ...Because that's the family trademark colour? Looking at these photos of a younger you, you seem to share that—"

"Hmmphh, I ain't ashamed of me family roots – only the weak branches that they grew. I lost me faith in them and them in me, long ago."

"Yet you still carry your burden for them? Won't you share it now? *We* are your family and will not turn away from you." I speak as softly as possible. Eve's face is screwing up, fighting back tears and I don't want to push her into her shell again.

"I save them *and you* with my silence. I may have lost faith in some people, but not the cause."

"In whose cause? The PTB's or the other '*them*'?"

"Both – it's one cause. Each has their part…each person their place in the greater map."

"I don't understand."

"You do, you just want a bigger picture." She's not wrong. The whole scope of my entire life has been dictated. I am desperate for wider horizons. "Your motive I believe is admirable, but the reality would not be so pure."

"Hang on!" Aunt Dora exclaims looking at me, "Are you saying Eve is Lady Fairfax's—"

"Great Aunt – yes."

"Wilson Sandhurst is me brother," says Eve. "He was a good man, rest his soul, he did good work. His granddaughter is a sweet girl – or was, she's not young now – but she remembers the value of family! Though none will know me now. President General Fairfax can't be tainted by the past. Hmmphh, maybe I wouldn't have them either. Priorities I suppose; we all laid them down long ago."

We all stare into the box. Maybe we are all hoping answers will jump out and somehow make everything clear. I know I am. There are too many thoughts and questions rattling in my head to form a coherent response. Nothing ever seems to be fully answered. Is there such thing as an answer that doesn't lead to another question?

Aunt Dora reaches into the box; there is a small jewellery box with a ring and pearl necklace inside next to various gadgets: "What are these, Eve?"

"The past. Souvenirs from the past and mostly no use now. If that upstart has upgraded tech to detect anomalies, my bracelets are only useful for laying at the bottom of the box. I suppose someone was going to override my codes eventually, pity she didn't wait until I was gone to manage it though. Hmmphh. I'm too tired to battle in ones and zeros now."

She does look incredibly weary. That is not surprising given how long she has been out and about today, but I can't help thinking the tiredness runs deeper – beyond exercise or illness. Her expression actually reminds me of Gee-Gee. Gee-Gee is obviously younger and far less frail, but they both have the mark of a worn warrior. Years of service in their different fields, taking its toll on body and soul. Neither giving away the burden of their mission, though at least with Gee-Gee, her mission is known. She may have struggles with science and characters such as Mary Rivers, disappointments from the like of Colin Evans, and family woes from – well, all of us, but we know where she is coming from and her mission for man and Earth is clear. Eve is a mystery.

Most of the gadgets in the box are unremarkable to my untrained eye; however, I suddenly spot yet another hidden compartment and find myself pulling out a strange synthetic material that almost feels like skin.

"What the hell is this?"

Eve quietly snorts air out of her nose and nods her head. "It's useful if you wanna be someone else." I stare at her, raising an eyebrow, hoping she will continue, however, like so many other questions, she waits to be asked 'how?!' before she answers: "It's an artificially intelligent sleeve. Add the barcode of who you want to be – and off you go."

I can feel my eyes boggling with surprise. Maybe I shouldn't be amazed. I accept the technological capabilities of so much: physical games played with people thousands of miles away; information recorded and shared within milliseconds regardless of location; food delivered whenever, wherever; food produced by machines; babies reared in pods; operations performed by a robot – so, why is a synthetic, independently intelligent skin surprising?

It really does feel like skin. When I picked it up, it was an off-white colour, yet I now realise it has altered to match my own colour. I haven't even laid it on my arm, and it has already mimicked my tone. I am in awe of the technology, but also the potential.

"Eve, what did you design this for? I can't imagine the PTB would be too happy – the possible security breaches with barcodes not reading true are endless." I look up and straight at Eve, hoping she will finally fully answer one of my queries, but yet again, her face has frozen over. The intelligent, knowing (even if not sharing), glint in her eyes has been replaced by a blank trance. I exhale loudly, trying to expel frustration.

Aunt Dora places a hand on my shoulder, shaking her head. "Let her rest. It has been a long day." I lean in and hug her, but the announcement of the security system makes us both jump. To be fair, hearing: 'PETER LLOYD, SECURITY HEAD' is enough to make anyone shudder. "I'll get it, close the box, and put it away. Then lay on my bed, you look like you need it."

I rush into her room, put the box under the bed, kick off my shoes and lay down. I sink into the mattress and were it not for my racing heart, I would happily fall asleep. I suddenly remember Eve is sat in her chair – should I try and get her to bed? No, she should be comfortable enough for a while. I need to calm down; people are just outside the door in the hall and if anyone comes in here, I do not look like I am resting at all.

"Okay, Mrs Harrison, we just need to scan each room – can you get everybody in here so they can be scanned, too."

"What is this about? What has happened?"

"Don't worry madam, we are just responding to a possible security breach, we are just ensuring peace and order is maintained in the Hub."

I don't recognise the latter voice; he sounds younger and far less arrogant than Peter, who undoubtably spoke first.

"Can we get on with this please? I've a whole neighbourhood to get around."

I hear footsteps and a light knock as the door slides open. "Maia, sorry honey, can you just come to the kitchen, there's a security check…"

"Maia?" Peter grunts as I walk into the hallway, "Oh, for heaven's sake, what are you doing here? Are you going to tell me how to do my job again?! Hmm, why are you never where you're meant to be?"

"Good evening Mr Lloyd, I am in SH1 with my aunt." I speak coldly and tilt my head at the end of my sentence. I'll leave him to guess the sentence I *want* to say. Gauging the angry expression on his face, he understands. Ignorant fool of a man. Why is his Deputy never around these days? Mark Jones is so much better at the job and nowhere near as disagreeable.

"What's wrong with the old lady? I scanned her, but she didn't move – does she need a doctor?" The young guard steps out of the kitchen looking genuinely rattled by his motionless encounter with Eve. Peter doesn't wait for a response from us and strides straight into the kitchen. Aunt Dora and I follow behind, stepping into the room just in time to witness the insensitive idiot poke Eve's upper arm.

"Mrs Addams is a very old lady, sir, she sleeps heavily. She will be fine when she wakens." I am not sure if I have said the right thing, but Aunt Dora nods to Peter and he seems pleased

I have called him 'sir.' The word choked in my throat, but if it gets rid of him quicker, my pride will have to wait.

"Get on man, scan this house and maybe we'll be done by midnight," grumbles Peter.

The guard does as he is bid. Aunt Dora and I sit down. I am not sure if it is just part of the cramps from my donation or fear, but the cold sweat I had earlier has come back with a vengeance. I try wiping my hands on my legs under the table, but they still feel sticky afterwards. I hope that box is as tech-proof as Eve thinks it is. Peter Lloyd would love nothing better than finding me with signal blockers and finally getting an unmistakable reason to arrest me for being the rule-defying brat he thinks I am.

"Clear," says the guard returning to Peter's side.

"Hmm, okay then – hang on, have you scanned her?" he says pointing his chin at me.

"No, sorry, sir, I thought you had scanned them."

For a second, I think Peter is going to hit his guard, but he pauses and instead swings his arm in my direction, scanning me himself. The guard doesn't seem shocked, I suppose he is used to his brash behaviour, but I am not sure that forgives it.

"Huh? Who are you? There's no room for you here!" Despite the potentially serious situation, Eve's sudden revival makes me smile. Peter was not expecting speech from behind him, and he cannot hide his surprise. Eve notices. "What you jumpin' for? I ain't in your house pokin' about, am I? Can't a lady sleep in peace?"

"My apologies," Peter says momentarily too shocked to be rude. "We are just acting to ensure your safety."

"Hmmphh, doubtful. Well, I'm safe, thank ye, can I go back to sleep?"

My amusement is short lived; if 'unguarded Eve' is the one currently awakened, she could land us in more than a little hot water. Peter doesn't seem amused and definitely looks like he is weighing up how harshly to respond to her – I think her age is the only thing making him question whether he can be bothered. Aunt Dora clearly shares my fears though as she jumps up, talking to Eve before Peter can reply.

"Sorry Eve, why don't I take you to your room?" She turns to Peter sweetly, "That is okay, isn't it?"

"Yes, yes, we're off – good evening." Peter nods to his colleague, then sneers as he turns to me: "Maia, I trust you will continue behaving as appropriate for your position."

ARRRGGGHHH! I want to scream at him.

No, swallow your anger.

Swallow it.

"Indeed."

FORTY

I wake up feeling like an old lady. Everything aches and the room is spinning. I have never felt particularly good after donations, but this absolutely wins the prize for most unpleasant aftereffects.

"Maia, honey, your breakfast drone is here," says Aunt Dora.

I groan, sitting up. I slept soundly, but do not feel rested. I stayed last night as the cramps increased horribly throughout the evening and travelling home just felt like too much effort. I messaged Max cancelling our plans; I hope he didn't mind, but even his embrace and a chocolate mousse wasn't going to save me then.

I had forgotten my delivered meals are continuing post donation this time. Apparently the PTB are not leaving anything to chance and want me in my absolute prime to ensure a quick pregnancy once married...*because a delay would obviously be dreadful.* A drone floats into the room, hovering in front of me, flashing my name. I lift my left arm so it can scan me and as it does, its cute little lid opens, exposing my food. I take my food parcel, the drones wishes me a prosperous day and floats out again, presumably being ultimately released by Aunt Dora. Breakfast in bed is nice. If only I had spent the last 24 years waking up in this room, being called 'honey' or just straight 'Maia,' but without the disappointed, disapproving tone my mum has marinated it with, then I might be sorrier to be leaving it in ten days' time.

"I don't think I can go into work today."

Aunt Dora smiles, "No, I've already called in for you." Wow, no, 'are you sure?' or 'don't be soft.' "I rang Max too, he is coming to see you after work – I said you'll still be here."

"Thank you. Is everything quiet outside now? The drones were still going over for ages last night, weren't they?"

"Yes, all seems back to normal. They found nothing, so I suppose they aren't going to waste so much energy for too long."

"But they will be suspicious about the area for a while."

"Yes. Eve cannot leave the house alone again. I am going to see if I can get the security system to announce when she leaves as well as when she enters. I don't want her to feel imprisoned, but that's what we will be if they catch her – well, maybe not for long: it would be the AIP for you and dead is more likely for me and Eve."

"Don't." I shake my head. Death is not something I want to think about – nor is being a full-blown brood mare. "Where is the AIP?"

"Nowhere you want to be."

"Okay, we all know that – but where and what exactly is it? Is no one curious to the actual details of the 'or else' we are constantly threatened with?"

Aunt Dora exhales sharply. "Was yesterday not exciting enough for you?!"

She is right. I know that, but despite being frightened yesterday for more than myself, I still can't make myself retire into my forthcoming role gladly. I roll my eyes, inwardly groaning at myself. Why is it, when everyone else seems content to take the role offered, do I still want to question, probe, and expand?

* * *

I have spent the day quietly watching Aunt Dora paint. We've spent hours in therapeutic silence. I think we have both asked enough questions and with no one to give meaningful answers, posing more seems fruitless today. Yesterday has taken its toll on Eve as her mental and physical state is delicate at best. Her outbursts have been sporadic, but even when quiet, she has not been settled; so much so, even the cats have chosen to sit by me instead of her for most of the day.

Max finally appears in the early evening, a little later than I was hoping, but his warm embrace and affectionate concern is just the tonic I need. I have been considering how much to share with him regarding – well, *everything* really. I have not forgotten my promise to him to share all and cannot honestly leave so much under the excuse of 'it didn't come up.' For now I just enjoy sitting back in an armchair, listening to him talking about his day, making small talk with my aunt, who seems as relaxed with him as she is me. Once again, in their combined company, I am filled with a feeling of genuine pleasure.

Having decided to stay the night here again, I walk Max to the door alone where he makes me weak at the knees with his kiss; thankfully, it doesn't matter because he is holding me up simultaneously. I'd quite happily bottle this moment.

"Hmmphh, young love." Eve is not wasting an opportunity to make someone jump!

"Good evening Mrs Addams, I was sorry to miss you earlier."

"Liar, but good boy for trying," she chuckles to herself. Apparently, her long slumber has renewed her good humour. I am relieved. "You marry soon?"

"Yes, Saturday week."

"Hmm, I won't go, sorry not to – but, well Missy knows it's best. But I wish you every happiness. Love long and loyal."

Max takes my hand and smiles as our eyes meet. "I intend to."

"Good lad. Okay then." Eve slips into the kitchen, leaving us alone in the hall again. Max is still looking at me and I him, gazing with the same expression that Tom is to Eve in their wedding photo. I have butterflies in my stomach – happy ones, replacing the gripping knots of earlier. If I thought I wanted to save the moment a few minutes ago, I want this one paused for eternity. Everything else in my life might confuse me, but amazingly, he doesn't.

"Maia?"

"Mmm?"

"I love you."

"I love you too."

"Will you marry me?"

I giggle. "Yes, next Saturday in fact."

FORTY-ONE

To be honest, I don't think the weather will overly influence how trying the day will be, but I am pleased to see a bright, sunny morning as I look out my bedroom window for the last time as single woman. I am finally happy for the husband, just not the public display and all the dictations that come with it.

Kate has agreed to brave my mother with me – a favour I will be eternally grateful for as Mum is in the weirdest of moods. I am so used to her disappointed niggles; I am totally unprepared for her hyperactive mother hen impression. I wish I could enjoy it, but after so many years of being her weak link, suddenly being the centre of her joy is equally unnerving. I was awoken far earlier than necessary by her excitement and have rarely heard her sing so enthusiastically. She assembled the family, willingly or otherwise, for breakfast – which to my amazement, went with no squabbling from the adults or children.

I have seen very little of Gee-Gee lately. Although we last spoke on good terms, there has been a tangible strain in our friendship and it hasn't been helped by the reminder when I was drifting off pre-donation that, as Director of Fertility, she will have been aware of, if not directly sanctioning, the use of my eggs – golden or otherwise. I rebuke myself for this line of thought: I have always known this, it is not news, but

311

I cannot shake the disappointment of her not openly pushing for my furtherment. A little voice inside again tells me off. Today being my wedding day *is* a direct result of her pushing *for* me. Maybe I am just an ungrateful lump. This morning she has sat next to me at the table and as I look at her, I worry about her.

"Are you well, Gee-Gee?"

"Quite well my dear, quite well," she says pouring tea. "Tired perhaps – I had a late meeting – but I am ready to watch you wed today. I know the future is bright with such a match." She smiles and I feel loved. Despite whatever reservations or disagreements I have, I know that I am loved. I do treasure that beyond words as I cannot honestly look around the table and say I feel the same unconditional affection.

Mum only vaguely conceals a groan when the security system announces Kate's arrival. I take the opportunity to escape, so I jump up and run to the front door. I was bridesmaid for her on her wedding day, but I was also still woefully subdued following Theo's departure so I am not sure that I was as much fun as I should have been; however, it was a beautifully simple ceremony with a small gathering afterwards – if only today was set to be as low key!

As I open the door to welcome Kate, I am surprised by Claire's enthusiastic greeting: "Maia?! Ah, lovely, lovely! What a glorious day! Are you ready to shine?! Of course, you are! I have your dress – and yours Kate, of course – how timely that we arrive together! I have been to the Hub Hall. Everything is so lovely. The press is there – you have my speech? Have you remembered it? The Committee have approved it, so try not to deviate. Max says he knows his – he recited it to me this morning, a little too fast, but he got it word for word – *good man*, I told him! Just make sure to deliver; we want the UNE to see the wonder of this match! And remind the next generation of the importance of our way and—"

"Claire," I say gently catching her waving arm, "I have read your speech and not only remember it, I understand it."

"Ha! Of course, lovely, lovely! Model couple! Couples like you will secure the coming generations!"

I cannot help wanting to add I might help secure more than my next generation if someone would unclip my wings and let me research properly, but Kate catches my eye behind Claire's back as she winks and mouths '*leave it, Maia.*' I have to laugh – she understands me too well.

"Have you eaten?" asks Claire. "I saw a lot of food downstairs."

"A little, I am not too hungry today."

"But you have been eating your deliveries?"

"From the drone? Yes, of course."

"Good, that's very important – we need you at maximum health for your husband!"

"You mean so I get pregnant."

"That's what I said! *For your husband.* You have read all your preparatory emails? No questions on, you know…*tonight?*"

"Schooling and emails have me well prepared." And freaked out.

"Lovely, lovely – just don't worry if a baby doesn't come in your first cycle. You are a little off kilter having your donation so soon – it's not impossible, but you may just have to use this as practice. The delivery drone will still deliver for optimum chances of course, but, well, you understand the importance of it all! I am sure the Committee won't need to counsel you on compliance – *will they?* That is always *so disappointing.*"

"I am sure that Maia and Max are ready to do their *duty.*"
I am struggling not to laugh as Kate chips in for me.

"Excellent, of course, lovely! Now, let's get you ready...oh!
I think you best shower first!"

And with that, I am scrubbed and primed. My hairdresser
and make-up artist appear like a genie at exactly 11 a.m.,
seconds after Claire said she would arrive in a minute. Mum
flutters around and coos as Claire directs. The rest of my family
dispersed to prepare themselves after breakfast, but as I make
my way downstairs, Dad looks up and, possibly for the first
time in my life, I think he looks proud. I am moved by the
sensation and feel my step lighten for a moment. He takes my
hand as I step in front of him and leans in to kiss my cheek,
whispering: "You are beautiful, Max is a very lucky man."

There are very few moments with my family that I would
like to hold on to, but this will undoubtably be one of them.

From there onwards, my time is a blur. I am whisked off
in the most elaborate SolarBug I have ever seen, followed by
smaller ones containing my family. Altogether they make a
strange procession of colourful bubbles. Abby makes some
snide comment wondering why I have such grandeur, but
for once Mum lands one of her tactless comments at her feet
instead of mine. "Hush girl, had you married better, you'd have
had more too!"

I arrive at the Hub Hall a nervous wreck. My earlier
confidence of remembering my speech has melted away and
only Kate's longest of hugs stops me from shaking violently
and averts the imminent danger of me losing my minuscule
breakfast. The guest list and media presence are unnecessary
at best, but I take a deep breath, take Dad's arm, and walk in.
Music is playing, all eyes are on me, but I look only ahead and

focus on the only pair of eyes that matter right now. Max is as handsome as ever as he holds my gaze, smiling as I approach him. With every step I count my blessings that he is the man I am walking towards and although I would strip away almost everything else here, I would not swap him for anything. I do not even feel regret later when I turn to see Theo – how quickly that scar has healed! Working with him recently in the lab has been a little odd at times, but mostly I just feel at peace, so I can honestly smile to him and Ella. The only churn of my stomach comes when I see her still wearing her enhanced bracelet, reminding me of hidden secrets that shadow everything.

Max and I are swept from group to group, room to room, stood in front of this camera, made to speak and recite into another. Everything is so far out of my comfort zone that I cannot put it into words, and although I say it all, I can only partially recite my speech with conviction. The system has, for this instance, worked, matching me with someone I can see a real partnership with. The PTB is working for a better, peaceful future with nature and humankind in balance. I still believe we can right past wrongs to our planet. But in my heart, I know I cannot sit back and blindly follow my mother's life. Pushing my children into decisions and making them feel less than worthy for who they are will not be my future. There is a way to obey the PTB mandate without trampling on individual's dreams. There is an answer to human fertility without turning people into mind-numbed broodmares and commitment doesn't have to mean absolute submission. *Surely?*

For now, however, until I find the key – or at least a firm thread to pull – I do as I am told. We eat, drink, and dance when directed. I can just imagine our wedding being used for schoolroom propaganda for years to come. Everything is beautifully choreographed in a surreal dream until I find myself finally alone with Max, in a home we are now told is ours, adorned with items we chose in a flurry weeks ago from a holographic catalogue, the day we both agreed to break free of our mothers' together.

"Well, Mrs Rivers, welcome home." Max scoops me up into his arms, a thrill I hope to never tire of. If either of us had been nervous after reading our instructive emails for newlyweds, we didn't need to be, and of all the future hurdles and tests that are ahead of us, marital 'compliance' is certainly not going to be one of them.

FORTY-TWO

Our first week of marriage has been the happiest time of my life. No one bothered us, no one told us where to be, what time to get up, or how to think. For six days we visited museums and parks, watched plays, and swam in the lake – all at the expense of the PTB as part of their honeymoon package. We have both received our thrice daily DDS (Drone Delivered Sustenance). Max came up with that; simple yet descriptive. I wish I had thought of it earlier, but either way, I am glad to see some equality in treatment – even if it is a stark reminder of us being enrolled in the next stage of a breeding programme. I have promised myself to ignore that element of life for as long as possible and just be thankful for the man I wake up next to.

We have another week of honeymoon and have every intention of using it to just be together; however, I left some tests running that I am eager to see and Max wants to check up on a project application he had pitched just before the wedding. So, deciding that we'd both like to check into work briefly, but not get stopped for long whilst still on holiday, we conclude that Sunday morning is our best window of opportunity.

My breakfast drone found me as I was about to walk into the foyer, so I walk into the lab absent-mindedly sipping on my tea as the lights ping on. I am about to sit at my desk when

I spot movement in the corner which almost makes me drop my cup.

"Hello?!"

"Ugh," a voice says from under a duvet.

I cannot believe it, someone has erected a camp bed in the corner of the lab. "What are you doing? You can't sleep here!"

"Maia? Oh, erm…"

"Henry?! What the hell are you doing?"

He rubs his bleary eyes. "Please, don't tell Mary you've found me here."

"I wasn't planning to, but what are you doing?"

"Never mind. Are you here to work?"

"Just to check up on – oh, it appears that Theo has checked into my system since I've been gone?"

"Ah, yes, he said he would as he thought you'd be gone longer. I didn't stop to see if he found anything interesting – is there anything of note?"

"Not yet." I skim over the data, but am distracted by Henry sitting up, causing a collection of empty bottles to rattle to the floor. "Henry, what has happened?" He is a sad, rather pathetic sight and I do not know what to do with him. Maybe I should call Max? I am considering my options when the door violently slides backwards and Mary storms in. Is there such thing as *good* déjà vu? If there is, I'd love to see it, because this does not feel like a good repeat of circumstances. Mary glares at me, then at Henry. She is clearly fuming. Still neat as a pin, as always, but her demeanour is nothing like her usual cool, stony expression.

"What are you doing here? I need to speak to Henry, *alone*."

"I was going to work briefly, but I'll be off."

"Good. Your working days are numbered anyway, so best leave it sooner than later." So much for any thought of her helping me. "My son needs a wife more than my husband needs a lab wench." Nice. It really is too early in the morning for this. I think her anger is more towards Henry than me, I just happen to be in the way; however, I feel myself flush red and choke back tears. How did such a person raise Max, he who is kind and considerate at every turn? Henry has those qualities, too, but looking at him now, I can see he is but a trampled fragment of the man he should be. The last time I heard them argue here I thought he was regaining some of his own sway, but seeing him now, barely sober and brow beaten, he seems more repressed than ever.

"Maybe you should both cool off before chatting again?" I gently suggest.

"Maybe you should mind your own business and f—"

"Mary, leave her alone." Henry's voice is a weary whisper, but it is powerful enough to send Mary flying towards him in a rage.

"What the hell are you doing?!" I scream, and to my surprise, it is enough to make Mary stand back, her chest heaving from the exertion. "Have you both lost your minds?!"

"GO." She grits her teeth at me.

"I cannot leave you together like this." Although I'd love to. Instead, I remain at my desk and turn to my computer. I don't look at Mary, but I can hear her seething. I try to at least act like I am focusing on my research and eventually she turns from me to Henry, who has barely moved since she arrived. As soon as she has her back turned, I video call Max, putting my volume off, so he can hear me, but I cannot hear him. I wait to see the call connected, put my finger to my lips, so he has half an idea something is wrong, then pull my coat sleeve over my watch, hoping that Mary doesn't catch sight of it.

"What are you doing?! Just look at the state of you! For shame man, get yourself together before someone else sees you. I have not come this far for you to ruin everything now."

"You have the twisted idea that everything is thanks to you, Mary. This lab is more of a home than with you will ever be. You sabotaged any chance of happiness I had long ago. I am tired, *so tired* of pretence. I have tried, Lord knows I have tried...tried to forget, to tell myself I, nay, *we*, have made our way to making amends, to right *your* wrong, but you can justify anything! – *even murder!*"

"WATCH YOUR MOUTH." Mary's eyes dart to me, then back to Henry as she answers him. Her tone is the most unnerving mixture of anger and resolution, each word delivered as a calm, decisive threat. Every hair on my body is standing on edge and I am seriously questioning the wisdom of choosing to stay. "We do not need to have this conversation in front of *her*."

"She deserves to know what level of manipulation she has married into."

"All I have done is for the greater good. Remember that, Henry."

"The greater good and your elevation are not the same thing."

"Funny, I didn't hear you complaining every time your budget or lab size increased. The end can justify the means, you know that."

"Tell that to Lydia."

Mary screams, throwing herself at Henry again. I have never seen such a crazed display. Shouting at her doesn't help, so without thinking, I run to her, grabbing an arm from behind.

I pull her backwards and we both struggle for control. She may be lightweight, but she is seriously feisty and nearly knocks me over. Henry finally moves, standing up, pulling us apart. The venom in her face is shocking, the veins on her temples are bulging and her nostrils are flaring with each breath. Through her rage, she snarls at Henry:

"*I will destroy you.*"

"Mum?!" Max's face is flushed, he has clearly been running, and his voice is strained with confusion. Max's presence has had a marked effect on Mary's demeanour. I cannot call it 'calm,' yet she is notably trying to control herself. Seconds earlier I was expecting her to fly at Henry again; now she sits down, shaking all over. "What is going on?" Max's voice echoes on his phone. He looks down, covers his watch with his left hand, and quickly ends the call I started. Mary takes a fraction of a second before clocking my trick, her eyes again flaring in my direction.

"You poisonous little cow! Trying to turn my son against me, huh? You married him, isn't that enough? Don't cross me little girl, you'll—"

"You'll do nothing to her, you hear? I don't know what the hell is going on here, but it stops now – are you listening? Dad, please, what is this?!"

"Your dad is a disloyal bastard, that is what is going on. You may look shocked, but it is true, he forgets the ultimate purpose and now he has the cheek to sit here pretending to be a victim."

"I am devoted to the UNE," says Henry. "The only one I was disloyal to was my wife and I will regret that until the day I die. You will make sure of that."

"I AM YOUR WIFE!"

"By manipulation and terror. Go, fulfil your destiny, just stop trying to reign over me."

"Mum, what have you done?"

"I have given everything to build a solid future for the UNE – *for you*." She looks oddly proud for a moment.

"How?" asks Max.

"By making note of human error, pushing for more and striving for better. If you want to succeed, you must keep your wits about you. Notice inconsistencies and follow them, you'll be surprised what intellectual gems fall your way. If life throws a happy coincidence or opportunity, take it."

"So, you rose up the ladder by knocking others down?" The scowl I receive makes me regret speaking, but Max reaches for my hand and gently, but reassuringly squeezes it. I hold onto him, silently letting him know I am on his side.

"I worked up the ladder with hard work and dedication – which was my right. My father ensured I had opportunities to shine; I just made sure I took them."

"And made good use of infidelities and greed that happened to come under your radar."

"I just said I utilised coincidence, Henry."

"Yes, to the point that your father disowned you, and your boss named you his successor for your silence."

Mary scoffs, "Frederic wanted to protect his family's innocence and I wanted what I was owed. Everyone was satisfied. Daddy didn't disown me; he understands the importance of holding one's status of influence, even if that requires sacrifice. Mamma isn't as strong and she put him in an impossible position. He had to save his marriage and he couldn't compromise The General."

"The President General?"

"No, Max, The Midlands General," corrects Henry. "You know your step grandfather is Captain of his Guard and his best friend – so good in fact, he pardoned Mary for—"

"ENOUGH!" spits Mary, "*If you go there again, that will be the last thing you do.*"

Silence. The kind that is so uncomfortable, you could cut the air with a knife. Max's grip is borderline too tight, but I think we could both slip free easily because we are sweating profusely. If Mary is willing to confess the less than flattering truth to how she succeeded as Director, how dark is the one thing she doesn't want Henry to share? 'If you go there again'… that would suggest he has said it already…I am replaying the last few minutes, trying to remember the gritted, screamed, and screeched words.

"Secrets and lies have clearly done you no favours. Why not clear them now? What is it, Mum?" appeals Max.

Mary makes no attempt to reply.

"Dad?"

"Forgive me, this is not the example of marriage I wanted to give. You can be happy and thrive despite us. The PTB need you two to do better than us." Why is Henry side stepping? I am not saying that he doesn't believe what he just said, but why come so far, to then protect Mary at the final hurdle? I do not understand. Suddenly a name comes to mind:

"Who is Lydia?"

All eyes shoot to me. One in pain, one in confusion, one in undeniable anger. The latter speaks first.

"A thorn in the past. Leave her there."

"My wife."

"Max's mother? The one you betrayed – how?"

"*Why, you!*" Mary throws herself at me, grabbing a chair and swinging it at my head. The leg catches my face, but the force of blow is deflected by Max pushing it and his mother aside. He drops the chair, but pushes her out of the door and slides it shut behind her. Henry, again late to react, now gets up and scans the door to lock it. Max is physically fit, but the stress and exertion has him puffing. Mary is thumping on the door, but no one answers her. We stand silently for a moment, staring in disbelief at each other. Max turns to his father; his face, filled with pain and confusion, tugs at my heartstrings.

"Dad, enough of the secrets, what happened?"

For a minute I think that Henry isn't going to answer, but we both remain silent, hoping that the cogs within Henry are aligning and he will shed light in the darkness. He is obviously mentally wrestling with himself, his eyebrows are flickering and eyes rolling, even if his mouth has yet to catch up. I take a deep breath as he sits down, looking up at Max with bleary eyes.

"Son, I am ashamed. For years I have justified my choices and hidden her secrets – our secrets – telling myself it is for the best, that we can do real good for the UNE, and that I can make amendments for past pathetic weakness. I have strived to be the man I should be, the father I should be, to protect you from my failures and give you the support to become the man, husband, and father I wasn't. But as she has become more powerful, she has also become harder. Maybe it is a coping mechanism. Sometimes I think she has forgotten she isn't really your mother, and it isn't just a front – she has twisted her own memories to fit her desires – which works as long as life goes her way. I hoped that this move, this job, for both of us would give individual freedom, a fresh start, but she is more controlling, not less, and I cannot breathe. We fought badly yesterday… her plans never stop. She wants a family empire at any cost and I told her I would openly disapprove of her interference. That didn't go down well. You've married, fulfilling her years of scheming, but that is just one stage in her design, and it has once again released the jealous Black Widow who took your mother 24 years ago."

"*Took...?*" Max's face grimaces as he takes in the potential meaning. I am struck not only by Henry's speech, but also his choice of words. He referred to Mary as a 'Black Widow.' Can it be coincidence that Eve used the exact same metaphor?

"The PTB rule works. It has formed a structure and plan for all life, but there is still human weakness to contend with. I have loved science since I was little – as you have architecture, Max. I saw the same natural spark ignite in you and I couldn't be prouder of the man you have become. But in my teens, I also fell for a bright, opinionated girl. She had plans to discover, expand, and conquer. I thought most of it just chatter, but I loved her spirit. She was pampered and doted on by her father. He shared her desires to make history and continue a family dynasty, so her older brother being totally infertile (though now doing well in the Army) did not go down well. When our grades were published, Mary's father took her infertility twice as hard, but nowhere near as badly as she herself did. We had been raised to excel and she had her plans of how to do it. Infertility and marrying a stranger were not included."

"But you did as you were told?" I ask.

"Of course, I took my match at the ceremony as I had been prepared all my life to do – and did my duty. I'm not saying that I had no regrets, but I knew my place." Henry pauses. I think part of him is relieved to be talking, but he also keeps glancing at the locked door, nervously checking for Mary, even though the silence suggests that she has left. "Lydia was a sweet unassuming girl, and we easily made a home together. I didn't see Mary for a while as we didn't part on good terms.

I heard her father called in some favours allowing her to defer marriage, focusing on her studies and future career. I didn't forget her, but I honestly felt we had both accepted our paths. One day I came home and there she was, sat at my kitchen table, laughing and giggling with Lydia. They had met at some meeting and become friends – Lydia of course totally oblivious of our past, having been raised in another school in the Hub. I should have told her. You have no idea how many times I have relived that first meeting – or the meetings thereafter, but I was weak, selfish, and pathetic."

"You had an affair."

"I did."

Poor Max looks nauseous, but I think he wants (or at least needs), to hear the rest of this story, once and for all. Henry, however, appears to have finished. He is rubbing his hands up and down his face, so I prompt him with a quiet: "And then?"

Henry sighs. "And then Lydia fell pregnant, and Mary went from an alluring (even if also conniving) mistress to malicious psychopath. Her jealousy consumed her and destroyed any real affection I had for her. I tried to do the right thing and end things, but it was too late. I came home from work one day to find Lydia at the bottom of the stairs in a pool of blood. Mary made it look like an accident, but I knew in my gut it wasn't. She pushed her and left her for dead." Cold chills are tingling all over my body and tears are rolling down all our faces. "The doctors tried to save her, but Lydia never woke up. You, Max, were transported to a SurrogacyPod for two months and I married again one week before you came home."

Max audibly swallows several times without speaking before finally whispering: "Why did you marry her?"

"The Genetics Committee told me that single fathers cannot have babies as it doesn't align with the family ethos, so you would be adopted unless I remarried immediately. I wanted you more than anything. Your mother and I had spent months anticipating your arrival with joy – you were everything we had been raised to revere."

"But why *her*, a 1? Why not another 3?"

"Because like the perfect actress she trained herself to be, she played the doting, bereaved family friend and got her father to appeal to The General for an exception. They are childhood friends, as were their fathers before them, and so, my fate was sealed. Mary's mother sensed foul play so she distanced herself, but Mary kept her word: she raised you as her own and pushed her way to the Director of Agriculture faster than anyone could. She has triumphed; and though ruthless, has been loyal to the PTB mandate – all the while, trampling my spirit. Sure, I would probably not have succeeded so easily if it were not for her, but I have earnt my position here, and refuse to declare myself totally in her debt."

I do not know where to go with this information. I have long mused on the mystery of Mary Rivers and how a 1 married a 3. Others must have noticed the grade difference in the last 24 years. Maybe that was one reason she was so happy to move Hubs: she would have less people aware of rumours and hearsay, especially as barcode reading becomes less interesting in those over a certain age and it is easier to dominate over strangers – even better strangers that hear rumours of your prowess, but have no extra knowledge – leaving you to spread only the impression you want.

I am at a loss to how to respond to Henry. Since meeting him, he has given me hope of an academic future – do I still have the right to expect or want anything from him? Would I be morally weakening myself by continuing such aspirations, knowing the foundation of his position? Now I know, do I wish I was still in ignorance? Possibly, but there is no 'unknowing' and whatever horror I feel, I cannot begin to imagine how Max is feeling after learning the truth of his origins. I turn to him and he just shrugs.

"Now what?" I am not sure who I am asking, but as no one else is speaking, I feel the need to say something. "Henry, what is your plan? Sleeping here forever? Can you go home?"

"I'll have to. I will have to work out a way to apply for official separation."

"Can you?"

"NO, HE CANNOT!" Mary's voice comes loud and clear through the door. "Let me in, you moron."

"Mum..." Max stumbles on the word. "Is that wise? If you attack anyone again—"

The door slides open, making us all stiffen. I would have much preferred her to agree to peace before re-entry. I would also have rather that she had come alone. However, rather than Mary entering, Peter Lloyd stands in front of us while Mary remains in the corridor. Why is this creepy man constantly appearing lately? He seems so pleased with himself, but we all look confused. Other than using his master door code, why is Mary risking so much bringing in yet another person? Or is she counting on us all retaining her secret?

"Right! Director Rivers has informed me of a potential issue. Dr Rivers, I would hope after your indulgence last night, you are now ready to make amends. The PTB would be very sorry to have any complications here. You can privately divide your home, but not the decrees of the UNE. One's duty is not something you can pick and choose when you want to comply."

"Do you know what you are asking me?" Henry asks sadly.

"*Do you?*" Peter spits back.

Mary looks pleased with herself. No remorse, no fear. Whatever she has told Peter, he has bought it hook, line, and sinker. My Father outranks this weasel of a man, but he stands there as if he were the President General.

"Max, your mother loves you very much and has worked hard to ensure your future. Your wife would not be my choice…" Peter pauses, smirking at me. Max looks ready to react, so I squeeze his hand tighter, encouraging him to let Peter finish his spiteful speech. "No, not my choice, though she is an excellent *specimen* for you. We want the union to thrive, we would hate for you, Henry, to jeopardise so much because of your *nerves*. You wouldn't want anyone here to join the AIP because of you or for you to be charged for obstruction, surely?"

"Obstruction of what!?"

"*Of anything that gets you gone.*"

"On whose authority? You answer to my father. I am certain he would stand up for my father-in-law," I demand.

"Not if he has sense. They will not protect an individual of spent value putting his nose in silly places."

I am disgusted hearing my dad referred to this way, but I am also struck by Peter's use of '*they*.' A few weeks ago, I would not have been; it would merely be a commonly used word for the collective PTB. The Powers That Be enjoy their cloak of secrecy as fear, command, and compliance comes with it, yet they also stand plainly for all to observe their rule. But now I find myself listening for reference to the secret fraternity behind them. Is there a classified society pulling the strings as Eve suggests? Or I am just distracted by the regrets of her past – valid as they may (or may not) be?

"Henry, can we go home now." Mary is not asking a question; she is telling him to get up – and what's more, he does. Henry packs away his things without a word and walks out of the room. I want to scream: '*What was the point of all that?! Why confess to so much just to step back into the shadows?!*' but a voice within tells me to save it for later.

"I trust this is the end of this," says Mary in a cool, triumphant voice. "Maxwell, darling, I will catch up with you tomorrow when everyone has calmed down."

Peter Lloyd is smirking like he has just won the lottery. How can he be proud of himself? He raises his left hand to his eyes, quickly turning two fingers to me, gesturing 'I am watching you.' Dad said that he had caught Peter tailing our family without authorisation. As she gently tugs on his hand, turning to leave, something tells me that Mary had more than a little to do with that.

Max and I are left standing alone in the lab.

I am shaking; he looks numb.

"I'm so sorry," I whisper.

Max nods in silent reply and hugs me.

I close my eyes and swallow the lump in my throat.

"I think we need to go visit Eve."

FORTY-THREE

As we make our way towards Aunt Dora's house with everything from this morning going through our minds, I cannot help wondering if I am about to overload Max with what might follow. I have had weeks to churn over mixed-up thoughts, half secrets, intrigues, and frustrations and it feels cruel to land all of it on his plate in one day. I am really lamenting not sharing more sooner. I have unquestionably considered it a thousand times, reminding myself of the promise I made him not to hold secrets and form a true partnership; but voicing my suspicions and concerns confirms their existence, potentially betrays others' confidence, and endangers him all at once. And, if I did not fear the severity of repercussions before, I certainly do now.

We have been largely silent since leaving the lab, occasionally exhaling heavily, or exchanging confounded expressions. We stop at the tram station, standing slightly back from those waiting to board the oncoming tram. As I look around at the people happily minding their own business, I envy their blissful ignorance. Panic suddenly rises within, clouding my determination for clarity, making me doubt whether my desire for so-called-truth is wise or selfish. I only have supposition, inconsistencies, and speculation – not anything tangible. Is badgering a 112-year-old woman for answers really the path to enlightenment? If I am willing to do that, I am not sure what kind of person that makes me…

"Maybe today isn't the day?"

"To share everything?" Max says looking sternly at me, "I think it is."

I suddenly feel a knot turn in my stomach.

"Do you think I—"

"Haven't shared everything to date? Yes. I know that, but I figured you would in time."

"I don't *know* anything – only things that don't make sense."

Max shrugs. "Then we'll know them together."

I squeeze Max's hand and nod. I suppose the only thing that has changed is the shared uncontainable desire for answers. I turn to see a tram pulling up at the station. People file off and those waiting patiently remain stationary until it is their turn to board. Suddenly a familiar face beams at me and her smile succeeds in producing mine, regardless of how stressful my morning has been.

"Maia! Max!" Kate calls, "How are you? How's married life treating you both?!"

"Well, thank you!" I say, hugging her. "What brings you to the Centre today? You look ready to work? I didn't think you worked on Sundays?"

"Ha! No, nor should I be, but once again Bruce has Tim helping him and I am collecting supplies. A lot of my team have been drafted in this time – they really need to get the engineers in gear though (*pun intended*). That blasted greenhouse caught fire yesterday!"

"What?!"

"I know! My beautiful plants! Months of work wasted – and Bruce said they were producing so well too!"

"Can we help?"

"No, no, I'm just grabbing a few bits and pieces with Jay here, we'll get a Solarbug back to SH3." Kate turns to Jay, who I rudely had not even noticed. He smiles warmly, but is as pale as he did the last time I saw him. "We'd best go – and you'll miss your tram if you don't hurry! We'll catch up soon, okay?!" I readily agree, hugging her again briefly as Max pulls me onto the tram just before it leaves.

We sit in silence. The couple behind us spot our newly altered barcodes on our necks. To be fair, it is hard not to: the new imprint takes a while to settle, making the freshly added marital code stick out like a sore thumb. It is annoying, but nice at the same time. I want people to know we are married, I am proud to be married to Max – but I'd prefer them not to gossip about us quite so noticeably. Surely it is possible to communicate quietly on a tram without alerting everyone around you? Apparently not today, as the people in front turn around to congratulate us, having 'really enjoyed' our wedding on TV. We smile and thank them; Max puts his arm around my neck – possibly to show true affection – possibly to stop anyone else reading my code for a few minutes at least.

We step off the tram at the last stop of SH1. We have a short walk to Aunt Dora's, but I am glad to have a few more minutes of fresh, quiet air before needing to attempt to discuss anything else. Max cannot know that I am waiting to fish out Eve's bracelets again, yet he seems to instinctively know to wait for our destination before asking questions or discussing the mornings revelations. To be honest, I think it will take more than a tram ride and a stroll to let that sink in anyway.

"Why, hello my dears! What an unexpected pleasure! Are you well? Do come in, Maia, you know you don't need to be invited!" Aunt Dora's welcome is a tonic, even if I do feel guilty as I prepare to lay woe at her feet.

"Aunt Dora, forgive me, but we have had a trying morning and need honest, loving family more now than ever. Your home is the only place I think we will find it. *Come what may.*"

Aunt Dora looks at me with concern, narrowing her brow, but she clearly remembers the last time she used that phrase with me. "There is nothing to forgive, my home is yours, always."

She hugs us both without another word, squeezing me in a way that brings a tear to my eye. I wipe it away and then point my left hand to my right wrist, ringing my fingers to symbolise a bracelet. Aunt Dora walks into her bedroom, returning with Pandora, walking past us into the living room where she places the box on the living room table. She pulls up the dancer, presses 5 and we all watch the little figure perform once again, only punching in the code once she has finished. Max is stunned into silence, and I do not encourage conversation until I have placed a bracelet on his right wrist. Apparently, Eve designed them with a woman's wrist in mind as it is a struggle to get it on him, yet he doesn't once complain.

I am resting a lot of faith on Eve's lap. Not only am I hoping she will be willing to share when she has previously made it clear that she isn't, but I am also banking on her having a lucid day and not being enveloped in the fog. So far, I am not encouraged as Aunt Dora manages to put Eve's bracelet on her wrist without her as much as blinking. Nevertheless, as we have mentally come this far, I cannot turn back now.

I begin by explaining to Max the purpose of the bracelet. To my surprise, he is not surprised. Apparently, my lack of digital response or availability when visiting here had made him suspicious of some such possibility, though by his own admission, he had been imagining a technical glitch rather than there being an active distortion of signal. I recount Eve's recent very near miss with Ella and security drones, reiterating that the bracelets must not go beyond these walls and now the PTB are searching for an anomaly, they can only be out of Pandora's box while our conversation needs serious censorship.

With that outlined, I move onto recounting to Aunt Dora what happened this morning. Max mostly sits without interruption unless I ask for confirmation. I think he has decided that it is easier if I narrate events for Aunt Dora, who is shocked and doesn't hide it: "What a despicable tale! I do not know what to say!"

"Nor do we."

"And Henry just walked away with Mary afterwards?"

"And Peter Lloyd, yes."

Aunt Dora shudders. "There is something very wrong with that scenario."

"I think she has him in her pocket in more ways than one." Max looks angry now. "I am disgusted by her, but I fear for my father. I always knew she controlled him, but we had our way of coping together – now he seems to have lost all will to resist."

"You must not sink yourselves with him; if she and Peter are threatening you, I would not assume it is done idly."

"I don't," Max says flatly.

"I am hoping Eve will illuminate us," I add.

Aunt Dora stares at me in surprise. "How? Why do you think she knows anything?"

"For two reasons. One, when she first met Max, she told us 'not all rivers run true' and came up with a metaphor about plucked apples being raised by another tree. I have thought about that a lot since, and I don't think that was mindless rambling. Max is the stolen apple. She knew what she was saying, even if she didn't really mean to say it to us."

"Hmmphh, think you're a detective do yer?" Eve says suddenly reanimating. "Don't you know it's rude to call someone mindless? – especially in front of 'em."

"Eve, I didn't call you mindless, I actually said the opposite, which you know very well." She grins at me and I am relieved not to have offended her. "How much of what I've said have you heard?"

"Enough to know you want answers to questions you shouldn't find."

"Pardon?"

"Exactly."

"Will you help us?"

"Yes, but you won't like it." We all unwittingly lean forwards a little in our seats, waiting for her to speak, but she says nothing.

"Eve?"

"I told you before: my silence is the only help you need."

I could cry. "Eve, we are beyond silence being of use."

She doesn't answer: instead she starts petting Smoggy and Squash, chatting inaudibly to them as they purr.

I look over to Aunt Dora in exasperation and she asks: "You said that Eve knows for two reasons. What is the other?"

"The Black Widow." Okay, there is no denying that means something to Eve as she immediately looks up. "Both you and Henry directly referred to Mary as 'The Black Widow' and I overheard the doctor who harvested me refer to Mary, telling her colleague 'that is a web you don't want to get caught in.' I do not believe that is a coincidence."

"Pfft, people want to watch their mouths," scoffs Eve. "Poison spreads fast you know."

"Mrs Addams, what does that mean? Won't you please elaborate?" Max's soft, manly but pleading tone obviously affects Eve for a moment. Her expression softens and she shakes her head.

"Young man, if I were not tied in a web of my own, I might explain more of yours, but I do wish you would believe me when I tell yer, it will not benefit you – neither of you. More than me has worked hard to establish the order that is around you now. Hmmphh, I know only too well it ain't perfect, there is much I'd change, but despite me reservations in some, the purpose is still clear. I have lost too much, my sacrifice is greater than it should be, but I must live with that. We do what we do for family and future. Your mum is a worthless rag and pretender, I can't say nowt else, but even she works for family. No, no, Maia, m'dear, I do think of you as family, so don't think I don't, you and Dora. My silence is *for* you – not against."

"But we are miserable in ignorance and under a rule so restrictive we are stifled of air."

"And yet you breathe. And the world breathes. And for our sacrifices there will be a tomorrow."

"Not for Tom or your boys." Aunt Dora delivers a much lower punch than I would have dared. It may only have been verbal, but it struck the poor woman, nonetheless.

"Hmmphh." Eve grits her teeth, shaking her head. I understand Aunt Dora's frustration, but I don't think that Eve will answer questions through guilt trips. The past clearly haunts her enough already – I need to find a different angle of enquiry.

"Who are *they*?"

Silence.

"Eve?" I wait, hoping against hope that she will relent, or I will ask the right question or remember the right phrase which she has said. I am sure that amongst her many ramblings, she has given away more clues than stolen fruit. The trouble is, how do I decipher the difference? "You know about a *'them'* beyond the PTB…and are angry at them when few others seem to realise *'they'* exist. So, you didn't just have a run in with them, *you are them.*" Eve darts me a look that I cannot define, but now I have a reaction, I am going to have to carry on. "Long ago, you said they owed you the right to die in your time, in your own bed, but they wouldn't respect that? Why?"

Eve sighs, "Maybe they are right…sick, blabbing old ladies *are* an issue."

"Don't say that!"

"Though, so it would seem, are arrogant middle-aged narcissists."

"If you are 'retired' from *'them,'* how do you know of the 'Black Widow'?" Max joins me in attempting to connect the dots.

"You don't need to still be *in,* to *know* about the Black Widow." She shakes her head again, looking at Max and sighing, I think in pity. "Look, my boy, your origin story – well, it can't be easy to have heard. She earnt that title, though most don't know why, just that her ruthlessness lives up to the nickname."

"That isn't comforting," retorts Max.

"I didn't say it was. You want comfort or truth? They are rarely compatible."

"Truth."

"Hmmphh."

The security system chimes 'DELIVERY,' making us all turn to the door. I glance at my watch and then Max's. They are both flashing.

"Ah, our DDSs."

"Pardon?" Aunt Dora looks at me anxiously.

"'Drone Delivered Sustenance' – that is what Max has dubbed it, we still get meals drone delivered. Max, we best both greet them at the door without our bracelets on."

"Keep those blasted drones outside, hmmphhing things make me angry, even if I did design most of 'em."

"You are a mystery and a wonder Mrs Addams." Max shakes his head.

Eve chuckles, looking pleased with herself while Max and I receive our meal from the drone outside. Aunt Dora makes something for herself and Eve and no one speaks again until we're sat down, bracelets reinstated, and all other technology free.

"They don't give you much, do they?" Aunt Dora clearly feels a little guilty as she compares our plates.

"No, but apparently it is packed with all the optimum nutrients for tip-top embryos!" I sarcastically jest.

Eve snorts, "Hmmphh, of course, they aren't gonna give you the dud batch, are they?"

I feel myself staring, wide eyed, heart racing at Eve. Max and Dora see my expression, but don't seem to be following my thought pattern. Eve has carried on eating, happily oblivious to my newfound inner turmoil. I swallow hard on the lump that has risen in my throat, desperately trying to find words, but Max speaks for me: "What do you mean?"

Eve glances up, sees my expression, and sighs in exasperation: "Oh, come on, don't look at me like that, Missy. Think about it! Why feed you specifically if all food is equal?"

Max calmly answers again for me: "To ensure we eat healthily. They have found certain foods are particularly helpful for human conception opposed to just maintenance."

"Your mother tell you that?"

In the milliseconds it takes the meaning to hit home, I feel like I have wasted my life entirely. I have dedicated my research to epigenetics. I have been *so* sure that more than pure genes are rendering humanity infertile. My Nature v Nurture argument has consumed so many of my thoughts and now Eve's short, throw away sentences have shed more light on my theories than years of experiments.

"*Nutrigenetics.*" I can only shake my head and groan. If the PTB are looking for the answers, *they* have them. "They control fertility through nutrition."

"Not control, *influence.*"

Suddenly Kate's destroyed plants make sense. "The drone crash was no accident."

"What?!" exclaims Max.

"It didn't ricochet into the allotment behind the houses. It was deliberately programmed to land there."

"What on earth for?"

"Because Kate had a new variety of homegrown, *chemical-free* veg there – and I am betting that is what altered those two young girls' fertility status, making those pregnancies possible."

I hold my head in my hands, staring forwards at Eve, hoping she will respond. She doesn't though. I think she is still conscious, but honestly, I cannot tell. She is breathing steadily, but nothing else is moving, certainly not her lips.

"And the SH3 greenhouse fire? Kate's plants are there too, right?" adds Max.

"Yes."

"My mother must be behind it – she has reviewed every corner of the Agricultural sector."

"It would seem she knew what she was searching for. And Ella? Analysing all the data, coming up with gadgets to detect anomalies? On who's direction is that? If she is working with Peter Lloyd – and he your mother…" I feel sick. I discounted nutrigenetics after a review of existing results as they seemed so thoroughly considered. Such care is put into every product – *of course, it is.* What do I do with this information? With no proof, it is as real as unicorns. I can draw a cone on a horse, but that doesn't make it real.

"If you pick a scab, be prepared to make it bleed."

"Eve?"

"You heard. I'm too old for bacon. Slaying the beast sounds heroic, but I'm not so sure you won't just blow your house into the river and then where will piggy swim to?"

"I don't know what you just said, but I do know my mother – *my stepmother* – has threatened my father as well as Maia and me due to his confession. If you know anything – anything tangible that can help us make sense of it all and avoid her betrayal – then please, *do tell!*"

"Flush them down the river, see if they can swim!"

Max's exasperation is palpable as he turns to me.

"Eve, are we safe? We have both obeyed PTB rule and followed it…and thought we are helping it. Are we? What is the point?! You once said, 'death comes to those who cross them.' Is Mary *them?* Have we crossed her irrevocably?"

Eve pushes her lower jaw forward and twists her lips together. Instinct tells me to wait. I have asked enough in one go and will now have to let her decide how to reply, even if I am physically shaking with anticipation. I cannot help fearing that my mother-in-law has dealt us all a blow beyond her own crimes.

"I don't know how deep the river runs these days, but I doubt it'll be allowed to swallow you."

"You think she answers upwards – so you think she isn't the top of command, despite being a Director?"

"I know it." Okay, well that is partially reassuring. "But I'd still rather see her sink."

"Then help us!" I exclaim.

"I have already said too much – *again*! Damn dementia and aging! I have held me tongue all these years!"

"Or maybe you have finally found family enough to speak out for?" Aunt Dora holds Eve's hand, speaking softly whilst Eve looks at her pouting.

"Hmmphh."

Silence takes hold of us all. I suppose we are all overwhelmed by thoughts, I know mine are muddled enough. I run through conversations and events; I see connections and mistakes. The unwillingness to learn from and acknowledge mistakes would be giving myself the greenlight to repeat them. I must not replicate the errors of others or myself, any more than I can now blindly follow them. I see the path I have taken and the one I should take if I want an unchallenged future, but I am still sure that there is room for another path, one yet unseen.

"Eve?" She doesn't look up, so I repeat her name softly until she does. "Remember when you got home the other day? You had just snuck past those guards and you laughed and said, *'you'd show them who the real revolution is'* – what did you mean?"

"I was just laughing at the guards."

"No, I don't think so. Who is the revolution?"

"You're asking the wrong question."

"What is the right question?"

"Who *isn't* part of the revolution."

"And?"

"*Everyone is.* Just some are more aware than others. That is the best way. *Enough!*" Eve waves her hands. "I have compromised too much – love of family past and present compels me to return to my appeal for silence!"

"Silence is not golden."

"It really is."

"Like my eggs?"

"What?"

"Apparently, I have Golden Eggs – or Chicks I think is what they actually said." Eve looks grave, but doesn't reply. "Does that phrase mean something to you?"

Silence.

"Please, I—"

"Who told you that?"

"That I have Golden Chicks? I overheard it at the clinic. The term 'Golden Goose' was knocked about the playground – everyone was told that is what they wanted to be, I just thought Golden 'eggs' and 'chicks' was an off shoot of that?"

"Hmm."

"Is it?"

"Probably."

"You're not very convincing. Is it more than a term for the most fertile 3s?"

No reply again.

"The doctor and nurses did seem rather thrilled to be harvesting me and mocked my application to donate to Kate, saying, '*Golden Chicks don't go to barren nobodies*'…Had I not been semi unconscious, I would like to have throttled them for saying that."

Eve remains tight-lipped, but Max is clearly indignant. "Hateful bitches! They'll actually get throttled if the wrong people know they said that in front of you, I've no doubt. Then being a barren nobody would be the least of their concerns. I bet even the AIP wouldn't have them."

"I've been intrigued and afraid of the AIP all my life. Mum made sure of that."

"Pfft. She did well then," grumbles Eve.

"No need for that now." Max takes my hand, smiling. Despite all the craziness that surrounds us, once again, I am relieved it led me to him.

"No, indeed." I squeeze his hand, returning the loving, reassuring smile he gave me. "For so long I feared I would be sent there for not complying like that poor girl, Lilith."

"*Who?*" Eve suddenly turns. I am not sure if it is fear or anger in her tone.

"Just some girl who refused her match."

"WHO! *Her name!*"

"Lilith, I don't know her surname. Her boyfriend was Jay, he is infertile, so they were separated by force at the Matching Ceremony."

"How old is she? What does she look like?"

"I don't know Eve, why?" Eve glares at me to continue. "Okay, poofft! I only saw her that time…erm, she must be younger than me, 18 I suppose, *if* it was her first year to be eligible for matching. I really didn't see her face well…she had red hair—" I am cut off by the hideous sound of Eve wailing. None of us can console her and for several minutes, all we can do is wait. Aunt Dora tries to hug her, but she throws her arm out with surprising force, only to start wailing again…with the only audible word being 'no' on repeat.

FORTY-FOUR

Max and I awake wrapped in each other's arms, a strangely familiar and welcome sensation, even if it has occurred so few times. I hope it will continue for a very long time, but I also hope to be back in our own bed soon, not in Aunt Dora's spare room.

Our discussions continued until late into the evening yesterday and I was glad when Aunt Dora suggested that we remained together for now. Eve's spirits did not recover from her outburst. She took a long time to fall asleep, but she didn't speak again. Both cats have refused to leave her side for any longer than a pee and dinner – and remarkably they have done that in shifts, proving the felines understand that they are needed as comforters now more than ever.

We are all subdued and eat breakfast with very little conversation. I am worried I broke Eve – mentally at least – for she still isn't speaking and although has awoken, she is not eating or reacting to her surroundings. I ask Aunt Dora if we should call for a doctor, but she says no, we must respect and honour Eve's request; for Eve had specifically asked to be allowed to slip away should she become unresponsive – her desire to die at home being as strong as her desire not to rally and risk saying the wrong thing in public.

After breakfast, whilst still sat in the kitchen, away from Eve, I show Max her photographs. He is fascinated by the architecture; I knew he would be. I draw his attention away from the backgrounds, asking him to focus on the subjects themselves, pointing out the number of red-haired family members.

"So, you think that Eve thinks Lilith is related to her?"

I shrug. "Maybe?"

"If she has vowed silence for her family's protection, yet she has been betrayed—"

"That could account for yesterday's response."

"Hmm."

I hear my name called, so immediately follow the voice into the living room. Aunt Dora is crouched in front of Eve. "Eve wants to talk to us."

We sit down quietly, merely responding "of course" as we do. Eve grumbles, but doesn't speak. She looks wearier than I have ever seen her. She takes a wobbly sip of tea before sitting back.

Eve holds my gaze, then nods gently. "It is always darkest before the dawn. I must ask you to step into that darkness and pray you step back out intact. If you want to take something out, you don't nip at its heel and hope it falls. You aim true for the heart and make darn sure it can't get back up. Do you understand?"

I nod. I may not understand exactly, but I do feel that if I remain open, Eve will illuminate my way.

"I believe that the girl you mentioned yesterday is my great-great granddaughter, Lilith. Her mother, Penny, denounced me on direction of her late mother after what happened, so I have never met Lilith, only glimpsing her from afar. I don't blame them really; although they don't fully know why they did it, it was the safest option and they stayed safe as long as I kept me silence and retired peacefully. I love me family, despite everything. Ultimately, we are all hardwired to want family to carry on beyond us – to leave our mark, a part of ourselves, for future generations. Convincing the infertile that their legacy is of value without kids, is a difficult task sometimes – even though it is true. It is not our right to fill the Earth beyond capacity, to take without giving – we must make our time count now, leaving our little corner better than we found it. That is where humanity went wrong and on an epically bad scale. We are working on that and more than not, we are succeeding." She pauses, shaking her head, as though she is arguing with herself. "But I *do* have family and they promised me that they'd leave her be, not put her in the AIP nor recruit her for anything. If they have broken that promise, despite knowing I break everything – *and risk you* – I will send you into the depths if you agree."

I do not answer straightaway. It is funny, when put this is way I begin to doubt how badly I want the answers – but I cannot deny that I want to know. I want to know if I can do more to leave my corner (large or small), better than I found it… and I can only do that by understanding and challenging the true state of affairs. So, I take a deep breath and say, "I agree."

Aunt Dora seems terrified; Max looks concerned, but equally determined.

"Dora, please fetch Pandora again."

As she complies, Max turns to me. He places a hand on my leg and rocks its slowly. "We will tackle whatever it is, together."

As Aunt Dora sits back down with the box in her hands, Eve says: "Dora, open her up and get the skin." Of all the gadgets in the box, the synthetic skin was not the one I expected to be of interest now. "If you want answers, you'll have to go underground – alone. No mole hides in the sun."

"Why alone?" asks Max.

"Because I only made one skin – and you ain't a girl, and she needs to be your mother."

"Excuse me?"

"I'm hoping you ain't denying your gender, otherwise the PTB have really dropped a— Oh, never mind," grunts Eve. "She needs to see things and she'll only get there using me skin."

"Can you make more?"

"Now? No. I don't have the time or resources. My husband was a suspicious man – what good that ultimately did him – but we experimented with tech before declaring it. I carried on after his death; it seemed wiser then than ever. Some technology will have surpassed mine, but tech only goes as fast as business allows – it often has to be economically viable for people to care. Well, I never was one to wait to see if it was useful, I made things for the *may be*. After all, no war was won with weapons made after the attack."

"What do you need me to do?" I ask.

"Save Lilith."

"From the AIP?"

"Yes, you need to record it and show everyone what it really is. The people think it is just a resource for fertility – it is so much more."

"No disrespect," says Max, "but how do you know? Were you a scientist or director of a division?"

"No son, I was more...*I was everywhere.* Scientists have their fields, directors their sectors to govern. I saw it all. Every one of them linked to data – to my IT and tech. Every element aided by a robot of some description. I may not have designed or operated them all, but I *saw* it all."

"So, what do I need – where I am going?"

"First, you need to find out Mary's exact barcode."

"I know that."

"How?! I don't even know it!" exclaims Max.

I gulp, this isn't my most flattering of confession. "I have a bad habit of reading codes and when I first realised you were not related, I read your family codes – *a lot* – to the point I memorised them." I grimace as I finish; it is embarrassing to sound like a stalker.

Max nods, chewing his lip. "Okay then."

"Well, it's handy you did as that makes the task move on faster. You need to go to the AIP – here take my necklace." I am handed Eve's pearl necklace, but I fail to see why. It seems unremarkable. "You may look confused, but put the skin on your arm – yes like that, it will wrap itself on your arm on its own…see, ha-ha, yes, it does feel a little odd. Now, twist the pearls on the necklace…keeping going… Ah, ha, there you go! What digits do you need?"

I have no idea how, but as I move the plain pearls, they activate, producing letters and numbers in the correct positions. All I have to do is choose the code and as I do, my arm displays what the necklace dictates.

"Neat, huh?"

"Very, but I am a little freaked out too – how do I get it off?" I say, tugging on the skin unsuccessfully.

"There's a tab you pinch – see? Only you can do it, though. The skin reads your marker, so will only act for the current wearer."

"So, I walk in as Mary digitally, but what is to stop anyone from spotting me – or Mary from finding me?"

"That is where Max can help – I am hoping he can call a 'family meeting' at home this evening. Staff will be minimal and not interested in you, so you can go in and record and get out."

"On my watch?"

"No, that is linked to the database – here have this."

A tiny, unassuming button camera is passed to me. "Won't this be on the network too?"

"No. It is free." Such a simple, but totally unique concept.

"Okay…but you haven't answered where I am going?"

"Under and out…until you find something incriminating."

"This plan, though intriguing, feels flawed, Eve. Maia can't just go pottering about hoping to bump into something, she is just going to get in serious trouble!" Max looks very uneasy.

"Change is never achieved by those who quit when things get tough."

"That's all very well from the old lady who is going to stay in her warm bed!"

Eve ignores Max and stares at me. "The road of real reckoning requires the revolution to reign."

"That's a tongue twister," I reply.

"Repeat it."

"The road of real reckoning requires the revolution to reign."

"Excellent – remember that – BUT only say it if a drone is threatening you."

"Why? What will happen?"

"Repeat it."

"The road of real reckoning requires the revolution to reign."

"Okay, let's go."

FORTY-FIVE

I am walking towards the hospital, wondering how on earth I have been persuaded that this is a good idea. I am dressed smartly in Aunt Dora's clothes with my hair brushed and slicked into position. It is the wrong colour entirely to be Mary, but Eve tells me that is not an issue as drones are not programmed to notice such things, they only need the unchanging data from barcodes, not skin or hair colour. So my altered appearance is purely for my reassurance. No one will bat an eyelid at me for the first few stages of my mission – I could be visiting for any number of reasons – so although I still feel like my butterflies have turned into full-fledged eagles within my stomach, and my heart is beating far faster than I'd like, I walk past multiple humans without as much as a 'how do you do?'

Eve is convinced that there is more beyond the maternity ward. The only sketchy piece of evidence that I can think of to agree with this comes from when I overheard Henry and Mary fighting the first time as he told her to 'relax, I only took her to the SurrogacyPods.' I am not sure that means the AIP project is beyond, but I guess I might soon find out.

It is 9 p.m. Max called his mother and arranged a family meeting. We were both relieved to hear Henry's voice in the background, even if he didn't sound particularly chirpy. I am hoping that meeting goes okay. To be honest, I think I am as worried for Max's safety as I am my own. Mary Rivers may be an intelligent woman, but I do not for one minute think she is a stable one. Hopefully, for this evening at least, she will remain stable in mind and geographical location.

I walk down the corridors, scanning my fake code as I go, every door opening for me despite the identity lie. I walk past civilians, staff, guards, and robots alike; none of them are interested in me. Eve told me to just keep walking, so I am.

I come to the main set of lifts by the maternity ward. As per my instructions, I take the middle lift and step in. No one is there. The AI system asks where I want to go. I look at the control panel; I don't see anything different to normal numerical options that are in all lifts until I wave my left arm near to the screen. Suddenly a downwards arrow appears at the base of the panel. I take the biggest breath I can as if I were about to dive under water and press the arrow.

It feels like an eternity, but in reality, it is probably seconds, certainly no more than a minute before the doors reopen. I had not meant to hold my breath, but I gasp as I step out of the lift. Looking around all is quiet and unremarkable. If I didn't know, I could have been stepping out onto a standard, non-clandestine floor. In the distance I can hear the gentle whirr of a drone, but I cannot see anybody. Eve has given me a rough guide of the turns I need to take, but as her information is several years old, I am concerned that there could be some interior changes. I glance quickly through windows and doorways as I go: all I can so far see is standard offices, a few storage rooms, the odd consulting room, a few labs; but without going in, I cannot see what they are researching. I do not see any wards, patients, and certainly no red-haired captives. I am wearing my button camera, so it will be recording everything I see, but until I get out of here, I am totally alone. I wish I had a familiar voice in my ear directing my path, but Eve quite rightly pointed out that using data linked technology is too risky. Dark and alone is the only way.

The last room I pass is huge. The walls are made of glass so I can clearly see it is a conference room. In the centre of the room is a videocall projector pointing a potential beam at each chair. This kind of room is in PTB governing meeting rooms so personnel from all over the world can be streamed into any meeting, anywhere. Apparently, several tonnes of building and earth doesn't stop the signal reaching down here.

I carry on walking. Even with dimmed lighting, it is surprisingly light and airy down here, but knowing that I am deep underground is beginning to make me feel claustrophobic. I am doing my best to stay on autopilot despite my legs feeling like they are lead weights when I begin to hear a strange yet familiar noise. A tram. I hardly believed Eve when she said the hall would lead to a tramway, yet the closer I get, the more convinced I am. Here, under the Central Hub Hospital, is a tramline. How the hell has this been kept secret?

Eve told me to board the tram. I have come this far, I may as well carry on. I step on, again expecting the AI to pick up on my fake code, but it doesn't. Four people get off the tram, all of them are busy on their watches and none of them are interested in me. I sit down, doing my best not to look around like a tourist. The tram doors close and it moves off. I glance upwards to see a map of the tram line: it is huge. I reach for my button, pointing it in the map's direction. I hope it sees all that because I am never going to remember it all. The track I am on seems to loop under the hospital and out. I want to study it, but don't get a chance to as we reach another stop and a man steps on. He is dressed in white, so I am assuming he is a doctor from another department. I can only imagine that there are routes to the underground from multiple positions in the hospital, as he gets off again at the next stop.

My heart is racing faster than the tram is moving. How on earth do I know when to get off? Eve said 'under and out' but didn't know how long it would take. "Hmmphh, like a good mole, you'll know when to come up for fresh air." I should probably question my own sanity following the advice of a woman whose directions involve mole metaphors.

In my bid to not seem lost, I hadn't noticed the sign at the front of the tram which names the next stop. 'SH1, Florists Drive.' Oh my word, there are stops in the SubHubs? Where do they come up?! If I hadn't got Eve's *"Follow the line and do not deviate"* ringing in my ears, I would possibly let curiosity take over – but I agree, one frightening mission at a time is quite enough. A few people get on the adjoining tram cart, but no one else joins my section. I cannot see any faces, but from the glimpse of their clothing, they look like they are wearing security uniforms. I remain seated and feel increasingly sweaty as I watch the sign indicate SH2 and then SH3 locations. It occurs to me this could be a widely elaborate lie; these dark underground tunnels could be anywhere or nowhere for all I know. All I *do* know is that I feel like I have buried myself.

Then, suddenly, the tunnel lightens up and the tram stops. The mole has come up for air. Oh, wonderful, I am thinking like Eve! Well, if that is the case, I think now is the time to get off the tram. I jump up and step on the platform. I am outside and can see the faintest clouds in the semi-moonlit sky. Straight ahead is a building…I seem to be in a station attached to it, rather than an entirely open area. The tram pulls away, turning downwards and back underground.

Like a mole.

Eve has been here.

I walk straight into the building, past an empty reception area. A sedentary robot springs to life as I approach a double door. I present my arm and it stands down. I wish my heart would calm down as quickly. What am I looking for? Eve wants me to save Lilith by exposing the AIP – but she was short on specifics. Everyone knows this place exists – just not what it does. Trial and error breeding plans: that is what I am after… proof humans can breed better than we are told. Suddenly I can hear my mum squawking 'fools rush in'…this might be one of the rare occasions she has a point, but in fairness, this isn't really an objective you can plan well for.

That is my excuse and I'm sticking to it.

I seem to have found a maternity ward. It looks identical to the one at the hospital as there are SurrogacyPods arranged in the same petal formation. There are only robots attending so I walk into the room, hoping they will ignore me. I have never particularly feared drones or robot security personnel before as they have always been such a constant presence in day-to-day life, and the ones at the lab are actually incredibly useful. Plus, I never felt like I was doing anything noteworthy, so had no reason to worry about my presence being logged. Now the thought of being scanned by one is sending shivers down places that I didn't realise contracted.

As I walk around the SurrogacyPods, the babies look peaceful. I stop to read the chart of one. She has a countdown ticking in the right top corner; her birth is so well coordinated they have it down to the second, like a baker waiting for a cake to rise or chocolate ganache to perfect. I glance over her DNA sequencing, her pedigree and future barcode. Everything is mapped out for her already. I move on to the next baby, reviewing the same details. She has the same pedigree. Sisters. Nothing overly remarkable there, until I view the next child and the next. Six full sisters and six half-sisters. All have the same mother. I am relieved to see the maternal code doesn't match mine – I know my code off by heart so rebuke myself for attempting to visually check it now – it is hardly going to match Mary's, is it?! Each woman will have multiple eggs harvested at once, but what are the chances of the resulting eggs all being female? I continue reading the sisters' notes. They have their families marked out, size of family, the schooling, location, feeding, prospective grading, number of donations and job or marital plan. The 'Nurture' of their existence is planned to the letter for the better part of three decades. As I read the last record, I suddenly notice that after grading she has no further plan plotted, just 'THE INTIATIVE.'

Mentally I am whisked back to lying in that horrendous bed, waiting to be completely unconscious, hearing my eggs described like mythical creatures out of science fiction novel. Golden Chicks. Why do I think that Dr Oldman is in charge of the use of Golden Chicks as part of this 'Initiative'? I could be adding two and two and making five, but somehow, I doubt it.

I hadn't thought to check for a signing doctor on the records until now, but the only repetition of initials is 'Oo' and that means nothing to me. I look through the glass to the next room – it is the same as this one and is again void of human activity. Are these babies reared by robots alone?

I enter and quickly read through the notes again. These babies are almost the same age as the previous, but this time are mixed gender and from two mothers. The first code means nothing to me, but the second makes me flush with confusion. They are mine. I have always known that my eggs are developed: this should not be a surprise, yet seeing them in the flesh is vastly different to their theoretical existence. I peer into the pod, surveying the baby before me. He is sleeping in his amniotic fluid without a care in the world. Without realising I am doing it, I find myself stroking the case of his pod, wondering if he senses that I am here and who I am. Whether I want to be a mother or not, six of my children are laid before me. Three of them are marked for the Initiative. Now more than ever, I want to know what that is.

A drone enters and I suddenly realise that I need to get moving. I glance into the next room, scan the door, and enter. I do not have time to leisurely read these pods as I suddenly notice human movement in the adjoining room: to my horror, it is Dr Oldman. His profile is one I will always remember, even if it is just a glimpse. I have to hope I have seen and recorded enough to be useful. I would love to go from room to room and take in as much as I can, but time is ticking by and I am risking too much by being here so long.

I scan the door, ready to step out into the corridor, but in my haste to look ahead, I do not notice the drone come up behind me until it has scanned my neck. I freeze as it spins in front of me. The mild-mannered, mint green coloured drone turns red as it shouts 'HALT – UNAUTHORISED PERSONNEL.' It repeats its angry message three times. I know what it is doing: it is searching for instructions on its system for how aggressive to be and how quickly it needs to call in backup.

"The road of real reckoning requires the revolution to reign."

"Precisely," says the drone.

Whatever the hell that phrase means, the drone immediately discolours and returns to its former assignment. I do not know how I remembered those words and I cannot claim to have consciously chosen to say them now. Eve has obviously sunken into my psyche more than I am aware of, but right now, I am relieved that she has.

I have definitely taken in enough information for one evening and want to get out of here post-haste. Only with a great deal of restraint do I manage to get back to the tram without running, but I do get there in one piece. The ride back to the Central Hub seems to be eternal and I am shaking the whole time, even though it is actually as peaceful as the ride out.

I am not built to be a spy, that is for sure.

I step out of the lift, breathing like I have been chased and make my way out into the street. I close my eyes for a second, then look up at the sky – the same semi-moonlit sky I saw beyond the Hub. Was I really beyond the fence? Did that just happen?

Time to be me again. Eve told me not to remove the synthetic skin until I get home, just slide it up my arm. I have no idea how the skin works, but as soon as I pull the tab and slip it upwards, Mary's code disappears. It might be tighter higher up, but it is certainly reassuring to see my own barcode again.

I walk to the tram station, feeling an odd mixture of burdened, but lightweight. Is it possible to be elated and overwhelmed simultaneously?

I check my watch for the first time since leaving Aunt Dora's. I turned off the sound and put the display on night-time for my mission; the last thing I needed was Mum calling me asking some ridiculous question like 'do you think you're pregnant yet?' If only she visited the ward where I have just been, disturbing as it is, there are grandchildren enough to please even her. Seeking a happier thought, I step off the tram rereading Max's message and smile:

'Am back at Dora's. Be safe. Love you xx'

It came in twenty minutes ago; I feel my chest heave with relief knowing that he is safely at my aunt's. I am so glad we arranged to stay there again tonight so we can discuss everything together in one (relatively) safe place.

"Well, here she is! Aren't you a slippery little eel?" I turn, following the sarcastic voice. Standing in front of a SolarBug is Mary Rivers looking anything but friendly.

"Good evening, Director Rivers, can I help you?"

"Indeed, my dear, you can." As she speaks, I hear the twitching of metal. I don't recognise the sound, but I instinctively know it is not good. Following the sound to my left, I see Peter Lloyd scowling, pointing a gun directly at me.

FORTY-SIX

The three of us just stand motionless in the dark. I am not sure what to say, I am certain that I cannot outrun them. I do not know how to disarm him (or her), so I choose patience. Terror-driven, statuesque patience.

"Do you have anything to say for yourself?" Peter sounds like the schoolground bully. Even now with a gun pointed at me, he is still the pathetic idiot that no one respects or cares for. I cannot for a moment believe that Mary thinks anything of him other than being a convenient henchman. I choose not to answer him. I can only imagine they know exactly where I have been, but until they lay their cards plainly, I am not laying out mine.

"I should have known you were trouble. Fertile or not, you are not good enough for *my* son and I should have insisted on a younger, fresher wife for him – someone who unquestionably knows their duty to family – and doesn't try to turn a son against his mother! You cannot topple me, do you understand? *I am more than you'll ever be!*" She sounds desperate. I can only imagine Max or Henry told her some home truths. If they did, good, I cannot pity her. I think she wants me to say I know she is special, and I revere her, but she deserves no such compliment, so I remain silent. "I don't know what spell you put on Henry, but he has one last opportunity to keep the faith, or he will…well, never mind him, *you* are my issue now."

"Why?"

"Why? *Why?!* Because you have been pretending to be *me*!" Mary is clenching her fists to the point that they are turning white.

Peter is sneering at me as he retorts: "You may roll your eyes and groan, little girl, you forget that I see—"

"So, you've been following me again when my dad told you to leave his family alone."

"That clueless tool doesn't know what is going on in his own household! I'll be governor before long and then I'll give him pointless orders – if he has a job at all."

"*Peter.*" Mary scowls. Okay, it is plain what his motive is. He is too stupid to focus on the more immediate task, but unfortunately for me, I get the impression that he thinks it doesn't matter if I know too much because my 'free days' are numbered one way or another.

Mary sneers at me: "How did you do it?"

"If you want answers to something, you will have to be more specific with your questions."

"Look, you smart mouthed brat, you have two options: 1) answer my questions and live in the AIP or 2) die and make my life *much* easier. One less fertile girl isn't going to tip the scale of humanity."

"Not even a Golden Goose?" I don't know why I think that is a helpful response, especially not in my chosen sarcastic tone. I am afraid. Mary's expression clearly shows that my demise would be nothing to her; but call it bravery, pride, or stupidity, something within me will not bow to her.

"*Is she?!*"

"Shut up man – how do you know that? What the hell *have* you been doing?!" Her face is turning a hideous shade of red. "How did you get on the underground? Peter saw you get off the hospital lift logged in as me – *so tell me HOW!*"

Peter jumps forward, grabs my left arm, yanks up my sleeve, and drags me towards Mary: "I saw her use her arm, look, does it match?!"

The following tussle is undignified and frankly embarrassing, but eventually they both step back, out of breath, angry and confused. Eve's artificial skin is amazing; it is so well adjusted to my own tone, it is not possible to see where it ends. Mary orders Peter to frisk me. She is too cowardly to do it herself and he is too repugnant to even blink at such a request and immediately complies. I doubt there is a nice way to do a full body search, but if there is, Peter has no interest in finding one, and seems pleased to leave me feeling violated beyond words.

"It has to be linked to that old IT witch – you said she has been spending a lot of time there? Let's visit her, shall we? I'd like some answers and taking out two or three birds in one go will suit me just fine." The spite in Mary's tone is petrifying.

I am again grabbed by the arm and propelled forwards with the gun poking me in the side. Suddenly fear for more than myself rises; I will not lead them to Eve, Max, or Aunt Dora. I will die trying to stop them terrorising anyone else.

"Leave my family out of this!" I squeal, trying to wiggle out of Peter's grasp, whilst lunging for his gun. He repeatedly tries to hit me; some blows I dodge, some I don't, but I manage to stay with him. Suddenly, he changes tactic; he is no longer trying to restrain me, instead he turns his gun on me and I am desperately losing any grip I have in my attempt to turn it around on him. A shot is fired, closely followed by a second. Peter's grip relaxes as he slumps to the floor, blood trickling down his forehead. I am too shocked to move as I hear steps approaching. I just stare at Peter's lifeless body on the floor next to me.

"Maia, Maia, we have to go."

I turn my head towards the approaching voice, but do not take in who I am seeing. I look over to Mary and vomit rises in my mouth. She has a matching bullet wound in her forehead.

"Maia, come on! That'll be cleaned up in five minutes, you can't do more now."

I must have the most blank expression on my face. I am not processing anything.

"They're dead."

"Yes."

"You shot them."

"I did."

"You saved me?"

"I did."

I stand, staring, not knowing what to say.

"Come on, just round here."

I am taken firmly, but kindly by the hand. My body just follows him. It is odd, only moments earlier something arose within me to resist abduction; now I am blindly aiding it. I am led through trees – I know the area, but I feel lost right now going off-piste in the dark. All my sensations are blurred, but suddenly a name is matched to the face.

"Mark?"

"Hmm?"

"Mark Jones?"

"Hmm?"

"You shot your boss."

"I did."

"Where have you been?"

"Watching."

"I don't understand."

"You will – here."

We step out onto a roadway. I can hear the river sweetly flowing by. How is it I always end up by the river? A car is parked on the road. A real one, not a drone or robot. The rear door opens as Mark gets in the driver's seat and from within a familiar voice calls into the night:

"Maia, get in."

FORTY-SEVEN

No one has spoken since I got in the car. Mark calmly starts the engine and drives away. I do not know where we are exactly, but after a while, the landscape becomes more and more familiar, and I realise that we are heading home – to my *old* home.

Still, I do not speak, I stare a lot, but no words come to me. I would say this whole day feels like a dream, but this evening definitely feels like more of a nightmare. The car silently pulls up my old drive and stops outside the house. Mark turns to us both, nodding to my companion.

"Okay then, good night, stay safe."

"Thank you, Mark, see you tomorrow."

I take the hint and get out of the car. Mark wastes no time pulling away, but gently steers his vehicle down the road, not rushing for anyone. I watch the vehicle disappear into the night, only turning to speak when I can no longer see his taillights.

"Gee-Gee, now what?"

"Now," she says firmly, "you learn. Come."

I silently follow like a lamb following its shepherd – I hope not to my slaughter, but I follow into the house, nonetheless. I am assuming nothing, for I feel like I *know* nothing.

I am led into the middle of her study – the room I have always been curious about, but rarely seen. The paintings are all hung the same as they were the last time I was in here, the one of the Earth again catching my eye more than any other. I soak in the image rather than looking for human conversation – for the first time in my life I find the depiction of Earth half destroyed less distressing than any company or truths more immediately surrounding me.

'Being Guardians of the Earth gives us no greater right to be here than any other species'

I find myself quietly narrating the inscription without premeditation. I remember being struck by the sentiment the first time I read it, but I think I perhaps underestimated the weight of it.

"Maia, this is not how I wanted this conversation to start. I have shielded you from the truth, hoping you would settle into a more stable, easier life than I have had, without the difficult choices which knowledge inevitably brings. But it is what it is, events around us have brought us to now. For better or worse, we must tread the path set before us. Come."

Gee-Gee walks over to Great Gramps' desk, running her hand along the front of the surface until I hear a popping sound. Behind the desk, but before my disbelieving eyes, a lift appears. Silently she waves her hand in the direction of the open door. With no words coming to mind, I step forward and she steps in behind me. She uses her barcode to bring up a command panel with the now-familiar downwards arrow taking centre position.

The door closes, the lift starts moving, and when the doors open, I find myself for the second time tonight in the tramline tunnel. Unlike the first time, I now look around openly. The design is simple yet gloriously effective. The smaller branches of the track have paths to the main tram line and there is a Solarbug waiting to escort us to it.

"How is it powered?"

"Solar packs; they just get recharged and brought down here."

"Oh." Why not? Something tells me that is going to be one of the least difficult things to believe today. Gee-Gee doesn't attempt to talk to me as we get on the tram. I notice her observing me; sometimes I think she is smiling, but she makes no effort to educate me on anything I am seeing.

We get off tram at the same place as I did before and despite it being dark, I try to take in my surroundings. Max would love the design of this building; it is more elaborate than some of the ones in the Hub and I think some of the plants are the ones that he was advocating the other week for their super carbon absorbing properties. Halfway up the building, I am sure that I can see the silhouette of a globe. I believe if seen in daylight it would prove to be another replica of the monument that is situated in the Central Hub. At every turn it would seem that the PTB ensure their mission is remembered.

Gee-Gee stops, standing directly in front of me, examining my face.

"Please tell me what is going on."

"I understand you have spent a lot of time with Eve Addams?"

"Yes."

"Hmm, I was nervous when I learnt that Dora had taken her in, I knew her health must be fading, and Dora would look to you for help if she needed care. However, long-time loyalty does not die overnight, and we all owe much to Eve."

"How so?"

"So, she hasn't told you all?"

"No, just riddles."

"Hmm, but she knows about Lilith being detained? That is why she sent you into the AIP, right?" I raise my eyebrows, stuttering a little, but not finding words. "I'll take that as a yes. I feared that if she found out she would break her vow of silence and action would be necessary. I did hope she would not drag you into her pit though. She has left me in an impossible position."

"Why do you not want to share with me? Am I such a disappointment?"

"Oh, Maia, no, of course not. Your Great Gramps' and my lifelong dream has been to have a family member to share our work with, someone to share our goal and continue what we have dedicated everything to. Had you been infertile, my dream may have been achieved with less heartache, I could have snatched you away from your selfish mother long ago, but to lament you being fertile is as ridiculous as is wishing the sky to be eternally grey. A part of me was relieved that you were *so* fertile. Our previous attempt at training our next generation ended in such epic failure that the pain of that was enough to convince us it is best to focus on *mission*, not personal dynasty. Too many have waivered for that pride." She pauses, tilting her head. "Though, by the by, through agonizing irony, it led us to today anyway."

She pauses again and her words replay in my mind – who is lost in the family? Great Gramps is clearly not who she means… "*Oh, my – Grandad?! You killed him?*"

Gee-Gee sighs. "He should have carried the torch after your Great Gramps, but he lost his way and there is no room for error. The decision was out of our hands. You do not understand the cause yet, so the rule will seem too narrow – *too cruel*. Come, Maia, I have much to show you."

I am swamped in a million questions, with as many emotions clouding every one of them. I follow her, noting that any staff (human or android), greet Gee-Gee with marked respect. Nobody challenges my presence; some look quizzically at me, but mostly I am ignored, even when I am led through multiple wards and laboratories – all without a word of explanation.

Finally, Gee-Gee stops in a ridiculously large room that has a viewing gallery overlooking a large laboratory. Although I cannot tell exactly what they are doing down there, I can see they are testing and producing some kind of vegetation. In the gallery itself is an enormous desk with the largest set of virtual TV screens, projectors, and controls I have ever seen.

"Welcome to the Real Revolution."

She waves her arm over the desk and projectors spring to life, throwing more images than I can take in across the screens in front of me.

"What is this?" Gee-Gee doesn't answer, instead she gazes upon the images with a look of pride. As I focus on individual pictures, I am awe struck. They are not just pictures, nor are they virtual or historic videos. This is no collection of fiction like when at the gym or when visiting a museum or theme park. "These are real images, aren't they?"

"They are. You are witnessing real footage from across Earth as we speak."

I am not looking at Hubs – not human inhabited cities or places of destruction, but of natural order and beauty. It is the most wonderous thing I have ever seen, and it invokes such a passion within tears well and spill from my eyes.

"The planet has recovered? Or were the wars a lie?" Suddenly I am doubting everything that I have ever been told.

"I wish they were. The wars were very real, the destruction more so. Here, I will show you other areas." Gee-Gee commands the system in front of her, bringing up camera upon camera, showing an overwhelming number of places across the globe – some in total disarray, some in recovery, some recovered. I am shown a map of Hub locations with positions of nuclear destruction overlaid, then finally she adds in the areas in which their work is operating.

"Are there people out there? That drone image seems to have human activity on, and it isn't a Hub?"

"Well spotted my dear, that is a research outpost. Many posts are android run only, but we have dedicated teams in certain places."

"I thought the Army wasn't that far out?"

"It isn't. The Army is largely the PTB's—"

"So, you are not the PTB?"

"No, we are the Real Revolution – or R&R as—"

"*Oh, for*—*!* You have got to be kidding me! *Your catchphrase?* What you have been saying all my life…that wasn't *'rest and relaxation'* at all?!"

"Well, it is, but for Earth more than me." I wish that Gee-Gee looked apologetic, but she doesn't.

"And Mary Rivers is in the R&R – you trusted *her* with all this, but not me?!" I feel ill.

"That was not my choice by any stretch of the imagination. We had tolerated her for grandfather and father's sake as they have been loyal members. We thought she would stay low level, not push constantly for more. I was outvoted regarding her promotion several times, but despite my abhorrence of her previous personal actions and some of her methods, she has (until lately), proved loyal to the cause. So, I hoped, if not believed, that I was wrong about her."

"But you still thought marrying me to her son was wise?!"

"Your genetics matched perfectly."

"Golden Chicks."

"You have been learning."

"By default, not design."

"Max is a good man, is he not?"

"The best."

"A blessing beyond pure science."

"That, and I wasn't poisoned," I retort sarcastically.

"Pardon?"

"So, you deny that you have been poisoning the population?"

"Ah. That is a little simplified, but no, I do not deny it." Oh, how I wish you had!

"I have spent years looking for the eureka moment to find that I am years behind because I have been blindfolded. Why bother getting us to search for what you already know?"

"Because the planet needs our population managed and the PTB need to see us attempting to achieve a breakthrough."

"You mean the people?"

"I mean both."

"So how do the PTB not know you exist? I thought there was only one database, one united nation and one united goal?"

"The R&R *is* the PTB. We share the same goal, just with slightly different shaped goalposts. We all want the success of the planet and human population. The R&R is called that because we are for restoration and revolution; rest and relaxation – for Earth, for Nature, *and* for us. The PTB is society's framework and moral compass; the R&R does what it cannot. You look at me as though I am the devil, but this organisation requires sacrifice – huge personal sacrifice – to give humanity the structure it needs to thrive peacefully, as well as give the Earth space to restore and keep her balance. That balance is hard won; but it is worth the fight."

"And worth dictating over people, stifling choice, and denying them babies? So many would still follow with just a *little* more information…even a better chance of an adopted child. Would it have been *so* difficult to donate a baby to Kate?!"

"So many, but not all. The masses don't always choose wisely, and democracy did not end well last time. As for Kate: such resources are delicate…your embryos are particularly—"

"Never mind what they are! You can still collect data from them, and they are certainly plentiful! I saw that plainly earlier as they are all loaded by the dozen in their Pods!"

"Hmm, did you now? Even so, I kept out of the Committee's decision on Kate…I thought it wise, maybe I will rethink, but I promise nothing."

I shake my head as a new question arises. "So, you have double agents within the PTB?"

"Monitors. They report to the R&R and influence certain events if necessary."

"Such as?"

Gee-Gee stares at me, but doesn't answer for a moment. "Come."

Once again, I follow her through corridors, down steps and through a large doorway. She pauses in the middle of the room. When I stop to take in my surroundings, I realise it is the room which I was overlooking a few minutes before. I suppose we must be getting near to daybreak, as people are working in here – unless of course, they work 24/7?

A handful of people are working at a station in the corner, but no one pays attention to us. I turn back to Gee-Gee, but she nods towards a workbench where a man has his back to me. Even from behind I recognise his frame, but I still wait for him to turn around, hoping more than believing I am mistaken. I feel the freshly healed scar of reconciliation tear open on my heart and the biggest knot forms in my throat. I feel my entire face crumbling in on itself and my vision blurs with tears.

Gee-Gee waves to Theo, calling him to my side. He looks nervous, regretful maybe, but not repentant. No one speaks. Apparently, they are waiting for me to fill in my own gaps.

"My work? You sabotaged my work?" I finally whisper.

"You've been getting too close to answers, so I had to keep track." Gee-Gee is totally unapologetic.

"You recruited him?"

"When you were both given your final grades. I knew that you were planning on defying the system. I had to act – to save you both."

"You watched me crumble for six years! – *six bloody years!* – under my mother's selfish, indifferent direction!" My thoughts are racing like an angry furnace. "And I thought Mum took my note…but it was *you*! Wasn't it?! You could have comforted me – *but you left me to rot!*"

"Maia, I had to. If you knew, you would have tried to follow and that wasn't your path – you have no idea how much it tore me to see you that way, Maia—"

Gee-Gee reaches out and I swing my arm, stopping her from touching me. My skin feels like it is crawling from betrayal. I was so happy to have put the whole Theo saga behind me. I was enjoying the idea of being lab partners without complication – discovering science to help the world. Now I find I have just been a pawn in their bid to distract the world.

I turn to Theo, quoting the last sentence he said to me by the river, after I finally read his note…suddenly it makes more sense: "*You only know what you need to, to serve.*"

"Maia," Theo stutters, "f-for what it is worth, I—"

"Don't bother!" I snarl. "I won't believe you."

Again, we stand in silence, although inside I am screaming. Gee-Gee nods to Theo. Thankfully, he takes the hint and leaves, only glancing back at me as he slides the door shut. I watch him go with nothing but anger in my chest. He has a (what I want to believe is genuine) tear in his eye as he turns, but genuine or not, it doesn't matter now.

Exasperated, I ask: "Why bring him back?!"

"That was not my choice either. I had him placed with Henry, watching his work. When Henry transferred with Mary, he insisted on bringing Theo – which the board agreed was of value and we promoted him upon his return."

"And Ella? Is she in your pocket too?"

"Not yet. Mary recruited Ella, but she thinks that she works for the PTB alone."

"*Not yet.* So, you plan to – because she is infertile and has wider potential than me."

"Maia, no." Gee-Gee shakes her head softly, but doesn't finish her sentence.

"So, why show me all this now? You have made it clear that it is not by choice!"

"Maia, I have seen many families try and bring their members into the fold, only to find that they do not share our resilience or determination for the cause. The very essence of our mission requires unwavering loyalty to being true Guardians of Earth – before anyone else, including ourselves. I can show you videos, I can even take you on field trips to impress our point, but be thankful that you did not live in the world that was. Humanity so badly lost their way, the planet groaned under our every step, and fauna and flora suffered and died as a result – some beyond rescue. Our arrogance and greed blinded our way, common decency seemed all but lost, and wars upon wars resulted in a mess so heinous that disease and destruction ground life to a halt. The PTB rose through those ashes, but the R&R guided them.

"The UNE works, Maia. Once you have sifted through the pain, you will see that. But I feared, yes, I will be honest, I feared you would not fully share the R&R's judgement and if you attempted to swim against them, only death would meet you. Your grandfather lost faith in the cause before he was sent into the radiation. Eve's family – her sons – were drone operators and flew the wrong way, finding things they shouldn't, then compromised their father and children by trying to expose all of the R&R's work. Thankfully, they didn't share Eve's supreme understanding for signals. They thought they did, but we caught them in their own web, resulting in Eve having to watch them all die in a faked accident. She is Great Aunt to Lady Fairfax – did she tell you that? Her remaining relatives all disowned her, thinking that the accident was her fault, but in truth, she tried to save them. She took the blame anyway. We let her stay with Ray, Dora's late husband; he was the only one faithful to her, but then history cruelly repeated itself. We found out too late that his error was an innocent one and his injury (and later death) broke Eve, prompting her to fully retire, begging the freedom of her remaining great granddaughter and great-great granddaughter in return for bowing out with no fuss. The Board owes her more than can ever be written or explained, so we granted her request."

"What did Eve do in the R&R?"

"She founded it. She and my parents were childhood friends. They grew up in the world when it was its most disastrous and they had the vision for change. A vision they shared with people who proved key across the globe in their varying roles. What Eve cannot do with IT or AI isn't worth knowing. Tom was good, but she was always better. I remember being in awe of her engineering skills. She was humble, too. Allowing Tom to take much of the credit must have bothered her, but she followed the PTB mandate for family values and put herself in the position of mother first."

"As all fertile women should do," I say sarcastically whilst scuffing my feet.

"Exactly. I know that will not sit well with you."

"You didn't do it."

"No, but that was in the early days of settling in the sciences, establishing the order, and there was much to do…but, yes, I agree I was lucky, most of the Governors and Directors were not allowed such leniency – although I paid for that in other ways. Do you not now see though, that the people must see unity?"

"I do. But I also see holes in your mandate…I see you allow extra testing on certain people – your own family members no less – on Abby and *on me*!"

"It so happens, our line is particularly fertile – I was harvested more for my 'Golden Eggs,' too. Trust me or not, Maia, I live honestly by my own motto: *'Only do unto others that which you are willing to do to yourself.'*"

Neither speaks. I am glad, for I need a minute. There is too much information being laid at my feet and I do not know how to sift through it. I said I wanted to see the bigger picture, but I now feel like my entire world has been upended. Oddly, I am also afraid that if I do not ask for as much information as possible now, I may never be given the opportunity again. So, trying my best to leave aside the consuming feeling of betrayal, I push forward with my quest for answers:

"So, are people really infertile? Or is that a lie?"

"No, they are."

"By your means only?"

"No, disease, viruses, and nuclear waste left hundreds of thousands infertile for decades. We found the vaccines for the majority of the known viruses, but still, even those who were fertile were giving birth to infertile children or hitting menopause unnaturally early. The degeneration of natural fertility is genuine. The work you do at the PTB is not meaningless."

"But when you think there is something interesting, you remove the evidence and continue it privately to avoid a real breakthrough?"

"Yes."

"Because you do not want the population to mushroom."

"Right. It needs to be a steady, manageable number."

"In manageable locations with controlled activity."

"Yes."

"But the population is still declining?"

"Yes."

"Because there are still too many of us?"

"Not quite, we haven't perfected the answer to infertility."

"Then why feed us poisoned food?"

"It isn't poison, it does not kill. It represses, neutralises, or enhances fertility to varying degrees, hence grading 0-3. We are trialling different control substances, but as yet, we cannot predict the grade people achieve. We want to fully map heritable changes caused by our research, but also that which is naturally occurring. There are some who are resistant, and we need to find them for our further studies."

"The Initiative?"

Gee-Gee raises her eyebrow and stares with surprise, but only stumbles momentarily. "Precisely. With the Initiative project we hope to use Golden Geese and their eggs to take the guesswork out of the next generation of fertility. Through our embryo studies, the R&R will select the optimum number of golden embryos to release into the population, removing the need for controls in the food as we will know an individual's grade before they are born and manage population size more efficiently."

"Oh, my goodness, I cannot believe I didn't see it before! I was so busy focusing on environmental factors affecting gene expression, but it is *you!* You are actively testing epigenetics on the live population! – without anyone suspecting a thing!"

"We are trying to make a healthier, stronger population. Our research extends beyond just who can breed. We want to control those factors and consistently choose the ones we wish to promote."

"You want to play God."

"Doesn't everyone?"

"No, I just want to understand more."

"And define it. Label it how you want, our goal is ultimately the same. You just think that yours is more noble."

"No, I am just not sure yours is."

"Then join us and restore the balance," Gee-Gee smiles proudly.

A new cold chill hits me. "What?"

"Why do you think I am telling you all this?"

"Are you not afraid I will be another family 'accident'?"

"We are beyond that point. I would be honoured for you to stand by my side and one day take my place when I am gone. Think...why do 'accidents' happen? Due to bad luck, a result of bad decisions, to spread fear and encourage obedience in those around – to remind people of their purpose. You do not need to succumb to any such accident. I do not want you in the AIP, but the R&R has no room for lost paths. There is but one. There is no selfish agenda. Humankind cannot go back to times of old. We are here as Guardians of the Earth. You are either for her restoration or not. You are either willing to make hard choices for the greater good or not. Now you know we exist, there is no forgetting. No turning back. You are either with us or against us. Do you accept your calling? Now is the time, Maia. Choose."

ALEXIA MUELLE-RUSHBROOK

Alexia Muelle-Rushbrook was born and raised a farmer's daughter in rural Suffolk, UK. Having spent her life as a stockperson, horse stud hand, and now dog breeder, Alexia has always had a passion for the natural world and an interest in genetics.

For many years she thought of writing a novel and was encouraged to do so by her husband, but it was only after their canine family members inspired Alexia to write poetry based on her love of terriers that she branched out and finally wrote her debut, speculative fiction novel, *The Minority Rule.*

Never really fitting the 'norm' as a teen or adult, Alexia has always found solace in books and her own storytelling. From an early age she enjoyed a variety of genres, but has always had a firm love of all things sci-fi and fantasy – the genres that she writes in.

Having finally found the courage to put pen to paper, Alexia now has no plans to stop, and hopes you will join her on further adventures throughout time!

ACKNOWLEDGEMENTS

I would like to thank everyone who has helped and encouraged me on my writing journey, but particular mention must go to a few people. To Kerry, Lucia, Roxanne, and Stephanie, you were all so kind and supportive when I asked you to read the first draft. 'Thank you' doesn't begin to cover what your encouragement, edits, and praise mean to me – you turned a very nervous wannabe author into someone willing to share Maia's story with the world. I have to add special thanks to both Anna and Paul for their help – you really have gone above and beyond to encourage your little sister and all the countless texts, emails, calls, edits and advice has been a true joy and pleasure. To my other sister, Elspeth, I humbly thank, not only for your support, but also your time spent scrolling through my errors and helping me hone my skills. To Miguel Muelle, again, thank you, not only for reading and loving the story, but also for your wonderful cover design and general edits – including pointing out and making me laugh at my repetitive grammatical mistakes…I promise to do better next time! *Hopefully.* To Belle Manuel for your brilliant editing and proofreading skills, and Scott and his team for setting it all together. Finally, my absolute thanks must go to my husband, Sergio, without whom I would never have dared dream to be a writer. Your love and support turned my floating idea of '*I should write this…*' into '*I have written…*' and you have unfalteringly been behind me every step of the way. There's no one I'll trust more to read my first draft – or anyone so pleased to mark errors with a red pencil!

Alexia Muelle-Rushbrook

THE MINORITY RULE:
BEYOND THE FENCE

Convicted by fertility
Forgotten by society
Only the repurposed have a life beyond the fence

Publicly revolting against the Powers That Be is never wise,
but for the remaining fertile, there's only one penalty. Naively
believing love will save the day, Lilith abruptly finds herself
torn from all she knew and dreamt of. Facing exile as a
breeding specimen, guided and guarded by androids, with the
mere mention of *before* banned, Lilith only sees a future that is
totally devoid of hope.

Welcome to the FARM.

THE MINORITY RULE:
INTO THE FOG

Condemned by fertility
Disillusioned by family
The wisdom in morality just got displaced

Maia wanted the truth and now she has it. Torn between fascination and repulsion, she must decide once and for all the path she wants to tread. Searching for a way to save herself would be difficult enough, but her loved ones and the future of the entire world hang in the balance as Maia wanders into the fog.

BOOKS IN ORDER OF TRILOGY:

THE MINORITY RULE

THE MINORITY RULE:
BEYOND THE FENCE

THE MINORITY RULE:
INTO THE FOG

Printed in Great Britain
by Amazon